DESPERATE BLONDE

Marta Selfron made a stupid mistake and married young. How was she to know that Vernon Cashion was a bully, and that his domineering mother would threaten to kill her! She got out of that relationship pretty damn quick, but to do so she had to come up with a grand, which she "borrowed" from her employer. To make matters worse, she naively confessed to the Cashions what she had done to come up with the divorce money. Now they're sucking her dry with blackmail money. And that's when she meets Dirk Delgar, a private investigator that might just be her savior—if she can avoid telling him about her own crimes.

DUNGAREE SIN

Binnie Riordan is hooked up with Mick Fogarty, second in command of the Red Rovers. She wants to be top Deb, but she's up against crazy Veronica, who may be chicken at heart, but is still in charge. So she needs to enlist Vince Kirby, the top dog, if she wants to get anywhere. She's already got Sugar Fernandez and Midge Daly in her corner. She and her fellow Debs are a ruthless group, unafraid to take out a stray drunk and roll him for his currency. But there's fat, lecherous Officer Yates to watch out for, and hostile gangs like the Dusters and the Happy Jacks to avoid. It's a kill-or-be-killed world, and Binnie is determined to get her slice of it.

DESPERATE BLONDE

DUNGAREE SIN

LORENZ HELLER

INTRODUCTION BY BILL KELLY

Stark House Press • Eureka California

DESPERATE BLONDE / DUNGAREE SIN

Published by Stark House Press
1315 H Street
Eureka, CA 95501, USA
griffinskye3@sbcglobal.net
www.starkhousepress.com

DESPERATE BLONDE
Originally published by Beacon Books, Sydney, and copyright ©
1960 by Magazine Services Ptd, as by Laura Hale. Revised and
reprinted as *The Marriage Bed*, Beacon Books, New York, 1962.
This edition reprinted from the Australian version.

DUNGAREE SIN
Originally published by Chariot Books, New York, as by
Frederick Lorenz, and copyright © 1960 by Frederick Lorenz.

"Lorenz Heller: Like Nothing You've Ever Read"
© copyright 2024 by Bill Kelly

ISBN: 979-8-88601-119-7

Book design by Mark Shepard, shepgraphics.com
Cover design by Jeff Vorzimmer, ¡caliente!design, Austin, Texas
Cover art by Al Rossi
Proofreading by Bill Kelly

First Stark House Press Edition: December 2024

LORENZ HELLER:
LIKE NOTHING
YOU'VE EVER READ

By Bill Kelly

Lorenz Heller (1910-1965), wrote over twenty novels and nearly one hundred short stories using his own name and five pseudonyms. His writing career, excepting a novel published in 1937, spanned only fourteen years from 1946 to 1962. Prolific during that relatively limited time period, Heller's output filled magazine stand shelves and drugstore spinner racks with both hardboiled crime fiction and fiction intended for the so-called "sleaze" market, i. e., stories with sexual content more explicit (for the era) than was typically encountered in popular fiction. Heller also supplemented what must have been a meager income by penning a handful of television scripts, using yet another pseudonym, Burt Sims.

Stark House Press has previously published nine volumes of Heller's work encompassing fourteen of his novels and a collection of short stories. Several of these volumes include critical essays and provide what scanty biographical information is known about Heller.

Until Stark House began reprinting his work, Heller was consigned to the overflowing Just Another Pulpster Bin. Reprinting his novels and stories has enabled those who value work with complex (but decipherable) character-driven plotting, in-depth characterization and page turner pacing, to find another writer to add to their list of favorites. Until relatively recently, critical appraisals of writers who wrote primarily for the pulp magazine market and paperback original market usually described most of these writers as hacks whose work wasn't worth reviving, either for rereading or contemporary critical appraisal. The gloss is that these "pulpster" authors would grind out copy per formula, rarely giving readers little in the way of anything new or refreshing, so why should a new generation bother reading their work? To some extent this negative evaluation was true, but contemporary reevaluation efforts focused on the fifty+ year run of the pulp fiction era has revealed that there were many writers who produced works for the pulp magazines and their successor, the "paperback original", and created fiction that was often comparable in quality to the best hardcover crime fiction of their era. Indeed some of the writers who honed their craft during their tenure in the pulp market, would eventually break into the "slick" magazine market with *Collier's*, *The Saturday Evening Post*, etc. and/or be published in hardcover. The twenty-first century has seen an increasing number of publishers who have not only revived the work of these previously neglected laborers in "the Pulp Jungle", but have also generated critical appraisal that not only examines why these writers were successful in their own time, but why their work is worthy of attention in any time.

While reading Heller's novels, one is always struck by the fact that regardless of what subgenre bin the book may be consigned to, e. g. Seagoing Adventure Thriller, Police Procedural, Heist/Caper, etc., there is always more at work, linguistically, stylistically and thematically, than one would normally find in a "per formula" pulp or paperback original guilty of a "creation" strategy designed to check various mandatory element and style boxes that would meet the expectations of the publisher and presumably the "typical reader." And writing strictly by formula of course, with no evident nuance or subtext, has the effect of making heist novels, for instance, interchangeable with each other, be they written by the same writer or by all writers of heist novels. Readers of Lionel White know that it doesn't have to be that way. White wrote several heist/caper novels, none of which bear any resemblance to each other, beyond the fact that the books contain characters who want to take what doesn't belong to them.

Those who wrote series works featuring the same characters were especially vulnerable, if not careful, to writing works that were indistinguishable from one book to the next or the one before it. Heller eschewed the series character in his novels and employed only one, PI Dinny Keogh, for his short fiction. To me, after studying Heller's work, it is not surprising that the Keogh stories are among the weakest he was to write. Uncharacteristic of his other work, the seven stories are, for the most part, predictable, show inconsistent characterization from story to story and the writing seems, atypical for Heller, sloppy at times, as if he was unsure how to proceed or was thinking, let me wrap this up and go out in the garden and do something comparatively more interesting like pick weeds. Heller may have found Keogh a bore or he was simply writing to keep an agreed format commitment to the publisher, as all stories were written for the same periodical, *Mammoth Mystery*. He must have also realized that the series character will impose certain constraints on the writer as all resulting actions and reactions to the events of every story by this character must be faithful to the characterization the author has created. Heller may have decided, for his novel writing at least, that this I-can-paint-myself-into-a-corner risk was potentially a hindrance to his potential as a creative writer.

The two novels in this volume, *Desperate Blonde* and *Dungaree Sin*, could have been, in the hands of another writer, potboilers fulfilling the basic ingredients for the sub-genres Romantic Mystery and Juvenile Delinquent Mayhem, respectively. At first glance *Desperate Blonde* seems to be describing what might happen to a Nancy Drew type character caught between adolescence and adulthood when faced with a dire situation. *Dungaree Sin* would appear, based on the title and the original cover art, to be another in a flood of juvenile delinquent sagas portraying the tragedy of slum life—and very late (so therefore stale) in a cycle that began, at least most notably, with Willard Motley's *Knock On Any Door* in 1947 (filmed in 1949). "JD" novel publishing maintained a fevered pitch throughout most of the 1950s, but these books eventually ran their popularity course. Heller may have pitched both these works to his publishers as standard fare in their niches, but the reader, while not being wholly cheated regarding content expectations, was in for an experience with far more depth of presentation and characterization than they might normally encounter from the normal spinner rack fare. Most of Heller's novel work shows a pattern: a stock/done to death genre situation made much richer and more interesting by continuous plot reversals and complex characterizations, and are particularly richer for the "minor" characters who are more than stock background personalities and often play a pivotal role in determining the outcome of the story, sometimes more so than the good and evil protagonists. The reader of a Heller novel (regardless of pseudonym used) is quickly aware that they are not engaged in reading a "Gee, this is just like that other book" experience. Heller was clearly motivated to not bore his readers, but perhaps more important to fully realizing his creative potential, he could not bear to bore himself with his own writing. I suspect this was an objective Heller may have believed a crucial and indispensable key to his success as a writer.

For *Desperate Blonde* (1960), Heller used the Laura Hale pseudonym, a pseudonym he used for *Kiss of Fire*, a double-crosses-galore crime thriller and *Woman Hunter*, an inversion of the woman-in-distress chestnut. In *Woman Hunter*, the man is in need of rescue with the woman determined to rescue him and, in the process, rescue herself. This story line of a woman initiating a course of action to achieve multiple goals will also be a key element in *Desperate Blonde*. Curiously, four of the Hale novels were slightly rewritten with racier titles and spiced up content for Beacon Books in 1961 and 1962. *Desperate Blonde* reemerged as *Marriage Bed*. Other reissue titles were *Lessons in Lust* (*Woman Hunter*), *Sensual Woman* (*Lovers Don't Sleep*) and *The Zipper Girls* (*Wild is the Woman*). Something was needed to make those cross-country bus trips more bearable and this was no doubt the publisher's intention. Such altruism.

As readers of 1950s paperback originals well know, book titles and *egads!*—that cover art—may or may not have had some resemblance to the content between the covers. For those avidly plucking these books off the spinner racks or snatching them from the ink-stained hands of Joe or Willy at the corner newsstand, I suspect that both the provocative titles, and the even more provocative cover art, were part of the fun with any later discovery of the irrelevance of either or both to the content of book emerging as a big don't care. For this Stark House two-fer the title *Desperate Blonde is* appropriate to the content, while *Dungaree Sin* is an entirely different matter, but later for that.

Marta Selfron is the titular desperate blonde, being blackmailed by ex-husband Vernon, "love child" and puppet to his mother, a "big hot blonde", who added to her other charms, is a paregoric addict. Marta's indiscretion, embezzling, was altruistically motivated, but she was foolish enough to put it all down on paper and send it to Vernon and Mumsy, hoping they would be moved by sympathy, but they are only moved to extort a sizeable amount of her monthly paycheck for their silence and are now upping the ante and Marta is in over her head. Confess to the authorities and be ruined or continue to pay and be ruined are Marta's choices. Up steps Dirk Delgar, a PI passing through town. Marta meets him, falls in love and looks to him for rescue, but on her own terms, as she fears losing him if he finds out she is a crook. Marta worries:

> It was an ugly story to unfold before the eyes of the man she was sure she loved.
> When Dirk learned the truth, what would he do?
> "Drop you," she said aloud.

Nevertheless Marta risks involving Dirk, asking him to investigate a different crime, one committed by her ex, for which he has yet to be caught as the authorities are of course stumped. Marta is a combination of naiveite, self-delusion and storybook romantic, but Heller also gives her an iron-will and an intellect that can rapidly adjust to the numerous setbacks and reversals she encounters as she continues to manipulate Dirk (or so she thinks) into performing the tasks she sets for him, while continuing to keep him in the dark as her own crime. Jim is on to Marta pretty much from the beginning but both characters emerge as poseurs leading both a surface life and an inner life hidden from the other, which adds another layer of tension and suspense to the proceedings. Love at first sight, yes. Trust at first sight, no. Both characters are principally motivated by a positive romantic outcome, but find the time to deal with the gnarly details of these pesky crimes.

However, what makes the book really entertaining is the cast of characters involved along the way. There is a zany sheriff running for office more interested in proving his homilies to be true than solving crime, Vernon's "father", enslaved to both Vernon and his psychotic mother, and the mother herself, devoted to her own pleasures and her son, the treasured "love child". There are several scenes, including a murder, bordering on the absurd and the whole work has a serio-comic tone, but Heller never steps over the line with the humor or irony, allowing the various threats to the heroine's happiness to edge closer and closer bearing their impending doom. Marta's machinations drive the story, Dirk sorts it all out, but not without help from some of the subordinate characters. For instance, Dirk is aided in his detection efforts by one Bertha Smathers, who tails people as a hobby and is clearly a woman he admires:

> She's not much to look at—scrawny, and I guess about forty years old. She has runs in her nylons and dreams in her eyes and a soft voice. . . . She's an avid reader of mysteries and that's how she got interested in detective games. She's much more than a nosy old maid, I found out. I'd say she was a good solid citizen. She's lived at Cashion's for three years and nothing has escaped her eyes and ears."
>
> Marta said curiously, "And she plays detective?"
>
> "That's right. Two years ago, she began to tail people. Anybody, just so long as she kept busy."

The story is populated with eccentrics whose behavior is taken at face value—they are all just folks you see—so regardless of what they do, the hero and heroine take it all in stride, which of course adds to the humor. Heller inverts the normal romantic hero/heroine device by basically having the two principals along for the ride while it is the actions of others that move the plot forward. Heller evenly balances the romantic elements of the story with the mystery elements and when the resolution comes, everyone is in place for their deserved outcome, per their character strengths and weaknesses rather than through any by-the-numbers plotting scheme.

Dungaree Sin (1960) was published using another Heller pseudonym, Frederick Lorenz. The content of this book fits most appropriately to the Lorenz pseudonym: novels published under this name were Heller at his hardboiled best, but the brutality and near nihilist violence of *Dungaree Sin* is in another category entirely. The title appears to be irrelevance at its paperback original best. What were they thinking? What does it even mean? Could there be any possible relation to the content of the book, or is the word "sin" merely there to make the title somehow provocative? A weak euphemism for the horrors perpetrated by characters in this novel? Mike Hammer at his most excessive is put to shame by the people who populate this book. An upgrade in title accuracy might be Dungaree Rage or Dante Dons Denim—to visit a recently added tenth Circle of Hell. The resemblance between this work and Dante's *Inferno* may appear to be ludicrous, but after comparing key characteristics of each, parallels actually do emerge. If we can once again assume that Heller was attempting to take a beat-to-death crime novel subject and breathe new life into it, using an older work that demonstrates the human price paid for various "sins" as inspiration, he responds by creating a society that has brought mankind to a further and deeper level of degradation.

As mentioned earlier, *Dungaree Sin* arrived late in the Juvenile Delinquent cycle and may have been written earlier, rejected and shelved. I only indulge in this speculation because the content of this book is so extreme in its violence and world view that the publisher of Lion Books, who published the other six Lorenz titles (the last in 1956) may have mailed it back as being excessively violent, even for them. The book was published by Chariot, a publisher much less likely to blanche at extreme content. In any case, they didn't blush and we have it today.

In *Dungaree Sin* Heller is at work developing a theme using juvenile delinquent crime as a starting point for expressing a social view that is much more dystopian than would typically be found in a book that is ostensibly a crime novel. The dystopian vision of a society that devolves rather than evolves often appears in science fiction writing in the fifties and would hit a peak in popular literature and the movies in the 1960s and 1970s, but still, in a crime novel . . .? Heller's vision of a society that produces the people that populate *Dungaree Sin* is definitely a step or two more severe than many of the books and movies depicting juvenile violence after World War II. *Knock on Any Door*, as mentioned earlier would help lead the way with the movie of course being more well known than the book. Both book and movie end with an impassioned guilt tripping shame-inducing speech that puts the entire blame for the protagonist's crimes firmly and wholly on society (you and me) using rhetoric that any social justice crusader would be proud of. Most juvenile delinquent books I have read feature some form of condemnation of "society" though many also look at the question of personal decision making/responsibility, e. g. not every 1930s Midwestern farmer's son became a John Dillinger. I deliberately use an example from the Depression era, because the problem of juvenile delinquency is cited as having its historical roots deep in the past, as far back as the Industrial Revolution. Nineteenth century immigration from Europe, the Great Depression and those fatherless after World War II all are alluded to as contributors to the problem. Heller of course would have been aware of this history, as well as its treatment by contemporary "JD" novels and Hollywood, so the challenge for a writer like Heller, determined to create something fresh, would be to create a novel that would be unique to the experience of those readers familiar with previous works on the subject. But is there any more to say?

Heller says more by creating a world that is fundamentally and irretrievably insane. Insanity reigns at every level of his society, with violence, often for the sake of violence, being the *only* common denominator between the good and evil. The word crazy is used thirty times in the book, often as a touchstone for people to "explain" or label the incomprehensible. There are no "root causes" and there certainly aren't any solutions. Those most feared are the ones that appear the most insane. All action is predicated on avoiding situations where these people are present or if present, being careful not to provoke them:

> Midge was worried. She didn't think Binnie could take care of Veronica. Everybody knew Veronica was half crazy. Her old man was in the nut house, her three brothers weren't all there, and her sister was one of the screwiest whores down at the Five Points.

The criminals who inflict pain, the cops who use authority as a weapon and to extort personal gratification may have been typical of any 1950s slum milieu, but even those who are innocents are driven to behavior that is extreme:

She was a decent Catholic girl, and never missed a mass, a novena or confession. She was crazy about confession. She went to confession every chance she got. She was particularly crazy about the decorated inside of the Church itself, all the colors and gold and everything.

In self-defense, flee the insanity of your own surroundings by creating a world as extreme as the one you are fleeing.

An honest and caring captain in the police force is basically rendered impotent by the horror of it all, becoming powerless in the face of its grotesque enormity:

Hell, he knew they were tough little girls but—Jesus God, they were still only little girls! And even tough little girls didn't make a habit of throwing those lye-and-coke bombs with the deliberate intention of burning the faces off anyone within range of the burst. But these little girls did, and some varied the formula with hydrochloric acid.

Those who have a family may be dealing with another layer of insanity when they come home:

Little Augie was crazy smart and some day would get killed doing a craziness. Not real crazy, but a crackpot, queer like all the Chavez family.

And the insanity can be communicative when a scapegoat for everyone's misery is sought:

Now everybody is crazy like Patsy. They blame everything on you, Ricki.

Heller does maintain a story thread (barely) as the mugging of a local resident in the beginning of the book leads to reprisal by the victim and a further reprisal against the victim by a gang killer, as no offense against the reigning powers of chaos can be ignored. For the most part, we see a nihilistic cycle of power struggles and betrayals with those seeking to survive driven to the point where all their efforts, to any purpose, become devoid of meaning. The only solution to any problem is violence.

What semblance of sanity exists in this environment is represented by a dance that is attended by two rival gangs with the understanding that there will be no warfare. This plan works as long as the two sides do not mix, obviously precluding any hope of peace and of course even this dubious refuge is soon shattered when a member of one side "defects" to the other. A society without hope.

Throughout Heller offers no explanations, theories or mitigating circumstances. JD literature and movies of the time usually offered some or all of these elements and/or hopeful alternatives, but I believe Heller was looking at the society he created as a pure distillation of evil in the human soul existing in a seemingly hermetically sealed universe, a universe revealing the final devolution of the human animal. Dante's Nine Circles of Hell each feature a particular sin, with Violence being the seventh circle, but there is more than violence or any of the other eight of Dante's sins at work. The issue here is not a litany of a specific moral wrongdoings but the total dominance of amorality as society's touchstone. Violence as the only solution is merely a symptom of a much greater ill. Heller employs no didactic elements: no lessons, no shaming, no fear mongering to encourage reform. Works depicting social ills are often cautionary tales, warnings against the spread of the condition being portrayed. However, the inmates in this asylum do not look to escape nor do they want what those on the outside have. If there actually is an outside world. Viewed through the lens of its own time the society portrayed in *Dungaree Sin* is a step *down* from the recently deposed totalitarian societies of World War II, which promptly gave way to other totalitarian societies, which if they did not have non-totalitarian societies to conquer and remake in their own image, might resemble the world of Heller's characters in *Dungaree Sin*, where all explanations are past the point of meaning, alternatives do not exist in the imagination and survival depends solely on the avoidance of powers that are more insane and violent than you are. The sin in *Dungaree Sin* is as inescapable to the Human Condition as were Dante's nine, and is a personified evil, or the essence of evil, residing in each human being as a total sum. This is what Heller seems to be portraying in this work. At no point does Heller condemn either individuals or society. As is said with wild animals, how can they be blamed for being what they are?

So once again it seems Heller looked at what had been done with works dealing with situations, events and themes well plowed by his contemporaries and produced a work that bears only a superficial resemblance to these works. Obviously, it is a dark vision, and one with no stated purpose of instruction, warning, redemption, etc., but as Heller seems to accept his characters (that we may fairly regard as monsters) as "normal" in the context of their own society, they are nonetheless clearly human and not cartoon characters, but twisted beyond a point anyone can be comfortable with.

Two books varying more in tone and content appearing together in the same volume would be hard to imagine, but their common denominator is the achievement attained by "pulp writer" Lorenz Heller when he stretches the limits of their respective genres and creates a work unlike anything readers have previously experienced. *Desperate Blonde* turns the intrepid romantic crime-solving couple story on its head and *Dungaree Sin* is a hyperbolic portrait of JD life, perhaps portraying the eventual devolution of life itself, with a vision that is indeed more horrible than any category of bad guy or fictional monster that can be created by the mind of man.

—Mesa, AZ
October, 2024

Bill Kelly has proofread many Stark House releases since 2017 and recently has contributed introductions to several volumes, including *The Deadly Pay-Off* by William H. Duhart and *Hollow Triumph* by Murray Forbes, as well as having edited short story collections by Helen Nielsen, Nedra Tyre and Lorenz Heller. Kelly received a B.A. in English from Columbia University and was a technical writer and illustrator for several corporations. His first exposure to crime fiction was the works of Raymond Chandler, Penguin UK editions, purchased in Singapore.

DESPERATE BLONDE

·············

LORENZ HELLER

Writing as Laura Hale

ONE

As the nude girl splashed and kicked, the sun sank lower along the far lip of the green hills in the west. Unseasonable warmth and dying light slanted across this virgin section of North Jersey.

On the shore, a Virginia creeper, having escalated to the top of a dead cutleaf maple tree, proclaimed with a scarlet shout that this was the second week of September and the first frost was a not-too-distant menace.

It was an isolated lake, surrounded mainly by open woods whose peripheral trees exhibited flamboyant *NO TRESPASS* signs. On the west side, bulldozers had cleared two acres.

There, a landscape artist had created ample lawns, following the pattern of a millionaire's whim; the grass was velvety smooth, like putting greens at an exclusive country club.

Beyond the lawns sprawled a riotous flower garden, along with profuse plantings of bush and rhododendron; there was also a cloistered summer house remote under the branches of a single elm.

The residence itself was a capacious ranch affair at the lake's edge. Girders projected over the water and supported a screened porch.

A railed promenade, six feet wide, extended from the north end of the porch to a swimming dock equipped with a low board and a ten-foot tower for high diving.

For a moment, only the frolicking girl was moving in this quiet arena of opulence. Then a wayward insect with twin sets of wings on a needle-shaped body set off across the water.

In the center of the lake, it hovered over the lone, lovely swimmer, whose face and white bathing cap were visible above the waterline.

As the insect winged shoreward, Marta Selfron's face clouded and she murmured, "Summer is down to her last dragonfly—damn it!"

Then, smiling, she added: "But September is such a nice month for vacationing that I'm glad I waited. Tonight the harvest moon will be full."

Although alone under sky and sun, cleaving deep water and facing the treachery of cramps, Marta was unafraid. And daring, in a way—because, except for the bathing cap, she wore nothing. Hers was a lovely face with full red lips and eyes a clear, constant blue. The body was just as lovely.

Her arms moved idly. Her feet kicked. Her shoulders lifted above the waterline. She sank down slowly until her chin submerged. A slight chill shivered upward from her toes, and she decided: "You've been in long enough, young lady."

With a flirt of long arms and an upward kick of feet, she turned on her stomach and swam toward the nearby dock.

She used a crawl stroke, arms knifing the water, a powerful feather-kick meshing with the arm-beat to propel her body steadily.

At the dock, she mounted the ladder nimbly. Water dripped from her sleek body. Unbuckling the white cap, she fluffed honey-colored curls with a careless gesture. A smile teetered on her lips, as if some half-formed thought amused her.

She pivoted for one last look at the quiet lake with its green girdle of maple and pine and oak.

It was so lovely and virginal here, she thought; such a sharp contrast to the ant-hill life of busy office and overcrowded city. She inhaled the warm air appreciatively.

Full moon tonight, she thought—and no man to share it.

Damn.

She walked between white railings and, opening the screen door, stepped inside and tripped half the length of a wide porch cluttered with thick grass rugs, aluminum-tubed beach chairs bright with sailcloth, scattered tables, and a deflated rubber sea lion in one corner.

Beyond the open door was a huge, dim living room which she crossed to reach a hallway that bisected the length of the ranch house.

She entered a bedroom on the left, furnished in knotty pine and with a baseboard-to-baseboard green rug, an inch deep, on the oak floor.

Thoughtfully, she pirouetted to a full-length mirror that formed the outside of a closet door. She inspected the image critically, like an envious woman searching for flaws in the superstructure of a rival. Every inch of her body was a rich tan. She turned sideways to the mirror. Her eyebrows arched at the reflection. She inhaled deeply and watched while the chest inflated.

Not bad, she thought.

She lifted on toes, arms extended. The stomach was flat, like a boy's. She wheeled full-face to the mirror. She walked closer to the mirror.

"No woman," she lectured the nude image aloud, "ever gets younger. What you need in your life is a man. You should marry again, understand? Since the divorce, it's been almost three years. You're twenty-two, Marta Selfron. Is there any valid reason for you to be wasting your charms on a mirror?"

The lips of the image murmured, "No."

"Your second husband won't fool you, will he?"

"No," the image said emphatically.

"Stop talking to yourself, understand?"

She broke it off . . .

Decidedly, the next husband wouldn't fool her—as the first one had so tragically.

And what would Number Two be like?

Tall, *umm!*

And dark, to complement her own coloring. Handsome? She had thought her first husband handsome, but she had been a child of only nineteen then and unprepared to recognize a real man. The next husband need not be good-looking.

But it was essential that he be a one-woman man, with appreciative eyes only for herself. Perhaps his eyes should be brown and filled with laughter, yet that was relatively unimportant.

What mattered most, actually, was that the second husband be a decent citizen, a man who could hold a job for more than a couple of months. A husband should not be a parasite on his wife's earnings, either. He should be—

She suddenly remembered something.

Going out for her dip, she had worn an old-rose two-piece suit. This she had thrown off when the urge to swim bare had seized her, and now she had forgotten it.

With a laugh, she turned from the mirror and ran back down the hall to the porch, thence out to the dock.

The sun, touching the ridge with gold and orange, threw brilliant fingers on the lake. As always at the sight of this bucolic majesty, Marta paused for a moment to gaze in awed appreciation at the scene.

She was just bending over to retrieve the old rose suit when she felt two arms thrown around her waist from behind.

Her first thought was that it must be Mr. Klee.

But once glance at the hands now clasped over her shocked midriff told her that they belonged to a younger and stronger man.

She opened her mouth and screamed.

"Go ahead and yell," growled her captor. "I've been watching long enough to know there's not a soul around here—"

Marta closed her mouth. She had recognized that voice.

"Let go of me," she squealed. "Vernon, you let go of me, of—"

"Yeah—or what?" He laughed coarsely. "Not a damn thing you can do, and you know it."

Tears of frustration rose to Marta's eyes. He was so right. "Get away from me. You filth. You dirty, rotten scum—"

One hand went to her arm and grabbed it. His other hand descended smartly on her rump.

"Don't talk to me that way, Marta. You look real toothsome." And again he sent a stinging blow to her buttock. The pain of it caused Marta to bawl. He threw a bear hug around her.

"Vernon," she shrilled, her nude legs kicking. "Vernon Cashion! Get away from me. You . . ."

His hard body falling on her knocked the breath from her lungs. He sent a stinging slap to her face. His hands pawed her. Her skin crawled at his loathsome touch, and she thrashed and kicked, trying to escape him.

But he was too strong for her. She had succeeded in turning over, and on her hands and knees was scrambling away. But he shifted quickly, sent a hand sweeping below, knocking the legs from under her and spilling her face down on the grass.

Vernon. Vernon Cashion. Once her husband . . .

Long after he had left her on the grass, Marta was still lying there. He disappeared into the woods, but she could not get herself to move.

But when at last the sun sank and reddened, and twilight fell, Marta stirred herself.

She rose up, walked the length of the dock, plunged cleanly into the lake.

The cold water shocked her into the realization that she was still alive. All might be hopeless, but nothing was ended.

It did not seem to her that the crystal waters of the lake cleansed her sufficiently. She swam to the dock.

Again forgetting the old-rose bathing suit, she ran into the house, her wet feet leaving marks in her wake.

Moments later she was in the shower soaping herself frenziedly under water as hot as she could stand.

The strange part was that she slept well that night. The explanation was her utter physical exhaustion, or perhaps the resiliency of the young.

But with the morning, although Marta awoke feeling refreshed, came that feeling of humiliation.

What was Vernon Cashion doing in the vicinity, anyway?

How had he known that she was here?

And it wasn't like him not to have mentioned the money—although Marta had not sent it this week, or the week before.

She spent the day swimming in the lake—religiously wearing the two-piece old rose; and she took no less than five showers between breakfast and the little dinner she cooked for herself in the elaborate kitchen of the ranch house.

She was wondering what kind of canned fruit she should open for dessert, when the wall telephone began to chatter.

She glanced at the electric clock on the wall. Ten minutes past seven. Would the call be from Hiram Klee, her millionaire boss?

"Marta," he would say in that imperious voice so characteristic of many fat little men, "I shall return from Canada tonight. I was forced to shorten my vacation because of business pressure. Besides, ah—my new redhead, who will be the fourth Mrs. Klee, has decided she does not care for the northern country."

With one hand on the ivory telephone, Marta hesitated.

Mr. Klee would never telephone in advance of his return.

He would swoop in unexpectedly and shatter the quiet with an assortment of house guests.

Who else knew she vacationed here? Well, maybe it was a call for Mr. Klee. She had better take the message.

She lifted the phone. "Yes?" she asked, and her voice was soft and cautious.

Silence greeted her ear.

She tensed.

"Yes?" she repeated.

"Did I scare the hell out of you yesterday?"

Her fingers tightened on the receiver until the knuckles stood out starkly white, like bleached bones on a skeleton. A lump formed in her stomach and, skyrocketing up her windpipe, blocked off her breathing.

She strangled slowly. Her free hand grabbed the edge of the table and that was all that kept her body from collapsing on the rug.

She said tightly: "Vernon!"

"Sure, your no-good ex-husband." Pause. "Speak up, Marta. Do you still hate me?"

Panic leaned over her shoulders and breathed ice on her body.

"Vernon, why are you calling?"

He laughed. It was an unpleasant sound over the wire.

"Thought we didn't know where you vacationed, hey? Listen, little pigeon. You forgot something since I left Newark and—uh, holed up for a while. I got the news from Ma. I hear you neglected to send the weekly letter to West Plank Road. We don't like that."

Long pause.

"We decided to teach you a lesson. We raised the weekly ante to twenty-five dollars. Get the letter in the mail tonight or—"

"Where are you?" she panted. "Where have you been hiding?"

"Wouldn't you like to know! Look, I may be a fool, but I'm a careful fool. You're not setting the cops on my trail—and you'd better forget I phoned, see?"

"Oh, I won't call the police," she assured him. Panic was crawling inside her body. She began to shake.

"Vernon, please listen. I've been sending your mother fifteen dollars a week for more than two years. Don't ask for twenty-five!"

"Twenty-five—or else."

For a moment, she gained some courage.

"This can't go on much longer. Haven't you and your mother bled me enough?"

"You've got plenty of blood in your arteries, Marta. Look, we're after money, all the money we can lay our hands on. That's a joke, see? If you don't think it's a joke, ask Hiram Klee, your boss at Aircrafter's, and wait until he laughs! Ma doesn't care for you, remember?"

Pause.

"Ma would like to wring your soft neck, see?"

Pause.

"Ma might decide to pay you a visit some dark, lonely night in the sticks."

Pause.

"Or I might drift over tonight myself, if you don't do right. I'm near enough to do it, too—you know that."

"For God's sake," she wailed, "why don't you leave me alone? I can't pay twenty-five a week. I—" He chuckled.

"The hell you can't. You raised a thousand bucks for our divorce, didn't you? And we know where you got it, don't we? That's why you have to do as we say, isn't it? Remember how you wrote a letter explaining where you got that money? We have the letter."

His voice hardened.

"The hell with you. Send twenty-five tonight and don't miss another payment. Or do you like jails from the inside?"

She was beyond panic. She was paralyzed into helplessness.

She gasped, "I work for my living. I'm not rich. I'm a secretary, that's all."

"We keep tabs. Hiram Klee pays you ninety bucks a week and we want our share. You can make it every week. You'd better make it." His laugh was a menacing sound over the wire. "Full moon tonight, Marta. Have fun."

"Vernon, is—is Prudence with you now?"

"Who?"

"Prudence Nason."

"That creep? Look, I've never had one woman for very long. Even you."

He broke the connection.

She leaned against the wall. Her strength slid down to her toes and leaked out on the rug. A sob shook her body.

It was a piteous, stricken sound that crawled through the dim silence of the empty ranch house.

After a moment, a busy voice said in her ear: "Miss, didn't your party hang up? Did you wish to make another call?"

She roused long enough to say dully, "Will you please connect me with the supervisor?"

"This is a rural exchange, miss. I'm the supervisor. Is there anything I can do?"

"Trace that call, please."

"Miss, it's against the rules and—"

"Please. It's vital. Life and death."

"Well—one moment, please."

She waited, every nerve tilted on raw edge.

If the operator traced the call, Marta promised herself, she would send the police to arrest Vernon. They would, too.

He was wanted because he had worked for Hiram Klee at Aircrafter's and, with the connivance of a secretary, Prudence Nason, had embezzled thirty thousand dollars.

Yes, and the police could arrest Vernon's mother at 1327 West Plank Road, Newark—because the mother knew where her son was and had not reported that fact.

If both the Cashions were in jail, they could not blackmail her any longer.

The operator said: "I checked the call, miss. It originated from a pay station in Hallstead. Do you wish the number?"

"Please."

"Hallstead 498. Is that all, miss?"

"Yes, and thanks."

"Not at all." Short pause. "Are you all right, miss?"

"Yes. I guess so." Marta cradled the phone.

But until she was free of the blackmailing mother and son, she would never be all right. They were bloody buzzards, feeding off living flesh. And why was she kidding herself?

She knew that she couldn't possibly set the police on their trails without opening prison doors for herself.

No, she could not notify the police that Vernon was in the vicinity and making threats.

How long had they been blackmailing her? Nearly three desperate years.

Her mind was so numbed from panic that she could not retrace the past except disconnectedly, but she went back over it again.

Nineteen years old, she had thought Vernon Cashion handsome in a Navy uniform. Oh, he had been smooth as silk. He could charm a girl, when he wanted to, and she had been completely innocent insofar as men were concerned.

They had married and gone to live at 1327 West Plank Road, his mother's rooming house.

The son had proved a complete tramp, the mother even worse. Marriage, except in the legal sense, had lasted two short weeks, at which time the mother had driven Marta out at the point of a gun.

A few months later, anxious to be free of them, Marta had begged for a divorce. Vernon was agreeable but had had no money. It would cost something like a thousand dollars, he had argued.

She raised the money—by taking the thousand dollars from a loose cash account at Aircrafter's, where she worked.

That had been her first mistake.

The second had been sending the money to them with a letter explaining how desperate she had been and what she had had to do to raise the money. Young and inexperienced, she had expected sympathy from them. Instead, she had received blackmail threats.

Only ten dollars a week, at first. Then fifteen. Now they wanted twenty-five. How stupid she had been to take that money, and more stupid still to write that incriminating letter.

Bit by bit, she had scrimped to pay back the money to Aircrafter's and Mr. Klee in a lump sum—and anonymously, because the money had never been missed. Today, she had no more than a pathetic four hundred dollars saved for the purpose.

Ironic, wasn't it?

Divorce was supposed to free a person from a horrible marriage to a criminal. Instead, it had enmeshed her in a deadly web.

Why, they might even come here after her.

She ran about, her body like ice, and flicked on switches until the room blazed with light. She stared at the grand piano. It wore a three-thousand-dollar price tag.

Money did not matter to Hiram Klee, sole owner of Aircrafter's. Funny, and she needed but six hundred dollars to square her conscience.

Suppose Ma Cashion did come here after her? Suppose Vernon came again?

Her chin jerked up defiantly.

"I've had enough," she said loudly, in an effort to bolster her courage. "I won't pay them any more. Let them come here. I'll never give them another cent, come what may."

She ran into the hallway and made her way to the master bedroom. It was a man's room, with leather-covered furniture and twin beds, with maroon walls to rest the eyes of the tired businessman on vacation. Tossed carelessly across one chair was a transparent raincoat and a battered felt hat, the only visible evidences of Hiram Klee.

He owned this ranch house, this lake, and two hundred surrounding acres. Just before he had departed for Canada with the new redhead, Klee had said: "I think a lot of you, Marta. You're my right arm at Aircrafter's. You're welcome to take your vacation at my place. You'll be alone—but if you ever feel unsafe, remember I keep a loaded revolver in the top drawer of my dresser. All you have to do is snick off the safety catch, close your eyes, and press the trigger." He had laughed. "In case a skunk prowls at night, you do that."

It had been a joke. It was a joke no longer.

She found the gun in the dresser, as he had said. It had a bluish barrel and a wooden butt inlaid with ivory. It felt solid in her hand, and magnificently comforting.

"I'll force one of them or both to come here," she thought. "I'll shoot to kill."

Wouldn't the local law side with her? She could build it up. She tried out a tentative line of defense. "I was all alone and it's so—so wild! I— I heard this sound at my bedroom window. I fired blindly. Of course, I warned the intruder first! And—and the gun went off, just like Mr. Klee told me it would, and I happened to hit him—or her!"

Tight, wasn't it?

And simple.

If she shot one Cashion, the other would leave her alone. If they came together—she would kill two skunks with two bullets!

If she had thought more deeply, standing there in Mr. Klee's sumptuous bedroom, she might have realized that panic had hidden temporarily in a dark corner. Now it stalked forth and, creeping silently across the rug, leered at her nude spine. Thinking of Vernon had made her feel soiled, and she meant to take another shower.

Back in her bedroom across the hallway, she picked up a towel and rubbed the chill from her flesh. When the skin glowed pinkly, she checked herself in the mirror.

She still had that beautiful body. But, Marta—that face! The clear blue eyes were haunted. The mouth was drawn and grim . . .

She couldn't stay here alone tonight, not even with the comforting gun hidden in her pocketbook. She had to get out and mix with people.

She might even get drunk and numb the feeling of menace inside her.

Pulling a nylon slip over her shoulders, she settled it in place and shortened the length by tightening the buckles. Next, she added a sheer white blouse with a square, low neckline and nodded approval.

She chose a short green skirt and white sandals. She omitted stockings because, uncovered, the tanned legs looked more seductive.

At the vanity, she sat and fluffed the honey-colored curls with deft fingers. She penciled lipstick carefully, filling out lips that needed no further accentuation. Red. Red was for courage, Marta.

She left lights burning in the living room, locked all the doors, and strode to the car parked on a graveled driveway.

It was a big Chrysler town car, one of Mr. Klee's. He had authorized her to use it as she pleased. In the glove compartment she located a map of New Jersey and pin-pointed Hallstead, population eleven hundred, a village on Culver Lake—only a twenty-minute drive away if Vernon Cashion decided to pay a nocturnal visit.

She glanced up. The sun had set behind the rim of hills. Twilight would soon be darkness. She switched on the ignition. The engine kicked over and purred obediently.

She drove off in an effort to escape, to escape the Cashions, to escape herself. The rear tires peppered the ranch house with gravel. The front wheels cut across the smooth lawn. She yanked the car back on course and steadied the wheel.

She turned left on a tarred road. The tarred road debauched on a main highway, and she turned right. The Chrysler shook itself and ate into the long upgrade of the ridge.

She had this car, she thought. She didn't have to go to the ranch house or Newark. She could just drive off. Disappear. She could find a hideout for herself, like Vernon Cashion did. She could get another job. He would never find her and haunt her again, or his mother, either. She ought to follow the road and lose herself. Then she thought—no, running away would not do at all. Not while she owed money to Hiram Klee and to her conscience. She would have to stay and fight it out until she had made restitution. That was all there was to it.

Her fingers tensed on the wheel of the speeding car. Besides, she thought, flight wasn't so simple in a modern world of fingerprints and social security cards. She would have to show the card to get work. And if she managed to procure another card under a different name, personnel managers still would pry into her background—and where would she get references?

She was trapped. Vernon Cashion and his mother had pinned her down.

Near the crest of the grade, she saw the familiar building that squatted under a platoon of red oaks. It had a green-shingled roof and imitation log siding and window boxes that flamed with geraniums. In there were people whom she knew casually.

She turned off the road, parking by a white picket fence beyond which a neat vegetable garden loafed in the twilight.

Over the door, a neon sign advertised: *FRED'S LOG CABIN*. It wasn't much of a place, of course. But it was the one to which she had been going sometimes when in the mood for a meal out or a drink or just driven by a need to hear human voices. Here at least, she told herself, she would be temporarily safe.

She slid out of the car with a flash of bare, tanned legs.

TWO

Up front, there was an ample dance floor flanked by many tables covered with white-and-red checkered cloths surrounded by wire-backed chairs, all empty, like a chorine's stage smile. Across the entire rear ran a lighted bar where backless stools waited for customers. A rainbowed jukebox offered tunes of the day and of earlier days.

Behind the bar lounged a fat man, quite bald, who wore a white shirt, a black bow-tie, a white apron, and a bored expression on his wooden face.

This was Fred, the owner. He rested fat buttocks against a partition and worried his teeth with a wooden toothpick.

As Marta swung across the dance floor, Fred frowned and spoke up. "Now I got to go to work, damn it. Don't you city people have any homes, Miss Selfron?"

"Hello," Marta said brightly.

"Look," he grumbled, "I been busy with vacationers all summer. Why didn't you come in August, like the rest? Don't you know September is supposed to be a vacation for me?"

"Quit grumbling, Fred. I need a drink."

They both laughed. Fred loved his little jokes.

Midway along the bar sat a hairy-armed ape man, his prognathic chin lowered over a glass of beer. The ape man turned slowly. His eyes ran up and down Marta's trim figure approvingly.

"If Fred won't wait on you," the ape man said, "I will."

He was a hanger-on, Marta knew. He haunted the place practically every night.

She smiled. "Hello, Harry. How are the muscles today?"

He rolled up one sleeve, grinning. He balled a fist, lifted his elbow and bent the fist towards his shoulder. His biceps balled into a muskmelon.

"I'm the strongest guy in Jersey," Harry bragged. "Anybody gets fresh with you, Miss Selfron, you let Harry know, see?" His fist moved back and forth. At each movement, the biceps leaped.

Marta chose a stool near the rainbowed jukebox. She laid her pocketbook on the mahogany. The purse was heavy. She'd get herself stoop-shouldered, toting that gun around. The lights reached her hands and bare arms, but missed her face and failed to highlight her loveliness.

"A rye and water, Fred," she ordered. "And go heavy on the ice, if you don't mind."

"Ice is the cheapest thing I sell," Fred said, and went to work. He carried the drink along the bar, set it down. "Someday," he offered darkly, "I'm gonna sell this joint and buy a farm and get away from all the troubles I hear."

"Do lots of people unburden themselves with you, Fred?"

"All the time. The stuff I sell loosens tongues."

Marta sipped the drink. It was cold and tangy. Outside, cars rushed past on the highway. Once a horn blew and a trailer truck lumbered in low gear up the grade. Marta set down her glass.

"Make the next one a double, please," she ordered. Fred obliged, and Harry said, "You drink what you want, Miss Selfron. I won't let no wolves bother you, see?"

He was a bore, she thought. The entire setup was a bore. Why had she come here?

She was halfway through the second drink, hitting it too rapidly on an empty stomach and not caring, when headlights stabbed in at the windows and an engine died on the parking lot.

"Stranger?" Harry asked, without turning.

Fred said: "It don't sound familiar."

The door opened, and Marta turned casually.

A young, hatless man strode across the dance floor. She did not know him. He was tall, rather solid through the shoulders, but narrower at the hips. He had black hair and black eyes. He wore a sport shirt and a tan gabardine suit with brown suede shoes. He crossed to the bar.

"Hot—there on the road," he offered sociably.

"Too hot for September," Fred agreed. "Travel far?"

The man's eyes swept the room. They flicked past Marta and she wondered if he had seen her. "Adirondacks. Late vacation," the man explained. "That means work tomorrow."

He grinned at Fred. Marta sipped. The man had a nice smile, seemed rather interesting, she decided. As she crossed her legs, she saw Harry staring at her with bloodshot eyes.

"Make mine rye and water," the man was saying. "First, squeeze some lime over the ice, and not too much ice."

"I don't have a fresh lime this time of the year," Fred explained. "Got some in a bottle. That okay?"

"Sure. My throat's like sawdust."

Fred went to work. The man spotted the jukebox. He walked along the bar and Harry's eyes followed him. Marta thought: why, that man didn't even glance at you, honey. Hmmmm!

The man examined the legends, spent a dime. The machine whirred. Lights flashed on. He leaned against the machine casually. He still had not noticed Marta particularly because his eyes were on the floor. But the added light from the jukebox spotlighted Marta's lifted foot, pointed toward him.

She sensed his eyes on her white shoe, then going up the length of tanned, crossed leg, and to the hem of the skirt primly over her knee.

He took an involuntary step toward her. His dark eyes were full of compliments. He started to smile, checked himself. Marta glanced at her unfinished drink.

The music started up. It was one of the show ballads, something catchy and romantic, a trumpet riding high over the swelling melody.

She saw his foot begin to tap and heard him murmur: "Good song, eh?"

He was talking to the floor. Or, the machine. No, he was talking to her.

She asked: "Did you say something?"

He grinned. "Good song," he repeated. He strolled to the bar. "Mind?"

"Of course not."

He sat down. "Thanks. Uh—I missed you when I first walked in. You sat in shadows, your face hidden. You shouldn't do that."

"Why not?"

He leaned elbows on the bar, faced her. "Because," he said softly, "you belong in spotlights. Am I being fresh?" He laughed. "In spotlights," he repeated. "Sounds corny, doesn't it?"

"Did you mean it to be?"

"No. I'm telling the truth. It's a habit of mine."

Fred padded along the bar, set down the limed drink. The man laid a five-dollar bill on the bar and Fred made change at the cash register.

"You like to dance?" the man asked.

"Sure."

"If I asked you to—I mean, would you like to dance now?"

"If you won't step on my toes."

He slid off his stool and waited. Marta uncrossed her legs, stepped down. He was reaching for her when Harry loomed at his back.

"You," Harry growled, "break it off."

The man turned slowly.

From behind the bar, Fred called: "Harry, back on your stool."

"She ain't dancin' with him," Harry said.

The man turned to Marta. "Let's go," he said. If he was scared, he did not show it.

"No," Marta said. She stepped closer to him, fingered the lapel of his coat. "Maybe we'd better wait," she whispered. "He's pretty tough. I don't know why he's interfering and I don't want trouble—please?"

His eyes grinned at her. "No trouble," he said.

"Get the hell out of here, you!" Harry said, and lifted a brawny fist. "Get out before I tear you apart, see?"

The man said easily to big Harry, "Why don't you go sit down?"

"Who, me?"

"You. Sit down."

"You got fresh with her," Harry said. He stuck out his chin and, without other warning, brought up a haymaker.

"Look out!" Marta squealed.

But the young man had stepped back and Harry's fist collided with air. Behind the bar, Fred picked up a bottle by the neck and started around the far end.

Harry straightened. The man said: "You're drunk, you know. Why don't you behave?"

Marta said: "Harry, go sit down!"

"Gonna throw the louse out," Harry raged savagely, and bored in.

"Sorry, miss," the young man said. His voice had picked up a flat, dry sound.

Ducking under Harry's high guard, the man threw a jolting left to the chin. Harry's head rocked back. A lightning right slammed into the pit of Harry's stomach. Surprise blossomed on Harry's ugly face, which proceeded to fall apart. The blow had shivered his spine, and without sound he plunged floorward, his two hundred and twenty pounds of beef all but splintering the oak under foot.

The juke box cut off.

Fred was standing beside limp Harry on the floor, bottle held high overhead.

And Fred, mouth open, stared at the young man. "Cripes," he said slowly, "I ain't never seen nothin' like that. Two punches, cripes!"

"I walked in here," the man said dreamily, "for a drink and a sandwich."

"You a fighter?" Fred wanted to know.

"No. Make it ham and cheese, please."

"That Harry," Fred grumbled. "Always pickin' fights. Cleaned out the place a month back. This is the last straw. We got State Police. They can cart him off, see?"

Fred waddled toward the kitchen, and the man turned to Marta. "Sorry," he offered. "I must have lost my temper."

"It wasn't your fault," she mumbled.

Fred called over his shoulder: "Gonna call the troopers, this time. Had enough of that monobrain."

"It was partly my fault," Marta offered. She shivered. "I want—to get—out of here."

She picked up her pocketbook. There were tears in her eyes as she walked past the young man. She heard him say, "Throw a bucket of water over him. He'll come to."

And Fred: "You sure you ain't in the ring?"

"No."

"Gripes, you're a puncher. How do you make your living?"

"Private detective. I'm supposed to be tough and—" His voice faded, and Marta stumbled out the door.

She sat in the darkness of the front seat of the Chrysler, staring at the tip of the moon beginning to lift over a ridge in the valley. She heard the door of Fred's Cabin open and close, then steps crunching along the gravel.

"Thought you were still here," the young man said. "I didn't hear your car start up."

He rounded the car, opened the door. "May I?" he asked, and waited.

"I guess so."

He slid in beside her.

"What about your sandwich?" she asked.

"Hell with it," he said.

"Uh—didn't I hear you say you were a private detective?"

"On vacation."

She thought about that for a moment, making up her mind. "I don't know why that oaf did what he did," she said slowly. "I don't live around here. I've been in the place a number of times, but—"

"You don't have to explain. I know why he did it," the man said.

Her eyes queried him.

"Because you're you," he said. "He thought I was bothering you and in his dumb, drunk fashion he imagined he was a knight on a white horse. That's the way you make a man feel. Look, I can climb into my own car and head for home in Newark. Or—"

He let it dangle.

Marta turned on the seat. She extended her right knee toward him, straightened the leg, then slipped her left knee over her right ankle. The skirt hem had hiked three inches past her bare knees during the operation, but she did not bother to lower the hem.

"You know," he said softly, "you interest me, and not just because I've been in the hills for three weeks."

He reached to the cowl, flicked on the dashboard light, and there was more light in the car.

She sat still while his eyes went over her carefully. She hoped he liked the honey-colored hair. She could see that he was more than casually taken with the thin blouse and the square, low neckline.

He shook his head, puzzled. "No wedding ring. The men you know must be blind." He leaned closer. "Don't turn away," he cautioned.

She looked him full in the face, and something seemed to jump the space between them.

"Nice eyes," he said thoughtfully. "Like the color of a summer sky, or the light's all wrong. And rather guileless eyes, full of innocence."

She laughed. "Are you sure Harry didn't hit you?"

"Something hit me, all right. Virginal eyes, like—like the first rain of September. I'll bet you've never been kissed."

"A poet with muscles," she mused, and his easy masculinity intrigued her. "So you think I've never been kissed. Am I that unattractive?"

"That's not the way I meant it, and you know it."

For Marta, it was a moment of decision. She could break things off right here and drive back to the ranch house alone. And he, whatever his name was, could drive to Newark and go about his business—the business of being a private investigator. The two words impressed her.

He was quick and hard with his hands, and he might be more than a match for the Cashions. Lord knew, she had no one else to turn to. Which led her to the alternative. Instead of sending him on his way, she—

He interrupted her thoughts, saying, "You're worried about something."

She jumped. "I am?"

"Yes. Something is disturbing you, preoccupying you—"

"How can you tell?"

"Instinct and training. Besides, it's all over your face." He laughed.

"I am preoccupied," she confessed, smiling. "I'm on vacation, you see, and I keep thinking that it can't last forever—"

She made up her mind. She needed him. Her fingers touched his coat sleeve. They inched up his arm and fiddled with the biceps muscle under the cloth. Hard, she thought. She pinched the biceps thoughtfully.

"You cooled that bruiser so fast that I couldn't believe my eyes. Are you always that good with your fists?"

"Just a free sample against a chump," he explained cheerfully.

"I liked it and Harry had it coming to him." She added casually: "I'm stopping at a private lake in the valley. Would you—I mean, why don't you let me buy you a drink?"

"If you don't stop playing with my muscles, I'll roll on the floor mat and lap your shoes."

"Then you'll come?"

"I'd be delighted."

She untangled her legs and settled under the wheel. Her pocketbook, on the cushion between them, slid to the mat. He picked it up, said, "Hey, this is heavy. You got an iron in there?"

She said lightly, "I carry a tommy-gun around for guys like Harry. Will you follow my car?"

"You bet."

He stepped out and closed the door. Marta started the engine, swung the car around and waited, facing downhill. There was an old green convertible, top down, parked near the fence. It looked honest. But instead of climbing aboard the convertible, he marched toward the Cabin.

"Not again!" she called, alarmed.

He walked to one of the window boxes and broke off a red geranium, then rejoined her. "Couldn't let 'em get away without paying for my exhibition," he explained. He tucked the stem over her ear, patted the curls in place.

"Makes you look like my little sister—except I don't have a little sister."

She studied him intently. "You're pretty tough, aren't you?"

"So I've been told."

"Tough and hard outside—and kind of soft inside."

"Look, you must have a name."

"Marta."

"I like it. And?"

"Selfron. Marta Selfron."

"Ask me my name, Marta."

"What's your name?"

He pulled out a billfold, opened it. "Take a look at the buzzer."

She held it under the dashlight. The buzzer was his identification, an official card behind a cellophane window. He was Dirk L. Delgar, Private Investigator, Prudential Building, Newark. He was thirty years old, a hundred-eighty pounds of bone and muscle. The official seal of the State of New Jersey was on the card. It looked so reassuring. She returned the billfold.

"Shall we go?"

"Right." He headed for his old convertible.

His headlights followed her down the long, steady grade. She did not glance back. Perhaps he would drive on to Newark immediately. Perhaps she had no actual attraction for him, except that she seemed to be offering quick and easy sex. Perhaps she had overplayed her hand and he would sense that this was more than a casual pickup. Perhaps he would think her so crudely wanton that he would say, "No, thanks."

She shivered, remembering the nearness of Vernon Cashion. Then she stopped shivering; the man's headlights were trailing her into the side road. And she began to think.

This stranger was quick and keen. "You're worried—" he had diagnosed. Of course, she was worried. Oh, she wouldn't tell him. There was a way out—whereby he could help her indirectly. But she would have to be careful not to let her secret leak out. Well, she would manage. Couldn't a good-looking woman deceive a man artfully, even if he were a private investigator? Sure . . .

THREE

As Marta parked in front of the garage, Dirk clicked off headlights and joined her in the half-darkness behind the ranch house. "Looks like a swank place," he offered. "All the lights."

"The lights keep me from being lonely."

"Who's here?"

"Just us two chickens. Come on in."

She unlocked the door and led the way into the kitchen. He stood in the middle of the room and inventoried the equipment. "Rather elaborate," he decided. "Plenty of everything, including refrigerators. Why two?"

"Parties," she explained cryptically. "Suppose you run out to the front porch and see if the moon is up? Take your coat off and relax. I'll mix that drink I promised you. Still hungry?"

"Starved."

He walked to her, touched her chin with a forefinger. It was a casual gesture, but Marta felt a shiver course up her spine. He asked: "If your name is Selfron, where does Hiram Klee fit into the picture?"

He doesn't miss a trick, she thought.

"Oh," she said, "you saw the name on the 'no trespass' signs. He's the principal owner of Aircrafter's in Kearney, and I'm his secretary. He's off vacationing with his new girlfriend in Canada. He let me come here for my belated vacation. He calls this his country cottage." She sighed. "Two hundred acres, the private lake, and this perfectly wonderful house."

"With his new girlfriend . . ." he mused.

"She's a redhead, and rather—uh—electric. When they marry, she'll become the fourth Mrs. Klee."

"If I were your boss—oh, skip it."

"Should I?"

He said: "Didn't you have a chance?"

She stared, startled at the idea. "Why, Dirk, he's short and fat and fifty!"

"And lousy with mink coats and Cadillacs and country estates that he calls cottages."

"I think you'd better retire to the front porch," she said tartly.

"Hey, it has a temper."

"Darn right, I have a temper! If mine were like yours, I'd—" She looked around for a suitable weapon.

He said casually: "The pocketbook?"

"Pocketbook?" she echoed, puzzled.

"The tommy-gun is in your pocketbook, you said."

"You idiot, to the porch with you!"

He walked off, nonchalantly, as if he owned the first mortgage on the place.

She busied herself at the refrigerator, slicing cold meats, arranging pickles and olives and cheese on a tray. She sawed off slabs from a hard-crusted loaf of bread.

She opened a bottle of rye, set it on a second tray and filled a silver cooler with ice cubes. Next, two glasses. She squeezed a fresh lime and poured the juice into a tiny silver pitcher with a monogrammed HK on the outside.

"Be nice to the nice man, Marta," she murmured. "He's keen and clever and strong. He's going to take the Cashion family off your back, if you play him right." She carried the two trays to the porch, pausing briefly in the living room to cut off some of the lamps.

It was dark on the porch, just one dim light from the living room. The

September moon had topped the distant ridge and started to pour gold on the quiet lake.

"Coffee table, please," she said, and he jumped up from a divan and arranged the low table. She sat down beside him, not too close and covered his thighs with a napkin.

"Try this," she suggested, and handed him a drink.

He sipped. He smacked his lips. The drink had hair on its breath, and he said: "Very good. Nothing like lime on ice, then rye and water."

"I heard you order at Fred's."

"Thanks. You're a darling hostess."

They ate and drank. Marta mixed another drink. She recalled that if you wanted to keep your wits, you always placed a layer of food in the stomach, then a layer of liquor.

More food, another layer of rye. The food was supposed to absorb the alcohol so it didn't rush to the brain and paralyze your resistance. But she wasn't too careful about the layers.

A warm glow spread through her body. Why not? With Dirk here, she was safe.

They smoked and talked idly—simple stuff, like who would win the pennant. The moon had mellowed into a ripe coin. It piled gold four feet deep on the porch.

They sat, silent a lot, and let time drift past.

"It's nine o'clock," Marta said. "I can tell by the height of the moon. The food and rye have settled. We could swim."

"I'd love to see you inside a bathing suit."

"Do you like to swim?"

"I had three weeks of it in lonely waters up north. I hate to think of work tomorrow."

"Why?"

"I liked it up there. It was quiet and lonely, like this spot."

"Do you go on a new case tomorrow?"

"If I'm lucky. September's usually a slow month."

She was shrewd enough to postpone her personal problem. "Were you alone in the Adirondacks?"

"One female."

She kicked off her shoes and stretched her legs and toes languorously. She stood up, then sat down on both bare feet, a woman's nonchalant trick in sitting. "Was she nice, Dirk?"

"One of the nicest females who ever ate salt."

"Salt!"

"Sure. That's the way to a doe's heart."

"This female was a—deer?"

"What did you think?"

She pouted prettily.

"Stinker, leading me into that trap. Aren't there any women in your life, Dirk?"

"Oh, here and there. All there, I guess. You see, I'm being perfectly honest with you. Don't get the idea that I love 'em and leave 'em—but I'm committed to no boudoir permanently. You?"

"Unlucky, I guess." A cloud scurried across her relaxed face. "No wedding ring, no diamond, and the boss is taking on a fourth wife. I'm worried. When a girl is twenty-two—"

He bent toward her. A strong forefinger tilted up her chin until her eyes met his. She knew what he contemplated. Her blue eyes filled with anticipation.

He asked quietly: "What's worrying you?"

"You."

"Okay."

He kissed her gently on the lips.

She teetered back. Practically the sort of kiss you received from a brother.

Careful, she thought. Don't let him see that you're worried.

"Bold, aren't you?" she chided, a challenge in the question.

"So are you."

"Me?"

"You wanted me to kiss you."

"I did?"

"Yeah."

"Mr. Delgar, can you X-ray a girl's mind?"

"Sometimes, but don't tempt me."

She felt reckless. She smiled, puckered her lips, closed her eyes, and moved toward him. Their lips met clingingly. *Ummm*, this was much better. His lips said so. So did hers. She had been alone with her complexes far too long. He had spent three weeks in the lonely mountains with only a doe.

Smile benignly, September moon!

They were sitting too awkwardly to hold the position. When they paused for breath, she lifted to her knees. That made her taller than he was, but she was sure he wouldn't acquire an inferiority complex.

She murmured: "Tell me something, please?"

"Anything for a beautiful girl."

"Dirk, I was bored here, alone. I wandered up to Fred's for a drink. I wanted to spend an hour somewhere before I took my nightly swim and went to bed. I didn't expect anything to happen—and then, you walked in. You looked so—so interesting."

"Go ahead. Flatter me. I love it."

She was leading him on, and if stroking his ego would do the trick, fine.

"I hoped you'd invite me to have a drink with you. I admit, that was forward. And you didn't even see me!"

He touched the cloth over her thigh with one strong finger. The finger described a circle. Her skin tingled as if the finger had been on her flesh.

"I didn't get a chance to order you a drink."

"Dirk, you didn't look at me until you saw my legs. Oh, I was thrilled when your eyes complimented me. You asked me to dance and that lout butted in with his muscles! I was afraid he'd hurt you. Dirk, you were magnificent against him."

Her hand toyed with his fingers.

"Dirk, will you tell me something?"

"Look, you've been telling *me.*"

"Dirk, I've seen a lot of private investigators. I mean, I've read mysteries and seen movies and television programs. Are you like those men?"

"In what way?"

"They're all so strong in a crisis—as you were at Fred's. So honest and understanding in a nasty world where people always have such difficult problems. Do all private investigators try to accomplish good against terrific odds?"

"A moon riding the sky," he said, and shrugged, "and you make with questions about my work. Look, I've been a private operator since I was twenty. It's four years now since I opened my own agency.

"Nothing big, understand—just a couple of shabby rooms in the Pru Building and no oriental carpeting and beautiful secretary like Hiram Klee has. I like the work, not the pay. No matter how inconsequential a new case seems on the surface, I give it the goal-line plunge.

"It's a challenge to whatever integrity and brains I have. Sometimes I stumble into danger, but not as often as those guys do in TV scripts."

He sat brooding, staring across the waters. His face had lengthened while he talked, and now his hands kept clenching and unclenching.

He began to talk in a monotone, as if he were alone; he was letting her see into his heart.

"Danger spices dull routine, I suppose. I'm no epic man. Certainly no heroic character that script writers invent to thrill lonely spinsters. I get an assignment. I try to do an honest job.

"When a case ends satisfactorily for my client, I feel good. A client often brings me stuff that he's ashamed to take to the police. The client hasn't done anything illegal, but simply involved himself through indiscretion or inadvertency or both.

"Society is full of predatory people who overwhelm an ordinary citizen. He dumps the mess in my lap. Often he withholds vital information that would help me and I have to grope in the dark." He laughed suddenly. "Do I bore you, darling?"

"No." Her mind fastened tight to one item he had detailed. "Shouldn't a client always be frank with you?"

"Not unless he wishes to be. I try to win confidence, but not necessarily confidences."

"If the client withholds pertinent facts," Marta persisted, "doesn't that increase your personal danger?"

"I've never looked at it from that angle. I'm hired. I'm paid to face whatever danger arises. I don't object to danger. If I were an incompetent operator, I'd go sell hardware and be safe behind a counter. Danger? According to vital statistics, the home is the most dangerous place there is.

"In the most prosaic task, there's an element of danger—like the risk of getting your finger caught in a wringer. We sit here talking.... Isn't that dangerous?"

What does he mean, she pondered.

"We're young. There's the moon. We drank three highballs. We've got red blood. We couldn't be in greater danger if we sat here drinking nitroglycerine. You know it and I know it. Why walk around it? Basic biology isn't a phrase, Marta. It's an urge. You have it. I have it. I'm merely warning, is all."

"Do I want to be warned?"

"That's your decision," he finished, and sat silent.

She touched his cheek lightly, where a small, white cicatrix marred his tanned skin.

"Did you get that scar in your work?"

"Probably."

"Tell me about it, please?"

"That's a nice way you have, always please."

"Please?"

He stared out at the golden water.

"Moonlight and us, and you talk about a scar. You may not like to hear it."

"But I do!"

"Okay. It was a blackmail case, as I remember. A blackmailer is a bloodsucker, the worst criminal in society, except for a sex criminal. He cultivates death-by-inches torture on a victim. Let's say he's picked up something on somebody who has been indiscreet. He moves in carefully. First, he tries to establish that he is a menace to security and happiness. To soften a prospect, he asks for a trifle initially. If the prospect pays off, that's an admission that menace exists. The prospect graduates to the victim class.

"Soon the bloodsucking blackmailer has sapped all power of resistance from the victim. The victim is helpless. He does whatever he is told to do. Each succeeding bite is deeper until the victim is picked clean.

"I've heard of victims who committed suicide rather than take positive action against the blackmailer. Lovely moon out there, Marta."

"Go on," she said breathlessly. "About the scar."

"Well, in this case, the bloodsucker acquired an incriminating picture. All bloodsuckers need evidence, like a letter, a record or a photo.

"Finally, the desperate client came to me. I tailed the leech. I let him take another bite to be sure of his *modus operandi*. When he moved in for another bite, I had the trap ready and sprang it. He was a big man, a tub of soft butter.

"But he carried a sleeve gun. Trying to escape, he used the gun. The bullet nicked my left hip. I fooled him by collapsing on the rug. He clipped me across the cheek with the barrel. So—the scar."

"Did the blackmailer escape?"

"No."

"What happened to him?"

"After he clipped me, he was off balance. I carried a .38 in a shoulder rig and pulled it. He fired once, but he was a poor shot and missed. I had to fire once. At the ceiling. He threw down his gun—"

She sat still, fingers interlaced tightly, measuring her own dilemma against Dirk's case.

Then: "Did he bother your client again?"

"No."

Teeth nibbled on her lower lip.

"Why not? I sound awfully stupid, I know, but how did you restrain the blackmailer?"

"I recovered the picture."

"That was enough?"

"No."

"Don't be so secretive, please!"

"I fired that one shot to scare him, Marta. It did." She stood up suddenly, unnecessarily smoothing the tight skirt about her hips.

"Don't run away. I'll be right back, and I want to hear more of your adventures."

"You going somewhere?"

"To the little girl's room."

She stooped suddenly and kissed him on the scar and caressed the lean line of his jaw.

"You're a brave man," she whispered, and left him.

Exhilaration welled inside her. Listening to the story of that case, she had become more certain than ever that Dirk could help her against the Cashions without his knowing she needed this help.

Be nice to him, she thought. Bind him to you . . .

Above the nearby ridge, the moon rode high across the vaulted sky. Against its pure mellow radiance, the stars were faded jewels.

The moon fingered the quiet ripples on the lake and laid gold flecks on the silent water.

From somewhere along the shore, a bird roused itself long enough to drop a silver *loo*, a sleep sound before slumber.

They stood on the dock, leaning against a railing and holding hands. Marta faced the moon, chin lifted, features relaxed. The moonlight patted her hair and changed it to gold. It highlighted her best curves.

"So lovely," she murmured, entranced with the beauty. "I hope it never ends."

"Lovely," he repeated, staring at her.

"The moon's like a gold coin, isn't it? A moon is wasted if there are no people to watch it. Would you like to swim?"

"Whatever you say."

"Want a canoe?"

"If you sit close."

"You won't splash water?"

"No."

Under the spell of her troubles, she had plotted a definite course that would bind him to her.

"Mustn't a man behave in a canoe?"

"He can beach the canoe."

"On a rocky shore?"

"Now you're being elusive."

She let recklessness explode, as if by accident.

"Maybe I don't want you to behave."

"Well?"

"We'll go canoeing and see what happens."

A canoe rode by the dock, bumping its ribs gently on wood. She released Dirk's hand and crossed to the craft.

She leaned down and stuck one bare foot toward the thwart.

"That's no way to board a canoe," Dirk said lazily. "It's light and tricky. Place your hands on opposite sides before you step down."

"I know how to do it."

He shrugged.

"Watch, please."

She knew all about the trickiness of a canoe. Balancing on one foot, she lowered the other and set it squarely in the center of the canoe.

She swung her body outward. The pressure accomplished what she wanted and the canoe moved inches away from the dock.

She lifted the foot on the dock and reached down for the opposite gunwale. Of course, the canoe did exactly what she had planned for it to do.

One moment, she teetered upright; the next, she had pitched headfirst into the water as the canoe upset.

She sputtered to the surface and brushed hair from her eyes.

"I'll be damned," she announced, as if she had been outwitted. "Why did the canoe upset?"

"Because it's a canoe?"

She pouted. "Why didn't you dive in to save me?"

"And place you in greater danger?"

She paddled around. The water sopped her clothes and tugged her toward the bottom.

"I'm silly," she said, laughing. "I didn't watch my step, did I?"

"Did you want to?"

She let her body sink and called, "Help!"

"Cry wolf," he offered, amused.

"I really am!"

"I should get my clothes wet?"

"Please, save me!"

"No, ma'am."

"Then I'll save myself. My clothes weigh a ton."

They laughed, and she swam to the dock.

He grabbed her wrists and lifted her easily to the boards.

The end of step one, she thought.

The honey-colored curls had plastered to her head like wet seaweed to a rock. The episode had done to her body what it was supposed to do. The sodden skirt gloved her hips and thighs. She stood sniffing, the water streaming to the dock.

"No canoe ride tonight, Dirk. We'd never get the laméd thing dry in time."

"Want to try?"

She switched to, "I must look terrible."

"You're beautiful, soaking wet."

"Like a drowned rat."

"Wet clothes on a woman don't leave much to the imagination. You're definitely beautiful, I can assure you."

"You say the nicest things, darling. Unlike a lot of men, you're not forward. Is that your line?"

"I have no line," he said quietly. "A woman's not like a man. You wait for her. If waiting doesn't do the trick, there's no point in playing a masterful role. A. woman will do what she wants to do and that's all there is to it."

She geared her mind for step two, and said suddenly: "And I wanted a romantic canoe ride with you."

"Canoes make a man behave."

"You don't want to behave?"

He countered, "What do you want me to do?"

"My clothes are—are clammy. Dirk, let's be reckless and blame it on the moon!"

"How?"

"We'll play a game. You must remember that there are rules in this game, Dirk."

"What's the game?"

"Turn your back, please."

He turned away.

"Walk toward the porch, please."

He marched off. When he neared the screen door, she called: "Don't turn until I give the word!"

"Can I guess what you're going to do?"

"No!"

Reckless fingers unzippered the skirt. She stepped free of its clammy weight. She pitched the skirt. It landed behind him with a loud *slosh*.

"Can't I look?" he pleaded.

"If you do, the referee will banish you from the game."

Agile fingers unbuttoned the blouse. She tossed it after the skirt. Then the slip joined the heap.

Starkly nude, she poised on the dock. "When I count to four," she explained, "you may turn around."

"You witch!"

She tiptoed to the diving board. She began to chant: —two—three—three and a quarter—three and a half—"

She dived. Before she hit the water, she shouted: "Four!"

The cool water shocked her heated body. She needed that coolness. The game had got beyond her control and the water might restrain the urges that were a hurricane inside her.

She swam down into colder, darker waters, but she was unafraid. Her legs kicked frog-like, and she swam toward the middle of the lake.

She warned herself, don't be a goose. You can't let him—not the first night. You've never acted like this before. Why you barely know him.

Lack of oxygen constricted her lungs. She bubbled to the surface, rolled over, and faced the dock. He leaned against the railing, motionless.

"You witch. Where did you have your bathing suit hidden?"

"What bathing suit?"

"You're—?"

"Yes!"

Pause.

She called, "Aren't you coming in?"

"With my clothes on?"

"Don't be silly!"

He unbuttoned his shirt and draped it across the railing. He kicked off shoes, yanked off socks. As his fingers unbuckled his belt, she called: "I'll be underwater!"

"You and your rules."

She flipped over, dug palms into the water and submerged. The water slid off her skin and she thought: Could she trust him? He had said he played a waiting game, which meant that it was up to her.

If she could really trust him . . .

She surfaced.

He swum toward her, crawling effortlessly. She swam slowly past the middle of the lake where the water was deepest.

On the far shore, the trees were molded into golden statuary by the moon. She stopped and trod water. Only her face showed above the waterline. Did Dirk know the rules?

Ten feet distant, he halted. He floated with his feet straight down, his arms flat on the water. "Isn't this nice, Dirk?"

"You are."

"You see only my face."

"I'm the imaginative type."

"I'm completely clothed by water. Clothes or water—what difference does it make what one wears?"

"Want me to tell you?"

They floated with simple arm and leg movements. They watched the moon. They listened to the quiet night.

Somewhere beyond the ranch house, an engine throbbed along the road and the water picked up the sound and magnified it.

Headlights slashed through the woods and died.

Two people about to watch the moon, Marta thought idly.

"I love to swim nude," she said casually. "And I often do, here. This lake is private."

"When are you going to announce changes in the rules?"

She let the question drift off. When the chill began to enter her toes, she said: "I'll bet I could beat you to the dock."

"What do you bet?"

"Wait and see."

"I hope I do," he said fervently. "You'll be a sight, all right."

She swam toward him, using a crawl stroke. As she streamed past, her face turned and she gulped fresh air. He had not moved. He was giving her a handicap in the race.

She swam powerfully, gloating at her silken passage through the unresisting water. At intervals, she heard his splashes in pursuit.

She stopped in the shadow cast by the low diving board.

"You're good," he applauded, stopping ten feet from her. "Swim a lot?"

"At the Y."

"Nude?"

"Very funny. Are you good at fetching?"

"Fetching what?"

"The water's twelve feet deep here. I'll bet you can't fetch up a rock."

"If I do?"

"You win the bet."

"What do I win?"

"Fetch a rock and find out."

He sank below the water, eyes closed. His hands flirted and he flipped over and drove straight down.

She grabbed the ladder and climbed nimbly to the dock. She ran along its length and scurried onto the porch. She shouldn't treat him like this.

He had been nice to her. She had promised him so much—and this was treachery.

He called: "Where did you hide?"

She found the towels and ran to the screen door.

"Where are you—under the dock?" he demanded.

She cracked the door open, pitched a towel across the railing.

"Here, Dirk. What did you want?"

"I got a rock," he bragged.

"You win the bet."

"What do I win?"

"That towel on the railing by your clothes."

"That all?"

"Dirk—"

"Cheater!"

"Please hurry and get dressed. Will you mix us a drink, Dirk?"

"I'll mix a drink. Damn right, I'll mix one. I'll make yours with cyanide."

She ran along the porch. She dared not stay. A girl has desire—and imagination. In the water, she had been sorely tempted by his nearness. A shame to treat him like this.

Where did they go next?

She wasn't sure.

FOUR

Through the open twin windows of her bedroom, the moon wafted in and lay down and lapped the rug.

She toweled vigorously, but there was nothing she could do about the dampness of her hair.

Warm and glowing, she waded through the moonlight.

The lawn and graveled court and garage waited, outside, quietly soaking up the radiance.

Full September moon, and a nice man to share it with—if she dared.

The panel between the twin windows cast a wide shadow in the room and she stood there idly. Nearby stood a pair of compact firs, dark on the lawn. They were close together, forming a solid mat.

A cloying sweetness siphoned in over the window-sills. She knew it for the perfume of nicotiana, a flower that closes its petals tightly during the day then opens up at dusk to drench the air with attar and—

She tensed—

Against those two nearby firs. A darker shadow?

She stood still, every muscle tightening. Danger prowled up her spine. Somebody hiding against those two firs?

Pressed into the blackness of the firs, the tips much higher than a person's head, she definitely discerned a darker shadow!

A scream formed around her heart and shivered upward. It rushed into her mouth and her lips opened. She stifled the scream before it reached her lips. Only air hissed between her chattering teeth.

Don't you dare scream, she chided herself. That will only scare the shadow.

Who was out there?

Then she remembered the dying engine that she had heard while she and Dirk had swum in the middle of the lake and the headlights that had lanced through the woods beyond the garage.

Somebody must have parked on Hiram Klee's lane through the woods and sneaked in here to peep. You've been very careless alone here, she scolded herself tardily. No thought ever about lights out when the shades were up and you were in the nude.

She moved her head slightly so that she could peer around the panel between the windows.

The figure wore a man's hat. Gradually, her eyes traced his outline. Yes, a man. Some local peeper who came here, night after night, to watch her undress? Or was it Vernon Cashion?

He wasn't very tall, she judged. Say, five feet, eight inches. Maybe nine inches. Not very wide through the shoulders, either.

It was a familiar figure. Marta gasped.

Vernon had driven the twelve miles from Hallstead to park his car off the lane and hide outside her bedroom window.

Not content to wait to see if she would send the twenty-five dollars to his mother in Newark, he had skulked in here again. Maybe he was intent on using his power over her once more. Panic crowded against her back. She stood rooted to the rug.

She retreated noiselessly, her body atremble. She managed to keep the panel between her and Vernon until she was beyond the moonlight on the rug.

At the dresser, she found her pocketbook, and her hand closed on the loaded gun.

She eased the safety off. She tiptoed back to the windows.

He was still there. This was her chance. He was a prowler outside her bedroom window, wasn't he? He might have a gun, mightn't he? He was a threat to your security and happiness, wasn't he?

How should you treat a blackmailer?

Shoot him.

The gun wavered on the dark target. She trained it low, to make sure of a hit in the stomach so he would suffer a thousand tortures as he died.

Just one shot, and you're rid of half the menace.

Wait, not in the stomach. That way, he'd live to talk before he died and the truth about her would have to become public. Steady, steady.

Her face hardened. Her finger began to tighten against the trigger.

Inside her mind, she heard a man's slow, implacable voice intone: "Miss Selfron, you spotted this prowler outside your window. You say you didn't recognize him?"

She heard her own voice. "That's right."

"Why did you go for the gun?"

"I—I was frightened!"

"Had you reason to believe he was more than a trespasser?"

"No." She couldn't admit to anything. She couldn't tell the facts without incriminating herself.

"Why did you go for the gun?"

"I—I was frightened!"

"Did he try to get in through the window?"

"No."

"He stood there motionless against the firs?"

"Yes."

"Miss Selfron, you weren't alone in the house. Why didn't you call Mr. Delgar?"

"I was frightened!"

"Why were you so frightened? Do you know this man . . .?"

The gun barrel sagged in her hand.

No, this wasn't the way to handle Vernon Cashion.

She crept back to the dresser and put the gun in her pocketbook. Catching up a white terry robe, she slipped her hands into the sleeves and knotted the belt loosely.

There was another way to handle Vernon Cashion.

Dirk Delgar.

FIVE

From the screen door on the porch, Marta saw Dirk at the railing. He wore trousers and stood on one foot, about to pull on a sock.

She eased the door open soundlessly, and whispered: "Dirk, don't make a sound. Come here."

He dropped the sock and padded to the door on bare feet.

"What's the matter—more tricks?" he whispered.

"Dirk, a prowler outside my window!"

Her teeth chattered. Oh, God, how would this turn out?

"Dirk, he's hiding against fir trees on the lawn. I—I saw him there."

He patted her arm. "It's okay. Sure this isn't another game?"

"Please. He's a big man."

"Yeah?" he mused. "Maybe Harry slipped down here from Fred's. As big as Harry, maybe?"

It might be a way out.

"Yes," she lied.

"I hope it is Harry. I'll clobber him. You wait inside."

He grasped the railing, swung under, and dropped on the lawn at the edge of the lake. He turned and waved. Relax, his gesture said.

You should have told him who it is, she thought numbly. Vernon Cashion is dangerous. He may have a gun.

You fool! Why did you send Dirk unarmed against a dangerous and remorseless opponent?

She ran through the house and, in her bedroom, retrieved the gun. She tiptoed along the panel shadow against the firs.

If he has a gun, she reasoned, you have a right to shoot him. If he moves against Dirk—pull the trigger.

She poked the barrel toward the screen. Suddenly, she thought: There's a better way out of this tonight, you fool!

Carefully she scraped the tip of the barrel along the wire mesh. It made a too-loud sound in the night.

She saw Vernon Cashion crouch, then shift position. She waved the gun in the moonlight and the barrel gleamed.

Vernon took a quick running step.

At the same time, Dirk's voice challenged: "You, there—stand still. Who are you?"

Vernon bolted around the firs. He fled across the lawn toward the gravel drive. Dirk burst across the lawn in pursuit. He was faster afoot than Cashion.

He gained with every lunging stride. If Dirk caught Vernon, would Vernon pull a gun? Now she could not help Dirk as she had planned.

Don't catch him, she prayed frantically. Don't catch him, Dirk.

Head and shoulders down, Vernon Cashion galloped manfully. A second later, Dirk reached the gravel. Instantly his head lifted.

He slowed. His knees jerked up. He was barefooted, and obviously the gravel was biting into his soles. He ran like a cat across a hot stove, feet lifting high and coming down lightly.

He lost ground rapidly. When Vernon Cashion disappeared around the garage, he had gained ten yards on Dirk.

Dirk picked up the speed after he reached grass again. If he trailed Cashion into the woods, Dirk faced a greater danger; he might be ambushed there.

She waited by the window, staring at the moon-flooded lawn and garage, thinking of the danger in the nearby woods.

A minute drifted past, then another. An engine roared on the lane and headlights swiveled and a car gunned off.

As the noise faded, Dirk strode hack across the lawn and picked his way gingerly across the gravel. She heard him mutter: "I'd have caught him if I'd had shoes on."

Breathing a relieved sigh, she replaced the gun. She reached the porch ahead of Dirk, greeted him at the open door.

"You shouldn't have chased him, darling," she said, shivering.

"I needed the exercise. I don't think he'll come back. How many days left of your vacation?"

"More than a week. Mr. Klee will be here part of the time."

"And his redhead?"

"Of course. Dirk, who was he?"

"Some local knight of the bedroom window, probably. A little guy, not nearly as big as Harry."

"He looked big to me."

"Shadows magnify. Any ideas about his identity?"

"No."

"Could he be one of the workmen who tend the gardens?"

"No. They're elderly."

She clung to his arm, not because of any fear, but contrite for having sent him, unarmed after Cashion.

"It—it gave me a fright. You don't expect anybody lurking at your window."

"Maybe it served you right."

"Why?"

"If you'd stayed until I fetched up the rock, it might not have happened that way. Thanks for the towel."

Her eyes widened. "But, Dirk, you didn't expect—swimming is one thing! I'm not the sort of girl who—please, I'm chilled to the bone. May I have a drink, please?"

"Sure."

On the divan, she sat close to him. "More rye and not much water this time," she ordered.

"The guy did scare you, hey?"

"Suppose I had been here alone."

"Isn't there a phone?"

"Yes."

"Probably he was only a harmless peeper. Here, drink some courage." She sipped greedily.

The rye warmed her stomach and headed for her brains. She drained the glass, slopped more rye on the ice, and tried to find security when it was sitting close beside her, bare-chested and stalwart.

She dug an elbow into his ribs. "Don't go away, please."

For the moment, she was the timid female. She needed the protection of a strong man and he was elected. As if he sensed what she was thinking, he set his glass on the coffee table.

His arm circled her shoulders. She sighed and rested her head on his shoulder, her hair against his jaw.

"Okay?" he asked.

"No more shivers."

He took her empty glass and set it beside his own. He kissed her lightly on the forehead.

"Too awkward," he said, taking over. "Let's get more comfortable."

He turned her sideways. She stretched her legs along the cushions and leaned back into the circle of his arms. The robe had slipped during the brief maneuver, but she was oblivious to her legs showing nudely above the knees.

She thought: *You sent him against Vernon Cashion's gun. Be nice to him.*

He kissed her lips and she responded more eagerly than when he had kissed her before. *That was for sending him into danger.* Her right arm crawled around his neck and pinioned his face tight to hers. *That was to keep him here.* It was a long kiss.

She pulled away regretfully.

"Like electricity," she murmured, and blood pounded her temples.

He let his lips move around her face and kiss her eyes and cheeks. She lay quiescent under his spell, the hot blood surging through her body and all thought of panic gone. She would not remember how it happened, exactly, but a little later they were lying on the divan with his right arm under her shoulders as they faced each other.

She had him for tonight, anyway, she thought. A delicious numbness invaded her body. Maybe she could have him for tomorrow, even for many tomorrows.

He whispered, "I was wondering about that."

"What?"

"What you wore under the robe."

"Just me."

"Beautiful you—"

"Your hand's on fire."

"I touched you, darling."

"Maybe we—Dirk?"

"Yeah?"

"Do you believe in love at first sight?"

"It happens."

"Maybe to—to us? Dirk—this isn't wrong, is it?"

"You're right—just right. Absolutely right for me."

"Dirk—Dirk—such a lovely name."

He kissed her throat.

There was yet time to escape. But he lifted his head and his lips met her lips and flame passed between them and there was no escape. She moved under his guidance, trusted in him.

Love, she thought dreamily, is Dirk and a full moon in September. Maybe a touch of panic, too.

"Darling," she said fervently, and the full moon smiled.

Some gold lay on the lake, but the moon had lifted off the porch and there was only serenity on the dark depths of the divan.

Dirk asked lazily: "Cigarette, darling?"

"Please."

"It seems as if I've known you for a long time." He placed two cigarettes between his lips. A lighter flamed. She wore the terry cloth robe again, but the belt was loosened.

Under the flame of the lighter, more of her showed than was covered. She murmured: "Big eyes."

"I can look, can't I?"

"Love me?"

"I don't know. I guess maybe I do. But is it possible? On such a short acquaintance?"

He fired the cigarettes belatedly.

"Yes—I think I've fallen in love with you," he said wonderingly. "It seems like something out of a story book. How could such a thing happen so suddenly—in real life, I mean?"

"Please, may I have the cigarette?"

The lighter flame died. She inhaled deeply and sat relaxed, the back of her neck propped against a cushion and legs across a hassock.

She mused, "Maybe it's the moon, Dirk?"

"We both saw the moon last night, but this didn't happen."

"We weren't together."

"I don't go for just any woman."

"Nor I for any man."

"You don't have to tell me that," he said.

"X-ray eyes again?"

"No. I know you're a good girl."

They smoked quietly awhile. Then he spoke again.

"When you first told me about the prowler, I had an idea you knew him."

"I wish you'd turn off the X-ray."

"Did you? Was he someone you recognized?"

"I wouldn't know his shadow again." She mashed out her cigarette on an ashtray. "Dirk, may I tell you what's been worrying me?"

"Prowlers?"

"No. It goes back two months."

That was the point in time to start the story. Two months ago—not years ago, when she had married Vernon Cashion too hastily. Dirk must never know about that, or about the letter used to extort money from her. He must never know that she was a thief.

"I'm sure Mr. Klee will not mind my telling you," she said. "He's worried simply sick and I want to help him,"

"Three ex-wives—that's a headache, all right."

"Not that."

"He's discovered something about the new redhead?"

Marta laughed. "It has nothing to do with Mr. Klee's personal problems. It's something that happened at Aircrafter's. Look, pal—Mr. Klee is awfully nice, really. Even if he is bald, short, fat—and fifty."

"So he's nice. Get on with it."

"You see, thirty thousand dollars were stolen from a safe at Aircrafter's—it happened early in July, a Friday morning about eleven o'clock. The police are positive it was an inside job involving at least two employees. One is a—" she hated the name— "a man named Vernon Cashion, who worked in Billing. The other was my assistant, a Prudence Nason. At Aircrafter's, it's my custom to go downstairs for coffee every morning just before eleven o'clock and to leave Prudence alone in the office. Dirk, I want you to get on this case. That's what I've been thinking about, and I've come to a decision. I want you to find the guilty persons and recover the money. Would you be free to start to work tomorrow?"

"Tell me more about it, first."

"Well, on the second floor, there's a main corridor. Parallel to that runs a shorter, narrower passageway from the treasurer's office—Mr. Ronstein—which passes a small fireproofed room where we keep important records and the safe. Next to that room is my office. The passageway ends at Mr. Klee's private office. When we're open for business, all the doors on this inner corridor are unlocked. Is that clear?"

"Crystal."

"That Friday morning, Mr. Ronstein and his assistant were not out of the treasurer's office at all. They could see anybody who walked into that inner passageway. They saw me go downstairs. When I returned, Prudence was missing, but I thought nothing of that at the moment. When she did not return in a half-hour, I asked Mr. Ronstein if he had seen her. He told me she had gone off five minutes after I had left. She had mentioned coffee, but she had not been in the cafeteria while I had been there. Prudence had been with us for four years. She was a conscientious, capable worker, certainly not a clock-watcher, except to be meticulous about appointments and hours of work. I worried when she did not return. She wasn't with Mr. Klee—nor with Mr. Truegate, whose dictation she would sometimes take in his office on the main corridor. I remembered that she had brought a weekend bag to work that morning and had mentioned something about a trip to the Jersey shore. I checked the closet where we keep our personal things. Her hat and weekend bag were missing. I was wondering what to do next, when Mr. Ronstein came in—all shook up. It seems that he had gone to the safe on an errand and had found the door open a crack. He had checked the contents, had discovered that the cash box, which had contained thirty thousand dollars, was missing."

"Had this Mr. Ronstein been in the safe earlier that morning?"

"Twice. Each time the box had been there."

"It was unusual to find the door ajar?"

"Very much so."

"When the Nason girl passed out through his office, why didn't Ronstein see her bag and hat?"

"I forgot to explain that. You see, there's a solid desk, like a partition, that runs four feet high across the front of his office. There's also a grillwork above the partition."

"This inner passageway begins and ends in his office?"

"Yes. Anyone coming into the passageway has to pass Mr. Ronstein and his assistant. They were positive that no outsider had entered. And it seems Prudence did leave the building early. She had been keeping company with this—this Vernon Cashion in Billing. Mr. Klee called the police. They checked in the Billing Department and discovered that Cashion had left his desk at eleven and had not returned. Later— I think it was Monday—the police found that the two had bought a new Buick sedan from Valery Brothers in Newark on Thursday, making the necessary arrangements for delivery on Friday. On Friday they picked up the car, paying cash for it—Aircrafter's cash. Dirk, it's been two months since the robbery. No trace of either of them, or of the money."

He sat silent for a while, then asked: "Was the cash insured?"

"No."

"Why not?"

"It was a special account, used principally to cash large checks when the banks were closed. Also, for Mr. Klee's convenience or to take care of special things that needed—uh, cash."

"Ice money?"

"Ice!"

"That's argot for bribes."

"I don't know about that," she said primly. "Aircrafter's is a reputable business and—"

He interrupted: "Did Mr. Ronstein have the bill numbers on file?"

"No."

"That means the police couldn't trace those two by trailing the money when it returned to circulation." Dirk shrugged, lit a cigarette. "Who knew the combination of the safe?"

"Three persons. Mr. Klee, Mr. Ronstein and Mr. Truegate, the executive vice-president. Because of the large sum of cash, they were always careful to keep the safe locked. Mr. Ronstein and Mr. Truegate have been with the firm for fifteen years. They're absolutely honest and—"

"Stop writing character references," Dirk interrupted dryly. "You've been writing a subtle reference for this Nason girl, too, yet the way you tell the story, she stole the combination and ran off with the money."

"But Mr. Ronstein and Mr.—"

He laid two fingers across her lips. She nibbled on them. He said, "But how would the Nason girl manage to get the combination? Or did she get it? Was it someone else, after all, who rifled the safe? I take it the cash was handled rather loosely by Ronstein and the others, so there could be shortages, right?"

Right, she thought despairingly. Three years back, when she had needed a thousand dollars for divorce, she had looked for and found the combination to that safe and had taken the money from that very cash account. No one had ever discovered her theft, except the Cashions. They wouldn't have discovered it, either, if she hadn't explained about it in a letter.

"I suppose they were a little careless," she agreed. "Maybe you can ask Mr. Klee about that later."

"See where that puts us, Marta? Someone else, not this Nason girl, could have robbed the safe. Who needed money? Where did Cashion fit in? Who figured the heist? Why couldn't somebody have depleted the cash over a long period, then finished the job when he was in so deep he could not repay the money? Truegate and Ronstein had access to the safe. One of them might have robbed the safe on Thursday. Or early Friday morning before the offices opened, because they would have the necessary keys to get into the passageway. And your Mr. Klee is not in the clear. He wouldn't be the first president who robbed his own concern. He—"

"Damn your suspicious mind," Marta snapped hotly. "I tell you, all those men are perfectly honest!"

"The police think so?"

"I don't know what the police think."

"I know. They wouldn't give those three men a clean bill of health without thoroughly checking their stories and their backgrounds. Believe me, the police and myself never accept any story at face value. The advantage we have over laymen is that we suspect every possible person, no matter how innocent that person may seem. Hell, you were in your office when that safe was ajar. What about you?"

The idea startled her. His X-ray brain again!

"I didn't take the money," she said tightly. "Do you believe me?"

"Sure. I'm only hurling rocks. The fact is that the disappearance of Cashion and the Nason girl is coincidental with the robbery. Naturally, those two are prime suspects. But to convict them, you must prove the Nason girl found the combination, took the money, shared it with Cashion. Either they confess to robbery or you catch them with the money in their possession. Suppose they turn up tomorrow with a likely story? *We went off on a honeymoon. Money gone from the safe? Why, don't look at us! Sure, we should have said where we were going, but we were so full of each other that we didn't think of it.* See what I mean?"

"You're silly, Dirk. This Cashion wouldn't marry Prudence."

"Positively?"

"Yes."

"Why not?"

"Because he—" Marta compressed her lips. "Prudence struck me as a nice girl. She wouldn't marry a thief," Marta finished lamely.

Dirk took another tack. "Who handled the police angle?"

"Mostly a Lieutenant James Dalgren."

"But he's Newark police!"

"Yes."

"I thought Aircrafter's was in Kearny?"

"Only the plant, Dirk. The office building is in Newark."

"I know this Jim Dalgren pretty well," he mused. "Went to grade school with him. He was graduated at the head of the class, while I was lost in the shuffle. He's a good man, and don't forget it."

"A good man?" She laughed derisively. "Mr. Klee said your Jim Dalgren couldn't find a watermelon in a basket."

"Jim's still a top detective and I'll tell your wonderful Mr. Klee that when I meet him." Dirk dragged deeply on his cigarette. The flame lit up the hard contours of his face. "Why did you tell me all this?"

"Because I'm worried and because you're a private investigator."

"That all?"

"You return to work tomorrow in Newark. You aren't sure that you will be busy—that there's a case awaiting you—"

"So?"

"It was an inside job."

"And?"

"You're the most exasperating man I ever met, Dirk Delgar!" She pouted prettily. "For heaven's sake, do I have to draw a blueprint? The office is—is like dynamite with a sputtering fuse. There are—rumors. They say Mr. Truegate plays the ponies and needs cash. They say Mr. Ronstein has just paid off a big mortgage on his home. They ask where does Mr. Klee get all his spending money, when there's the income tax? That's the way the gossip goes. And I suppose," she continued, "there are stories about me, too. Anyway, the office morale is shot. Mr. Truegate won't even speak to Mr. Ronstein. It has to stop."

"What do you want me to do, Marta?"

"I told you. Try to solve the case—since the police have failed. I'm sure Mr. Klee would be glad to pay you a percentage for what money you recover. What's the usual fee?"

"Ten percent, if I'm successful at recovery. If not, expenses and a day's pay for each day I work. I like the first arrangement."

She rested a hand on his thigh. "Then you'll try?"

"I'll need a letter of confirmation from your Mr. Klee. I have to have a client in the background or the police will give me the brushoff. Besides, Jim Dalgren's my friend. I'm not going to antagonize a friend by working without authorization. When's Klee fetching his redhead back from Canada?"

"Next week, I think. Dirk, I don't want you to wait that long. I want you to get started right away."

"Maybe I can give it a whirl tomorrow, at that," he decided thoughtfully.

"Oh, thanks, Dirk. You won't be sorry."

He asked casually, "Why don't you like Vernon Cashion?"

"I don't like him?"

"No."

"I hardly know him," she protested.

"And you don't like him. Why?"

She said angrily: "Because I'm convinced it was he who duped poor Prudence. She's a nice, honest girl. Does that answer your question?"

"You don't have to blow up. You don't like Cashion and I wondered why. Meanwhile—"

He shrugged, and let the word drift around.

Marta ventured, "Do you have to drive to Newark tonight?"

"No."

"There are extra bedrooms here."

"Mr. Klee won't mind?"

"Of course not."

"Will you?"

"Will I what?"

"Will you mind if I stay?"

"Oh. Why should I?"

He stood up. "It's been a long day on the road and a lovely night. Let's hit the mattress."

"What time do you want to get up?"

"Noon."

"Can't you get an early start on the case?"

"All right."

"Dirk—are you strong enough to carry me?"

He picked her up easily. "Which way?"

"To the right. Up the hall."

He carried her off. At her bedroom door, she murmured, "In there, please."

Moonlight bathed two small squares of the rug.

Nicotiana perfumed the room.

SIX

The kitchen clock said it was seven a.m.

Wearing a yellow playsuit, Marta Selfron tripped lightly about the kitchen. She had already straightened up the front porch.

She also had a morning dip in the lake; nude, of course.

She was sorry that Dirk had not been awake to see her—uh, dive! The coffee was almost done, the eggs out, and the bread ready for the toaster. She returned to the bedroom.

Dirk lay covered by a sheet, only his black hair in view.

"Time to get up," she announced cheerfully.

He mumbled, "Go away."

"Look, you character, it's seven o'clock already. Breakfast will be on the table in three minutes."

He sat up and rubbed sleep from his eyes. "Are you always so difficult in the morning?"

"Not difficult. Just practical."

"Come here."

"No."

"Afraid?"

"No, but breakfast is almost ready."

She retreated to the sanctuary of the kitchen. Last night, she thought, you wanted to use him for your own selfish ends against the Cashions. Now you're puzzled. You're not sure what you want.

Yesterday he was a stranger.

Today he's in your blood.

She promised herself that she would keep him off for a while—long enough to give herself a chance to think.

After all, she was a grown girl now. She knew perfectly well that love could not come so quickly to two who had been strangers only a few hours ago. Or could it?

When he joined her, he was fully dressed except for a coat. His hair was sleekly combed. His face was smoothly shaved.

He kissed her lightly, sat down at the table. The four-minute eggs waited, the toast was browned and buttered, the coffee poured, and the bacon crisp.

Afterwards they smoked a cigarette, then washed the dishes together and tidied the kitchen until it was immaculate.

She asked, "How soon can we get started? I want to drive you in and bring you back."

"You do?"

"My sister lives in Newark." That will keep him away at least one evening, she thought. "I'll stay the day with her—then bring you back here."

"But why?"

She couldn't tell him that she wanted to keep tabs, wanted to prevent his finding out what she didn't care for him to know.

So she said, "I want to make sure not to lose you."

"But what's all the rush? This case has dangled for two months. It's a cold trail."

She wanted to blurt: Dirk, they're after me. Twenty-five dollars of blackmail is due at 1327 West Plank Road, not later than tomorrow. Dirk, if I don't send the money, they'll come here. Vernon was the rat you chased last night.

That's the reason for all the rush! He'll attack me again. Or he'll get me sent to prison, because he has a letter . . . Dirk, I'm in danger!

Instead, she said: "I don't want Aircrafter's to be upset any longer. And I want the money recovered, for Mr. Klee's sake."

She did not add that she had got Vernon Cashion the job at Aircrafter's in the first place, and so felt responsible for the whole thing.

"Well, I'll have to see Jim Dalgren and see if he'll give me what he has. I can't get far if he doesn't shell out. You know, you're darned good-looking in an apron. And that was an excellent feed, Miss Selfron. I thank you kindly. Hah, the doomed man ate a hearty breakfast!"

"Doomed?"

"I met you. Do you like to cook?"

"Yes."

"And wash dishes?"

"I can stand it."

"Housework?"

"I have two rooms, and I keep them pretty clean."

"Rather work for Klee or manage a house?"

"Dirk, am I being interviewed as a prospective wife—or as a maid?"

He laughed. "Let me kiss you."

He held her close. His lips were hungry. Once his arms were around her, she was soft as hot wax.

He said, "Sorry about last night?"

"No."

"Good."

"Am I a—hussy?"

"Uh-uh. Just a shameless wench."

She laughed. "And that's what you love about me, I suppose."

"What else?"

She had to ask. "Dirk, what's love?"

"A mirage. Maybe a rainbow. I don't know. I've never found it, either, until . . . I mean, this might be it. But—" He stopped, lit a cigarette, puffed thoughtfully. "Marta, last night, were you entirely frank with me?"

"About what?"

"About Aircrafter's."

"Yes," she said, too quickly.

"Nothing more you want to tell me?"

"Not that I can think of." She opened her eyes wide. "I'm not a detective, you know. I might have overlooked something—but I don't think so."

"Okay. Uh—you know that I don't consider Hiram Klee my client, don't you?"

"You don't? Then who is?"

"I'm doing this for you."

"Not for ten percent?"

"That, too. But as I've said, something else is bothering you. I want to get you off the hook. If there's anything further on your mind, tell me."

"Nothing, Dirk," she lied.

"Okay, client." He grinned suddenly. "Suppose I help you dress so we can get out of here in a hurry."

"If you did, we wouldn't get away from here, ever."

"Who wants to go?"

"Us. Give me ten minutes. Would you go out to the dock, please, and dump the water from the canoe?"

"The canoe? Sure. Well—guess I'll have to hold out until tonight."

"Tonight," she promised, and knew it was another lie. When would she be able to be utterly frank with him?

Tomorrow, yes.

In Newark, an abnormal heat wave had drifted in from the south and turned the busy city into a blast furnace.

Marta sat in the parked Chrysler. Dirk had left her on a shady side street while he visited Jim Dalgren at Police Headquarters. There was nothing to do except think, and she didn't want to think.

"Only be a minute," he had said, before going off. "Can you wait that long?"

"For you, yes."

She checked her wristwatch. It was almost ten. His minute had expanded into a half-hour. What kept him so long? What would Jim Dalgren tell Dirk about her?

Dalgren was a slim man, rather handsome in a quiet way, she remembered. He had made many visits to Aircrafter's offices.

His short, curly hair was black and liberally salted with premature gray. Lines etched the flesh at his mouth corners, pin scratches on the oak coloring of his lean face. He had dark-brown eyes, rather sleepy, and a habit of smiling shyly, as if he were unsure of himself.

She had sensed an alert brain behind those sleepy eyes. He had not fooled her. She had been very careful with her answers.

Little of her personal background had entered into his questioning, for which she had been thankful. There was one fact in particular that she had not wanted to let slip. It concerned the reason Vernon Cashion happened to be working at Aircrafter's.

It had been simple.

Mrs. Cashion had phoned and said, "Vernon is out of work. You're to use your influence to get him a position at Aircrafter's, understand? What's that? Oh, you won't do it? Listen, you'll do it, all right. Have you ever seen the inside of a prison? It's not pretty. We've made photostats of a certain letter. If Vernon doesn't get that job, the copies will be mailed anonymously. One to your boss. One to the Prosecutor. One to—"

Her resistance had crumbled at that point and once again she had bowed to coercion. She had been not only a thief, but a coward.

It had been remarkably easy for her to get Vernon a job. She had bypassed Mr. Truegate, in charge of Personnel, and gone directly to Hiram Klee with a lie. Mr. Klee had nodded.

"Friend of yours?" he had asked.

"No, a friend of a friend. On his mother's side."

"What can he do?"

"He's been a clerk."

"I'll drop Truegate a note."

Simple, except that Vernon Cashion had then proceeded to worm his way into the heart of Prudence Nason and use her as an instrument with which to rob Aircrafter's.

After the robbery, Marta had mentioned to Mr. Klee that it had been she who had asked for a job for Cashion.

He had been very nice about it. "Could happen to anybody," he had said. "I don't like to lose the money, of course—but charge it off to experience, Marta."

She had vowed in his presence: "I'll never, never recommend another person for a job."

"Forget it, I said. Now, about this deal with Parks-Hutchinson in Chicago. It's a new account and—" That's the way it had been.

If she had stood up to the Cashions, no money would have been stolen. She remembered something that Dirk had said last night. *Once the prospect becomes a victim, he loses all power to resist.* They had robbed her of all combative strength down the years, had bled her until she could bleed no more.

Her only hope now was that Dirk would find Vernon Cashion, would be able to handle Vernon . . .

At her elbow, Dirk drawled, "Why the long face, darling?"

She turned, startled. "Oh, I thought you'd never come! Did I have a long face? It's because I missed you."

He slid in beside her. "Someone is looking very chic this morning, despite the heat. Nice black dress. And a whistle-whistle neckline." His eyes roamed down to where the dress hem showed bare, golden legs. "That's plenty of good leg you're displaying, Miss Selfron."

"I want to keep you interested. Did you learn anything in there?"

"Jim's a good egg, Marta. He gave me the scoop."

"They make any progress?"

"Not too much. But Jim feels he's getting close. He's expecting to make an arrest soon. Cashion, and maybe the Nason girl. He—" He stopped suddenly. "Now that's an idea. Why do I keep calling her a girl? She's no chick—and you kept that fact back, client."

"What fact? I told you all I know."

"Not about Prudence. Now look—I learned this Vernon Cashion is no cream-puff. He has a record as a juvenile delinquent—stealing cars, things like that. He took a petty larceny rap at nineteen but got off with a suspended sentence. The Navy found it necessary to give him a dishonorable discharge. Twice after that he was arrested for armed robbery, but was released because of lack of evidence. His prints are on file."

Dirk snapped his fingers.

"I didn't realize the manpower shortage is so critical that personnel managers are scraping the bottom of the barrel. Did you know that Cashion never held a job longer than three months?"

She tensed inwardly. This was why she had been wise to ride to town with Dirk; she could keep up with developments, steer things a bit.

She asked quietly: "Why did Aircrafter's hire him?"

"Jim told me he asked Hiram Klee that very question. Klee said a friend had recommended Cashion, which explained why Personnel hadn't checked him more closely.

"But about this Nason girl—that is, woman. Now, she's something— and you didn't tell me. Jim did, though. In her late thirties. Round-faced, flat-chested, wears bifocals. Only five feet two, but weighs a gaudy hundred forty pounds and must look like a barrel. On the other hand, Cashion would be handsome in the eyes of some women. Now I know why you were so positive Cashion wouldn't marry her. Imagine waking up in the morning and seeing her!"

Marta said sharply, "Is that the way to judge a wife?"

"No."

"Is marriage only the bed?"

"No."

"Then don't talk about Prudence like that."

"Hey, how did I get into the middle of this?"

"You said you wouldn't marry Prudence and—"

"No, no," he interrupted. "I said Cashion wouldn't marry her. You know who'd fall for Cashion? Well, an old maid desperate for a man. Or some brainless chippie who didn't have sense enough to add two and two.

"I figured this Nason dame was some witless kid like that. Instead, she turns out to be a fat, lonely spinster with no more sex appeal than an eggplant."

He drummed fingers on the leather cushion and muttered: "How would he get rid of her, do you think?"

"What do you mean?"

"The moment Cashion got his loose fingers on that thirty thousand dollars, the Nason dame was strictly surplus baggage. It's been two months now—and no trace of either of them. Her parents haven't heard a word and they're worried. They should be."

A chill began to crawl up Marta's spine.

"Don't you think you'll be able to find Prudence?"

"I'll find her—if I find Cashion, first."

"Dirk, he wouldn't—wouldn't kill her, would he?"

"It may not be that bad," Dirk said. "Maybe he just booted her out of the new Buick so he would be unencumbered. Prudence wouldn't dare return to Aircrafter's or her family, not after robbing the safe."

"Prudence was my friend," Marta said. "You've got to find her."

"All right. Suppose we get to work. Jim thinks that Cashion's mother at West Plank Road is the logical place to start. She runs a boarding house there. She has a mousy husband who does all the housework while she polishes her toenails. Jim has a hunch the mother knows where the son is hiding and communicates with him. He hasn't been able to get anything out of her—but I'd like to try. Drive me over there, will you?"

"To West Plank Road?"

"Yeah, Dirk dipped a hand into a coat pocket. "Where did I put that number? You remember it, Marta?"

She nearly blurted it out, but restrained herself in time; Dirk had not mentioned the number, only the street.

He dredged up a scrap of paper, and said: "It's 1327, so this says."

Balling the paper, he tossed it over his shoulder.

"Do we park in front of the house?" she wanted to know.

"Wait and see."

She started the engine. Cutting the wheels, she asked: "Did Jim tell you anything else important?"

"A couple of details that wouldn't interest you. Uh—he admitted that he took a shine to you, though."

"Me?"

"Want to hear what he said?"

"Yes."

"That you're a pretty nice chick, and good-looking."

"I thought he was pretty nice, too."

She nosed the car out, cut smoothly into a gap in traffic and drove off along Broad Street. She had driven half across town before she realized she had headed reflexively toward the Cashion home.

She slowed, and said nonchalantly: "Am I driving in the right direction? Where is West Plank Road?"

"I thought you knew where it was."

"I'm not sure."

"Take the next turn left. It's a little longer that way, but we'll avoid traffic." He glanced at her appreciatively, and said, "When you drive, does your skirt always hike up like that?"

"I don't know. I haven't been taking notes."

"Want me to cover them?"

"And pile us into a tree? Keep your distance, please."

Twice, she was thinking, he had almost trapped her. Once, when he had tested to see if she would let slip the number of the Cashion home. Next, when he had let her drive off without giving the necessary directions to reach West Plank Road. Yet anybody might know where that street was.

She bit her lip. Don't let your guilty conscience conjure up groundless fears, she admonished herself. Besides, if you did know the number, it could be because Vernon Cashion had worked at Aircrafter's; it would be perfectly logical for you to remember it.

Most likely Dirk had not been setting traps for her; that had been her imagination.

She concentrated on driving. They reached an intersection and he said, "This is it."

She slowed. "Which way, Dirk?"

"The numbers run toward the river, I think. Go left."

There were several factories in the vicinity, and West Plank was cluttered with trucks. It led downhill. She drove slowly, saying, "Let me know when we near the place."

"Drive right past the house. I don't want to be seen if Mrs. Cashion happens to be out front. Jim said she was a pretty hot number, forty-five years old and well preserved. One of those big blonde types with a yen for the men."

"At forty-five?" she protested.

"So Jim said." The car rolled down the grade, until he cautioned: "Next block. Take it easy."

Marta followed a gigantic trailer truck, lumbering in low gear, and the needle dropped to ten miles an hour.

The house was the third one in from the next crossing, a three-story affair with a box porch and high steps.

She spotted the familiar, neatly clipped privet hedge out front and noticed the porch was deserted.

"Easy," Dirk warned, and leaned to the open window.

Marta turned away. All the house meant to her was nightmares. How could any man possibly find Mrs. Cashion interesting? How easy it was to fool a man. Like she was fooling Dirk.

"Around the next corner," Dirk ordered suddenly, and she swung off West Plank into a side street.

"Park," he said.

She stopped at the curb and cut the switch.

"I don't know how long I'll be," he said, opening the door and stepping out. "You wait—okay?"

"You're going in there?"

"Yeah. She has a sign in the window about a vacant room. That's for me. If I'm to cover her, I can do it best from the premises. From now on, I'm Donald Dwenger, a law clerk in the offices of Quakenbush & Lindabury, Attorneys. Do you know what a tort is, Miss Selfron?"

"No."

"A tort," he explained smugly, "is any wrongful act, not involving breach of contract, for which a civil action will lie. That's lawyer jargon, Miss Selfron."

"Suppose she does rent you a room. What then?"

"I'll stick a dictograph in her bedroom or hide under her bed in case she talks in her sleep."

"You won't get away with it."

"Why not?"

"If she does know where her son is, she'll be on guard."

"I'm glad you came along, Marta. You're so encouraging."

He grinned mockingly, and strolled off. At the corner, he turned and waved.

He was a nice guy, she thought, and he was doing his share. Why deceive him when he was her sole hope to escape the greedy clutches of the Cashions? Yet what good would it do for her to tell him that she had been married to Vernon, that she was being blackmailed? How could he use that information to catch up with them?

It made more sense for her to keep her mouth shut.

The minutes dragged past, like tired old men.

What was keeping Dirk? He had been gone ten minutes. How long did it require to rent a room or be refused?

Worry began to build up in her mind. She opened the glove compartment and found a whiskbroom. "I'll clean the car," she decided. The front seat was clean, but there was some litter on the floor mat. She brushed the dirt into the street. She checked her watch.

Dirk had been gone fifteen minutes. Mrs. Cashion was out buying a girdle and he had to wait for her to return. Or the sign was a phony and Dirk was trying to rent a room in another boarding house.

From the curb side, she opened the rear door and leaned in. The felt floor mat didn't need cleaning, but she brushed it anyway and that's how she spotted the tiny wad of rolled paper. She opened it. She turned it over. This was the scrap of paper that Dirk had pulled from his pocket.

The paper was blank on both sides. Dirk hadn't needed to ask the number at West Plank; he carried it in his head.

That meant he had set a trap for her. *What was that number, Marta?* Then Dirk did suspect that she was withholding information.

She re-wadded the paper and, leaving it on the mat, returned the whiskbroom to the glove compartment.

How much had Dirk learned? How much was he concealing from her? Did Jim Dalgren suspect that she knew more than she had told, and had he tipped Dirk off? A clever man, Dirk. How long would she be able to deceive him?

"You're lousy as a liar," she chided herself.

She slammed shut the car doors and walked along the sidewalk to the corner. She glanced toward the Cashion house. She saw the neatly clipped hedge, but no Dirk. Had he gone to the Cashion's at all?

She checked her watch. Twenty minutes!

That was long enough for Dirk to rent a room, rearrange the furniture, scrub the floor, and hang fresh curtains. Where was he?

She started back toward the car. She did not notice a car swerve across the street.

Brakes screeched, and she glanced up in time to see the car park on the wrong side of the street in front her.

A middle-aged man leaned from the window and said:

"Hello, Marta!"

Startled, she said, "Why, Mr. Cashion!"

"You remembered me."

"Of course."

He was a small, wiry man in a battered felt hat and a faded blue workshirt. He wore thick glasses and sported a luxuriant brown moustache. He had always been nice to her.

When she had first left the Cashions, he had called her a few times to say hello and find out whether she was all right. But she had not heard from him in a couple of years.

"Good to see you again," he was saying warmly, while his jaws worried a cud of tobacco. "Haven't clapped eyes on you in months. Thought about you, though. How've you been?"

"Good. And you?"

"Tolerable, considerin' the way I have to live," he said darkly. "What are you doing out here at this time of day? Don't you work at Aircrafter's no more?"

"I'm on vacation." She drummed up a reason for her presence here. Not that the reason mattered. Mr. Cashion wouldn't tell his wife that he had seen her. "A friend of mine is trying to locate a girl she used to work with. I told her I'd take a look, since I'm familiar with the neighborhood."

He asked abruptly, "Any news of Vernon?"

"None that I know of."

"Police didn't turn him up, huh?"

"Not a sign of him since he quit at Aircrafter's."

Mr. Cashion snorted. "Not since he robbed Aircrafter's, you mean," he snapped. "Marta, he never was no good and I'm glad you got rid of him. And she ain't no better. They ever bother you?"

"No."

"Taint like 'em not to bother you. They're always scheming and up to no good, like that Aircrafter's robbery."

"You mean your wife helped plan that robbery?"

"She's always settin' Vernon up to things, so I wouldn't be surprised. And you can bet she knows where he is. They got some way of communicatin', but I ain't found out what it is yet. When I do—" Mr. Cashion brandished a puny fist, which promised doom. "Say, did I ever tell you why I never liked that Vernon?"

"No."

"It goes back a long spell of time. The year I was fool enough to marry her, I had a good job as second mate on a ship. I was gone thirteen months. I come back and she had this month-old baby boy. Me gone thirteen months and him a month old, see? I shoulda walked out then, but I give up my good job and stayed home to keep an eye on her. Her love child, she called the brat."

He spat again, savagely.

"I took all I'm gonna take from them two. He ain't no son of mine. I hope I catch up with him before the police do."

"Why do you tell me this?"

"To make you understand that I don't have no more truck with my family than I got to have. If they bother you, just let me know."

Marta changed the subject. "Plenty of roomers, Mr. Cashion?"

"Too danged many to suit me. I get the dirty end. That bitch, she won't even dust a chair." He shrugged. "Guess I better get back to work. Scrubbin' to do and I gotta fix her lunch. She's on a diet. I oughta feed her some arsenic."

Dirk may be along any moment, Marta was telling herself.

"Well, it was nice seeing you," she said. "I've got to run along, but call me once in a while, the way you used to."

He sat with thin shoulders hunched over the wheel, a haunted expression lengthening his face.

As if he had not heard Marta, he muttered, "You got to stop this going on in your home. You was a second mate on a ship and now you're mess boy on a—a garbage scow."

He shook himself so violently that his glasses tilted on his face. He righted them carelessly. Then without a word or a glance, he drove off.

If they bother you, he had said, just let me know. Marta sighed.

What could this weak, inoffensive man do against his dominant wife and vicious son—well, not quite his son? But in their grip, he was as powerless as she. Poor harmless man, suffering so patiently in that horrid house down the years, now resorting to vapid threats to bolster his courage to carry on.

She sat in the Chrysler, wondering why little Mr. Cashion had not run out on his wife years ago. Strange, too, that such a tiny man should have married such a big woman, and—

Dirk reached the car. "Miss me?"

"You were gone long enough. Did you meet Mrs. Cashion?"

"Did I meet her!"

"What happened?"

"I escaped," he said succinctly, and sat down beside her.

"What's she like?"

"Big-boned, almost as tall as I. Blonde. Bland. Like Jim said, remarkably well-preserved. She'd pass for thirty or so with no trouble, if you didn't know her son was twenty-six. Fortunately for me, her husband returned a couple of minutes ago, so I was able to break away."

Marta purred. "What's the husband like?"

"A study in contrast. Small, a shadow man compared to her. He's such a nonentity, it embarrassed me. He sneaked in so quietly that he was standing at her bedroom door before I spotted him."

"Standing *where?*" she asked, astounded.

"In Mrs. Cashion's bedroom."

"Why?"

"She was showing me the house."

"But why?"

He leered. "I'm a handsome man and irresistible to the woman."

He had been gone a half-hour, Marta thought. She started the engine angrily. "Where would you like to go?" she asked, staring straight ahead.

"Look, I couldn't rent a room and then run off just because she wanted to show me her bedroom."

"I'm not interested."

"Uh—she's quite a number."

"Where do you want to go?" Marta repeated.

"She's quite voluptuous. She has beautiful legs. And those tiny feet that often characterize buxom women. She's very graceful even though her hands look like they could throttle a man."

"I'm not one bit interested in her charms."

He continued calmly: "Strange—the rest of the house is threadbare, but her bedroom is beautiful. The walls are pink and the window drapes costly. There's an enormous bed with a pink coverlet. The rug is an Oriental and looks like an original. It has an air-conditioning unit, too."

Marta sat stonily silent, gripping the wheel.

"When we first went in," he rattled off, "I spotted an empty bottle on the dresser. She must have forgotten it because she tried to slip it into a drawer without my seeing it."

In spite of herself, Marta asked: "Gin bottle?"

"Paregoric. Know what that stuff is?"

"Soothes babies, or something."

"In teaspoonfuls. Paregoric is an anodyne—and contains tincture of opium. If you guzzle a bottle of paregoric, you walk around in dreams and she must have downed the contents of that bottle. When she moved, she seemed to flow. Her eyes were so vague that at times she scarcely knew I was there. High in her dream cloud, Marta."

"Where shall I drive you?"

"Pru Building. When will you go to your sister's?"

"Later."

"I'll be over there tonight."

"My sister won't invite you into her bedroom."

"Are you trying to be adolescent, Marta?"

"Why did you go into her bedroom?"

"Because she asked me."

"Do you go into the bedroom of any woman who asks you?"

"For God's sake, drive me to the Pru Building. It's in the center of town. On Broad Street and the corner of—"

She gunned the Chrysler off viciously.

"I'll pick up some law books—window dressing," he explained.

"For whose bedroom?"

"On a case," Dirk replied quietly, "a man has to do a lot of things he'd never dream of doing in his personal life. That's the way it is with a private investigator. She's a hot number? So what! She—"

Marta closed her ears.

But her mind was racing. To obtain evidence of a crime did Dirk have to let himself be seduced by an old hag? And she'd thought he had taste! And restraint. Control over his basic biology. And she had given herself to him last night. Served her right. On such short acquaintance. In the future, she—

He interrupted her thoughts. "What are you worrying about?"

"The price of eggs."

"You sore?"

"Should I be?"

"I don't know. But when you frown like that, it makes me want to kiss you."

"Don't you dare try it."

SEVEN

Night brought no break in the heat wave.

In Marta's small apartment, an electric fan whirred, but it failed to dent the temperature appreciably. The living room was square, bright with colored drapes, a tapestry, and several pictures.

There were two straight chairs and a small table, a maple two-seat divan, one club chair, a bridge lamp and a rug.

At one side of the room, an alcove posed as a kitchen so a landlord could gouge an extra fifteen dollars per month in rent. Opposite the kitchen was another alcove containing a single bed. An open portiere might be drawn across a wire to hide milady's sleeping quarters.

A night lamp glowed by the bed. With two pillows propping her back, Marta rested on the sheet and glanced carelessly at a newspaper. PLANE CRASH IN EUROPE. Too many of those, lately. SENATE CRIME COMMITTEE REVISITS NEW YORK. Were they interested in blackmailers? MODEL SUES MILLIONAIRE . . . She flung the paper aside and lit a cigarette. Maybe the heat wave would subside by tomorrow.

A shame to swelter here. She ought to be enjoying the moon over the ridge in North Jersey. But with Vernon Cashion so near? No, thank you.

Why hadn't Dirk called? Was he—

The phone rang on the night table. She reached hungrily for it. "Yes?"

"Hello, darling," Dirk said cheerfully. "I'm tied up with Mr. Cashion for a while. Beer together, but I doubt he knows anything about you-know-who. Miss me?"

"Yes."

"Still sore?"

"I'm not sore."

"You were when you left me this morning."

"Just a moment, please." She laid a palm carelessly over the mouthpiece. "Will you children stop squabbling when I'm on the phone?"

Pause.

She removed her palm. "Yes, Dirk?"

"Who were you talking to?"

"Oh those darn kids . . ."

"If you'll give me your sister's address, I'll be right over."

"No. It's too crowded and sticky here."

"Why not pick me up in the car?"

"Sis is out. I'm babysitting."

"You don't want me to come?"

"Dirk, the place is a mess. Any progress?"

"So soon? This is a cold trail. I've met some of the roomers, but didn't dare probe. Uh—one is a too-nosy spinster on my floor. I'm going to mine that lode, believe me."

She yawned delicately into the phone.

"The heat and the children have me exhausted. Can we postpone things until tomorrow night?"

"If you say so."

"Call me, if you need the car."

"Okay."

She cradled the phone.

Why had she turned him down tonight?

She swung off the bed and kneeled by the fan.

She left the fan and, at the refrigerator, opened a can of beer. Back on the bed, she sipped beer and finished the cigarette.

It wasn't too late to get Dirk to come over, she mused. That's what the New Jersey Bell Telephone was for. To call a man and—

Suppose she did phone 1327 West Plank Road? The old hag would answer.

Old hag: "You wish to speak to Mr. Dwenger?"

"Yes," in a disguised voice.

"Your name?"

"He knows."

"Don't you wish to leave your name? He's out and—"

That would make a simple phone call sound too mysterious and Mrs. Cashion might have an extension from the phone in the downstairs hallway. She thought of a more appropriate phone call.

"Mrs. Cashion? Listen, you old bitch. This is Marta. Why don't you come over to my apartment and blackmail me some time? I'd love to have you! There happens to be a gun in my bag. I'll drill a hole in your belly so the paregoric can leak out on my rug. I'll—"

Drivel, she decided. Like Mr. Cashion, she was uttering vapid threats.

She fluffed the pillows, clicked off the light, and stretched out deliciously. She was tired from the heat.

Tomorrow night.

But tomorrow came, and tomorrow went and there was no phone call from Dirk.

Here it was ten p.m., and still no call.

Tonight is our night together and there are cold cuts in the refrigerator and fresh lime juice ready to pour over ice cubes exactly the way you like it, darling. On the table, two lighted candles, two places set, and where are you?

Dirk, I love you! Why didn't you phone today? Dirk! Dirk!

Like this new nylon thing? I hope it's sheer enough!

It's been such a long Thursday, darling, and I love you!

Eleven o'clock!

Damn.

I can't spend another night away from you. Please phone. Tell me where you are and I'll break all the speed laws to reach you, darling! You can't do this to me, understand?

Dirk, Dirk . . .

The phone rested on the night table, mute as a Buddha god.

Oh, hell!

That was the way Thursday passed. And Friday passed that way too, except that Marta went out for a while.

It was twilight when she unlocked the apartment door and stepped inside. She clicked on a switch, set the lock, and heeled the door shut at her back. The phone started to ring, and she rushed to it.

"Yes?" she said impatiently.

"Darling," a guarded voice said. "I've only got a minute. I tried twice to get you, but you must have been out. Listen, I think this thing is going to break wide open tomorrow. The damnedest thing happened last night and that's why I didn't call.

"Listen carefully and don't interrupt. At the top of West Plank Road is a corner drugstore. Marlow's is the name. Can you drive me—uh, there's another passenger—to North Jersey tomorrow morning?"

"To stay?"

"Yes. Can you get away from the sister and the kids?"

"I'll manage."

"Wait a minute." She heard him calling to someone, then: "I'm in a hurry. Tell you later. Be at Marlow's at eight o'clock tomorrow morning. We've struck gold, Marta. You got that?"

"Yes, but—"

"'Bye, darling," and the receiver clicked.

No Dirk again tonight, she thought dully. But— Dirk tomorrow. Except that three would be a crowd.

Who was the mysterious passenger, anyway? North Jersey—that meant Dirk probably had picked up the trail of Vernon Cashion. Marta had last heard from Vernon near Hallstead, a dozen miles from the lake and Mr. Klee's ranch house.

How had Dirk located Vernon's trail?

She switched on the fan. She unzippered the black dress, wriggled it over her head and flung it at the bed. The petticoat followed the dress. She giggled, kicked off her high-heeled shoes, stood in the cool stream from the fan, and stretched.

At that moment, soft as a lover's kiss, knuckles tapped outside her door. She pirouetted. Dirk was here! Could it be?

Long pause.

Tap, tap—pause, tap.

Dirk at her door!

She tiptoed forward, her face aglow with expectation. He had phoned from nearby! He had fooled her, telling her he could not get here tonight, and here he was!

Tap, tap—

Pause, and then the knob began to turn slowly. Almost a full turn, then back again.

Tap, tap, tap.

But Dirk doesn't know where you live. You gave him only the telephone number, not the address of this apartment—because you did not want him to come that first night, you wanted time to think.

The knob rattled.

Well, Dirk might have phoned *Information* and asked for . . .

A fist smashed against the door.

That wasn't like Dirk! It couldn't be Dirk!

She froze against the wall, making no sound. Her head began to spin. She took a deep breath, and pressure built up inside her and she heard no further noise outside the door.

A minute crawled past, and then another.

Something whispered under the door. She stared down. A bit of folded paper slid over the sill. The paper moved inward another inch, then stopped. She did not stir.

Then, in the bare corridor outside, heels clicked off. As the footsteps faded, numb fingers jerked at the slip of paper. Marta ran to the bed, switched on the night lamp. Her hands trembled as she opened the folds. The scrawl said:

> *I know you're inside. I saw you come upstairs. You can't get away. We know wherever you go. You didn't mail that letter. Next time I'll have a key, understand?*

She sat immobile, the blood drained from her face. Then she picked up the phone, dialed slowly. She would never forget that number.

A woman's voice said: "Hello."

"Is Mrs. Cashion there?" Marta asked softly.

"One minute. I'll see."

Pause.

She heard a woman's voice calling: "Mrs. Cashion. Phone, Mrs. Cashion."

Pause.

"Sorry," the strange woman's voice said, "but she seems to be out. Did you wish to leave a message?"

"No," and Marta cradled the phone.

Mrs. Cashion had been outside the door, trying to get in. Marta was certain of it. But how had Vernon's mother learned that she, Marta, was here? Had Mr. Cashion told of the meeting near West Plank Road?

Marta dropped to the bed. Rolling over, she buried her face in a pillow. Why didn't they leave her alone? They had thirty thousand dollars of Aircrafter's cash. Wasn't that enough for them? Why did they insist on blackmail money, hush money?

A stifled sob emerged from the pillow. Except for the whirring of the electric fan, it was the only sound in the apartment.

EIGHT

At eight o'clock the next morning, she sat with Dirk in the Chrysler, which she had parked in front of Marlow's on West Plank Road.

"Damnedest thing that ever happened to me," Dirk was explaining. "The name of that woman in 2C is Bertha Smathers. She's not much to look at—scrawny, and I guess about forty years old. She has runs in her nylons and dreams in her eyes and a soft voice. Seems she's a country girl from Elmira, where she has an uncle. She clerks at a stationery store from noon until nine, without relief. She's an avid reader of mysteries and that's how she got interested in detective games. She's much more than a nosy old maid, I found out. I'd say she was a good solid citizen. She's lived at Cashion's for three years and nothing has escaped her eyes and ears."

Marta said curiously, "And she plays detective?"

"That's right. Two years ago, she began to tail people. Anybody, just so long as she kept busy. It was a game at first. For instance—what does that crafty Mr. Enders do every day, she wondered, and tailed him one morning. He's a roomer on the third floor, see? Well, she found out that he met a married woman. Seems Enders worked at night, the husband of this woman in the day—and so on to trouble."

"What does Enders have to do with it?"

"Nothing. It's illustrative of what I barged into unsuspectingly. On Thursday morning, I had to pick up some stuff at the office. Bertha tailed me. Thursday night, after work, she cornered me in my bedroom and called me Mr. Delgar. She floored me! I guess you have to see Bertha to realize that she could tail practically anybody and not get caught.

"She's so innocuous to the eye. It looked as if the investigation would blow up in my face until she explained that she hated Vernon Cashion and had promised herself to find out where he was hiding out so she could inform the police."

"Bertha's offered to help you?"

"Right. As soon as she learned I was an investigator, she decided to throw in with me. She wants to do some real investigating. She knows the mother controlled Vernon in everything he did. And she decided she could locate Cashion by finding out how the two communicated with each other. Bertha's very clever, Marta."

"Did she find Cashion?"

"Yes."

"Where is he?"

"Take it easy," he said, grinning. "I'll get to it." Dirk looked at his watch. "Wonder where she is. It's five minutes past eight."

"Imagine any woman late for a date with you, darling."

"Deflates my ego. Bertha figured that the Cashions were still using the mails to communicate. She knows the local postman. Early every morning, she'd waylay the postman up the street and he'd let her leaf through the mail for 1327—ostensibly looking for a letter addressed to herself. Last week, she noticed that two letters had arrived for a Miss Rose Kessinger. But no Kessinger lives in the rooming house. On Tuesday, this week, there was a third letter for Rose. Bertha beat the postman back to 1327. When he left the mail, she came right down. Mrs. Cashion already had the mail. She let Bertha sort it for the roomers. Of course, the letter to this Rose Kessinger was missing. Do I draw a diagram, darling?"

"Such a simple trick! Nobody would suspect."

Again he looked at his watch. "Hey, she's ten minutes late. That's not like Bertha."

"Dirk, how did the letter tell her where Cashion is?"

"The postmark, my dear."

"And where is he?"

"Oh. Bertha didn't tell me that."

"What an anti-climax! Why are we heading for North Jersey, then?"

"He's somewhere up there—some hick town. Bertha was afraid, if I knew the postmark, I'd run off without her. 'I want to be in on the kill,' is what she told me."

"Or get a chunk of reward money from Mr. Klee."

"If he pays out any reward money. He hasn't offered a reward yet, has he? Anyway, you don't understand. This is the damnedest thing I ever ran into. Bertha isn't interested in money. She said that to take money might impair her amateur standing. In fact, she wanted to pay me twenty dollars to let her go along. How do you like that?"

"I like it fine—if it leads you to Cashion. Can you find him from a postmark? Suppose he drove fifty miles to post the letters?"

"I'll get him. Where the hell is that Bertha?"

The time dragged. Dirk fidgeted and chain-smoked. At eight-thirty, he snapped, "Let's get out of here. Drive down West Plank and I'll see what happened to her."

They drove off, and Marta parked a block above 1327. As she watched him stride off, she sensed the change in him. Before, he had been relaxed and easy-going. Now he seemed like the man she had seen in action at Fred's Log Cabin against tough Harry.

She lit a cigarette and relaxed and waited. She was halfway into the second cigarette when she saw him marching up the block, his face dark.

He slammed into the car, almost smashed the glass as he closed the door.

"The godamnedest rotten luck I ever had!" he exploded. "Bertha ran off to Elmira to visit her uncle. She got a phone call from Western Union during the night. There was a telegram saying he was sick and she was to come immediately. Why did the old goat have to get sick now—if he is sick. I checked Western Union just now, and—"

"How did you find this out?"

"Bertha left a note in my mailbox. She explained why she had rushed off and said we'd have to wait until Monday to check those new books." He glared at the inoffensive windshield. "Now what the hell am I going to do?"

Marta smiled secretively and drove off. She was a dozen blocks towards Montclair, when Dirk roused and snapped, "Where the hell are you going?"

"North Jersey."

"What for?"

"There'll be a moon tonight and I could use a cool swim."

"I'm not going along. This is urgent. I—"

"Don't be so peevish, small boy," she interrupted. "While you were at Cashions, I got the postmark for you."

He grabbed at her arm. "You what?"

"I got the postmark."

"How?"

"It was so easy, Dirk. I used my head."

"Damn it, what's the name of the town?"

"Please, Dirk. I'm driving. You said the postman came around early on West Plank Road and that was the way Bertha got her clue. I merely stopped the postman, said I was a friend of Rose Kessinger, and did he know why she hadn't answered my letters, and please, was my last letter to her with the batch he carried? He fell for it and there was a letter and—"

He demanded hoarsely: "What the hell's the address?"

"My, my, but you get excited when someone else is exasperatingly slow. If I pay you twenty dollars, may I go along for the kill?"

"Please, Marta!"

"What's the rush? It will take us nearly two hours to reach North Jersey. Do you love me?"

"Women!" he snarled. Sulking back against the cushion, he stared straight ahead.

In Montclair, Marta continued to the top of the ridge, turned right on Route 23 and reached open country. Of course, the postmark was easy. Vernon Cashion had phoned from Hallstead the other night. So easy to fool a man. She felt a hand suddenly spread itself on her arm.

Dirk's feeling better, she thought. The first time this morning that he's paid any attention to me.

"Please," she protested. "I'm driving."

The Chrysler slid down a long grade. His fingers probed.

"Dirk!"

The fingers now tweaked. "Hmmm, whadda you know? Soft as—"

"Damn you. All right—it's Hallstead. Now, stop it before I wreck the car!"

He opened the glove compartment and yanked out a map, which he spread over his knees. A fingernail coursed across the map.

"Hallstead," he muttered. "Let's see. Scale, ten miles to the inch. I make Hallstead fifteen miles from Hiram Klee's lake, Marta. I can drop you there, pick up my own car, and get in some licks today."

"No time for a swim, darling?"

"No time for anything. I didn't finish telling you—but that telegram calling Bertha to Elmira was too damned coincidental to suit me. I checked with Western Union before I returned to the car. Know what?"

"What?"

"The telegram originated in Newark. On Thursday night, Bertha and I might have been careless, discussing our plans. Somebody must have overheard what we knew. Somebody got Bertha out of town before we could run up to Hallstead. This thing may be touch-and-go. Somebody will try to reach Vernon at Hallstead and tell him to hit the road. But I ought to have some time. They'll figure I can't locate Vernon without Bertha's help. Won't this bus go any faster?"

"Isn't seventy fast enough?"

"I guess so."

"Will you be busy on the case tonight, Dirk?"

"Not unless I find Vernon today."

"There's nobody at the ranch house."

He smiled, and slid closer to her. "Been pretty busy, haven't I?"

"And I've been the loneliest girl for three nights, darling. You'll be at the lake with me this evening?"

"You bet."

"There's something I want to tell you."

"Go ahead."

"Not now. I want the moon to hear."

Ahead of them, the concrete highway seemed to be dividing under the hood and vanishing there as the big Chrysler ate up the road.

NINE

High in the night soared the full moon of September. It gilded the ground.

For the sixth time, Marta Selfron paced the graveled driveway at Hiram Klee's ranch house. Why hadn't Dirk returned? It was past nine o'clock. What was keeping him?

At her back, light blazed from every window. Parked cars lined the lane and intruded the smooth lawns. A record player was blaring inside, but not loudly enough to drown the wild bursts of laughter and the raucous voices that poisoned the quiet of the night.

From somewhere on the moonlit waters, an off-key soprano hit a high note. *When you're in love with someone . . . It's the love—li—est night in the yearrrr!* Too much liquor and not enough harmony, thought Marta.

Splash . . . from the middle of the lake.

A female trilled, "Help. Help!"

"I hope she drowns, whoever she is," Marta muttered viciously. But the calls of the female had already changed to delighted giggles. And Marta knew the night here was spoiled for her and Dirk—if he did ever arrive here.

At noon, Hiram Klee had barged in with the redhead. "Celebration tonight," he had announced. "Marta, I'm going to get married and we're going to let the world know about it. We phoned Sherry's, the caterer, to prepare for a hundred guests. No, you don't have to do a thing. Everything's taken care of. On the way down, we stopped at every telephone and invited guests. They'll start pouring in pretty soon. Some fun!"

And the sultry redhead had drawled: "Hiram-boy has invited a dozen show girls, Marta. Just to spice the party."

No old convertible yet stood among the parked cars. And if Dirk did come, Marta asked herself, what would he think of this revelry?

She returned to the kitchen.

The caterer's crew was working busily. Waiters bustled in and out, wearing harried, set smiles. Food cluttered many tables. Everywhere were cases of scotch and champagne. "How many are here?" Marta asked of a calm majordomo.

"Eighty-six at the last count, Miss Selfron," he detailed. "It's rather impossible to estimate accurately because the—ah, guests are so widely dispersed. We'll manage, however."

She threaded through the kitchen. "Would you?" a waiter asked, and presented a tray filled with mixed drinks. She took one and sipped. Strong with Scotch, she thought. In this madhouse, an unattached girl must be careful to keep her wits or—

Propped against the wall by the arched entrance to the breakfast nook, Marta noticed a small, dark woman with a hard face. Through clenched teeth, the woman muttered: "I'll fix that fat little bastard."

A bare arm stretched along the corridor wall. She tried a sliding step towards the central hallway.

A waiter passed, and Marta handed him her glass, and he murmured: "Thank you, miss," and hurried off.

"Do you have a match, Alva?" she asked.

Alva, who had been the second Mrs. Klee, was pinned to the wall with alcohol. "Huh?" she rasped.

"A match, please."

"Who wants a match, me?"

"No, me," Marta corrected.

"Oh, me. Got a cigarette, Marta?"

Marta placed a cigarette between the slack lips. Alva inhaled. "Good," she muttered, but the cigarette was unlit.

"Some party," Marta offered.

"I'm gonna cut his eyes out," Alva promised.

Marta's fingers closed around a wrist and pressured. Alva's hand opened. A potato knife clattered to the floor. "Pick it up, you interferin' bitch," Alva ordered thickly. "Gonna cut his eyes out."

"Whose?"

"That fat bastard I was married to. Invitin' me here to tell me he's gonna marry again! I'll fix him! I'll—"

A middle-aged man stumbled into the corridor. "Hey," he blared, spotting Alva. "Been lookin' for you." He grabbed the woman and, pulling her away from the wall, bent her backward and planted a kiss on her lips.

"Too public," he announced. He gave Alva a push and they staggered off together. Marta heard him say: "Old Klee didn't appreciate you, but I do."

Marta shivered. What a collection.

Couples littered the central hallway. Wild laughter erupted through an open bedroom door. But two bedroom doors were shut, Marta noted. What would Dirk think if he came here tonight?

She strolled into the living room, closing her eyes to the minor orgy going on there, but unable to dial the racket from her ears. The living room was sheer bedlam.

They had shoved back the furniture and turned the rug into Yankee Stadium, with a pillow for home plate and a tennis racket for a bat. The feminine players had kicked off shoes, hose; their skirts were pinned high above their bare legs. Toeing the pitcher's slab was a round man with a bald head and overstuffed stomach. He wore yellow shorts, Argyle socks and garters, and blue sneakers.

He was Hiram Klee.

At the plate posed his sultry redhead. She wore a bikini that could have been stuffed into a thimble. Some of the male guests were standing around just ogling.

Hiram served up the tennis ball. The redhead swung. The ball took off and smashed through a lamp shade. The bulb exploded and the room rocked with noise. The redhead strutted toward first base. The baseman grabbed her. Their bodies glued together and their lips cemented. Hiram Klee did not seem to mind. "Safe!" he roared.

A tall man reached for Marta. "You're goddammed cute," he announced, but Marta shoved him into the arms of a golden blonde wearing a red playsuit. The tall man was not at all put out. His arms happily circled the willing blonde, who was supposed to be the third baseman.

"You look good enough to love." The tall man laughed.

"You have to go around the bases first, you know," the blonde reminded him.

At first base, men had lined up to take a turn at Klee's redhead. On the mound, Hiram Klee stood slack-footed, belly sagging over the belt of the shorts. He might have been smiling or simply reflecting an overdose of scotch. He wheeled slowly, spotted Marta.

He stumbled over, muttered: "Marta, you seen Joe Beggs?"

"No."

"He's here—with his wife. Look, do me a favor. He's whining over that last shipment from Aircrafter's. Cool him off for me."

"All right."

Klee patted her arm absently.

"You look swell. And listen, this stuff is too rough for a nice girl like you. You keep out of this, understand?"

"I'm trying to."

"Your man arrive yet?"

"No." She had told him that she was expecting company.

"Handle Joe Beggs for me." Klee turned away, grumbling. "She's goin' too far." He meant the sultry redhead. He moved off purposefully.

The tall man had backed the golden blonde against the wall and clamped a half-nelson around her neck. As Marta moved off, an unattached woman bumped into her. "Sorry," Marta offered.

"Oh, Miss Selfron! I'm Mrs. Beggs. Have you seen Joe?"

"No."

"I can't find him. Will you help me?"

"Of course."

"I—I'm worried. This is so—so disgusting." Mrs. Beggs brushed a lock of gray hair from her worried face. "I'm worried about the twins at home. A new maid, and I can't trust her. You'll find Joe for me?"

"Yes," Marta promised.

Why had the woman brought her husband into this, Marta wondered. If I had a husband, I'd keep him home, she told herself.

It was less noisy on the porch.

Marta wandered around among the couples there, murmuring: "Has anyone see Joe Beggs? His wife wants him."

Nobody answered her. People lolled on chairs and swing divans, and four filled a strung hammock. God, Marta thought, and I invited Dirk here to share the moon. I can't take any more of this.

She pushed open the screen door and walked to the dock.

Girls in bathing suits were playing a game with men who tried to keep from being pitched into the water with their business suits on. One middle-aged man—she recognized Truegate, executive vice-president at Aircrafter's—had no luck. With his arms wrapped around a girl, he plunged overboard. It was nice, clean fun—so far—even if pretty wet.

At her elbow, a voice said bitterly, "Look at that fool Truegate making an ass of himself, Marta." She turned to a tall, lean man with a cadaverous face. He wore a sport jacket with a houndstooth design and was swilling from a tall glass inside one bony hand.

"Good evening, Mr. Ronstein," Marta said to the treasurer of Aircrafter's.

"That bastard doesn't have a brain in his head, Marta. Never did like him." Ronstein's voice lowered confidentially. "Did you know he bets on the ponies every day? Why, he coulda got his hands on that missing thirty thousand bucks and—"

She interrupted sharply. "That's a hell of a thing to say, Mr. Ronstein."

"A lot of people are saying it," he muttered.

"And a lot of people are saying things about you, too."

"That's Truegate spreading his gossip about me! Sure, I just paid off a big mortgage on my new house—but it was all my money, not that cash from the safe. If the lousy police had any brains, they'd have solved that robbery long ago and—"

Marta interrupted. "Have you seen Joe Beggs?"

"No. I hear he's been whining about the last shipment. You want him, Marta?"

"Mr. Klee asked me to talk to him." She made a sudden decision. "If you see Joe, tell him I'll be in the summer house. I can't take any more of this party."

"Don't blame you. Sure, I'll send Beggs out if I see him."

Marta swung under the railing and dropped to the lawn.

"Dirk," she murmured sadly, "please come!"

She strolled past a bed of rhododendrons, her steps silent on the moonlit grass.

The summer house would be a nice place to wait and smoke a cigarette—until Dirk arrived.

It was a couple of hundred feet from the ranch house, squatting quietly under the graceful trees at the lake's edge. It had a conical roof of cedar poles and sides of latticed cedar. Rank vines covered the lattice. Marta went inside the dark doorway.

No one was inside.

She sat down on a cushioned two-seater divan and lit a cigarette. She could still hear the noise, but it was subdued. Thank God for the vines and the distance.

Soon she would check again to see if Dirk had arrived. A moon like that, and no Dirk.

TEN

"You know that last shipment from Aircrafter's wasn't up to specifications," Joe Beggs said smoothly.

He sat on the cushioned divan close beside Marta inside the summer house. A hand patted her knee and rested there. "Sure, materials are scarce and top-grade labor hard to keep, but I don't intend to let Klee cheat me, understand?"

She captured the hand and held on to it. *Handle Joe Beggs for me,* Hiram Klee had said.

He should have said: *Defend yourself from Beggs.*

"If there is anything wrong with that shipment," Marta said, "you know Mr. Klee will make good. We're an old, established firm and we keep our customers happy."

"That's what I want you to do. Keep this customer happy."

"Why, Mr. Beggs . . . Did you see your wife, Mr. Beggs? She's looking for you."

"I deliberately lost her."

She had all she could do not to slap his face. But she owed Mr. Klee so much.

She did not want to offend one of his biggest customers.

An arm circled her shoulders. Moist, avid lips plastered to her cheek.

"Please," she said, too loudly.

"Damn it, relax."

His lips glued to hers.

Silence.

What did a girl have to do to "handle" Joe Beggs? Let herself be mauled in a summer house?

His arm left her shoulders. She pushed against him, and the hand stopped for a moment.

"I was hoping to get next to you tonight. Glad I bumped into Ronstein and he told me you was waitin' for me here. Smart girl! Honey, I operate on a lush expense account and there's enough for the two of us, see? Goin' to Cleveland for three trips. You come along."

She pressed her palms against his chest, braced her back against the divan, readied herself to shove him to the ground and—

A woman's voice said, outside: "You, there! Have you seen my husband?"

Beggs groaned. "Shhhh, it's the wife, damn it!"

Marta freed herself.

"No," Dirk Delgar's voice said outside, and Marta shuddered. How long had Dirk been there? What had he heard?

"I can't find him anywhere," Mrs. Beggs shrilled. "I'll bet he's with that blonde tart, Marta Selfron! Will you help me find my husband?"

"Certainly."

"Do you know him?"

"No."

"How are you going to find him?"

"What does he look like?" Dirk asked.

"He's small and thinks he's dapper," Mrs. Beggs explained. "He's dark and a customer of Aircrafter's."

"Suppose we try the summer house. I think it's occupied. Let's just see who's in there, okay?"

Joe Beggs groaned again. He darted through the doorway. "There you are, Gwendolyn, darling," he said. "I've been searching everywhere for you. Where have you been?"

"Looking for you," Mrs. Beggs said waspishly. "Is that blonde bitch in there?"

"No. A guy grabbed her at the dock. I wandered out here for some quiet. Let's go get a drink, all right?"

"I'm going inside that summer house, first!"

And Dirk said smoothly: "He's telling the truth, Mrs. Beggs. I was looking for someone and checked the summer house. There was no one there a moment ago, except Mr. Beggs."

"That's right," Beggs said. "Let's go, Gwendolyn, darling."

Marta heard them arguing as they drifted off.

Pause. No sound from outside.

What was Dirk thinking?

A lighter flamed. Through the vines, she saw his face, outlined as he lit a cigarette. The lighter flame died.

Pause. Did he know she was here, she wondered frantically. What had he heard? What did Dirk think of this wild party?

"For God's sake," Dirk said, "why don't you come out? His wife saved him from the blonde tart and there's nobody here but this wolf."

She went out with a rush. Her hands reached and clutched the lapels of his sports coat. She lifted eagerly on tiptoes.

"When did you come?" she asked. "I went out a dozen times to look for your car! Oh, Dirk! I missed you so!"

She lifted her face.

He had the cigarette between his lips. He blew smoke into her eyes. "Were you lonesome?" he asked.

"Please, put the cigarette down! I want to—"

His body was like steel. He asked: "How come the mob?"

"Mr. Klee spoiled it by coming here unexpectedly. He's going to announce his engagement to the redhead tonight."

"Some redhead. I saw her. Does she neck with everybody?"

"When she gets the chance. Dirk, did you locate Vernon Cashion?"

"No. This is a pretty wild party. There's a girl swimming and ten guys trying to catch her. Did I interfere with your work just now?"

"My work?"

"Yeah. It was work, wasn't it?"

"Dirk, what do you mean?"

He stared down at her, his face dark. "Come out in the moonlight," he suggested, "so I can see you."

When they were on the bright lawn, he stared at her and said thoughtfully: "Beautiful eyes, so innocent—and blue. Rather a low neckline on the dress. "

"Dirk, why don't you kiss me?"

"I was smoking." He flung the cigarette away savagely.

She lifted on tiptoes, breathed: "You're not smoking now, darling!"

"No."

Weight sagged, and Marta lowered her heels.

"How long were you outside the summer house before Mrs. Beggs came?" she asked in a tiny voice.

"Long enough."

"Eavesdropping?"

"Yeah. And wondering how far you'd let him go."

"Dirk, you're angry."

"I certainly am not!"

"Please, not so loud."

"I'm not being loud!"

"Please—you're shouting."

"You think nobody heard you two? Hah!"

"But you don't have to shout. Please, you—"

"Is that part of your, job, to soothe disgruntled customers?"

She pressed in against him, her arms around his strong shoulders.

"Listen to me, darling. That man doesn't mean a thing to me. He got one kiss, period. If a single kiss smooths out a business difficulty, then what's a kiss?"

"You don't need to apologize," he said more quietly. "I'm no prude, either. Personally, I'm not hanging around. There's a motel near Hallstead where I can spend the night more profitably. Did you get a letter of confirmation from Klee?"

"Yes. It's in my bedroom."

"My car's parked down the road. I need that letter to show to Jim Dalgren. If I wait five minutes, do you think you can fetch it out?"

"Yes."

"If I don't get the letter, to hell with Aircrafter's. I don't like your boss and I don't like his parties."

"That's an ultimatum?" She released him, stepped back and waited.

"A statement," he said flatly. "You've got five minutes—if you can spare the time." He turned toward the nearby garden. He sniffed the air. "Nicotiana. That's a dead-white flower, five-pointed, like a star. Opens only at night and cloys the air. It has broad, oblate leaves and belongs to the tobacco family.... Well, that's enough botany for one night. You have five minutes."

He waded across the moon-drenched lawn.

Oh, God, she thought bitterly, this is the end. Damn Hiram Klee for asking me to handle Joe Beggs. Damn Aircrafter's. Damn everything.

She fled across the lawn, her knees flashing. She had five minutes before Dirk went.

From the direction of the lake, a baritone bellowed, "Last one in the water is chicken!"

A female wailed, "But I don't have any bathing suit!"

Padding silently down the driveway, Marta listened bitterly. She had to square herself with Dirk for that stupid episode in the summer house.

She saw his car, the top down, pointed toward the wood, the engine running.

She reached him and said, breathlessly, "Afraid I'd missed you." She tossed an envelope on his lap. "There's the letter. Mr. Klee is glad you're working for him, Dirk."

He stuffed it carelessly in a pocket. "I'll probably be seeing you some time," he said.

"When, Dirk?"

"Oh, when I get the case cleaned up I'll be around to Aircrafter's to collect."

"Aren't you going to kiss me?"

He slid across the seat. She leaned into the car. His lips were quiet, but not unfriendly.

She said, drawing back: "I don't kiss other men like I kiss you."

"Okay."

"Know why I didn't let you come to see me on Wednesday night?"

"You were at your sister's, and the place was mussed up."

"I don't have a sister," she said. "I wanted time to mull over what had happened between us. I couldn't think with you near and I wanted to be sure."

"Of what?"

"You and me. It was lonely without you. It was lonely here tonight, even with this crowd." Her hands gripped the top of the door. "Dirk, this isn't just something that happened—and suddenly is over. It can't be."

"Why not?"

"Because I—oh, damn it. Good night, Dirk."

He slid under the wheel. Marta leaned down, picked up an overnight bag that she had been carrying, and dropped it on the floor mat. Dirk glanced up, startled.

Before he could say anything, Marta stuck one foot over the door. Her leg followed the foot, and then she tumbled on the seat beside him. He hadn't moved.

She righted herself, snuggled close to him, and purred: "I was afraid I'd miss you because I had to pack the bag and fight off two wolves and rush out here and—and—" She stopped to pick up air, and then laughed.

"Where you going?"

"With you," she told him.

"Who says so?"

"I do!"

"Why?"

"Dirk, I love you."

"Now wait a minute. We've known each other a couple of days and—"

"Dirk, I love you! Nobody else in the world."

"How do you know?"

"A woman always knows."

"Why does a woman always know?"

"Because she's not a man, silly."

"What do you want me to do now?"

"Drive off, please."

He drove.

ELEVEN

The light streaming from the business office of Paradise Motel was left behind as the convertible followed a narrow lane that passed neat one-room-and-bath cabins, with a darkened car in each port. In most of the cabins, the lights were off.

"It's way at the back," Dirk said, driving slowly. The convertible entered another lane and the headlights picked up a screened cabin.

The car stopped, and Marta exclaimed: "Dirk, I think it's positively lovely."

"And quiet."

"Blessedly quiet, after the lake."

He rounded the car and opened the door. "Out with you," he said.

She handed him her bag. He opened the trunk and took out a suitcase. She tagged along to the steps, and he unlocked the door behind the screen porch. He stumbled around inside and found a switch. A bulb glowed behind a bilious yellow shade. This cabin had a single bed on either side, one chair, a bureau, rag rug, green walls, and a small closet full of wire hangers.

Dirk dropped her bag next to a bed, said: "Yours." He set his suitcase on the other bed, opened it, and added, "Mine. Uh—you mind if I take a shower?"

"Be my guest."

He took some things from the suitcase, eyed a closed door. "Well, be seeing you."

"Yes, darling."

He opened the door, stepped in.

And he didn't once try to kiss you after you chased him here, she thought. Oh, well. The night was young.

She heard water running. She switched off the lamp. She got out of her things. She opened her small bag, found a nightgown. It settled over her shoulders and nestled against her body.

Barefooted she walked out to the porch. There was a swing across one side, and she sat down on lumpy cushions. This wasn't a bit like the front porch at the ranch house; yet it was infinitely better. That was because she was alone here with Dirk.

Wasn't that proof of love?

And, he must love her! Please, God, make him love me! After all the lonely years, please make him love me . . .

"Marta, where are you?" Dirk called from inside.

"Out here on the swing, darling."

"Decent?"

"Not quite. And you?"

"Shorts."

He walked out barefooted. The full moon outside the screens sifted through the arms of a gnarled apple tree. It was so quiet that they heard a katydid sassing a katydidn't and the katydidn't sassing right back.

Dirk asked: "What are you thinking about?"

"Katydids. They sass each other all summer. Which is the female—the katydid or the katydidn't?"

"The katydidn't."

"How do you know?"

"It's the female who usually says no." He chose a lump on the cushion and sat down.

"Dirk, do you like me like this?"

The gown was sleek under his hand. It had a short, flared skirt. It was opaque. Two abbreviated straps narrowed at bows atop each shoulder. The neckline was high and square.

He said huskily: "You look stunning, and you know it."

She leaned against him, and his lips found hers. His lips were avid. His heart thumped against hers. He drew back, and shook himself.

"Cigarette?" he asked.

She stirred deliciously. "Try mine. They're cork-tipped."

"They should be asbestos."

"Why?"

"Your lips scorch."

He lit two cigarettes, handed her one. She wondered what he thought when her cigarette flamed as she inhaled—but, she did not ask. Instead: "Glad I came along?"

"Yes."

"You're so quiet."

"It's quiet here."

"You like that?"

"I don't like clambakes."

She remembered something. "What luck with Vernon Cashion's hideout?"

"I asked around cautiously, but no one recalled him. Somebody will recognize that new Buick, though. Cashion will drive it around. That means stops for gas and oil, air in the tires, and some service station attendant will remember him, and I'll pick up the trail."

"Clues—right?"

"Not so much that as Cashion. You see, I study people. I leave the clues to the smart boys at Headquarters who have the manpower and the laboratories. I'm interested in subtleties of character. Cashion is a no-good guy spoiled by his possessive mother. He likes to spend money. Suddenly, he has thirty thousand dollars in his hands and his fingers itch to toss it around. In a hideout, he has time on his hands. What good is money if he doesn't spend it? You see, I'm inside his mind. So I know that temporary safety will lull him into an attitude of false security. Why sit around and rust? There's no danger. You're safe, see? That's what he'll tell himself—and act accordingly. He's got to break out of that cage, because that's what people who have never had money will do when they get big money."

Dirk mashed out his cigarette.

"For instance," he continued, "I remember a study a prominent psychologist made some years ago with a case-method investigation of all the big winners in the Irish Sweepstakes over a ten-year period. Mostly, they were little folk, like you and me and Vernon Cashion, and unused to cash in lumps."

"What did this psychologist discover?" Marta asked lazily.

"That eighty-five percent of the big winners were worse off within one year than they had been before they'd got lucky. The first thing they did was tear up the roots, quit the job, and tell the boss to go to hell. They plunged into an environment they were unprepared for. One guy in particular sticks in my mind, a butcher in Hackensack. Before he won a hundred thousand dollars, he had owned a butcher shop and an apartment house. In nine months, he lost everything he had owned, including the hundred thousand. Just one year, Marta, and he was a pauper."

"That sounds impossible."

"Fast living to which the butcher was unaccustomed—that's what cleaned him."

"Did he get another job as a butcher?"

"No. He blew his brains out."

"How awful!" She turned the facts around in her mind. "You're figuring that Vernon Cashion will break loose, toss his cash around, and so enable you to pick up his trail, is that it?"

"Right. In the morning, I'll show you how I work on a case." He leaned back, stretched his legs. "What do you know about the high cost of living, Marta?"

"All I know is that a dollar is worth only forty cents and getting cheaper every day. So the newspapers advise. Apartment rentals are awfully high, too. We could live in mine—or yours, until we had enough saved for a larger place. I'd continue at my job for a while because I have a personal obligation I must pay. That way, we could pool most of our wages and—"

Pause.

A cloud obscured the September moon. They sat inside a pool of pulsing darkness. They held hands, like lovers, and smoked idly.

Dirk said, around a yawn, "It's been a long day in the mines and we have to work in the morning."

She patted his knee, and stood up and stretched. She rose on her toes, like a dancer, her long legs liquid with grace. She lifted her hands. "I can almost—touch the ceiling," she murmured. "Can you?"

He stood and laid his hands flat on the ceiling. Her arms circled his waist. She kissed him on the bare chest. "Stop tickling," he chided, and she released him.

"Carry me inside, please," she murmured. "Like last time."

He carried her through darkness and laid her on the bed. "It's supposed to be a Beauty Rest," he murmured.

She stretched arms and legs languorously. Where was he? She sat up and extended a hand. No Dirk. The springs creaked on the other bed. "Dirk," she called, "where are you?"

"Safe here."

"Dirk?" a tiny voice, she said, "Don't you love me, Dirk?"

"That's not the point."

"What is?"

"Remember how you went away and wouldn't let me come to your apartment because you wanted to think about us? All right, you've made your decision. I'm not prudish. I'm not careful, either. But I must have time to think my side through, just as you did."

He's found out something that links me to the Cashions, she thought despairingly. He'll learn to hate me because I told him lies. Maybe he's found out that I'm a thief.

A long pause, then: "Dirk, good night. I love you, darling. Always and all ways."

His voice was troubled as he answered. "Pleasant dreams, Marta."

She rolled on her side and faced the wall. The mattress was soft and enticing, but she wanted none of it. She swung her legs savagely to the floor, the springs creaking a protest. She stood up and whipped the suddenly hateful gown over her head. It rustled to the rag rug.

"Asleep?" she whispered.

He did not answer.

"Damn you," she sobbed.

She flung open the lavatory door. The place was built to house a dwarf, but there was a shower stall. She turned a faucet.

Cold water hit her like an electric shock, breast high. She stayed under the spray until her teeth chattered.

She toweled her body dry. Her skin was cold to the touch, but her heart was still on fire. She walked out quietly. She could see his dark hair against the pillow. He hadn't bothered to use a sheet, but had stretched out, facing the wall, in his shorts.

She drifted to his side. "Asleep, darling?"

"Yeah."

She sat on her bed and gazed at Dirk. Her eyes misted over.

She was thinking: "You have been deceiving him, and that's no basis for love. Tell him the truth tomorrow. He'll find out anyway."

TWELVE

Sunday started out humidly hot.

The convertible drifted along a two-lane macadam road that wound through the rugged, woody section west of Culver Lake.

It was too early to meet the local drivers on tour, not late enough to face the threat of road hogs returning to the cities. The convertible had the road pretty much to itself.

Marta wore a dark sweater, darker slacks, and black sandals.

She murmured: "Ho-hum, there's another service station."

"Move over and act like a married woman."

"That's the way I want to act."

"Married to a husband who deserted you, remember?"

"That role." She sniffed. "Am I doing wrong?"

"So the law says."

"We'll get married."

"On Sunday?"

"Tomorrow!"

"That's wash day."

"Tuesday?"

"In New Jersey, you wait three days after you get the license."

"Be difficult! Dirk, is detective work always as boring as it is this morning? We've tried all the service stations in Sussex County and no one remembers Vernon Cashion or Prudence Nason."

"We keep trying," Dirk said patiently, and parked beyond a triple gas pump.

An elderly man wearing a soiled jumper walked out and asked: "Can I help you folks?"

Dirk nudged Marta.

She leaned on the door, smiled, and said: "I hope you can. If you help, you win the ten dollars. If you don't help, you win only five."

"Sounds interesting."

"I'm looking for a new Buick sedan, blue, with fog lights, whitewalls, and a mounted spot. It's my car. He's twenty-seven years old, about five feet eight, hundred and fifty pounds, light-brown hair and eyes. I want to find the woman, too. I'll scratch her eyes out! Have you seen my husband in my new car?"

"Run out on you, huh?"

"You're so right."

"Must be a fool. Well—is he transient, local or foreign?"

"Foreign?"

"City folks. That's what we call 'em up here."

"He's foreign."

The man pondered, pursing thin lips. "He don't hit my mind atall. See a lot of cars, but don't remember that one."

Marta extended a five-dollar bill. The man reached for it, stopped his hand in mid-air. "Nope," he decided, "I don't want nothin' for the nothin' I give you, missus."

"Why thank you. You shock me."

The man turned away.

Dirk shrugged. "Let's try the next place."

"Do we have to?"

"Know a better way?"

"Yes."

He eyed her curiously. "Let's hear it."

She had been thinking about it all morning.

Now, she offered: "They drove that new Buick right off the showroom floor, Dirk. New cars need more attention than older ones. Wouldn't the Buick need a thousand-mile check at a Buick service station, and all the fixings, like a motor check and so on?"

"Maybe you've got something," Dirk decided.

Marta called out, "Wait a minute, sir. There's one thing more—"

The elderly attendant shuffled back to the car. "What's on your mind?"

"I've got to locate my husband," she explained. "He's in this area, and the Buick is brand-new. For five dollars where would he take a Buick for special servicing?"

"New Buick, huh? Try Hal's Repair Shop. That's a mile beyond Hallstead, main road. Everybody knows Hal. He's up-to-date, with a neon sign, *Buicks a Specialty*, and he gets all the local Buick trade. I got nothin' against a Buick, but I always drive a Dodge. Had one since I was old enough to drive and—"

"Thank you," Marta purred, and handed over the bill. This time the old man cheerfully accepted it.

"If my husband wasn't at Hal's, what's the next best place to try?"

"Sparta—but you try Hal first." The man smiled. "Mind if I ask you a question, missus?"

"No."

"You want him back—or the Buick?"

"The Buick," Marta said quickly, and Dirk drove off.

They spotted the sign atop the roof of a roadside barn that had been converted into a garage and gas station at the invasion of the motor age. Dirk parked.

A young handsome man in a peaked cap and jeans strolled out. He took off the cap and grinned at Marta. He had close-cropped blonde hair, blue eyes, red cheeks, and a grease spot on a chin that had been shaved that morning.

"My lucky day," and his eyes admired Marta.

"Are you Hal?" she asked.

"To my friends."

"Hal, I understand you're very good with Buicks."

"Everybody around the lake knows that."

"You see a lot of Buicks?"

"Not enough to suit me but quite a few."

"I'm trying to locate a blue Buick sedan, brand new, probably a Jersey plate. It has fog lights, whitewalls, and a spotlight."

"Sounds like Judge Vanderplatt's new job, only he don't have the spot. This isn't local?"

"No."

"Who's driving this new job?"

Dirk leaned on the wheel, and said, "Here's the description of the man."

He detailed the facts about Vernon Cashion.

He added, "Maybe there's a woman with him. She's a faded blonde, bifocals, a trifle over five-feet tall, rather heavy. We'd like to talk to this man."

Hal thought it over. His blue eyes said nothing, but his lip asked,

"You a cop?"

"Private."

"Car theft?"

"No."

"Payments overdue?"

"No."

"Hit-run?"

"No."

"On the lam?"

Dirk said slowly, "He's a no-good guy. You sound as if he'd been here and you didn't like him."

"This Buick," Hal mused. "Two fog lights, you said?"

"Yeah."

"It was last Sunday morning, early. A fellow drove in with a new blue Buick, Jersey plates. It had a mounted spot, whitewalls, but only one fog light."

"What did he look like?" Marta asked.

"I was telling you about the car, see? He had skidded off the road on Saturday night, he said, and smacked a tree. He had a whisky breath so I figured he told the truth. The car had a rumpled right front fender and he had blown a shoe. He was in a hurry, wanted the car fixed in fifteen minutes. It took me most of Sunday to do the repairs and he paid me a bonus. I never did get that other fog light back in place because he hadn't fetched it along."

Dirk's nostrils quivered. "Brown hair and eyes?"

"Sure."

"Was the dumpy blonde with him? What name did he use? Where is he hiding out? How do I get there? Does he—"

Hal grinned.

"You must want him bad. No woman with him. I drove the car to his place when I was finished and I didn't see this woman there neither. I'm naturally curious. What's he done?"

"Ran out on his wife," Dirk explained.

"You the wife?" Hal asked Marta, and she nodded. "I hate drunk drivers—and he was a wise guy. What's his address worth?"

"Twenty bucks," Dirk said.

"Cash?"

Dirk extracted a bill from his wallet, passed it to Hal. "How do we get there?"

"Like this," Hal said, and detailed the route.

"Thank you very much," Marta said.

"That's okay. I figure the guy belongs in jail."

Dirk drove off, heading back towards Hallstead.

The sky had darkened. Thunderheads reared in from the southwest to erase the noonday sun.

Marta shivered. "I wish I had a coat."

"I'll buy you a mink if we catch Cashion."

West of the lake, a dirt road hugged the indented shoreline. It was hilly wilderness broken by a few scattered cabins, most of them boarded in preparation for the winter.

Tall, primeval white pines marched majestically down a steep slope and headed for the lake.

With the sun gone, it was like twilight under the pine canopy.

Dirk parked on a lane leading to a boarded cabin with a sign that said: *IDLEWILD*.

"This road ends about two-hundred yards further along," he exclaimed, remembering Hal's instructions. "It's the last one. They can't see us from here because of the pines. If Vernon Cashion spotted you, he'd recognize you immediately?"

"I would think so."

"You're to stay here with the car. If another car comes along the road, keep out of sight. They may be at the cabin or they may be out for a ride and coming back. If they recognize you, they might run off and I don't want them flushed."

"Yes, darling."

"There's no danger."

"No, darling."

"I won't be long."

She kissed him on the lips, caressed his cheek, and whispered: "I'll worry every second while you're gone, darling."

"Don't."

"Are you taking a gun?"

"No. They don't know me. I'm only a real estate agent scouting around for vacant cabins that I can rent for the winter season. We have excellent skating and ice fishing here, and lots of city people rent cabins for the weekend. You sit tight. If you get scared, there's a .38 in a shoulder rig in the glove compartment. Know how to shoot?"

"Heavens, no."

"You won't have to."

"I'll worry about you, agent darling!"

"Yeah, an empty whisky bottle might bite me." Dirk stepped out. "It may take time. I'll stop at the cabins between here and where Cashion is. I want to learn what I can. And you keep out of sight."

Dirk strolled off along the lonely, quiet road. When he glanced back,

Marta blew a kiss. Dirk waved, and disappeared behind a laurel screen.

He shouldn't go after Cashion without a gun, Marta mused, worried. Unarmed, how can Dirk capture him?

What could she do to help Dirk?

She picked up her pocketbook. Mr. Klee's gun still weighted it down.

She couldn't use it, but if she were with Dirk, the gun in her hand would be a threat. On the other hand, Vernon Cashion must not see her. She thought back to Hal's description of the cabin.

If she could circle through the pines, reach the cabin from the rear—

Carrying her pocketbook, she left the car. She strolled down the road to the screen of laurels. There was Dirk, fifty yards away, talking to a man in front of a cabin. Keeping the laurels between them, Marta left the road and climbed the slope.

Dry pine needles muffled her steps. She made no sound as she walked along, paralleling the road.

From behind a tree trunk, she saw Dirk leave the man at the cabin and continue on down the road to a cabin that sat close to the lake shore.

She moved ahead, careful lest he see her. Fortunately her clothes were dark, and here under the trees she was almost invisible. Up ahead, a rock wall jutted into the lake.

The dirt road ended near a cabin. Pines guarded it and continued up the slope.

Near the cabin was the back of a single garage.

Marta circled higher, avoiding stones and boulders under the pines. From time to time she studied the cabin, but saw no one.

It was a one-story affair, with several annexes, as if the owner had added to his dream castle whenever he had accumulated more crates.

A screened porch was tacked across the side facing the road. In spots the wire had rusted through and some genius had plugged the holes with bits of newspaper.

Now, as she moved high above the cabin, Marta kept the pine trunks between herself and anyone in the ramshackle cabin who might be on the watch. There were two windows, shades drawn, at the end of the cabin toward the slope. She was safe. She glanced back to the road. There came Dirk, strolling along by the garage.

She had to get closer to the cabin. If she approached from the rear, Dirk would enter at the front. Perhaps she might get near enough to identify Vernon Cashion and Prudence Nason and might even overhear what was said.

Silently she circled, always with a tree trunk for protection. Across the back wall were two windows and a screen door standing ajar.

Orange crates filled with bottles stood against the siding.

A path wound under the trees towards the rock wall that formed a rampart at the rear. The path stopped at a small outbuilding with a weathered shingle roof, shiplap siding, and a closed door with a half-moon-shaped opening cut in the wood. It was the privy.

From her vantage point behind a trunk, Marta could not see Dirk at the front. When she heard voices out there, she would move in closer to eavesdrop. She would—

An inquisitive chipmunk scurried in back of the cabin and mounted a crate and disappeared. Then from inside the privy came a thumping sound. She tensed. Somebody in the privy? Had the door moved inward?

Maybe the wind blowing the door and the door thumping against the jamb. But there was no wind under the dark pines.

She stared at the privy. Was Cashion there? In that instant, she caught a movement behind her. She whirled. Vernon Cashion stepped from behind the trunk of a tree, and hurled himself at her.

She could not scream, because his hand was already over her mouth. His arm encircled her, holding her fast though she struggled wildly.

"I don't know what you're after," he chuckled, "and I don't know how you got here. But I sure am glad to see you. You let out one peep, and I'll choke you to death . . ."

He pulled her back from the path, found a grassy spot under the trees, and threw her to the ground.

As she felt his weight come down on her, she scratched and struggled. As usual, he was much too strong for her, knew too much about fighting, especially dirty fighting. A minute of this wrestling left her breathless and helpless. Vernon laughed.

"Remember—if you make a sound, I'll kill you."

Now Marta was paralyzed with fear. Tears were rolling down her face.

Marta opened her mouth and shrieked.

Vernon jumped to his feet.

At the same time, someone stepped out of the privy.

He was small. He wore a felt hat low over his face, a dark coat with the collar high around his neck—and he carried a rifle.

Vernon stared. The man lifted the rifle. An explosion shattered the air.

Cashion spun. His mouth fell open. His hands dropped.

Without uttering a sound, he pitched forward and hit the path face down.

My God, Marta thought. She opened her mouth and screamed wildly.

One of the little man's hands left the rifle and pushed the hat brim off his face.

Marta recognized Mr. Cashion—the weak, inoffensive husband—and he had just shot . . .

From the back of the cabin, Dirk called: "You there. What's going on?"

Mr. Cashion turned. Swiftly he climbed the slope, darting from one tree trunk to another. Dirk must have seen him, because he sprinted up the path and yelled: "Stop. Stop, or—"

Mr. Cashion whirled. He pointed the rifle, fired. A bullet whined through the trees. The man had deliberately fired much too high.

But it was a warning that could not be ignored, and Dirk dropped to the path.

Mr. Cashion started up the slope, and Marta lost sight of him.

She waited, scarcely breathing, her thoughts frantic. Mr. Cashion had killed Vernon! How had he found him here?

Dirk was on his feet. He dodged forward on the path and kneeled at Vernon's side.

Then he ran to the privy, peered around a corner, and took out after Mr. Cashion. Marta moved forward on numbed limbs.

Don't follow him, Dirk, she was begging mentally. He has a rifle. You're unarmed.

She dared not call out and let Dirk know that she had disobeyed his instructions and followed him here. What should she do? High up the slope, the rifle cracked again.

Marta tensed. Unarmed, surely Dirk would not attack in the face of that rifle. He had too much sense. He knew Mr. Cashion. Had he recognized him?

She forced herself to Vernon's side. She kneeled, her body trembling. Under the left ear, she saw a hole and a trickle of blood.

Vernon did not move.

He will never move again, she thought. Mr. Cashion hated him and killed him. She stood up, appalled by death, even the death of this criminal.

She dared not linger here. She ran down the path, around the cabin. She reached the road. The garage had no door. Inside was a dust-covered blue car, the evasive Buick. She fled along the dirt road, remembered that she must not race past the nearby cabin where Dirk had been talking to a man. She forced herself to walk, her chest heaving with emotion.

There was the man, down by the crude dock. Had he heard the rifle? Would he call the police?

No. He was casting a line into the water. He hadn't taken alarm at twin shots. Probably vermin hunters, trap shooters and target bugs made rifle shots fairly common in the vicinity even before the deer season.

At the parked convertible, she crawled on the front seat and sank back exhausted.

Vernon Cashion was dead.

What would happen next?

She could not guess. She could only wait for Dirk.

Dirk soon returned. He said: "Some stranger killed Vernon Cashion with one shot from a .22 rifle. I chased him up the slope, but he got away. He had a car parked off the main road on the far side of the ridge, but I don't know who he is. I didn't check the cabin to see if Prudence Nason was there. I hustled to a cabin down the road where there was a phone, so I could notify the police."

A single tear slipped from her eyes and skidded down her cheek.

Dirk asked, "You're crying?"

"Because you're back safe," she whispered.

THIRTEEN

Marta leaned against the side of the cabin and tried to overhear the voices on the path behind the shack.

There were four men on hand—Dirk, the coroner, a constable named Baggs, and a hulking young deputy called Ackersmith.

They were standing near the privy.

Marta heard the coroner say, "He's dead, all right. Good and dead. Any idea what time he died?"

"I phoned in," Dirk said, "at twenty minutes past one. Let's say that was about half an hour after I heard the shot."

"So he died about ten minutes to one," the coroner decided. "I'll do a PM later. No sense my staying here, Baggs. I have to go to the hospital on a case, anyway. When's the prosecutor coming?"

"He's on vacation," Baggs said. "I didn't call the State Police yet. You want to do that when you get to the hospital?"

"Sure. I wish you luck. What you know about solving a murder could be written on a parking ticket."

Baggs growled, "I know enough to have got this feller's story. He says the police wanted the deceased for robbery in Newark. He says maybe there's a woman in the cabin, but he didn't bother to check. We will. Be seeing you, doc."

Marta moved around to the rear of the cabin. The coroner, carrying a bag, walked past her and smiled.

"Know him, miss?"

"Vaguely. I happened to be along with Mr. Delgar."

"Nobody can help that Cashion now except the mortician." The coroner went on his way.

Baggs was saying: "Ackersmith, you go in the cabin and see if there's a woman. No, you don't need no gun."

Ackersmith lumbered down the path, and Baggs and Dirk followed more leisurely. Ackersmith grinned at Marta. He flung the screen door back against the siding. He retreated three steps, lowered his shoulders, and plunged forward. He hit the door like a pro fullback. The wood snapped off its hinges. Ackersmith followed it inside.

Baggs drawled, "The door was probably unlocked, but Ackersmith wanted to show off his strength, Miss Selfron."

The constable was a big man in a rumpled suit, Marta noted. He stood with both hands on his hips, the coat open. The barrel of a gun was stuffed inside the top of his pants, only the butt showing.

He wore a badge the size of a plate. His eyes were good, keenly gray, like the wind off the river ice, and his smile was friendly. When he had first driven up, Dirk had introduced himself and Marta.

They listened to Ackersmith thumping around inside, slamming doors, and hollering: "Hey, anybody here?"

"Good man," Baggs said. "Thought maybe I'd get a chance to show off with this .45, but—"

Inside the cabin, a woman shrieked.

"Hey," Baggs snorted, "there is a dame!"

"Let's see who it is," Dirk said, and moved towards the door.

"Just a moment," Baggs bawled. "You was in Hallstead yesterday, Mr. Delgar, and you passed through today. Why didn't you come to me in the first place?"

"Is this your territory?"

"It could be over the township line a mite, but I ain't got the time to fetch a surveyor out here and find out. If I wanted to, I could figure you was more interested in locating the cash than in arresting Cashion. You coulda gunned Cashion yourself, collected the loot, then run to a phone."

"Do you want to give me a nitrate test?" Dirk asked.

"You mean to find out if you fired a gun. If you was going to kill Cashion, you'd know enough to wear gloves."

"I already told you I came in unarmed and left my .38 in the car."

"Yes, you did tell me that. So your gun's a .38, is it? Well, maybe you shot Cashion with a .22, pitched it into the lake, and the county's got to hunt for it. What about that?"

"Ask the lady," Dirk snapped.

Baggs asked, "What about it, Miss Selfron?"

"Dirk told the truth," she explained nervously. "I wanted him to carry a gun because this—this Vernon Cashion was dangerous. Dirk refused and said he could handle Cashion—if he were here. And—"

She checked herself in time. If she weren't careful, she'd be telling them that she saw Mr. Cashion.

"I know Dirk didn't kill this man. The killer was a stranger," she said.

"You know he was a stranger?"

"Dirk said he was. I believe Dirk."

"Kinda like him, don't you?"

"Like him, my foot."

"I thought—"

"I love him, Mr. Baggs."

"Aw," Baggs grunted. "Let's go see what Ackersmith caught."

Dirk said, "Stay outside, Marta."

"But I want to see if—"

"Stay here," he repeated, and followed Baggs into the shack.

A moment later a hysterical voice shrilled, "Does he have to—to point that gun at me?"

"Put it up," Baggs ordered.

Gingerly, Marta walked in behind the men and waded across the splintered door on the floor. It was not much of a kitchen—empty bottles and dirty dishes and soiled linoleum and flies. She reached the doorway of the shack's main room, where two naked bulbs hanging from the ceiling shed light on the three men clustered near a decrepit daybed. Near the bed were a pair of bare feet and sheer pajama legs.

Marta peered around Dirk and saw a young face, the eyes two black holes in a white mask, the hair blonde.

"Why, that isn't Prudence Nason!" Marta exclaimed, and the men turned to her. "Where is Prudence?"

Baggs growled, "Who? Who's Prudence?"

"I never saw this girl before," Marta said. "I worked with Prudence, and this one isn't Prudence! Where is she?"

"All I know, dang it," Baggs grumbled, "is there's a young feller, brown hair and short pants dead on the privy path."

The blonde's tongue licked her pale lips. "He was Freddy Jones to me," she mumbled numbly.

"Was?" Baggs snapped, picked up the verb.

"Was," the blonde repeated. "This—this hick told me Freddy was dead. Look—wasn't that his real name?"

"Real name was Vernon Cashion," Baggs said. "What I want to know is who killed him?"

"I don't have any idea," the blonde muttered. "I was sleeping off a drunk. I didn't hear no shot and I didn't hear no noise. And I tell you he was Freddy Jones to me."

"See any strange men hanging around?"

She shrilled, "I was sleeping off a drunk!"

"Found two empty bottles on the porch," Ackersmith announced, smacking his lips. "Another was half-full when I come along, but it ain't now. Good liquor, too."

"Thought I told you not to drink while you're on duty," Baggs growled. "Young lady, you know this other man with me?"

The girl's eyes lifted slowly and dully. She seemed numbed from the effects of whisky and panic. "Never saw him before," she mumbled.

"The name Delgar mean anything to you?"

"No."

"Ever hear this dead feller mention a Prudence Nason?"

"No."

Baggs shrugged. He was at the end of his rope. He nodded at Dirk, as if suggesting that help would be welcome.

Dirk said, "You're not the girl we expected to find here with Cashion, the fellow you knew as Freddy Jones. You're too young. What's your name?"

"Julie Warnick."

"Age?"

"Twenty. What's that got to do with it?"

"Where's your home?"

"You mean before I met Freddy?" she countered.

"Yes."

"Allentown."

"Where'd you meet him?"

"On the road. Highway 23, I think it was."

"Pick-up?"

She flared. "I was only waiting for a bus and he drove along in a new Buick and stopped. So I didn't have to take a bus."

"When was that?"

"In the morning."

"What morning?"

Julie Warnick crossed her legs man-fashion, with an ankle on one knee. She had an attractive body and the sheer pajamas obscured very little of her figure. Color spotted her cheeks.

"Who's got a cig?" she asked.

Dirk handed her one, flicked his lighter.

Julie sucked in smoke greedily. The cigarette seemed to revive her.

"You're kinda cute," she offered, rolling her eyes.

Dirk closed the lighter.

"I asked you what morning Cashion picked you up on the highway."

"It wasn't yesterday."

"How long before yesterday?" he probed.

"Oh, sometime in July."

"Early in July?"

"I can't really place the date. Hell, this has been a pretty high life with that guy. It was after the Fourth. Maybe a week after the Fourth. I dunno. I don't carry a calendar around."

"Then you've been here about two months?"

"Okay, copper."

"Did he fetch you directly to this cabin? I mean, did he have the cabin rented when you arrived here?"

"He brought me right here from the highway if that's what you mean. We only stopped once to pick up some whisky."

Dirk turned to Baggs. Julie Warnick couldn't see his wink, but Marta saw it.

"She's on the big spot," Dirk said smoothly. "She knew Cashion was heeled. She tipped off an Allentown friend about this easy mark and he drifted over, knocked off Cashion so they could split the cash. She—"

"Like hell!" Julie interrupted. She spat a nasty name at Dirk. "You can't pin this on me."

Baggs said sadly, "Swearin' on a Sunday."

"Go back to your farm, pop," she sneered.

"She lived with him for two months," Dirk continued. "She knew his right name. She knew about the money." He wheeled suddenly on her. "Where's Prudence Nason?"

"I don't know."

Baggs suggested, "They must have knocked her off."

The tart from Allentown screamed. It sounded like a fire siren at midnight.

Ackersmith slapped her face. "Shuddup," he advised, and the screaming stopped.

In the silence, Baggs said: "I'd kinda like to check that Buick in the garage. Yeah, and I'd like to check the far side of the ridge where the killer parked his car. I'd kinda like to do all this afore the troopers are here, if you get what I mean."

Dirk nodded. "They'll take the investigation out of your hands."

"Quick. I ain't had a murder afore, only a chicken thief. Do we have to search to see if all that money is layin' around?"

Julie Warnick sat up straight. "You've been talking about a lot of money since you first come in here. How much money?"

"Thirty thousand in cash," Baggs answered.

"He had money, but not that much."

"How do you know?"

Her eyes narrowed. "I checked his wallet and—"

Dirk snapped, "So you did know his right name?"

"Sure, I knew it. I didn't like him too much. A girl has to figure her own future, don't she? I didn't know he was hot. I thought I'd skip out some dark night and head home, so I checked his wallet."

"How much cash did he carry?"

"Two-three hundred dollars. But he used to hint about all the money he had. That was when he was drunk. We'd spend a lot—still, he always seemed to get more. He told me it came in the mail, every week or so."

"Smart," Dirk said.

"How?" Baggs asked.

"His mother was in this up to her ears. She probably kept the money and passed it out to him in dribs. That's a possible answer, if this tart is telling the truth."

Julie screeched, "Don't you call me names!"

"Ackersmith," Baggs roared, "get her out of here."

"Come along," Ackersmith ordered, grabbing the girl's elbow.

Julie stood up. "On a stack of Bibles," she said more quietly. "I told you all I know. You can't frame me with this. Okay, if I walk off when I get my duds on?"

"You stay here until the State cops take over," Baggs said heavily.

"What's the charge, pop?"

"Suspicion of murder, robbery, prostitution, vagrancy and—and swearing on a Sunday."

She smiled cockily. "Is that all, pop?"

"I'll think up some more later. That's enough to hold you. Go get dressed."

She linked an arm through Ackersmith's. "Come on in, big boy," she leered, "and watch the show."

"You bet," Ackersmith said.

"And don't let her hide nothin' in her bag," Baggs warned. "If there's money here, you watch out for it. I'll be back pretty soon."

Ackersmith lumbered into a dark room. The girl stopped in the doorway, turned. "I'll keep him busy, pop," she promised, and closed the door.

Baggs shook his head. "A pretty tough kid," he grumbled.

Dirk asked, "Can you trust Ackersmith?"

"Sure. He's married." He turned around and saw Marta. "I thought you'd gone out," he said, and flushed.

"It's all right," Marta said.

They made their way to the garage. Marta walked with Dirk. "What about Prudence?" she whispered.

He shrugged.

"Do you think she's—" She could not finish the thought.

"Before there was some hope. Not now, I guess."

Dirk had brought along the keys for the Buick. He backed it into the dirt road. First he checked the trunk, and found nothing. In the rear seat there was an accumulation of candy wrappers, dead cigarettes, and an empty pint whisky bottle. Dirk lifted out the front cushion.

Baggs looked inside. "Hey," he announced, "look at this." He held up a new dime. "I'm getting paid for workin' today," he said, and slipped the dime in a pocket.

"What's this?" Dirk asked curiously, and Marta moved closer.

He held a bobby pin. Atop the loop end was a crystal shard. She said: "Some women stick pins like that into their hair. The crystal catches the light and flashes."

"Probably Julie Warnick's."

She watched him paw through the dirt on the floor mat. There were chunks of dried gum, burned matchsticks, red strips of cellophane from packs of cigarettes, and blobs of mud.

"Ouch," he muttered, and glanced at his finger.

A drop of blood clung to the flesh. He used a burned match to scratch around carefully. He held up something.

It was a tiny, triangular piece of glass.

"Mean anything?" Baggs asked.

"It could be nothing, but you'd better save it for the troopers. Prudence Nason wore bifocals."

"Piece of broken lens, maybe?"

"Could be. I noticed dark stains on the seat cushion. A technician can determine in the stains are blood and—"

"Look," Baggs interrupted nervously, "I'd kinda like to check the far side of the ridge afore I get finished with this case. Doc said he'd phone the trooper barracks from the hospital. Let's shove off while we got a chance."

They drove off in Baggs' car, dropped Marta at the parked convertible. She trailed them along the road, around the ridge, and onto the main highway.

Baggs drove slowly and she could see him peering at the roadside. Then he parked on the shoulder and, stopping the convertible, she joined them.

"Along about here he had that car," Baggs decided. Bending at the hips, he studied the roadside.

Autos hummed past. Curious eyes stared out. Baggs halted at an opening in the brush under the trees.

"In there," he decided, and followed ruts into the woods. "Been some car in here lately."

Impressed in the red dirt was tire marks. There were capital X's along both flanks and three straight furrows for the middle pattern.

"That's known as a symmetrical pattern," Dirk explained. "It's not one of the new patterns—possibly made by a real old tire. It's perfect for a plaster. Don't step on it, Marta."

Dirk hurried out to his convertible, returned with a piece of cardboard. He laid the cardboard over the pattern, set a rock on the cardboard.

"The troopers will find the killer's footprints on the slope, maybe where he hid by the privy."

"Here's something better'n that," Baggs said, and pointed.

The grass had been trampled down. "I'd say he stood there for fifteen-twenty minutes," Baggs decided.

They'll catch Mr. Cashion, Marta thought. And he did right to kill Vernon. It wasn't murder—just ridding the world of a nasty crook and—

Dirk was saying quietly: "I think I've got the answer."

"Who the killer was?" Baggs asked eagerly.

"Who the killer was. Chief, would you like to clean this murder up today and beat the prosecutor and the troopers to a headline?"

"Hell, yes."

"You may get a headache out of it. It's a chance."

"Never had a headache in my life, an' I'm sixty-four. Pop, that tart called me. Why, I'm a grandpop!"

"We'll have to take a little trip."

"Where to?"

"My territory. Newark. There's a detective lieutenant, there, Jim Dalgren, who will help us—but you'll get most of the credit."

"Let's go."

Dirk turned to Marta. "Do you mind driving back to the ranch house in my car?"

"No, darling."

He kissed her quickly. "I'll phone the developments." She could see he was excited. "We can clean up tonight."

"Darling, is there any—any more danger? I mean, you went after that killer unarmed! You took a dreadful chance! You—"

He wasn't listening.

He said: "I'll phone later tonight. I'll need the .38 in the convertible, but you'll be all right with Mr. Klee and his redhead."

He strode from the woods, joined Baggs.

She followed slowly. Baggs turned his car around, stopped for Dirk. Dirk waved. She lifted a numb arm, waved in return. The car headed south in a hurry.

She slid behind the wheel. Her pocketbook lay on the cushion where she had left it momentarily. She would be all right. She had a gun in the pocketbook. She started the engine.

They'll arrest poor Mr. Cashion, she told herself wearily. The trail will lead to Mrs. Cashion, whom Dirk thought had the money. Mrs. Cashion was alive.

She has the incriminating letter that will link you to the robbery.

When Dirk reached Newark—specifically 1327 West Plank Road— all the soiled linen would be hung on the line.

Dirk would learn that she had lied repeatedly to him—that she had obtained the job at Aircrafter's for Vernon Cashion—that she had been married to Cashion—that she had stolen a thousand dollars from Aircrafter's to pay for a divorce—that for three years the Cashions had been blackmailing her.

It was an ugly story to unfold before the eyes of the man she was sure she loved.

When Dirk learned the truth, what would he do?

"Drop you," she said aloud.

The traffic thinned. She swung the car into the road, made a U-turn. She checked the position of the needle on the gasoline gauge. The tank was two-thirds full. That was more gas than she needed to reach the ranch house.

She drove off, headed south. Beyond the end of the ridge where the dirt road cut toward the shack where Vernon Cashion had lived, she met a speeding radio car, the siren wide open and two troopers on the front seat.

She made a sudden decision and did not take the turn that led to the ranch house.

This case would be only half cleared up with the death of Vernon Cashion and the arrest of Mr. Cashion. Maybe she might reach Newark ahead of Dirk. Yes, and before Jim Dalgren joined up with them for the denouement.

And if she did arrive in Newark first, what then?

She did not know. She would think of something.

FOURTEEN

It had started to rain.

West Plank Road metamorphosed into a wet, black ribbon. The street lights wore halos in the night. Cars hummed past with headlights cutting swathes.

An empty bus rumbled downhill, air brakes hissing at intervals. A jeep crowded with teenagers rushed past and young voices shrieked in the night as it swerved around a corner.

Marta sat in the parked convertible, the top up. It was sticky damp because the rain had slanted in before she had got all the windows raised.

Fifty feet ahead, diagonally across the street, was 1327 West Plank Road with the box porch and high steps, dim light behind drawn shades on the first floor, the neatly clipped hedge by the sidewalk, and a starved maple by the curb.

The front door opened and Marta lowered a window. The rain pattered her hot face. A shadow trotted down the high steps and reached the sidewalk. Marta raised the window.

Just some roomer coming out and going off. Probably young, judging by the brisk pace. And a woman, too, with a raised umbrella.

What did you expect to find here, she asked herself.

Mr. and Mrs. Cashion. Dirk and Constable Baggs and the Newark police. She had seen neither of the Cashions during the hour she had waited here after night had fallen. And no Dirk or Constable Baggs.

The only police had been a patrolman on his rounds and he had not bothered to glance a second time at the parked convertible.

She glanced at her watch. Twenty minutes past nine. Where were they? What had detained them? Hadn't Mr. Cashion returned to Newark? Suppose he had run off to hide after he had used the .22 rifle on Vernon.

She hoped the police would never catch up with him. Yet murder was uglier than robbery. Murder should never be condoned, under any circumstances.

Despite the beating rain, she lowered the window again. She leaned out to refresh her face. The rain felt good, clean.

Across the street, a man passed on the sidewalk. She sensed his curious stare, then he veered and crossed the street toward the convertible. She withdrew her face, cranked up the window.

She was setting the catch, when he changed his mind and passed in front of the car. He took a dozen steps, glanced back.

She turned away. He was unimportant. Every man was unimportant to her, except Dirk Delgar.

A car crawled down the opposite side of the street, only the parking lights glowing. It stopped in front of the house next to 1327, close to the curb. She spotted the dark light on the roof, just over the windshield, and tensed suddenly.

Police car?

Headlights approached from the rear. They splashed against the parked car, and she read the license. The numbers didn't matter.

The letters after the numbers did. MG, which meant Municipal Government. That covered the Department of Sanitation, the Board of Health—and the police.

Shadowy figures left the car and stood in a tight knot under the slanting rain. She counted. One, two, three. She recognized the slim one—Lieutenant Dalgren. The chunky one—Constable Baggs. Her eyes glued to the third man, tall, wide-shouldered, hatless In the rain. Her Dirk.

Whose Dirk?

Not yours, she reminded herself.

They moved in a tight group toward the front of 1327. But where was Mr. Cashion? Had he escaped them? And what proof did they have of Mrs. Cashion's complicity in crime? With Vernon dead, what proof could they have against her?

Marta opened the door as the tight group mounted the high steps. One by one they passed inside where a dim bulb, glowed in the lower hallway.

Marta stepped out of the car, closed the door behind her. Where would they go? Shadows passed behind the drawn shades in the living room. Right in to see Mrs. Cashion.

She dared wait no longer.

The rain was damp on her sweater. Her hair and face were wet. She ran across the street. She made no sound mounting the high steps. She listened outside the door. Not a sound from inside. She inched the door open. It failed to creak.

There was the familiar hallway, unchanged. Racks for the roomers' mail on the side wall by the half-closed door into the living room. A coat rack. An umbrella stand. A narrow table by the back wall. A lamp on the table and a limp-leather book under the cone of light.

She slipped inside and closed the door without sound.

Drive to the ranch house, Dirk had said. *I'll phone . . .*

What would he say if he saw her here? Well, he wasn't going to see her here. She knew a way to listen in. She had to listen in.

She had to know what was happening and where she stood. On quicksand, probably. Prison doors clanged shut inside her head.

She stood motionless and listened at the partially opened door.

"—returned home unexpectedly from a weekend," Dirk was saying. "You told me to drop in and see you some time, remember?"

Pause.

Then, Mrs. Cashion's muffled voice. "I'm not dressed. But you may come in."

She was in the bedroom just off the living room. Marta scowled.

"There's something I want to show you out here, Mrs. Cashion," Dirk said.

The muffled voice. "One moment, darling."

Darling!

In God's name, what had been going on at 1327?

Just inside the door, she heard Jim Dalgren grunt: "Come right into my bedroom! I'm not dressed, darling! But you may come in!" Jim chuckled. "A good thing your new girlfriend isn't here. She know you're a heller with the women?"

"Shut up," Dirk said. "You want to tip her off?"

"Who," Jim jeered softly. "The girl—or Mrs. Cashion?"

To the right were the stairs that the roomers used. Marta tiptoed across a frayed rug. She bent her head low, climbed swiftly and silently, her back toward that half-opened door, her breath held.

She whisked around the turn, risked a backward glance.

No one had seen her.

A 40-watt bulb tried to pierce the gloom of the second-floor hallway. She hurried past closed doors on either side. At the back, she turned to the left into a side passage. A light inside an opened door said this was the lavatory. She wasn't interested in that, but in the closed door on the left.

There was a sign on this door. It said: *USE THE FRONT STAIRS ONLY*. She opened the door. Steep stairs ran directly down. She felt along the railing, lowered her weight from step to step. At the bottom, he opened another door and peered out. This was the kitchen. It was in darkness. The motor on the refrigerator started up and startled her.

Hurry, she thought. You might miss something.

She took two forward steps into darkness, stretched out her left hand. No wall. An opening. That was a doorway. She tiptoed along an ebony hallway.

To the left, she remembered, lay the pantry.

To the right was the cubicle where Mr. Cashion slept on an army cot. With one hand ahead of her body, she felt for the door that closed off Mrs. Cashion's bedroom. Her fingers found the wood.

She hesitated.

Here she was. What next?

If she reached the bedroom, she could hear the conversation. Was Mrs. Cashion still in the bedroom?

Marta, walk in and say: "Dirk, it's Marta! I want to tell you something!"

The knob turned under the pressure of her fingers. The door cracked open. Light leaked out softly from the bedroom.

She dared go no further, and then she heard Mrs. Cashion say from the living room: "I didn't know you had brought guests, darling. Who are these folks?"

Dirk said: "Mr. Baggs, Mrs. Cashion. Mr. Dalgren—"

Marta pushed the door wider. Soft golden light dimmed the room. There was the ornate bed and the pink coverlet. She glanced across the room. The door was wide open into the living room, and she saw Mrs. Cashion in the middle of the rug. Marta stepped in and closed the door at her back.

It was cool in here. Air-conditioning. Maybe it was you who paid for that, Marta. And for the bed and the drapes and the thick rug that muffled your steps.

She crouched against the wall, and watched.

Mrs. Cashion was a big-boned, blonde, bland woman, not an ounce of surplus suet on her king-sized chassis. She stood in the glaring lights of the living room and her eyes were soft and her face dreamy.

As she turned from one man to another, crystal sparkled in her hair. There was a half-smile on her full, sensuous lips and a languor in her movements. She was a dream girl, and paregoric made her dreamier.

Marta sniffed. There was a sickly odor in the bedroom.

"Pleased to meet you," Jim Dalgren was saying.

Mrs. Cashion nodded. She wore a sheer nylon nightgown and a negligee over the gown, but the negligee was open carelessly and there was little left to the imagination about her physical self.

"Yes?" Mrs. Cashion asked dreamily.

Dirk said bluntly, "Your son is dead."

Every muscle under the gown stiffened. She took a single backward step and her feet rooted her to the rug. Her body swayed.

Her mouth hung agape, her eyes widened with horror, and her face was like paste as the blood drained off.

"Did—you—say—dead? Vernon—dead?"

"Your husband found him at a lake cabin near Hallstead, New Jersey," Dirk said in a tight voice. "He waylaid him. He shot your son with a .22 rifle. One shot, Mrs. Cashion."

She lifted on bare toes. She was graceful, despite her size. Slowly she sank down on her heels. She was dreamy again, her face changing with the return flow of blood, steady on her feet, like a ballet dancer after a big moment.

Jim Dalgren said, "You'd better sit down, Mrs. Cashion. This isn't going to be pleasant."

She smiled absently. She moved toward a club chair, changed her mind and headed for a divan covered with brocade. She sat down. She crossed her legs. They were good legs; the feet were small and the toenails blood-red with lacquer.

One hand relaxed on top of her crossed knee. The other fiddled with her yellow hair.

"Yes?" she purred.

"My God," Baggs stammered, "is she real?"

Dirk said, "She drinks dream stuff. She's wrapped in a fog."

He stood in the center of the rug, flanked by Baggs and Jim.

"Mrs. Cashion," he began, "we know you're mixed up in the robbery your son pulled off at Aircrafter's. We know you have most of that money. We found very little cash at the cabin where he was hiding out with a woman. The woman told us your son received money every week from you in a letter. You're an accomplice under Jersey law. Maybe a principal by the time we finish picking your brains. Before we dig it out of you, what did you do with Prudence Nason?"

"Prudence Nason?"

"Drop the corny act," Jim interrupted savagely. "She was the woman who stole the money at Aircrafter's and handed it to your son. They were seen together and identified by the Valery Brothers, from whom they bought that Buick."

"I don't know what you're talking about. Prudence Nason? Oh, yes. My son did know her, but he didn' steal any money. A Buick? He bought a Buick?"

Baggs chuckled. "First we get her husband and he's a mute. Then we get a talking machine. It evens up, I been telling you men."

"Where's Prudence?" Dirk insisted.

"Isn't she with Vernon?"

"How did you know that?"

"You just said he was with a woman, didn't you?"

Dirk walked forward, stopped in front of her. He pulled something from one pocket, held it out.

"This is a bobby pin with a crystal shard. It's like the kind you wear in your hair, the kind you're wearing right now."

"But the one you have isn't mine. They bring out the highlights in my hair. Do you like them?"

"I guess so."

"I'm glad."

"We're all glad," Dirk said. "Jim, you'd better mark this one for her trial. It's evidence."

Jim took the bobby pin.

"Mrs. Cashion," Dirk said, "were you ever in that new Buick your son bought after the robbery?"

"Why, no."

"Did you ever see that Buick?"

"No."

"Did you see Prudence Nason in that Buick?"

"Of course not!"

"Or your son in that Buick?"

"No."

"You're lying. This bobby pin we have is exactly like the ones in your hair. I found it under the front seat of the Buick."

He clenched his fists.

"I'll take you back over your part in this. After the robbery and the purchase of the Buick, your son and Prudence met you. You sat on the rear seat. They drove off with you in the car—probably to some lonely spot in the country. At that spot, you leaned forward and throttled Prudence, or maybe you clubbed her. In the scuffle, one of the bobby pins slipped from your hair and lodged under the front seat. In the scuffle, Prudence's bifocals were broken. Your son was rather careless. We found a tiny bit of broken lens on the floor mat. The bobby pin and the bit of lens, Mrs. Cashion! Were you on the back seat of that Buick?"

Silence.

She leaned her head far back so that her hair touched the wall. Her eyes narrowed. The right hand slid off her knee and fiddled with the seat cushion.

"That was a long speech, but not a very good one, Mr. Delgar," she said. "I think you should write mysteries, your imagination is so over-stimulated. Your facts—"

Dirk interrupted. "You slipped, Mrs. Cashion. The only name I ever gave you was Dwenger—a roomer here. How do you know I'm Delgar?"

Her right hand slipped under the cushion. When the hand returned to sight, it wore a nickel-plated .32. The snick of the released safety sounded like thunder in the suddenly silenced room.

She leaned forward from the hips and uncrossed the svelte legs. Her body stiffened.

Inside her hand, the gun was steady. The barrel swiveled.

"Dadgum," Baggs said hoarsely, "I warned you two! Said the first one come too easy and this one would be trouble and—"

"Shut up," Mrs. Cashion snorted.

"Yes, ma'am. You bet."

"Don't move," she said. "The gun is loaded and I know how to use it. So you gentlemen want to know what happened to Prudence Nason?"

She laughed musically, not the slightest hint of worry in her tone.

"You have a moment left—just long enough for me to straighten you out. Vernon did meet me after he bought the new Buick. Why shouldn't my talented son have a beautiful new car for his very own? Yes, I rode in the back seat. We drove into the Reservation above South Orange. You know, it's very quiet and lonely there, so much woods. But I did not throttle Prudence. I did not club her. With this gun, I shot her behind the ear."

She spoke casually, like a housewife describing the death of a fly under the blow of the swatter.

"She fell forward against the dash. She broke her bifocals and there was blood on her cheeks, but a lot more under her ear. The broken bit of lens does not matter, nor the bobby pin. Nothing matters, except my son. I loved my son."

Her voice began to rise.

"I gave him everything a mother can afford to lavish on her love child. My husband didn't kill him! He's a—a weakling. He wouldn't have the nerve. One of you killed my love child! Tell me the truth? Which one?"

Pause, while she lined them up for a coffin. The gun barrel moved in a tight arc.

Her voice rose to an insane fury. "Which one of you bastards killed him? Which one, damn it!"

"Your husband shot him," Dirk said. "He's locked in a cell, charged with murder. He said Vernon wasn't his son—just yours, and that's why he killed him."

"You lie! My husband wouldn't dare kill my love child. Which one of you did?"

No man spoke.

"All right," she said. "You'll all get it. The hell with—"

Marta Selfron, who had been listening silently, was numb with horror. That ugly heart inside that beautiful body!

Not only was Marta horrified; she was furious with herself. In her haste to leave the convertible, she had left her pocketbook behind—and the gun in it.

From the living room floated Mrs. Cashion's voice.

"—hell with you. I'll kill you first, Delgar. Then you two others. I've got nothing to lose. If my love child is dead, I want to be dead. So here goes. I—"

Marta's hand moved in the half-light to the top of the triple-mirrored dresser. Her fingers closed over a hairbrush.

"—I'm sending you to hell, Delgar," the dreamy, deadly voice announced. "You killed my son—"

Marta's mouth opened. A sound welled up her windpipe. When it exploded on her lips, the scream rocked the bedroom and slammed into the living room, and Mrs. Cashion turned stupidly toward the open door. In the same instant that Marta screamed, she took two running steps across the rug and flung the hairbrush straight at the gun. The brush caromed off the woman's hand. In that split second, her finger tightened around the trigger and the gun went off.

Sobbing, Marta tripped on the rug. She plunged headlong, saw the edge of the dresser coming to meet her face. A clap of thunder burst inside the living room and a second scream poisoned the air.

Marta's head struck something hard. Darkness closed over her eyes.

She stirred. The pounding had eased inside her head. Cold bit into her closed eyelids.

She heard Dirk say, "She's coming out of it." He removed the chill, wet rag.

"Good," Constable Baggs monotoned. "She threw that brush just in time. I knew dadgum well that woman wasn't comin' so easy, like her husband did. Things even up, I always say. It's a good thing you city fellers had me along. I can ping a bird on the wing with that .45."

Marta did not open her eyes.

"I never argue," Dirk said, "with a man who shoots like that."

"Funny," Baggs mused, "this girl in the bedroom. How come?"

"She's in love with me. You know the way women act when they pick a target. She knew this address because she was along when I first came past and rented a room from Mrs. Cashion. She knew we were coming here. She was afraid that something might happen to me, so she did a silly thing and tagged along. Probably found the back door unlocked and sneaked into the bedroom to see if I was all right."

"Saved your life, didn't she?"

"Yeah."

"You in love with her, son?"

Marta's heart pumped as she waited for the answer. Instead of answering, Dirk said, "She's conscious. Marta—"

She did not move.

Knuckles rubbed against her cheeks. "Marta," he said softly.

Her eyelids fluttered. She tried to sit up, but a strong hand on her chest pinned her down.

"Take it easy," Dirk advised. "You got a nasty lump on your forehead. You hit the dresser when you fell."

"Dirk, are you all right?"

"Sure. Why shouldn't I be?"

"I heard her gun go off. She was going to kill you. Did the bullet—"

"Hit the wall," Baggs said heartily.

"I'm glad, Dirk."

"That's two of us. Feel better?"

"Much."

"Want to sit up and talk?"

"Please."

A strong arm lifted her and the strong arm propped her back. Her head lowered and rested against him. She heard a door close.

"What was that?" she whimpered.

"Constable Baggs left us alone."

"Dirk?"

"Yeah?"

"I lied to you."

"I know."

Her chin lifted. Tears misted her eyes. "You knew I lied?"

"Sure."

"How did you know?"

"I've been around. How's the head?"

"Better."

Her fingers found one of his hands. She held on tightly. "What happened to—to her?" she whispered.

"Constable Baggs pulled his gun and shot hers out of her hand. It was a good shot, from the side."

"He didn't hurt her?"

"We wanted her alive so we could hear her story."

"She'll talk?"

"She already did, but not quite enough."

She bent down and kissed his hand.

"Ooh, my head hurts," she moaned.

"Lie down again."

"Isn't this her bed?"

"Yeah."

"I'm getting out of here."

"Take it easy, Marta. Do you know how long you've been out?"

"I'm getting out of her bed!"

"For God's sake, be adult. You've been unconscious a half-hour. You didn't know that, did you?"

A half-hour. How much had Mrs. Cashion told them?

"Dirk, is she in the other room?"

"Jim took her away."

Pause.

Then, a tiny voice: "Dirk, how did you know I lied?"

"I'm good at guessing games. Did you hear the way I told Mrs. Cashion off?"

"You trapped her."

"Most of it was guessing."

"How did you know I lied?"

"Oh, most clients do lie. They hold something back. When I had that ruckus with Harry at Fred's Log Cabin, you interested yourself in me. I was flattered—and on guard. I wondered why you had picked me. Was it because you knew I was tough and a private detective? Then, in the car, your pocketbook was heavy, remember? I asked if you carried a gun, and you thought I was joking. You laughed it off with a crack, but that didn't satisfy me. At the ranch house, you seemed distraught, worried about something. When I went to the can while you were on the porch, I peeked in your pocketbook—it was in your bedroom. Well, you did have a gun. That gave me food for thought. I couldn't figure you out, and I had the feeling you were trying to use me—you were playing some game. Then, you came running with a story about a prowler at your window. Uh-huh, I thought. This is why she wanted you here. So I didn't jump the prowler, but yelled at him from the safety of the house. Who was he—Vernon Cashion?"

She nodded. She could not trust her voice.

"You were awful nice to me afterward," he continued. "I think the psychologists call it compensation. You send an unarmed guy into danger, and then your conscience bothers you so you try to reward him. After that, you sprang that Aircrafter's deal on me. Hell, it was all too obvious! Did you finagle that job for Cashion at Aircrafter's?"

"Yes," she said, and choked.

"There's a lot more to it, of course. A couple of times I set traps to get you to admit you knew the Cashion family, but you eluded the traps each time. How did they hook you into the deal?"

She cleared her throat. "A long time ago," she whispered, "I was nineteen, and innocent, and I thought Vernon was—handsome! We married in a rush. He brought me to this house to live, and I met his terrible mother. She hated me from the first. I had come between him and her. She threatened me with a gun. She chased me with her fists. It—it lasted two weeks—hardly a marriage. After Vernon's dishonorable discharge from the Navy—" subconsciously she began to hold out information again—"he divorced me and I was free. When Mrs. Cashion came to my apartment to persuade me to get a job for Vernon at Aircrafter's, I had to do it, much as I hated it. She would have killed me, otherwise." Marta trembled. "You understand how she could scare a person, don't you?"

He grinned. "Don't tell me! When her finger tightened around that trigger, the barrel looked like the Holland Tunnel. I wasn't merely scared, Marta. I was paralyzed!"

"And I sent you into danger against her!"

"Don't be silly," he said, amused. "Constable Baggs warned us that she'd be tough to take. She outsmarted us—and that was our own fault. Do you have any idea how Prudence Nason obtained the combination to the safe?"

He never lets up in a case, she thought.

Marta said slowly, "Mr. Truegate is rather forgetful. The combination is changed several times each year and he writes the new one down. I've seen him at the safe reading off the combination from a scrap of paper. I think that's the way Prudence learned the combination." An idea startled her. "Dirk, you don't think that I gave Prudence the combination?"

"Did you?"

"I didn't know it, thank God."

"That all of it?"

"One more thing." She had suddenly made up her mind to get everything off her chest. "You see, that divorce I mentioned—well, it cost a lot of money. The Cashions are bloodsuckers, and—"

Knuckles tapped on the closed door.

Dirk called out: "Who is it?"

"Okay to come in?" Jim Dalgren asked.

"Sure."

Jim entered and walked to the bed. He was slimly handsome, his eyes sleepy. "How's the head, Miss Selfron?"

"Better."

"Feel like a new man, eh?"

"Yes."

"I want to thank you for your help. We were suddenly in a difficult situation that we had not foreseen. Your diversionary tactics rescued us."

"I didn't do much."

"You did plenty."

Dirk said, "We'll all pin medals on her. Jim, she has a car out on the street. She's all shook up and needs a rest. Okay for her to go?"

"I guess so. I have most of it."

"Does Marta need to get any publicity from this?"

"What sort of publicity?"

"She's here. She helped."

Jim laughed. "You mean let them print that setup in the living room when we were chumps enough to let a dame get the drop on us? Don't be silly, Dirk. Miss Selfron isn't here and she never was here. That's the way it has to be. I like it wrapped up the way it is, a foolproof package for the D.A. Nothing is going to cloud the case, nothing. I'll bet that dame is going to be the first woman ever to sit in the electric chair at Trenton. She murdered Prudence Nason as callously as a person stepping on an ant—premeditated murder. Take Miss Selfron to her car. You coming right back?"

"Sure."

"We need you. To take a trip. Up to the Reservation."

"That won't be pretty," Dirk said.

"Two months under ground."

Dirk helped Marta to her feet. She wobbled, but that was so Dirk would keep an arm around her. "The back way, pal," Jim said. "The front room is full of reporters—and Miss Selfron isn't here, remember?"

"Right."

Dirk led her along the hallway, now brightly lighted, and into the kitchen where a uniformed patrolman guarded the rear door. Jim warned: "Polhoski, you didn't see this woman, understand?"

"Yes, sir." The patrolman smiled.

They went out into the drizzle.

In front, the curbs were lined with parked cars. Two police cars showed red winking eyes. A few patrolmen were drawn up in a loose circle to keep the steps and porch clear, and knots of curious spectators huddled motionless and silent in the rain.

A traffic officer in the middle of the street, his slicker sleek in the rain, halted cars and let Dirk and Marta cross. She slid under the wheel.

"Feel all right?" Dirk asked.

"Yes."

"I want you to go to your apartment and get a good night's rest, understand?"

"Yes."

"Tomorrow morning, drive my car up to the lake and finish your vacation. You heard what Jim Dalgren said. As the case stands now, it's clean and simple, which is the way he wants it. Can you do what you're told this time or do we have to send a plainclothes man along to watch you?"

"I'll do what you want me to."

"Good."

"Dirk, when Jim walked in on us, I was about to tell you something. I—"

"There you go, complicating things again," he said sharply.

"But it's important, and—"

"Stop talking, for once. Don't be a woman. You know I have to get back to Jim."

She subsided against the seat. "When will I see you again?"

"We've got a long night ahead of us and not a pleasant one," he said. "Then—let's see. My own car is at the lake. Suppose I come up and get it, okay?"

"When?"

"Tuesday or Wednesday."

"I'll wait."

"You do that, sister."

He leaned elbows on the door. He's going to kiss me, at last, she thought, and closed her eyes. He doesn't hate you, after all . . .

"You know, when we were checking service stations in Sussex County this morning, Marta, you must have been really amused."

She opened her eyes. "Why?"

"You were playing the part of Vernon Cashion's wife. That was a touch of unintentional irony on my part, believe me. I knew the Cashions had you in some sort of trap, but never suspected that marriage was part of it."

He strode off across the wet road, a tall and wide-shouldered young man, his black hair shiny with rain, and every forward step was carrying him further out of her life.

He doesn't love you and you can't blame him, she thought sadly. How could he love you?

She started the engine, cut the wheels, and edged the convertible from the curb. The traffic cop understood. He tooted a whistle. Traffic halted impatiently, and she drove off.

FIFTEEN

It was Tuesday, and she had heard no word from Dirk.

Outside the ranch house, the late afternoon was lazy with slanted sunlight, but the air had acquired a tang which hinted of colder weather in the offing that would redden the sugar maples and gild the birches.

In the bedroom off the graveled drive, the double windows were open.

Marta tugged a simple house dress over her head and dropped it on the dark-green rug. All yesterday and today, she had been busy outside the house, working feverishly until every muscle ached. Hard work had numbed the persistent pain in her mind.

Her shoes were dirtied from the garden where she had been pruning fall flowers and trimming hedges.

Tiredly, she walked to the full-length mirror on the door and inspected herself. Every inch of her body was evenly coated with golden tan. The face was smooth, the brow unwrinkled. The blue eyes tried to smile back at her.

A smile hovered over the full, red lips, but failed to materialize. Why couldn't she smile joyously, as in the past?

Was that a freckle on the tip of her nose? She rubbed fingers on the freckle. It vanished, leaving a faint line. Only a fleck of garden dirt. What difference did it make?

"You've changed," she murmured.

She inhaled. The body hadn't altered during the hectic days past.

The stomach was flat and the hips full but neat. The soft thighs and the lithely muscled calves were the same. So the outside had altered little. But how she had changed inside in a few short days!

Her body seemed only a shell, a beautiful protection, not at all the true reflection of her guilty inner self. Was she being too severe, she wondered. Her mind had matured under the impact of the tragic fate of poor Prudence Nason.

If Vernon Cashion had never worked for Aircrafter's and met Prudence, wouldn't the girl be alive today? Marta shuddered. Two months in a lonely grave. But Prudence had not been forced to succumb to the wiles of Vernon Cashion. She had had a choice.

You, Marta, never had a choice, she remembered. You were blackmailed into doing what you did. The web had tightened about you, constricting your decisions, and that had not been true of Prudence . . .

Her thoughts reached out for Dirk. It had been so glorious with him under the spell of the September moon. Yet like the moon, the romance had faded. Next week, there would be only the ghost of a moon—and the ghost of love, Marta.

She shook herself. Her body was chilled. Returning to practicality, she announced loudly: "What you need, young woman, is a bath. Stop scolding yourself and try to come alive again. A bath."

She donned a white bathing cap and tucked in the honey-colored curls. Remembering the tang hidden in the outside air, she pulled a one-piece bathing suit over her obvious charms and hid them inside old rose. Cake of soap. Towel. Terry robe over one arm to ward off a chill after the water. Then?

Another lonely meal inside a lonely house.

She hurried through the dim rooms. Where had Hiram Klee and his redhead gone after that insane party? There had been no note left to explain their absence. The redhead. There was a woman who knew what she wanted. Money, security, mink coats and Cadillacs—in exchange for favors to a fat, bald man. Wasn't that prostitution, exchanging yourself for a millionaire's checkbook?

Outside, the dock lay wrapped in lowering shadows. The water had darkened and lay slate-grey. On the far shore, the last rays of the sun fingered the tops of the trees. As she watched, shadows walked up the trees.

There!

High over the distant ridge, the September moon still rode in the soft sky, although something had bitten deeply into the upper edge. Nothing strange about that. Time and the changing season had altered the orb, and time would soon finish eating the moon and it would be gone.

She dived into the lake. After the chill air, the water was warm, but she recognized that as an illusion. She climbed to the dock. She lathered her body until it was covered with soapy snow, then soaped under the old-rose bathing suit. Lastly, she set herself on the edge of the dock, closed her eyes and lathered her face.

Here goes!

She dived blindly. Down, down, she swam, kicking and wriggling to rinse off the sticky soap. Then, up to the surface again. She did not venture away from the dock. The warm water was deceptive, like a man's kiss and caresses. The water could tease you into trouble at this time of the year.

Back and forth she swam lazily, using a crawl stroke, until she tired.

For a moment, she floated and rested. Twilight settled over the lake, and night was a half-step distant when a voice mocked from the dock: "What, swimming in a bathing suit?"

It was Dirk. He had returned from Newark.

She rolled over on her stomach. There he was, leaning nonchalantly against the diving tower. He grinned down at her. Her heart tried to high-jump into her throat.

"I didn't know you were there," she said. "When did you come?"

"Just arrived. How come so dressed up?"

"It's cold today," she explained.

"Not in Newark."

"Want a swim?"

"I'm no polar bear."

Could they, she wondered, recapture the beautiful moments they had known together—regain the friendly intimacy that they had once shared? Or would this degenerate, with emptiness afterward?

She paddled to the dock, climbed the ladder, and stood dripping water on the boards. She did not go to him. The next move was up to him.

What was he thinking about her?

"Put on the robe," he suggested. "You're shivering."

He picked up the garment, opened it. She turned. Her hands found the sleeves. The robe settled around her body. She waited. He patted her shoulder, nothing more.

She turned and faced him.

"Cigarette?" he asked.

"Please."

So close together, yet so far apart.

He lit two cigarettes elaborately. When he handed her one, his fingers were warm.

"Wow, your hands are really cold," he exclaimed. "You shouldn't swim alone, this time of the year. You could get a cramp."

"Worried?"

She dragged deeply on the cigarette. That was supposed to relax you, wasn't it? She was tense, her fingers like sticks. What was he thinking behind the mask of his face?

He asked casually, "How've you been?"

"Busy and lonely. I hoed the garden, raked leaves, burned trash—things like that to keep busy. See?" She extended her hands, palms up. "Blisters."

"You should have worn gloves."

"Didn't think, I guess."

"Is it always wise to think?"

"Probably not."

"Blisters turn to callouses. Unless they break."

"I don't mind, Dirk. Had dinner yet?"

"No."

"Hungry?"

"I could eat a horse. Does your boss keep horses?"

"He keeps sirloin steaks. Interested?"

"Sirloin broiled over charcoal?"

"There's an outside fireplace. There must be charcoal."

"Char the outside of the steak," he murmured dreamily. "Seal in the juices. You like steak rare?"

"Very rare."

It was so banal she wanted to scream.

He dragged on the cigarette, said, "No questions, Marta?"

"About what?"

"About the case? Jim said the D.A. liked it. A neatly tied package. Let's sit on the porch and I'll finish it up for you."

They sat on the porch. There was a foot of space between them, and the terry robe was tight around her body, only her bare legs showing under the hem.

He's a stranger, she thought sadly. The mood is gone.

"Prudence?" she asked.

"We found her. Skip it."

"The money?"

"We found twenty-six thousand dollars inside the mattress of Mrs. Cashion's fancy bed. I guess that bitch liked to hear the bills crinkle when she rolled over. Your boss was pleased. I saw him this morning. I'll get a check later, a full ten-percent recovery fee. The money is evidence, held in escrow. Jim Dalgren wouldn't take a dime, but said I could buy him a new hat. Constable Baggs said not to cut him in because he had found a new dime in Cashion's Buick and that paid him off. He's getting a million dollars' worth of publicity in the newspapers. Says he's going to file and run for sheriff."

"Did Bertha Smathers return from Elmira?"

"Yeah. I saw her for a few minutes. The telegram was just Mrs. Cashion's trick to get her out of town. Bertha was disappointed to miss the kill, but glad Vernon Cashion got his reward. I'm going to buy her a new fall outfit."

"Mr. Cashion?"

"Still in jail. He'll be brought to Sussex County for trial. Won't be more than a manslaughter charge—and I doubt the jury will convict."

"You do?" Marta did not feel any elation.

She was in full sympathy with the little man but, after all, he was a killer. Killing was not to be condoned under any circumstances—and she said so to Dirk.

"I fully agree," he said.

"Mrs. Cashion got crazily jealous because Vernon had taken a girl to the shack in Hallstead. She gave Mr. Cashion directions, told him to go out and break up that cozy arrangement. His instructions were to bring Vernon back to Newark, where his mother expected to hide him in some furnished room. But Mr. Cashion didn't follow instructions. In her hysteria, Mrs. Cashion had spilled too many beans, and he decided to rid the world of a monster. A jury will probably sympathize— unwritten law, and all that—"

"How did Vernon know I was at Mr. Klee's place?"

"I think Prudence must have overheard you making arrangements, and she told Vernon."

"And to think that I got myself associated with them . . ." She bit her lip. There was still something very much on her mind; to wit, that incriminating letter which had let them blackmail her. She dared not ask Dirk about it directly.

"Dirk," she said timidly, "what about Mrs. Cashion?"

"We have her safe."

"Did she talk?"

"Enough."

"What else did she say?"

"Nothing important." He shrugged in the darkness and his shoulder touched Marta's. "She won't get the chair. She's in a padded cell. Her brain snapped. She babbles and nobody listens to a maniac. Oh, Jim sent you something."

Dirk pulled a letter from an inner pocket. He flipped it on Marta's lap.

"You'll need light," he said. Standing up, he switched on a porch lamp.

Her fingers trembled. It was a plain envelope, sealed. She ripped off one edge. Inside, she found a second letter. This one had been addressed to Vernon Cashion, 1327 West Plank Road, Newark. The stamp was cancelled, the date old, and the outside rumpled and soiled. She took out the letter, knowing what it was.

Tears misted her eyes. She could not read now the foolishness that she had written—how she had stolen that money from the safe at Aircrafter's, how she wished them to understand—

"Did you look at this?" she asked dully.

Dirk said, surprised, "Why, no. Should I?"

"They blackmailed me with this, Dirk."

"There's usually a picture or letter as the basis of blackmail."

"I want you to know what I did. Long ago, at Aircrafter's, I—"
Fingers pressed against her lips.

"Shut up," he snapped. "I don't want to hear it. You've suffered enough because of them. Here." He pulled an ashtray closer on the coffee table.

"Do you want to save that letter?" he asked.

"No."

Dirk snapped on his cigarette lighter. "Here's to peace," he said softly.

The flame ignited a corner of the letter. Marta laid it on the ashtray. It burned brightly, charring the foolish words she had written. Then the letter was gone, and there were only ashes on the tray.

Dirk stood up. "Jim sent you a letter and I brought a present. It's in your bedroom. Want to see it?"

She stood up. She led the way through the dark house. Her step was buoyant. She was free again. What had Dirk brought her?

In her bedroom, he said, "Lights, please."

She clicked a switch. Lights winked on overhead.

"Surprise," Dirk said. "Like it?"

Propped against the side of the bed was a weathered sign.

FRED'S LOG CABIN
one-quarter mile
DRINKS AND DINNERS
STOP IN

Marta faced him slowly. "I—I don't understand."

He laughed. "That's the sign I saw on the road the other night. If I hadn't seen the sign, I might not have stopped at Fred's. It's the small boy in me, Marta. A trophy to hang on our bedroom wall."

She stared. "Our bedroom? Ours?"

"That's right. Married folks don't usually sleep in separate bedrooms, do they?"

She could not move. The blood rushed to her head.

She swayed. "Dirk—you—I mean, after what I did—you want me?"

"Sure. Something happened to me the first time I saw you. I went over to the jukebox, used a nickel. I saw your feet, then your lovely legs. When I looked into your eyes, I was—well, gone. Darling, come here to me."

She walked forward in a dream. "My bathing suit," she stammered. "It will get you wet—"

"We'll remedy that later. Here."

She was safe inside his arms. They were strong arms, crushing her close. His lips were on hers. They were wonderful lips—eager and searching. For a long moment, they clung there. Then: "Too much light, Marta."

They got rid of the lights . . .

"Dirk, can we get married tomorrow?"

"Got to get the license tomorrow."

"Thursday?"

"Wasserman test."

"Friday, please?"

"Only the third day. Can't you wait until Saturday?"

She lifted on one elbow. "I owe some money," she said. "I'll have to keep on working. Six hundred dollars."

"Take some of my recovery loot. You earned it."

"This isn't your debt. I'll work it off myself. You see, I have to get together that much because—"

"Forget it. I don't want to hear about it. What's past is past."

"But Dirk, there is one thing—far more important than money—that I must tell you about. It's on my mind. It's on my conscience. I couldn't marry you unless I told you."

He kissed her. "Spit it out, then, chick. I'm listening."

"Dirk, I want you to know that Vernon was the first man. He took me by force, one night—but I thought that I must love him. So we got married. We lived together only a couple of weeks—but almost every night he would beat me, humble me, make me do awful things. He would order me to fight back as hard as I could."

Marta took a deep breath. She was telling her deepest secrets to Dirk, as if he were a psychiatrist or something. But she wanted to get it straight with him.

"Get to the point, Marta. What are you trying to tell me?"

"Simply this, Dirk. I love you. I want to marry you." She hesitated, then forced herself to blurt, "But I'm afraid I'm no good. I'm spoiled—rotten."

Dirk rolled away from her.

Marta waited nervously for him to speak. It would be unbearable to lose him. At last, he spoke again.

"Listen to me Marta. You were innocent. You're not spoiled, or anything like that. You can be untaught. You just leave that to me. I'm going to recondition you, make you know what real love is. I'm going to teach gentleness, consideration. The past is the past, and the hell with it. But the future is ours. Just rely on me—"

"Oh, I do, Dirk—I do." She threw herself into his arms. "Dirk, I love you. You're the dearest man alive." All her fears and hesitations were gone. Her mood had suddenly become gay and mischievous. "When do you start lessons?"

"Right now!"

THE END

DUNGAREE SIN

LORENZ HELLER

Writing as Frederick Lorenz

ONE

Binnie Riordan stood in the shadow of the closed wooden newsstand on the corner of Hacksher and Summit and watched fat Patrolman Ed Yates come slowly toward her on Summit with that deceptively heavy, swaying gait that made him look like a big old shaved pig in a sloppy tan uniform. He walked as though his feet were killing him and, carrying all that hot grease, he couldn't get off the dime, no matter what.

"But never let him jap you, baby-O," Mick Fogarty had warned her. "The fat slob can move like a goosed goat, and he's got the arm on you before you know it. I mean, he can *move*. Don't let him, sugarmouth. He'll break you up."

Mick was Number Two in the Red Rovers, next down from Vince Kirby, the war leader. He had all the cops tabbed, and made Binnie memorize the list. But all the guys hated fat Yates. He was the one cop you didn't let yourself get taken by, because most times you never got to the station. He heaved you in an alley and broke you up. They said he bored a big hole down his club, filled it with BB's and plugged it tight with plastic wood and varnish, so's to make sure he did break you up.

Binnie Riordan watched, and huddled closer to the dark green side of the newsstand, glad that her dress was dark green, too. She wasn't too much afraid, because she had a good spot—close enough to the bus stop to give her a reason for being there, but hidden from the street light by the newsstand, so she didn't have to be seen if she was careful.

Yates moved with tormenting slowness, stopping at every closed store to try the doorknob. Binnie wondered what he'd do if he found an open one, though she figured she knew. He'd go in and fill his pockets for fair, and maybe go out and come back a couple times before phoning the store man to get down and lock up.

Binnie wished she knew for certain. It would cut him down a little.

It took him forever to pass, and she had to move along the shadow of the newsstand, so he wouldn't spot her. Except for the big neon-splashed Modern Times Bar and Grill, this was a dark stretch of the Midway, which was what everybody called Summit Avenue. The real clip joints and traps were clustered at the Five Points, the end of the Midway right across the street from the main gate of the steamship fence. That was the Butt's wide-open creep pad and welcome swamp for seamen off the freighters with a fat leather full of back pay. The ones with brains took the uptown bus and closed their eyes and ears, because the whores came right up to the windows and said, "Just stop for a second, you great big handsome muscle, and I bet you can think of better things to ride than a bus. Don't go 'way, handsome man. There ain't nobody round here with a muscle like you and I been waiting a long time. I don't want nothing but love and I got steaks and bottles and bottles all put aside and just for you."

Using the handkerchief soaked with Whorehouse Number Five put under his nose on the windowsill, she could talk a good percentage right out of the bus again. But if she didn't slip the bus driver a fin, the next time he didn't stall around long enough for her to make the pitch.

Binnie didn't like the Points. It was too bright, in the first place, but that didn't really count. It was whores' territory and if they got the idea you were cutting in, it didn't take two minutes to get slipped a mickey, even if you drank coke right out of the bottle. And the mickey was the worst way to get ranked in front of everybody and they laughed their heads off when you ran for the john and it happened while you were still yanking at the locked door. Binnie knew that if she ever got the mickey, she'd go out of the Butt and never come back. But she'd never go to the Points without Mick Fogarty, and a girl going in with a guy was all right.

Anyway, it was better here in this dark stretch on the Midway because Friday was payday and the men who went into the jukebox-happy Modern Times Bar and Grill seldom lost any more than a few bucks at the "25" tables, and nobody ever got kayo drops in the Modern Times. It was operated on sound business principles. The bartenders never took more than half a guy's pay. Then the guy's old lady wouldn't put up a stink so he'd knock her around and get stuck in the jail and not come back for a couple weeks or more. When a guy came out of the Modern Times he might be falling-down drunk, but he'd still have some dough, and if there'd been overtime and he was a foreman, it mounted up.

Binnie had her eye on a big, bony man who'd been hanging on the bar with his elbows so long, it was just about time for the bartender to give him the easy brush and send him stumbling home. He had on a necktie, so she knew he was a foreman, and the funny-colored stains on his hands and pants and shirt told her he was from the chemical factory. The chemical factory was best because the Union and the quick loan guys didn't give their pay envelopes a shave and a haircut like they did with the waterfront stiffs.

She was satisfied to end with the chemical foreman. She and the other Debs waiting around the corner half way down Hacksher had made four easy scores and there'd be a nice split when they came to the flat.

She crossed her fingers that the foreman wouldn't come out while fat Ed Yates was plopping along, trying doorknobs. Yates stopped to light his cigar, dawdled and poked and yawned until she was wound up enough to throw rocks at him. He stopped under the red, blue and yellow gush of neon and stared into the Modern Times. It was not a really hot night, but she could see the reflecting shine of sweat on his big face and its soft underhang of chins. He was always dripping and you could smell him clear across the sidewalk. It took a cold day to dry him off.

She watched narrowly and, from the way his thick lips moved as though washing each other, she knew what he was thinking—it was a sticky night and a cold beer'd go good. At the long bar inside, the arms of men in the crowded line were moving up and down like the pistons of a busy machine, lifting dripping seidels of beer, putting them down, lifting them, putting them down, never breaking the tantalizing rhythm. Cold, thirst-satisfying beer sloshed down a hundred throats, and six bartenders in white shirts and little white aprons trotted up and down the bar, refueling seidels.

Yates pulled his hand across his mouth and turned abruptly toward Jackson Street. He walked faster now, and didn't stop to try any more door knobs. There was a side entrance to the Modern Times' kitchen on Jackson, and that's where Yates was heading. He'd have a hot pastrami on rye and wash it down with a big beaded seidel of brew, and afterward the short order cook would give him a handful of coffee beans to chew to take the beer off his breath. It usually took twenty minutes—but no more—for Yates to reappear, licking the last flavor of pastrami and beer from his mouth before chewing the coffee beans.

Impatiently, Binnie watched the big foreman wilt lower and lower against the bar. He should have been eased out home before this, but the bartender was too busy to notice. Then she watched how the bartender worked his station. Five minutes, she thought, five minutes. She felt better. She had time to spare. In five minutes the foreman would be on his way home while he was still able to walk. Binnie knew the operation and most times had it timed almost to the second. Timing and experience were important when you set up a sucker to be mugged.

Binnie was an old hand at this. She was seventeen years old and a Roving Hotshot Deb.

TWO

At the northeast corner of the City, where the Paskack and Tenn Rivers flow parallel before emptying into Coyts Bay, is a stubby, gnarled peninsula called the Butt. At the far bay end are the neat geometric patterns of steamship lines' docks and warehouses.

This property and its Ali Baba caves of rich warehouses are grimly isolated from the remainder of the peninsula by a tight, thick-gauge wire fence, twelve feet high and topped by eight twisted strands of barbed wire on iron braces that overhang the fence at a forty-five-degree angle in both directions, forming a "V" which cannot be scaled without the use of cumbersome equipment. Armed watchmen patrol the enclosed area around the clock in eight-hour shifts, and every inch of the fence and waterfront is brilliantly lighted from earliest dusk to late dawn.

This defensive vigilance cannot be relaxed, for immediately outside the fence lies the worst district in the City and one of the most notorious in the country.

The Butt is not merely a choked slum of tenements, crumbling warehouses, slatternly shops, gin mills, dope pads, whore houses, and blind alleys, twisting streets, garbage and nameless filth. It is a hideout for fleeing crooks and killers, and a dubious refuge for dips, whores, pushers, addicts of all kinds, muggers and other varieties of thieves, whose hunting grounds are the parks, shaded streets and quiet homes in other parts of the City.

The growing threat in the Butt came from a direction that would have made mobsters laugh in the old days. It came from the kids, kids of eight and nine and upward through the late 'teens. But these weren't kids from the old days. Times had changed and so had the kids. They were probably no tougher than slum kids had ever been, but they had learned a dangerous fact: if two of them worked together, they were twice as effective as two working separately.

And ten were better than two, and twenty better than ten, and a hundred could just about control their neighborhood. There were a few lessons still to be learned, and they still feared the law, although they had no respect for it or for the cops who enforced it.

One of the biggest street gangs on the Butt was the Red Rovers, whose territory was about a fifth of the peninsula, from the fence on River Road west to Ridley Street. They, themselves, did not know their exact numerical strength but it was approximately a hundred, counting all units. At the top were the Seniors, boys from fourteen to eighteen. They were naturally the leaders of the gang—but they did not call themselves a gang; they were a club. The next male group was the Juniors, the ten to fourteen-year-olds. At the bottom was the formless and least disciplined unit, the Nits, kids of any age under ten. Their numbers fluctuated because of their youth; although they liked to hang around the bigger boys, they were just as likely to dissolve into the shrill squabbles of a stick-ball game or wander off aimlessly to walk barefoot in flooded gutters after a rain. The older or more precocious Nits, however, were excellent spies, decoys and messengers.

There was a new factor of which the old-time street gangs never dreamed—the girl gangs. Never before had girls banded together in any serious quantity, except for frivolous social purposes.

Now, there was not a gang on the Butt that did not have a female auxiliary or affiliate. In fact, there were few street gangs anywhere without their units of Debs—the fanciful name by which these teen-age vixens were generally known.

Few bands of Debs function entirely apart from a boys' gang, but many of them are independent organizations, have their own names and choose their own leaders.

The Red Rover Debs called themselves the Roving Hotshots and their uniform was a pair of skin-tight blue dungarees and a white nylon blouse with the monogram R-H embroidered prominently in red on the left breast pocket. There were about thirty girls in the Hotshots, most of them between sixteen and eighteen years of age, but there were several precocious twelve-year-olds among them. A full dozen of the oldest girls fought beside their males when the Rovers went into a rumble with another gang. This was one of the reasons the Rovers were known as a tough pack. The Imperials, at the westernmost end of the Butt, never took their Debs into a rumble. But then, the Imperials were not a real fighting gang, possibly because the grim, red-brick 15th Precinct Station House was in the middle of their territory on Summit Avenue between Bridge Street and the Cross County Turnpike.

The Rovers and their Hotshots were contemptuous of any gang that did not use its Debs in a fight. The handwriting on the wall was as big and black as front-page headlines. Just as modern total warfare outmoded the old-fashioned Little Lord Fauntleroy type of conflict, total gangs were superior to limited male outfits. In the final rumble, it would be only a total gang that could take and hold the entire Butt as its territory.

There were guys who'd punk out on a rumble, but never the Debs. They had a real taste for it, and fought savagely. They were not partial to guns, but preferred such refinements as lye mixed into a bottle of coca cola, a terrible weapon when hurled against a brick wall just over the heads of the enemy, for it literally exploded in a shower of burning liquid.

Captain Gahagen was one of the toughest cops ever to command the 15th Precinct House. His nickname was Ironhead because he was shockproof. He had been a rookie in the gaudy rum-running days when the mobs doused a would-be hijacker in gasoline and lit him with a match. He had seen more than one charred victim in the city dumps, the favorite and logical spot for such executions. He had seen almost every form of violent death that mobdom could invent, for the City was the battleground of what was then known as the beer barons. That was the liberal education that earned him the degree of Ironhead Gahagen.

His opinion of all Debs was succinct. "Those little bitches are twice as bad as the punks."

He had been saying that for several years, using the same sequence of words, and the same heavy tone in which there seemed to be an incredulous echo. Incredulous? No, not Ironhead Gahagen, not after the things he'd seen.

Hell, he knew they were tough little girls but—Jesus God, they were still only little girls! And even tough little girls didn't make a habit of throwing those lye-and-coke bombs with the deliberate intention of burning the faces off anyone within range of the burst. But these little girls did, and some varied the formula with hydrochloric acid.

So, although he never admitted it even in his most private thoughts, it was the little girls who finally shocked Captain Gahagen.

THREE

She was a small girl with not-quite-black curly hair cropped close to her head, blue eyes and the fine, creamy complexion that has been the heritage of the Irish for centuries; since the Spanish Armada was wrecked on their shores. The sailors scattered the length and breadth of the countryside, and the eager girls found them bold and fiery companions in the hours of the night when the village louts were swilling poteen and pummeling one another senseless in the taverns. There was Irish pride and Spanish fire in Binnie Riordan.

She looked younger in the dungarees-and-blouse uniform of the Debs, but in the dark green dress she was a beautiful woman ripening. The dress fitted snugly to the high, provocative lift of rounded breasts, and was tight over the slim hips, and showed the rich flare of tapering thighs, with a hint of the voluptuous crest between. Her mouth was wide, beautifully molded and generous, and in moments of excitement a passionate intensity glowed in her high-boned face. At such times you could see how deeply the passion ran and know that here was a woman who could torment a man. When her hair was touched up with an artfully feminine comb, and her rich mouth brushed with lipstick, she could walk down the street or across a room, head lifted, breasts high and swelling, hips in rhythm with the soft clenching and unclenching of small buttocks, thighs forming against the fabric of her skirt, curves flowing in the continuity of step after step, and the eyes of men yearned after her, some with longing, some feverishly lecherous, and many filled suddenly with hope, overcoming the dead expression of eyes old and tired and full of regrets.

Binnie knew this. She knew all of it. She knew what could be done with it and what it was worth and how to bring a man to his feet with the pull of it and the ways of drawing him after her. And when she chose, she knew how to enrich a man with herself and his own manhood when he needed that.

Of course she knew these things. She wasn't a Nit or a Junior any longer. She was seventeen.

And there was something else she knew, and had always known, it seemed. She used it as a gimmick to get around people for the purpose of the moment, whether it was to make mush of hard suspicion or simply to obtain something she wanted. It was this: she had the rare gift of charm and innocence, luminous in widened blue eyes, incandescent in a smile. She could spread her eyes, look up shyly and slowly let her smile envelop the man or woman who happened to be the sucker. This was better than a sexy wiggle or breathing her breasts out and up at a man. There were times and places for pussies and boobies, but it wasn't always and everywhere.

The other—it was always good. It never failed. It had taken her through that lousy P.S. 26, and she was a teachers' pet, but it almost got her raped by the crazy big janitor, who caught her sliding a carton of brand-new pencil sharpeners through a basement window to Midge Daly outside. He'd have slapped the face off any other kid and dragged her up to the principal, but he didn't do that to her. He ripped the clothes off her and threw her on a table in the boiler room. The dumb clunk, he was begging her not to scream but to look at him and smile just once like she always smiled at him, when a couple of the men teachers broke in, took one look, and beat the living hell out of him and turned him over to the cops, who beat the living hell out of him again.

There were a dozen big, new, shiny pencil sharpeners in the carton and she and Midge Daly got four bits apiece for them from the hockshop on Rabb Street.

It made her laugh to think of the things she got away with in P.S. 26. She could get away with anything. All she had to do was open her eyes wide and smile....

She looked sharply into the glare of the Modern Times and swore. The chemical foreman was drooping lower and the bartender was back at the spigots, drawing a beer for somebody else. There wasn't much time left.

A flicker of white at the corner of Hacksher caught her eye and she turned her head. It was tall, thin Veronica Ferenc, leader of the Debs, and the flicker of white was her blouse. She was one of the two who were waiting down the street for Binnie to bring another sucker. She signaled urgently with her arm and jabbed a finger at her wristwatch, telling Binnie to call it off, it was getting too late. Binnie shook her head and held up five fingers, meaning five more minutes. Veronica shook her fist angrily and disappeared back into the shadows of Hacksher Street. So long as Binnie stayed, Veronica and Sugar Fernandez, the other Deb, would stay too, but Veronica didn't like it for a cent. It had been like that for the past few weeks. When eleven o'clock came, Veronica wanted to quit and get back to the flat as fast as she could. Chicken punk, thought Binnie automatically.

She was always the one who called it off. Binnie turned her own wristwatch to the light of the Modern Times. Only ten to eleven. She'd thought it was later. Ten to eleven, and Veronica was punking out. Binnie smiled secretly, enjoying and savoring this moment. Well, what do you know. Old Veronica punking out the odds.

A shift of men at the bar brought her eyes back sharply to the wide-open doors of the Modern Times. The bartender was talking smoothly to the chemical foreman and giving him a buddy-buddy pat on the arm, the big grin, the brush-off. He gathered up the loose change on the bar and made a big gesture of handing it to the foreman.

He seemed to be saying, "Aaah, be a nice guy and go home and give the wife a break. It's payday and she's been waiting since six o'clock. You know how women are—they worry. She works hard, too. Give her a break."

The big foreman fumbled the change into his pocket, grinning foolishly. It was a fact. She was a good wife. She was the best wife in the whole damn world. The bartender was a right guy, yessir. He *knew*. The foreman looked affectionately at him, threw a buck on the bar and nodded solemnly, agreeing with every word the bartender said. Yessir, it was time he went home. Right was right. The wife, she'd be worrying and that wasn't right. It wasn't the way to do. The bartender waved him off cheerily.

So long, pal, sweet dreams, see you tomorrow. Bring the wife some night. We got a nice place in back with tables for ladies. Show her a good time for once. She'll be your ever-loving hot patootie. We put out a nice meal. Show her a time and she'll show you one. Fair exchange is no robbery, ha, ha.

The foreman turned, straightened up, but hesitated as though reluctant to leave, now that the party was just beginning to go good and he was getting to be pals with a smart man like the bartender.

That fractional hesitancy told Binnie exactly what was running through his mind. He'd go home and the old lady'd be worrying and before he could open his mouth, she'd light into him and the next thing you know they'd be going at it hammer and tongs, another goddamn scrap.

Binnie knew it by heart. Her old man was always coming home half-lit and the old lady'd give him merry hell and he'd holler and bang things around and the neighbors'd come barging in to break it up. The old man and the old lady'd tell them to get their asses the hell out of there and the neighbors'd get sore and yell back and stamp out and the old man'd look at the old lady and they'd bust out laughing and she'd put on her hat and they'd go downstairs and get soused together, and come back the next day, still laughing, and that night or the next they'd be going at it again at the top of their lungs.

That's what the dumb hunky foreman was thinking, but with that dumb sad face, he didn't look as though he ever laughed. He started to push heavily through a crowd of men at the "25" table.

Binnie gave her dress a tug, looked quickly up and down the empty street and crossed the sidewalk. She moved slowly with a lazy come-and-get-it swing in her hips, and stayed with the blast of light from the Modern Times so she'd be the first thing he'd see when he came out. He'd know what that slow walk and swinging hips meant and he'd look at her figure and start to get hungry, knowing there wasn't anything like her at home.

It worked. It always did, and a sucker like this was a setup. She heard the scrape of lurching footsteps behind her, and kept moving, so they'd be out of the light and near the corner when he made the pickup. She was practically at the corner when she felt his fumbling hand on her elbow.

"Jussa minute," he said thickly, "jussa minute lil girl, jussa minute. You don't hafta run away."

"Who's running?" she said, stirring him up with the throaty invitation in her voice, making him easier to handle. "I'm just going along, that's all."

"Yeah, yeah. Me, too. Going along. That way, hah?"

"No, not that way. My room's down here," she pulled against his loose grasp on her elbow, leading him toward the mouth of Hacksher Street.

He held back. "Jussa minute, jussa minute. We have a drink, hah? We go the—the—go Jimmy's Round Bar, have a drink. Okay. Sure. Nice place. Girls."

Oh crise, she thought. He wasn't even half sober. He was stoned, really stoned. She could just about understand him, the way his words slushed together. He spoke in the wuh-wuh-wuh mumble of a drunk at the edge of passing out. He stood hunched in the shadows and she knew that if she said the wrong word, he'd turn stubborn. She had to get him down Hacksher Street. He was too big and heavy for her to move if he didn't want to move, and they couldn't take him out here on the Midway. That fat cop Ed Yates'd be coming out of the Modern Times any minute.

"We'll both go to the Round Bar," she said swiftly. "We'll have all the drinks you want. But I got to change my dress first. I spilled something on it. It'll only take me a minute."

"Yeah. Have drinks. Now."

"Ah, be nice," she wheedled. "Let me change my dress, please, huh? You want to be nice, don't you, man?"

"Sure. Nice. Lil girl."

"That's right. I'm a girl. Take a good look. I'm better than any girls at the Round Bar. You want a girl, don't you?"

"Yeah. Girl. I know."

"And I've got lots of drinks up in my room."

"We go have a drink."

Now he let her lead him, convinced that she was doing what he wanted to do. As they finally turned the corner, a reflection of light from the Modern Times gaudy neon front caught the planes of his cheeks and highlighted the jutting, knuckly-looking cheekbones, high on his face.

It was a shock. That was all she felt at the sight of his face. He wasn't the sad-looking foreman at all. She had the wrong guy. Two or three of them must have come out of the Modern Times together, and this had to be the one that followed her. This—and then she felt a chilly touch of panic when she suddenly recognized him. She knew him. Not to talk to, just to see. He lived on Midland down the next block from her sister's. His name was Slaughterhouse Salaski, the kids made fun of him. But he didn't really work in a slaughterhouse. He was in that meat packing place at the end of Elm on North River Road, facing the Paskack. Almost every day she saw him trudge round-shouldered home from work with something wrapped in butchers' paper under his arm. The kids made believe it was a bundle of guts from the slaughterhouse and ran around in front of him, holding their noses, yelling "Pee-yoo, he stinks."

Binnie's chill of panic vanished. Hell, he didn't know anybody in the neighborhood or even the flat where she lived, never made friends with anybody, never said nothing. Anyway, he was too stoned to see who she was, in the first place. He was too stoned to see anything. Abruptly, she was angry. He'd gypped her out of the chemical foreman, and the place he worked was almost the same as the slaughterhouse, and the jerks that worked the slaughterhouse didn't get paid hardly nothing, worse than a ditch digger. She was furious. This was the same as getting the laugh on her and that was the one thing she couldn't stand.

She snatched the fingers of his left hand in a grip Mick Fogarty showed her and hustled him down the street toward the high dark steps to the warehouse office where Veronica and Sugar Fernandez were waiting to take him. He bleated in pain because it was a finger-busting grip when you leaned on it, and he lurched and staggered faster and faster alongside to keep from getting busted fingers. He *had* to keep moving.

Then, just when she got him to the dark steps, she did lean on it; didn't feel much different than popping a knuckle. She was disappointed; busted fingers ought to be worse than popping a knuckle. Salaski bent forward, like Mick said a guy did when you put on the pressure downwards, and she jabbed her knee into his face as hard as she could. Mick said that'd straighten him up and back, and told her what to do then. She did it, and he screeched like a woman when her spiky heel got him in the groin. He doubled over, and she sent him sprawling into the blackness at the far side of the cement steps with a hard, experienced two-handed shove.

She waited a second till she heard the two familiar meaty smacks when Sugar Fernandez busted him over the head with a hunk of plugged hose stuffed with BB's, then another kind of smack when she got him in the snoot. Sugar got kicks out of working over a guy's snoot with that hunk of hose. Binnie wanted to stay for the rest of it—the way he gypped her out of the chemical foreman! But that wasn't her part of the score. She whirled, pulled up her skirt and ran toward the corner of Hacksher and the Midway.

Binnie slowed down and dropped her skirt when she got to the corner. That sprint up the block was just in case a police cruise car turned in and got Veronica and Sugar in the headlights. That was Binnie's part of it. She was supposed to run screaming to the car, yelling they were beating up her guy, but at the same time making sure to hang on the edge of the open window with both hands, so the car couldn't take off without dragging her. She was supposed to hang on and keep screaming till they peeled her off, and by then Veronica and Sugar would be down the next alley, over the fence and into any Jackson Street tenement where guys in some of the flats'd let them hide. The guys in the flats were okay and usually didn't make the Debs put out.

Binnie looked back and stooping a little, she could just about make out the silhouettes of Sugar and Veronica against the greasy shine of the Paskack a half block beyond. It looked like Sugar that was bent over Salaski, her arm moving sharply up and down. Yeah, that would be Sugar; she liked to work over a guy when he was out. Then the silhouettes tangled angularly, and Binnie knew Veronica had Sugar by the arm and was pulling her away, so she could get out of there and back to the flat fast as they could make it. Chicken punk—that sure was Veronica all over.

Binnie made certain nobody was around before she eased warily out into the Midway. This was ticklish because the bulls could give her a bad time if she was spotted coming out of a street where a guy was mugged. But this part of the Midway was pretty quiet at night and the only spot for blocks both ways was the Modern Times and the men coming out usually clustered at the corner bus stop. The johns knew better than go for a walk in the Butt after dark; they took the bus.

It was okay for Binnie to walk cross-Butt. She was a Hotshot Deb. Even so, she went along with her right hand in her opened purse. She always carried a few little rubber balls filled with ammonia. A guy wouldn't even know it was in her hand till she squirted his eyes, and even if a guy got at you from in back, you could squirt over your shoulder and just getting his face was usually enough, let alone the eyes. Ammonia was best. It didn't eat holes in your handbag, like muriatic.

She saw the shadows of a few guys on the way, but all she had to say was a snapping, "Light a rag, crud," and they laughed softly and said, "Hi, little Binnie. Why you don't you gimme a break, doll baby? You're big enough for a man now." Sometimes they warned her to keep an eye out for this guy or that, who was sweating for a fix or was higher than up on muta, or tipped her that there was a stakeout of bulls around the Atlantic Transit Garage on Grove, on account of they had an idea there'd been some hot iron coming and going. Atlantic Transit was a sometimes a drop where stolen cars were given a bath—that is, a fast spray paint job—before moving them out.

These soft voices in the dark were right guys, actually, and she'd know them in the day, but by night they were disembodied half-whispers from a doorway, an alley or a fence-end, and they never showed. It wouldn't pay, in case they pulled a score and there were kickbacks. They all called her "little Binnie" and she knew they'd be right there with it if she put out, but not otherwise. Part of it was Mick Fogarty, but most of it was the Rovers. She didn't kid herself about scaring them with Mick Fogarty. The Rovers wouldn't stand still for anybody messing up a Senior Deb. These guys were *people* and, looking at it one way, kind of escorted her home.

Her sister wasn't home when Binnie reached the flat fifteen minutes later. Loretta was never home nights. She worked in some kind of nightclub uptown; first one, then another. Binnie had stopped trying to keep track of the names of them, Loretta shifted around so much. It used to be a stinking old railroad flat like all the others, but Loretta fixed it up with a lot of nice stuff she got from Junkie John. Junkie John wasn't really a junkie; they only called him that because his front was a junk business—scrap iron, bottles, old newspapers and the rest of it.

Junkie John had other businesses, too. Binnie didn't know all of them, but he'd buy almost anything you brought him, no questions asked and no answers wanted, just so long's he got it for a dime and turned it over for a buck.

For a hundred and a half, Junkie John gave Loretta four rooms of practically new stuff, most of it with the tags and labels still on. Genuine crisscross curtains, guaranteed Oriental type rugs, modernistic furniture, lamps, pictures, and believe it or not, a real hot water heater, white enamel, two feet high, and an honest to God modernistic bathtub. The next day four steamship sailors off a freighter came and hooked it up in the kitchen. Nobody in the Butt had their own hot water heater and a modernistic bathtub. Crise, nobody had hot water. The flats had one bathroom on a floor that stank on account of guys missing the john, drunk or sober, and the old cracked tubs were so crummy, you'd have to take a bath with your clothes on.

Binnie was fifteen when the old man told her to get a job or get out, he was sick and tired of her eating him out of house and home. On the sly, the old lady sent her to live with her sister. Loretta was fun, good-natured and always making what-the-hell jokes and laughing, but except for her clothes, they didn't come sloppier than Loretta and the flat was a garbage dump. Binnie cleaned it up some, but she didn't like housework any better than Loretta, and after a little while she began staying in other girls' flats for a night, then two or three. Then she came home after a week with Midge Daly and Loretta grabbed her and hugged her and started bawling and said she'd been worried sick all last night, and what was the matter, didn't Binnie like her anymore?

Binnie said bluntly, "The couch I sleep on worse than stinks and the whole flat's so crummy, what do you want me to get, lung poison? I'm going over to Sugar Fernandez' tonight."

Loretta tried to say something but all she could do was bawl. Then she hugged Binnie again and whispered, "That's okay, honey-baby. Leave it to your big sister. You'll see."

The very next day the whole flat was cleaned out with shovels, scrubbed and calcimined, and Junkie John had the new furniture and stuff in before dinner. The morning after, the four sailors hooked up the hot water and bathtub in the kitchen. It looked like a department store front window. When Loretta saw Binnie was crazy about it, she was so happy she busted out bawling and laughing and singing, "Happy Days Are Here Again" way down in her chest, real hot and sexy.

The four steamship sailors came for a date—they'd pooled twenny-fi'bucks, one said—but Loretta laughed and told them to shag their asses back to the Points, this was her night with the kid sister. The end sailor looked around her and gave Binnie the up-and-down with a whistle at the end. He grinned and started to say something about maybe getting another twenny-fi' bucks, when Loretta hauled off and smacked him so hard with her fist that his nose shot blood all over the other three and the wall and everything else. Loretta yelled something about leave her kid sister out of this and called them the worst names and hauled off again, but the sailors apologized almost on their knees and almost fell downstairs getting away.

Binnie was scared, she'd never seen Loretta so mad in all her life. In fact it was the only time she saw Loretta mad. She slammed the door with a swing like she wanted to throw it downstairs after the sailors. Then it was all over and in a couple minutes she was dancing around the new parlor, singing, "You Been A Good Ole Wagon But You Done Broke Down."

Then she and Binnie drank beer and ate sandwiches and had a real ball. When Loretta got going, she was better than a TV show. She didn't have any dates the next three nights, and stayed home with

Binnie, but Loretta, she was the kind who got restless when things didn't change.

The fourth day she went out in the morning, came back after lunch and told Binnie she had this swell job uptown, but it was nights. If Binnie was scared to stay in the flat, she'd tell them the hell with it. By this time Binnie was in the Debs and it took more than being alone in the flat to scare her, and anyway she'd get Midge Daly to stay the nights Loretta had to work.

So Loretta really fixed up the flat for Binnie because just about the only time she came was Sunday morning and afternoon, and went back to work after dinner.

When she was fifteen, Binnie thought there was nobody like Loretta— but you can't stay fifteen forever. Now she was seventeen, and knew you had to keep double-entry book on people or be satisfied with a half-ass answer. There still wasn't anybody like Loretta. She'd give you the shirt off her back, which was okay for you and better than paying for it, but the best you could say for Loretta was, she wasn't very bright. She never learned. She still had the same routines, the same jokes, and that deep way of singing wasn't hot or sexy anymore. It just sounded like a bellyache set to music for the squares. To get right down to it, she bored Binnie. So far as Binnie was concerned, the best thing she'd done so far was stay away from the flat all week. Binnie could put up with those few hours on Sunday because she slept till late afternoon after the big jazz of Saturday night at the clubroom and the biggest back at the flat with Mick Fogarty. The biggest jazz. She was getting Mick into the right groove.

He still needed some touching up and tried to give her a bad time, but she had the double-entry on him, man, the whammy. It was getting easier—just give it to him cool off the elbow and hold out when they were alone and she could hear him breathing. Hold out. Nix the jazz. The big-eyes and the little smile. "But I got the rag on, Mick."

"Again? It was only last week...."

"You never been a girl, Mick. It's complicated. You can read it in a book."

Baffled, frustrated, boiling mad—tough Mick Fogarty. The tougher they start, the tamer they end. She was getting him in the groove like a roller coaster.

When she walked into the flat from this last one, Midge Daly, in panties and bra, was gawping at TV on the sofa. Alone. That was Midge for you. She had the flat to herself for five hours and she gawped at TV alone, and crise knows she wasn't a mutt. She was five-one, an inch shorter than Binnie, the littlest Senior in the Debs, and very light-boned. She looked like a scrawny Junior in the Debs daytime street outfit, but there was nothing skinny about her in panties and bra. The guys'd never call her Bubbles, but her breasts were fuller than you'd think. High, swelling and rising with a special-plus shapeliness that nobody had but Midge. She slimmed down at the waist, started out again at the hips and her legs were a clean line from there to the ankles, not just all thighs, although the thighs had a long and sensually subtle rondure, and once you got them in your mind and heart and marrow, there'd never be any other thighs in the world for you. She had a figure of delicate and infinite feminine grace, apparent only when she was dancing. Most times she slouched or flopped around, like now on the sofa, and couldn't be bothered to make an effort. Or so it seemed.

She had deep chestnut hair, straight, warm gray eyes and again that subtle promise in the width of her mouth. The slender delicacy was also in her face but without make-up, it looked thin below the length of her eyes. She never wore lipstick, either. She seemed to go out of her way to talk and act and look like a thin, wiry tomboy, when she wasn't anything like that.

If the guys could see her now in panties and bra, sensuous, half asleep and curled up in a corner of the sofa, she'd never get rid of them. They'd be climbing in the windows.

But they never would see her in panties and bra. She was Midge the runt, and always would be, slouched against a lamppost or building, sitting cross-legged on a curb, or just flopped any old way on the tenement front steps. It was as though she didn't know there were better things to do with a guy than fight him.

Still, a fierceness burned in Midge and it was close enough to the surface to burst into brilliant flame one day.

She sat up and yawned drowsily and kicked at the extension cord to turn off the TV when Binnie came in. "You're early," she said. "A slow night?"

"A good night," Binnie snapped. "But Veronica punked out."

"Veronica? Oh sure. Just like Mick Fogarty's joining up with the Debs with bobby pins in his hair."

"I'm telling you." Binnie walked into the bedroom, unzipping her dress at the side. "What's more, she's been punking out the last four, five times." She hung her dress in the closet and her breasts swelled voluptuously as she reached up between her shoulders to unclip her bra. She stood nude and worked her breasts with soothing fingers. The bra was new and a little tight for a hot, close night. The light massage felt good.

Midge watched. "If I had your figure," she said. "That's all. If I just had your figure!" She didn't say why, but it had been her attitude since they were kids: Binnie had the most of the best, and her role as Midge the runt was played in the shadow of Binnie. Without envy, she thought Binnie was beautiful.

Binnie took her time poking in the closet for something to put on. She liked going around naked, and liked to be looked at, and there was more to it than just kicks or vanity. She finally put on a cotton print housecoat, a present from Loretta. By this time, Midge had draped herself in her usual old blanket bathrobe. She always put on something when other Debs came to the flat.

Binnie came back into the parlor, tying her housecoat at the waist. "So you don't believe it about Veronica."

"She didn't run out on you or you'd of said so."

Binnie said, "Sugar Fernandez'd bust her head if she ran." She lit a cigarette and lolled indolently in the soft lounge chair, resting one leg over the arm, stretching the other before her. Her housecoats never stayed closed and, legs apart, she was exposed all the way. Most people had some last personal privacies, but Binnie didn't care how open she looked. Midge took a cigarette and kept her eyes on the weaving smoke. "Veronica'd kill Sugar," she said.

"She keeps wanting to come home earlier all the time. She don't like it outside after dark."

"Me neither. Not the way you and her and Sugar go out. So that makes me chicken, too."

"That's different."

"But what'd she *do?*" Midge persisted. "I still don't know what she done. She must of done something."

"Well, tonight she started calling me off at ha' past ten," Binnie shaved off twenty minutes. "It's been the same thing the last four, five paydays. A month ago it wasn't even ten. Remember?"

"She was sick. That was the night she puked all over the toilet."

"I seen guys get the same kind of sick before a rumble," Binnie jeered. Then, thoughtfully, "That's when she started, a month ago. That night. Before then, she never wanted to come in. Crise, onct she kept us out till almost two. That was right after that bastit Ironhead Gahagen told the bulls to bust up any Debs or guys on the street after eleven, and she ups and keeps us there till almost two. Now it's a different story. She can't get in early enough. What kind of jazz is that?"

Midge frowned and muttered, "A month ago, a month ago . . ." as though turning it over in her mind. "What happened a month ago?"

"Eight boats came in at onct, six from the warehouse fire down Jersey City. The dock stiffs got time and a half and double time, and their pay envelopes were like a deck-a cards. We pulled one score on top of another, five hundred bucks almost. But crise, two o'clock! The matrons down the Station would of killed us if there was anything left after the lousy bulls got done."

"Then I don't see her punking out, Binnie. Honest I don't."

"You sticking up for her against me?" Binnie demanded in a voice like broken glass. "Or maybe you think I'm seeing things."

"Ah, don't be like that, Binnie. You know different. If she's chicken, that's one thing, but if she ain't, I don't want to see you get busted up for ranking her like that."

Binnie didn't like this turn in the conversation. It gave her a funny feeling. Furthermore, she'd been sure that Midge'd back her up. Not that Midge always agreed. She didn't. She was a shanty Irish pepper. But this time Binnie wanted Midge right there with her. Midge didn't take nothing from nobody, little as she was, and the Debs and guys didn't mess with her. They knew better.

"She won't bust me," said Binnie uneasily. "She won't even try, and never did. You know that. She let every other Deb have it, except you and Sugar—and me."

Yes, Midge thought, Binnie could take care of herself. She wasn't wild like Veronica or Sugar, but she never came out on the short end of a fight. She looked so little and scared with that white, bunched-up smile that in the beginning the Debs got an idea they could walk all over her till she exploded in their faces and did things. Even when they'd got her down and it was all over, or looked like, the next minute they were screeching and rolling around in the dirt and holding themselves someplace. Like Gert-the-Dog with an eye out. But Binnie didn't stand a chance and had no other way. Gert was some kind of ginzo and her old man was a Black Hand. She had a ring she stole from her uncle who was a packer in Bergland's Department Store, a special ring just for packers. There was a little sharp curved knife on it for cutting rope. Later she stole two, one for each hand. You couldn't get close to her in a fight, and the only way Gert Luccini knew to fight was close. She was short and wide and strong, like a lot of ginzos, and first she'd butt you with her head, then hold your arms and bite you.

That's why she was Gert-the-Dog, the way she wound it up with biting. You couldn't duck her all the time and every so often she just *had* to get somebody and cornered a Deb and bit something off, usually fingers, but ears too, and once it was a nose. Mostly she went for Debs of the Happy Jacks that had the territory just up the Butt.

Then this day, Binnie, Sugar and Veronica were all dressed for a date with three guys in the midtown Oasis Club and Gert-the-Dog wanted to tag along. Binnie gave her a snappy brush-off and Gert went at her with her head down like a locomotive, yelling and cursing. The yell alone was from Weirdsville, it paralyzed you. Binnie might of turned white in a fight, but she was an ice cube. She didn't paralyze, ever. She didn't like to fight. When you came to think of it, you couldn't call what she did fighting. It was something she tried to get over and done with fast. Gert-the-Dog was over and done with in ten seconds. She never got to butt nothing. Binnie slipped it with a footwork shift, like a pug, and the next second Gert was screaming and running around in circles holding her face and the blood coming through her fingers.

Sugar Fernandez said Binnie only put up her hands to hold Gert away and Gert's getting her eye out was an accident. Everybody went along with that, including Midge, but down deep Midge *knew* Binnie did it deliberately because she wanted to and got a big charge a when it worked.

She knew because she was the only Deb Binnie was close to, and sometimes in the evening when they were alone in the flat and drinking beer and horsing around, Binnie'd grab her fingers in a special way and Midge'd go down on her knees with a yell. Binnie'd give her the big-eyes and ask what happened and she didn't mean it and all that. After just so much of this kind of horsing around, Midge found out how Binnie did some of that stuff. Midge wasn't a nutsy fagin, and Binnie cut it out after Midge gave her a taste of the same thing a couple times. That's how Midge knew there was no accident with putting Gert's eye out. But what else could Binnie do? Just stand there and get bit?

Midge was worried. She didn't think Binnie could take care of Veronica. Everybody knew Veronica was half crazy. Her old man was in the nut house, her three brothers weren't all there, and her sister was one of the screwiest whores down at the Five Points. So far, Binnie's protection was Mick Fogarty. If you laid a finger on Binnie, you had to take care of the Mick too, the worst fighter in the Rovers except maybe Vince Kirby, the war leader, and that was a toss-up.

Veronica steered clear of Binnie on that count, but if it came right down to a fight, she didn't care what she did. She wasn't in her right mind, and it'd be too late for Mick Fogarty to do anything after Veronica ruined Binnie's face with an ax handle.

"Aaah, leave it lay," she told Binnie. "Let somebody else do the dirty work. Let them get the lumps. If she's chicken, the word'll get round.

Hell, you know what it'll come to. Vince Kirby'll turn her over to the guys that know how. He won't stand for a number one Deb that's chicken. He can't now that the Happy Jacks sucked in the Apaches. That gives them Bellevue Street and our line is one block down, on Grove."

"What're you trying to do, ootz me off the elbow?" asked Binnie sullenly.

"I'm not ootzing nobody, Binnie. Look at it this way. Who takes the Hotshots into a rumble? Veronica. That means she's gotta know the time and place and everything. The way it's gonna be done. Let's say she *is* chicken. She's been on top so long, she knows what Vince'll do to her when he finds out. But she's always sure of at least a handout from the Happy Jacks if she tells them the score. So what's the choice? She goes over to the Happy Jacks."

"Is that supposed to be news? I know how it goes better than you do."

"But to get away with it, Binnie, you gotta be half chicken to start with. If they got it on their mind, it don't show. But when a Deb like Veronica goes chicken, it's written all over her, and Vince'll take care of her like *that*. It's the top ones like Veronica that really get busted up. You know that, too."

Binnie nodded and shrugged, the way she did when something began to bore her. "Hell, let's forget it," she said indolently. "Maybe she's right and I'm wrong. Who wants to get picked up by fat Yates? That's a one-way trip up the alley." Her slim face was smooth, drowsy-eyed and empty, an expression she could hide behind when her mind was busy with something else.

She could even hide herself from Midge. Midge didn't know everything.

FOUR

Veronica and Sugar Fernandez showed up about ten minutes later, and Veronica began screaming and yelling at Binnie before the door was closed. Her thin face was congested and she really did look crazy, with those washed-out, faded gray, staring eyes. She stood in the middle of the room and screeched at the top of her lungs, so crazy-mad that she clawed the air with bony fingers as if Binnie were up there a few inches above her head.

Sugar stayed with her back to the door in a wary, defensive crouch. Her glance darted about the room, as if seeking a safer refuge. She was plainly terror-stricken.

Veronica ended on a furious, inarticulate howl and flung herself into the kitchen, slamming the door so hard that it sounded as if she had battered it with a sledge hammer.

Binnie stared at the door, her mouth still agape with astonishment. Midge leaned over the back of the sofa and also stared, slowly becoming aware that her right hand hurt. She looked down and saw that she was so tightly gripping the neck of an empty beer bottle that her fingers were white. Very carefully she leaned over and placed the bottle back on the floor beside the sofa. She looked at Sugar and canted her chin at the kitchen door.

"What's it all about?" she asked.

Binnie recovered more slowly and all she could say was, "Crise—"

Sugar shook her head. "She's mad," she said.

She was a dark Latin angel, was Sugar, radiating such infinite vistas of sex that she didn't need brains. Which was fortunate, because she was literally a moron. It made no difference, no difference whatever to the males, and there were many males in Sugar's simplified life. She was all curves, from the red blossom of her mouth, the rich heavy languor of her breasts, the swell of her belly, soft hips and buttocks, to legs that moved slowly and looked as if they'd rather lie horizontal than walk. The guys she went with didn't talk about her the way they talked about some Debs, but there were hints that Sugar had something special all her own and, man, she could really bust a guy up.

She watched the kitchen door and when Veronica didn't come running out in another crazy rage, she gradually relaxed.

"Wuh!" she said with a meaningless grin. "Wasn't that something."

"Yeah," said Midge. "It was something—but what?"

"Yeah, what?" demanded Binnie angrily. "Who the hell did she think she was yelling at?"

"You," said Sugar. "She was real mad all the way here. I was scared to come with her. She goes crazy, somebody gets hurt."

"She picked the right place," said Binnie. "Let her try it again and she'll find out. But what's the jazz, stupid?"

Sugar moved her hands in a placating gesture. She didn't want to be in the middle between Binnie and Veronica. "Well, you know that last guy you brung? His name, it's Salaski. It was in his wallet. His address, too. That's why she's mad, his address. He lives right down the block from here, Binnie. This is twenny-four and he lives a hunnert-nine. So maybe he knows you. Maybe tomorrow he tells the cops. You don't know him?"

"Sure I know him," said Binnie arrogantly. "So what? He was too stoned to know himself, much less me. Anyway, he never did know me."

"Hokay, sure. But Veronica, she thinks you're nuts, taking a guy from your own block. You get us all a bad time with the cops."

"Salaski?" Midge looked narrowly at Binnie. "Slaughterhouse Salaski?"

"I didn't take him on purpose, Midge. I thought it was somebody else."

Unconsciously, Midge gave her head a small shake, as if to rid it of something she did not understand. A mugging had never bothered her before. Almost everybody she knew had gone out mugging at one time or another. The small, good-looking ones, like Binnie, usually acted as decoys; the muscle babes, or those who liked blood, cooled the mark and lifted his leather—although cooled was hardly the word when Veronica slugged them with an ax handle and Sugar beat in their faces with a garden-hose blackjack and sometimes stamped on their testicles. Not all men; just the big, gross, jowly ones, as a rule....

The unspoken word was that Sugar had been raped regularly every week for years by her uncle Pete Fernandez—ever since she was twelve, ripe and busty. Sugar's parents had gone away and stayed there, leaving her to live with her uncle in two dark, wet-cement-smelling rooms in the basement beneath the Good Luck Cafeteria, which Pete owned. Whenever she forgot to lock and bolt the door of her room, and wedge a chairback under the doorknob, Pete appeared, clad only in his socks. He never took off his socks, even for love; you could catch a nasty chill from the damp cement floor. Sugar whimpered at the far edge of her old-fashioned brass bed, and later screeched, for Pete Fernandez was a big, thickset man in every way. His lovemaking was strictly Neanderthal: if she wasn't docile enough to suit him, he laid her out cold with a right hook to the jaw, and then fell upon her full length, because he liked to start out that way, taking great pleasure in the sensation of smooth feminine warmth beneath him. When she recovered enough to struggle weakly, he found a slow, sensuous pleasure in that also. It gave him an unneeded but exciting excuse for excursions into various amatory brutalities. The cafeteria did not open until noon on Sundays, so it was usually on Sunday mornings before late mass that, his huge feet decorated with gaudy nylon socks, he clasped the impotently struggling Sugar in his powerful, black-maned arms and after prolonged preliminaries that only a descendant of Torquemada, the Inquisitor, could devise, he seized Sugar inexorably and plunged into the wrenching climax with a triumphant bellow, taking her taut, heaving breasts in both tremendous hands as he spread his elbows and legs and drove mightily, a gargantuan maniac under the knout of his own passions. It was then that Sugar thrashed and screeched.

Now, Pete Fernandez was not close-fisted and could pick and choose among the women within his particular orbit, but he never gave them a passing thought. He was a primitive, a real atavist, and he was obsessed by Sugar, who was his niece. He did not know that almost any Senior of the Red Rovers could bed her whenever he took the notion. They were kids, and kids didn't count. He was Pete Fernandez. He was a *man*.

Sugar did not have to endure the things he did to her—and even after five years, it still was rape. She could have walked out of that dank bestial cellar, and if Pete Fernandez came after her, she could have told him flatly to go to hell. She should have known that if she flung the. word "cops" in his teeth, he'd have departed hastily (scrammed; lit a rag; copped a sneak; hit the grit) and for good. She'd been twelve and he thirty-five, when first he chased her around her subterranean bedroom, knocked her down with a swing of the sodden chicken-feather pillow, threw her on the bed and hurled himself upon her.

She was nubile and eagerly ready at the age of twelve, but not ready enough for the carnal violence of a monolith. It was almost a week before she could walk, painfully and slowly, by clinging for support to bedposts, chairbacks, and the walls.

Pete was scared. *Madre de Dio*, how could you call in a doctor and say the dumb little chick slipped and fell on something in the crotch? They were all stooges or stoolies for the cops anyway. Rape was bad enough, the way the cops looked at it; slipping it to a punk kid was worse, but when you put it to your own punk niece, her only twelve, and practically bust her gut, hell, the Chair was the least they'd give you. Crise, you'd be glad to get the Chair long before Cap Gahagen and the wreckers got finished showing you the goldfish down the cellar of the station house.

A flat, intensifying shine swept his protuberant brown eyes of everything but the growing hunger behind them. She was only a kid, sure, but she was his own niece, for crisake! She couldn't walk out on him or nothing. He was practically her old man and she had to live right there with him where he told her, in one of the rooms down the cellar next to him. *Right* next to him. Mother of God, he could have it a dozen times a day with no more trouble than kicking the door down, if it went that far!

Every day he went to her bedroom, bearing a tray of the Good Luck Cafeteria's choicest viands with elaborate ceremony. He soon learned, however, that she liked nothing better than meat loaf, mashed potatoes with anonymous gravy, canned peas, apple pie à la mode and a bottle of coke.

"Your most favorite platter, *cara mia*," he said with a dismal attempt at gaiety in Spanish. "See, this is green apple pie, none better."

At first she would not talk to him, but she soon found it unmitigated punishment not to chatter at something, anything, even to *Tio* Pedro Fernandez.

"Green ain't ripe," she said sullenly, eying the heaped plates greedily, her mouth watering.

What she needed, he thought heavily, was a clout in the snoot. But the time wasn't yet. "Eat your meat loaf while it's hot."

She told him what to do with the meat loaf and everything else on the platter, particularly the coke bottle. But she was careful not to arouse his anger. She was afraid of him. He was a man of authority, he owned the big restaurant, and you never knew. Furthermore, he was her uncle, a more important man than her owl father, and in the house, what he said went.

She dreaded the hour when he would come at her again, wearing nothing but socks, and put her through *that* all over. It was bad, it was against the Church, but he was her uncle and if he took off her clothes and did *that* to her, well, that was what uncles did, and when your uncle was *Tio* Pedro, you did it or got your teeth shoved down your throat. The world of morons is as elementary as that. People that went to the cops got thirty days in the workhouse. Girls that ran away from uncles got drug back and the hell beat outen them.

And then, to her surprise, two and a half weeks later, the second time was nothing like the first. Pete Fernandez came in, wearing the same old socks. She huddled against the wall, expecting a clip on the jaw. By this time she was sure that if Pete Fernandez set you up with a poke in the snoot, well, that was how it was done; everybody started off like that.

But he didn't beat her up or nothing. He had a funny kind of smile that kept sliding around on his mouth, and when he spoke, it was in a thick woolly voice, not like Uncle Pete at all. He sat on the edge of the bed and patted the inside of her thigh high up and said don't be scared. This alone was unusual for Pete, and must have taken quite an effort. All she had on was a skimpy cotton nightgown he'd bought for her at the five-and-dime, on account of her other clothes had got all ripped off the first time. She was ashamed for a man to look at her in a nightgown like that. It showed everything she owned. She wanted to cry. The nightgown was against the Church. She was a decent Catholic girl, and never missed a mass, a novena or confession. She was crazy about confession. She went to confession every chance she got. She was particularly crazy about the decorated inside of the Church itself, all the colors and gold and everything. If she had a million dollars, she'd build herself a church just exactly like St. Mark's up in Brookline. Like she always said to Father Mahon, she never had no ambitions, only to be a nun, and finally he said maybe she'd do better in some other line of work, he said, and anyway, the nuns she wanted, the ones with the pretty clothes and the nice brick place in Bergen Fells, were full up, and she'd have to go into a different kind of nuns and scrub floors and all the time take Vows of Silence.

It didn't do no good, thinking about the Church and stuff. Uncle Pete was taking off her nightgown and his hands were shaking and heavy and the nightgown got all tore up like her first clothes. His thick hairy hands were all over her, specially places she never let nobody look, and she realized in horror that if she was against the Church, it stood to reason the Church was against her too. She could never go back to St. Mark's or confession or anything. How could you go to confession after you done things like this with Uncle Pete. You couldn't, that's all, you just couldn't....

All the people living in the one flat, three rooms, her mother and father and brothers, there used to be four but one got cut and now the other three were in jail, not reform school, on account of they sold pot to high school kids, and they'd-a been high school kids themselves oney they dinn go, and there was her sister Angel and her husband Jake and their two kids and another one on the way, and her other sister Evita. She got to be a Mexico Air Lines hostess. Every time she come home, *ay de mi*, such a big fight, 'cause always Evita, she tries to take Mama away, the minute she comes in she say, *"Mama mia, por Dios*, you don't have to live this pigsty, this place. *Porque no va a mi vivienda, Mamacita? no trabaja*, no nothing, just have a good time for once, Mama, live in a nice place, invite your friends."

And that's when it really busted up with Evita and Papa, with Papa yelling, "Whore, whore, get out, get out, go back to your this-and-that with your gringos, whore, whore!" And Evita called him worse things, and defied him to throw her out. But Papa wouldn't dast do that or lay a finger on that gray-and-silver airplane uniform, 'cause that'ud be against the government, and against the government was worse than just against the cops, and maybe even than against the Church, too, 'cause Father Mahon, never scared of nothing, always said, never-never-never, as you live, go against the government.

Even the three dark brothers, that almost laughed at cops to their face, used to duck in the kitchen fast when they heard Mama let Evita in the parlor door. Four brothers at first before Ricki got cut back of the bowling alleys. Little Sordo, that was the youngest brother, snitched with Ricki's wallet before the cops got there, and there was a lotta secret talk with Mama and Papa and the brothers in the closed kitchen, and it seems they couldn't go down and *in*dentify Ricki in the morgue place with a lotta other dead guys. Ricki was a gangster, that's why; you dinn *in*dentify gangsters—they got after you.

Ricki had been a gangster, sixteen, all grown-up, and had a genuine piece, a *real* piece, not just a zip made out of a hunk-uh old pipe. And Ricki was a real big shot, too, in the Essex Dusters before he got cut, a great big gang down near the Butt, juss this side, oney one precinct in between. He dinn haffta smoke reefers no more, to show the kind'a big shot he was; he got all the 'H' he wanted down-Butt. When you were a big shot, people were scared *not* to walk up and give you things, like 'H' frinstance.

Crise he was handsome, *real* handsome. An she was his own favrit, too. Him, he was the one, the guy her the name Sugar, and that's what it was ever sinst. Sugar. She always took pains the days he was home, when she was practicing to be a nun in a remnant of muslin sheet and bits of black cloth she got from a busted umbrella. She rubbed her cheeks with vaseline to make them shine. A nun's face, it hadda be shiny. She was practicing walking with her eyes looking down at her still pudgy knees, calves and ankles. When there wasn't quite enough muslin sheet or umbrella cloth, her nun's dress started above the kneecap, and the less fabric, the higher the hem line. She'd never dream of skimping on the voluminous, poke bonnet style headdress she had devised. Never onct she ever seen a nun, her face wasn't shining from the shadows of her coif.

Her legs stuck out, so what? It wasn't her fault. Anyways, they wasn't fat no more. Sometimes when she stood not quite frontways and not quite sideways, but sorta in between, you could see they were getting a real nice shape to them, a helluva more shape than lotsa grown-up high school girls that thought they was showin off something in tight bathing suits down the municipal pool, now it was summer. Sugar wanted to go down the pool and all over, but you hadda practice, honest to God practice, every day like the piano if you wanted to be a nun. Wouldn't those girls down the swimming pool be jealous when Father Mahon said she could be one of the pretty nuns.

FIVE

Father Mahon, the scrappiest priest in the parish, yelled from the pulpit that—and the Lord would forgive him!—he'd take a fire ax if necessary to get rid of any street gang of boys and girls that tried to get together and take over *his* parish, as the depraved, vicious little animals were endeavoring to do in other precincts of the city. Aye, a fire ax!

He reached under the pulpit and brandished an actual fire ax over his head. He was a powerful red Irishman and he flourished the heavy ax like a tennis racket. It seemed a very special ax, hurled to earth by Jehovah, God of Vengeance. *I am a jealous God!* It sheared through dust motes into a shaft of sunlight and flashed like lightning, splitting the sky, just as Jehovah might split the sky in a wrath too vast and mighty even to imagine.

No one doubted for a moment, including Father Mahon himself, that he literally meant every word he said. The twelve- and eighteen-year-olds alike in the parish of St. Marks, plus a still more hardened nucleus that had already begun to foment, also believed without a single scoffing murmur that Father Mahon would break up their very first club meeting with a fire ax. It gave them a funny feeling.

Anyways, how could you fight a priest, for crisake? A priest is a priest. You didn't have to like him, but he was a priest all the same, and priests stuck together. What was behind them? Not the Squaresville Fife & Drum Corps, man, and that's no jazz. Behind them was the Holy Roman Catholic Church, itself. Crise, the spires of the Church pierced Heaven and were transformed into the mansions of gold, like it promised in the Bible, and who was in charge? His Holiness, the Pope, with an interdict in one hand, excommunication in the other, and the blackjack of Eternal Purgatory to make it stick. That ain't the jazz, man.

"Tonight's the big dance, man. You I don' know. Doyle? Glad to meet you, Doyle. It's what they give me to do tonight—cheer up the mutts. Me? Oh, the name's Fernandez, Ricki Fernandez. Yeah, just another greaser. Awright—awright, you dinn mean nothing. Nobody means nothing. But shove off, I'm busy, see Patsy over the piano there...."

"Gladdameecha, Doyle, but I'm up to *here* right now, see you later an—hey! dinn I see you someplace?"

"I'm inna ring. Slaughterhouse Doyle, the Harrison Butcher Boy.

That's me. Golden Gloves city champ turned pro, won six, los—uh, a light-heavy, I tole you, dinn I? Yeah. A light-heavy. One-semny-eight."

"You must slaughter 'm, Doyle," Patsy yawned.

"Naaah. I ain't slau— It's the goddamn promoter over the Arena. Put me down like, Young Jack Dempsy the Manasta Mauler, I tell him, and he says, him and Dempsey is frens and he wants to keep it like that, so he puts me down Slaughterhouse Doyle, the Harrison Butcher Boy. Ain't that a helluva note?"

"Yeah, but there's the piano. Get yourself in tune."

"Get—oh, a joke, huh? Haw, haw. I get jokes, see? Hey, c'mere, ben' down. That spik at the table, nex' the door. Yeah, him. Some talker. I dinn unnerstan hardly nothing he said. Boy, is he ever squirrel bait."

"Tell him," Patsy suggested blandly. "He'll be interested."

"Not that joker. I cun' get a word in sideways. Yeah, and he was snotty, too. I never heard no spik ack like that in Harrison. His name really Fernandez?"

"I dunno. Maybe. Mostly the guys call him Mack the Knife."

"Mack the—uh. Why?"

"He makes his own from metal saw blades. You should se 'm. Got one this long but oney that wide. Says all he needs is to get a little of it in an'e can feel all round your insides like with a finger."

"I'd bust him," said Slaughterhouse Doyle, "I'd masacrate 'm."

"He makes a different kind-a knife for everything. His old man's night watchman inna machine shop. One knife's just for fighting big guys, made on a bend like this, not alla way round. One thing he can't stand, it's them big muscle-benders. But he don't leave them no muscles. That's why the knife is made with that special end. He gets it inna guy's arm, gives it a push up to set it all around the bone, n'en pulls straight down the wrist with both hands. And there's the guy, shoulder to wrist, no muscles, just the bone cleaner'n you could hew the meat off'n a turkey leg."

"I'd slaughter 'm," said Doyle with diminishing enthusiasm. "I'd moider 'm foist."

"Thinking of tying in with the Club, Doyle?" Patsy's question was bright and eager.

"All I'm thinking is, where's the crapper?"

"Pul-ease, Mr. Doyle. We usually have Debs at a dance, and they might find your language in objection, a they're ladies, each and every one of them, but stinking tempers, some of them, like Rafaela behind you. She just so happens to come with Mack the Knife, and they's others come with other guys, and you know the chicks, they get on their high horse and tell their guys you insulted them and wotta they gonna do about it, so six, sem guys lay for you after the dance and give you a workout."

Doyle's chunky, battered face looked merely impatient. He didn't give a damn about six, seven guys laying for him outside. "All I want is where is it, so come on."

"It won't be just six, sem guys. When Mack the Knife is there, nobody else gets a look-in. Puts on a real show. He's a ham. It's little cut-cut-cuts all the time, little cuts, till the other guy's gotta keep throwing back his head to breathe. Mack could cut his throat a million times. That, he's best at. But no, he strings it out till the guy ain't got a dry square inch on 'em. Now don't make trouble for us and give yourself a bad time in the bargain."

Doyle looked Patsy over, as if looking for a spot to lay one right on the button. "Come on, crisake, I ask where is the lousy crapper? Any objections?"

Patsy had objections, but Doyle was standing there flatfooted and stolid, like a cop ready to smack your jaw up into your eyeteeth, and the sonuva bitch, he was just too goddamn big, and a pro pug, at that. And even a fair to lousy pro could break you up onct he found out you couldn't get to him.

So Patsy grinned and said glibly, "The john's out the door, to the right to the first corner, turn right again to the next corner, don't take the stairs but turn right, but keep going till little more'n the middle and there it is on the left hand side. But here in the 'Y' it ain't the crapper. On the door in gold letters is *Men*."

"Thanks, buster, but wouldn't I save myself a run around the block if I just turned the left corner, took a few steps, and there I was?"

"I guess so, but the guys take the other way on account there's an apartmin house acrost the street, and there's this redhead, if you catch her just right, the lights on and the shades up." He made vivid rounding motions in the air with his hands.

Doyle looked at him, wooden-faced. "Sonny," he said, "if I was you, I'd start wearing boxing gloves to bed. And the name ain't Doyle. The name's Vince Kirby. No hard feelings. I was just nosing around."

He turned and walked toward a group of about twenty Red Rovers, the really tough pack from down-Butt. They stood watching impassively, excepting a tall, wide sandy-haired guy, who threw back his head and laughed, hard flat laughs that shattered the silence that had amassed under the empty noise of the three-piece band.

"Save it, Fogarty, save it, save it. Don't bust up Junior's nice dance in the YMCA."

"If I had your funny bone, Fogarty . . ." Vince Kirby stopped and shook his head and grimaced. He didn't know the right words. What would he do if he were Mick Fogarty? Just what the hell *would* he do? Buy a couple yards of sense, for one thing. Stop giving it to that Binnie Riordan piece every time he got her skirt up, for another. At the rate he was going, he'd have it worn down to a nubbin before he was twenty; when it wasn't Binnie, it was first come, first served.

Vince was war leader of the Red Rovers, and Mick Fogarty was supposed to be his second on account of he could beat the living hell out of anybody in the Rovers, 'cept him, Vince Kirby. But now that Vince was at the top, he found he had to keep out of fights, out of trouble and, within reason, even out of the Debs, and some damn good-looking snoots among them, Binnie Riordan the best. But he hadda cut down to two, three times a week. He'd always been watchful, 'cept Saturdays and Sundays and then it was all day long, thru dawn, through dark and all night, too. Crise he'd been too bushed on Monday even to think about the Rovers and the Debs. Now he was top man, he couldn't take Mondays out no more. Too many packs wanted the Butt for their territory, and the Rovers had to be on top of them every minute. Thank God for the flying squads of Nits and Juniors that watchfully patrolled Orchard street.

If anything looked funny, the way Vince had it set up, the Seniors began drifting into the danger area in five minutes, keeping to the shadows, to their posts on roofs that commanded the area.

The first ones there crossed the borderline and made setups out of themselves, just to find out if the Imperials or big Happy Jacks were moving down the Butt to take the corners of Orchard Street on a tryout rumble. If the Red Rovers let them keep those worthless corners that'd be the beginning of the end for the Rovers, because from then on, the Happy Jacks would take one more corner after another, knowing that small weaknesses outside meant big weaknesses inside. The Happy Jacks were always reaching, to find out. If some dumb Happy Jack punk took a shot at one of those decoys, word of it was immediately run back to Vince Kirby in the Rovers' clubhouse, where by now Vince had the best of the fighting men in reserve.

Here was where Mick Fogarty shone. He was a wild man in a rumble and was known to have routed, single-handed, two separate squads of infiltrating Jacks. He was a fighter. There was no doubt about it, and Vince let the membership puff him up into the Number Two position, where he'd of been fine if there was no more to it than fighting and laying, but there was a hell of a lot more; there was detail work. The Rovers had over a hundred and fifty members, counting the Debs and the Nits. These groups were always on the move, yet Joey Groff could just about put his finger on any specified one of them, almost any time of day. It was necessary. Dues and percentages had to be collected by the week or by the day, and Groff had trained a tough "Gimme" Squad for that job. Vince Kirby's real Number Two was Joey Groff. Mick Fogarty was the showpiece.

They didn't nickname Joey the Brain for nothing. Joey was just about the only Rover that read books. The rest waded through the sports section of the *Essex Morning News*, and the Debs got their kicks out of magazines that featured stories like "I Loved Too Much" or "I Didn't Know I Was For Sale". Joey Groff was the one that loaned Vince that special book all about street fighting. Some Russian Commie schmo had wrote it. Street fighting is the dirtiest kind of fighting and Ivan McSchmo knew all the tricks; the book was right up to the minute.

Vince read the book, but didn't know how to use it. Joey Groff did. So who planned the series of rumbles that swept the Butt clean, from Orchard Street east to the steamship lines' high wire fence fronting Coyts Bay, of every warring club except the Red Rovers? Joey Groff. Mick Fogarty was all for beating the bejesus out of guys already beaten and kicking them the hell out of the territory. The guys had given the Rovers a good but disorganized battle, and again it was Joey Groff that told Vince that he'd only be turning over a whole mess of real fighting men to the Happy Jacks, so why not take them into the membership, but scatter them around the districts and make sure they didn't try to reorganize against the Club? Vince had to admit they were loyal though first he thought they'd turn on the Club the first chanct they got.

So it was Joey Groff that should of been Number Two, but Vince had to keep Mick Fogarty because he was so popular with the membership. Fogarty was a bastard in a fight, and there was no doubt about that; but there were at least twenty Juniors that could of kicked the living hell out of Joey Groff, even just horsing around, and there was no doubt about that, either. Fogarty was the big hero, and Joey the undersized mutt with glasses who did the thinking.

Vince's next step would be to get in the di Lucca organization, the real big guys in the Butt. Di Lucca had big money, and contacts in Essex. He was in solid with the county outfit that tied in with the Eastern Seaboard syndicate. Vince did not intend to go into the di Lucca pack as a punk errand boy. That was why, with Joey Groff's help, he was trying to make the Rovers the best organized fighting club in the city. It gave him background and importance; he wanted to be in charge of something when he went to di Lucca. Also, sooner or later, he was going to give di Lucca the works and take over.

After that it'd be one step up after another. Hell, the syndicate, or whatever it was, had to have a national tie-in, didn't it, so in the long run, what he really was after was a solid *in* with the main syndicate.

Vince Kirby was ambitious, and he intended to take Joey Groff up with him. He could do his own thinking, and in some cases better than Joey, who sometimes got out of touch because he'd rather read a book on how to talk to the right people than actually get down to it and *talk* to the right people. But he needed Joey. He'd found out all he wanted to know about the sprawling Essex Dusters pack, and was ready to go; he didn't like dances. On the other hand, he knew the guys would sour up if he said, "Let's get the hell outta here," and it only ten o'clock....

So, when he left Patsy Sean, war leader of the Dusters, and rejoined the attendant Rovers, he heh-heh-hehed a laugh of policy when Fogarty clowned, "If you had my funny bone, Vince. Hell baby, you wouldn't know what to do with a funny bone—except maybe clout somebody in the snoot with it." Fogarty was always clowning and getting the center of attention, but lately Vince was beginning to notice a whole flock of little digs at himself among the shenanigans. Fogarty couldn't of thought up that dodge by himself—why bother thinking when a guy could fight or lay?

Somebody was pushing Fogarty, and Vince Kirby had a shrewd idea it was the Mick's mouse, the one with the smoldering anthracite hair, the handful of breastworks that curved out front and the little pratt that curved just enough in back. Yeah, and that beautiful snoot and the big eyes, and the way she could make her eyes and mouth look hot for you, only you, or if the time wasn't right for that, her next best look was the I'm-a-poor-helpless-girl-and-I-need-a-big-strong-man-like-you-only-you.

She'd already tried her entire repertoire on Vince, but he was on his agonizing three or four a week sex schedule then, and the chicks he had, they didn't keep after him for one thing or another.

Binnie Riordan sometimes ran the Mick ragged, and it showed. She wasn't just another greedy dame; she wanted something big and wanted it bad. She was after Vince Kirby, the Rovers' Number One, to start with.

Thanks, sweetheart, but I ain't shopping....

Vince said, in quick explanation of his little talks with Ricki Fernandez and Patsy Sean:

"The Dusters're nothing but a pack of tough monkeys that don't know what to do about it and—this'll give you a charge—even Joey the Lover that breaks in the fresh meat for the Debs, is twict as tough as Patsy Sean, the Dusters' war lover. The guy to ootz outta here and in with us is that fairy-looking spik at the table near the door. Sean tried to scare me with a hunnert and fifty percent build-up of the guy, but that Ricki Fernandez is one tough greaser. And get that dumb grin off your snoot, Fogarty. When a greaser's tough, he's *tough!*"

Fogarty's grin drew in narrowly. "I can take the toughest greaser that comes."

"Sure, your way," Vince dismissed it casually, "but could you take him *his* way? He's a specialist. Nobody can take him his way, me included. I want that spik in the Rovers. Where's Joey Groff? I want to talk to him."

Somebody drawled, "Outside—up to what ain't possible."

"What?"

"He took a mouse out in the bushes, but nobody'll never send her no Mother's Day card."

"Brother," breathed Vince, grinning. "Now look, you guys, have yourself a ball tonight, we'll close the joint if you want, and anybody short on moo for liquor or anything, all he has to do is ask. The party's on me, tonight. Any questions?"

The usual comedian sang out, "I need a G-note the worst way, Vince. How's about it?"

Unsmiling, Vince said, "Oke," took out his wallet and offered ten hundred-dollar bills.

The slightly pudgy boy of seventeen shook his head, looked as if he wished he'd kept his big mouth shut, and leaned way from the proffered bills, giving the impression that he'd taken three long steps backward. "Oney kidding, Vince, oney kidding," he muttered. "I got lotsa scratch, honiss."

"You're sure?"

"Sure, I'm sure. Look." He hurriedly brought out his own wallet and showed a finger-thick sheaf of bills. "See. Just kidding. I dinn mean nuttin', Vince."

"He means," grinned Fogarty, "he's scared you'd bust him in the puss if you found out he was carrying that Michigan roll."

"There's no strings attached when I say a party's on me, Mick. Get it?"

"That's talking, man. Take us all to a whorehouse."

"I said, the party's on me, Mick, no strings attached. Want me to get the Brain to explain it to you?"

Fogarty flushed at being called, although knowing he'd clowned it over the line, as though anybody who took up Vince's offer was sticking his neck out. He'd pulled a boo-boo and didn't like the disadvantage.

"Anybody that don't take your word needs his puss smacked, Vince," he said, holding his grin. "I mean it, man."

And he really did mean it, Vince thought. It was just that Mick Fogarty would foul up anything, even his grandmother's funeral, for the sake of a wisecrack, if he was in a clowning mood. The Mick was a lightweight, but basically okay—if that bitch Binnie Riordan didn't have her hooks in him. Now Vince couldn't trust him, and if it got worse, he personally would have to cut Fogarty back to his hat size.

"Sure, Mick," he said. "How're you fixed?"

"Who needs scratch in this penny-ante joint?"

"You do, for one. It's cash on the line for beer or sauce in the alley downstairs, and a growing boy like you gets thirsty."

"Now don't get sore, Vince, for crisake. I was just giving you the jazz. I got a couple bucks."

"What you guys been drinking anyways? Giggle-water. Everybody's full of wisecracks. Let's see your couple bucks, Mick. I wanna see 'm."

"I was to promote fat-boy there for a sawbuck. That okay?"

"After I said the party's on me? No, it ain't okay. When I said all you hadda do was ask, why dinn you ask?"

"Aaah hell, Vince, why the production? You want I should ask for a lousy sawbuck right out in front of the guys? Hell."

"Nobody said you hadda ask in front of nobody, Mick. I'll be here as long as you guys, and is it so tough to whisper in my ear you need a sawbuck? Are you mixed up or is it me?"

Now Vince Kirby was leaning hard. From here on in, he wanted no more of Fogarty's sniping. If the Mick had an idea he could take him, okay; they'd go back to the club and have it out. He hadda be sure the guys saw him make the Mick put up or shut up, or be a half-ass war leader like the Dusters' Patsy Sean.

"Am I mixed up, Mick?" he asked softly. "If it's me, tell me where I went off the beam. I'm open to suggestion. *Any* suggestion." He emphasized, so there'd be no mistake.

The Mick all but ground his teeth. He wasn't scared of Vince Kirby. He wasn't scared of anybody, and that was the real truth. He wasn't. But with Vince, it wasn't a fight. It was a nightmare. You hit the son of a bitch with everything you had, you chopped him up like hamburger, you had even his fingernails bleeding, the bastard should be out cold till Christmas, then—*blam!* You woke up a week afterwards in Hackensack with the docs still trying to figure out which part went where on what was left of you, like a jigsaw. It wasn't fighting, the way Vince did it. Fighting was the pure joy of the fierce blood singing in your head, win, lose or draw. There was no joy in a go with Vince.

"Hell, nobody's mixed up, Vince," he said with that muddy melancholy of the Irish. "It's just I don't like YMCA's and their lousy tambourines, or's that the Salvation Army? Sure, I can use a sawbuck, man, and thanks for the party."

Vince gave him a twenty and said, "The other sawbuck is to tip the towel boy. Anybody else? Okay, but if you run short, just mention it to the Mick if you're bashful and he'll relay it to me and mention no names. Here's another thirty, Mick. If these millionaires're so loaded, you can give me back the change tomorrow. Now have a ball. I gotta ask the Brain how to spell pussy—with an 'ey' or just a 'y.'"

He left, a little confused, and went outside to smoke a cigarette in the unstale night air. Here he'd had the Mick all figured out, then Fogarty had to go and wind up being a right guy.

When Vince left, Patsy Sean hurried across the room to Ricki Fernandez. "I hope the hell you know who you sicked on me, Spanish," he said peevishly.

Ricki canted his lean, light ivory face. "You mean that slap-happy pug? That what you're sore about?"

"Slap-happy pug, huh? Man, you can sure pick 'm. That slap-happy pug is Vince Kirby and them twenny other slap-happy pugs with him is all Red Rovers and that big bird with the grin is Mick Fogarty, who just about ruined the Lions by himself in that last rumble."

Ricki whistled. "*Chinga!* What's Red Rovers doing all the way up here, Patsy?"

"We sent them an invite to the dance, dinn we?"

"How many invites we send them before this, hey, Patsy? Fifty, I betcha. So now they come, all in a sudden. Why, hey? *Porque?*"

"Christ only knows," Patsy worried. "It ain't to dance, and that's for sure. Their Debs're in the john smoking pot or shooting craps, and the Seniors keep standing around like that, all together. Gah *damn!* How many guys we got, Spanish? Just in case."

"Everybody. All of them. Thirty-one Seniors, ten Juniors, forty-one Debs. Altogether, eighty-two. Twice them."

"I wisht it was a hundred and two twict them, dammit."

"Hey, Patsy."

"What?"

"You worry you'self too damn much, hey? They ain't here for no fighting or bust-up. They got on their best suits, very expensive like the shirts and ties, and shoes all shined, too. You shine your shoes when you go mess up somebody's dance, hey, Patsy?"

"They ain't made no trouble, but the dance ain't over yet."

"Hokay. They take out Debs from the guys yet? They take *any* Deb an' give her a bad time?"

"Hell, they hardly moved from that spot since they got here."

"No trouble, Patsy, no trouble. They come to look us over, is all. Five'll get you ten."

Patsy digested this slowly. He did not like being looked over by the notorious Red Rovers, but he had to admit they hadn't busted any heads or cherries or anything—yeah, and actually were ladies and gentlemen compared to some of their own membership, like Vi and Dave, who had just been found all undressed and fast asleep together on the floor at the end of the locker room. Lucky it was a Duster that found them. The bastard had probly slipped it to Vi himself while she was out like a light. Yeah, him and all his stink friends, too. It wouldn't of been the first time they had a ball with a passed out mouse—and charging an extra buck if you wanted to watch the others, in the bargain.... But Spanish was right: the Rovers weren't here to make trouble. All Vince Kirby wanted to do was look the Dusters over, the way the membership had been going up.

"No bet, Spanish," he said. He thought of Vince Kirby's solid menace and the wild man threat of big Mick Fogarty and the closed faces of the rest of the Rovers. Patsy wasn't a Brain by any means, but very often he had ideas about things. "Y'know, Spanish, I'm glad we ain't that tough. It's a responsibility. They take us in a rumble, the guys all say, them lousy Rovers, always picking a soft touch. We take them, the guys all say, them lousy Rovers, all they ever had was a fake rep. They can't win no more."

"They figure a way round, you watch. Why you theenk they come and look us over, hey? Maybe they take this territory an' squeeze the Jacks in between."

Patsy would have laughed, if he felt like laughing. "The river bend cuts us off, and oney one bridge. They'd get slaughtered trying to cross that bridge. Y'know, it just come to me. I know what they're looking for now—our best guys. Would *you* nix an offer, Spanish?"

Ricki shrugged. "Big club, big trouble. You know."

That was too subtle for Patsy and he took it that Ricki would nix an offer. "I'm glad to hear you say that, Spanish, 'cause be a son of a bitch if I don't beat the brains outta any crud that even thinks about going to the Rovers. They're not going to leave us here with nothing but some puking Juniors and Debs."

Ricki's dark hot-chocolate eyes shadowed to black. He felt depressed. Patsy was getting too old for the Dusters. He was twenty. Ricki was sixteen and always ready for any kind of fight. When you got too old for it, like Patsy, you started looking over your shoulder before you went into anything. He wondered if they'd tap him for the Rovers. Compared to the Dusters, even a chicken punk in the Rovers was a big shot.

Vince Kirby was lounging against the building, smoking in the sidewalk shadows, when he heard the click of a girl's heels come from the entrance, and he leaned forward to see who it was. It was the Mick's little mouse, Binnie Riordan, rubbing her eyes. She started at his movement, and stepped back quickly, defensively, her hand darting into her purse. She was probably carrying the Mick's piece; most Debs carried their guy's piece, shiv, or sap. A cop'd fan a guy, but the Debs hadda be searched by a matron. Vince leaned back against the building and continued smoking without saying anything.

"Who's that?" she demanded sharply. "That you, Joey?"

"Joey's out in the bushes," Vince laughed softly. "You'll have to stand in line, girlie. There's no stopping Joey when he gets going."

"Oh, it's you, Vince." She made a big show of taking a relieved breath. "You scared me. I never feel right outside the territory. Some Debs don't give a damn what they do, but I guess I ain't built that way. Lend me a cigarette, will you, Vince? I'm out." She walked toward him, half-smiling, very feminine.

And Vince knew it had all been the malarkey—her start, her quick back step, her scare, her relief. She was good, he had to admit it. He might have fallen for that poor-little-helpless-girl line if he didn't know for sure that she'd deliberately come looking for him. This wouldn't be the first time. One way and another, she kept turning up by accident when she could ambush him alone. Debs were always making a play for him because it'd make them big shots. Hell, they tried to plop it in his lap every chance they got. But this one was smart. She went just so far, then stood back and let you work yourself up to it. Except for one thing, she was just what he wanted. She was the kind of bitch that'd smooch up a guy, then make him a nutsy Fagin when another guy came along that'd do her more good. That he wouldn't take from no mouse.

"What'd you want Joey for?" he asked, as though he believed her.

"He's the Brain and I wanted to ask him a question, but you got it all over him, Vince, and do you mind if I ask you? I'd rather ask you. You're more, well, more a man."

"And that's a fact." He pretended to go along with it. "On the other hand, I gotta be. What's the big question, baby?"

"I don't know how to come right out with it, Vince. I don't want to give you wrong ideas. But you're smart enough to know the difference.

It's, well, it's Mick. I don't know what to do."

He was instantly more intent. "Do about what, Binnie?"

"I hate to bitch to you, Vince, honiss. It's personal stuff. You wouldn't be interested."

"I'm interested," he said. She was about to give Mick the knife and she'd do it so slick, you'd hardly see her slip it in.

"It's just about me and him, Vince, that's all. Nothing with the club. I can't put up with it much more. I'm tired. He wears a girl down, and I don't mean what you think. It's the way he does and I'm tired in my bones. Maybe sick and tired of being stuck in a dead-end."

"You don't want to talk to me or the Brain, Binnie. Write a letter to the broad that runs the love advice stuff in the *News*."

"Don't give me the brush-off, Vince, please. That's what I get from Mick, the brush-off. He brings me to a dance. I like to dance and he dances good when he's in the mood, and the mood is crise knows when. So here we are again, a dance, and he ain't in the mood again. He's in the mood to get stoned, and there they are, him and his schmos, back in a little room they busted open, playing poker and slopping the sauce like crazy. Gah damn it!" she blurted. "I try to talk to him for a second and what's he do? Sends me down the alley for a half dozen pints. I bring them back and he kisses me in mid-air, not quite making it, and says we'll have a dance a little later. That's what I'm for—going his errands, carrying his piece, and being around, just in case. I'm a mope."

"There's other guys to dance with. Go dance with them."

"Oh yeah? Come inside and watch them break their necks to not dance with me. Mick don't like guys dancing with his mouse. He busts them in the snoot. You know something? When they want a dance, they ask Mick first. From now on if they ask Mick, they can go right ahead and dance with him. Oh crise, now I spose you'll tell Mick what I said and I'll wind up with one of his smacks."

"He won't hear it from me, baby. What's with him and you's your business."

She hadn't moved closer. She was still standing on the same spot two feet away. But she seemed a hell of a lot closer. The smell of her insinuating perfume filled his head, and she was a beautiful little mouse, and passionate as hell, he knew, because he could feel the pull of it hardening his loins, and crise how he needed it. He needed it all the time, but had to cut down, just had to, and not go back the way he used to be, day and night, and no good for nothing else, and just about dead Mondays.

"You're having a bad time, baby," he said thickly. "We'll ask the Brain. He knows answers to answers. He's in there."

"But I—" and then she saw that he'd pointed his thumb at the little walk-around next to the "Y" building. It was thickly grown with broadleafed rhododendron, and wide branches canopied the ground. "Yeah," she said, "yeah. Let's get it settled."

There were several paths winding among the rhododendron. Here in the darkness, she felt the urgent violence in him, and when he drew her down under one of the huge bushes, she had her skirts up over her hips so that he would not tear the sheer orlon.

He was in an almost mindless rage of voracious lust. He had suppressed his sexual drive so ruthlessly that his continence was an agony, and when he allowed himself relief, it came in shattering violence and was another kind of agony in itself. After their first experience with him, some of the Debs were deathly afraid of a second, but Binnie, dainty though she seemed, answered his urgency with a wanton gluttony that actually fed on his violence. They were both momentarily exhausted after the smashing climax, but Vince Kirby knew that he could go on and on, now that he had let himself become aroused. He looked down and saw the light ivory gleam of her legs, open and relaxed, wanton, quiescent, but there was still a faint undulant rhythm in her hips. He'd heard there were chicks like that who never really stopped until the very end, but he hadn't believed it until now.

Abruptly he rolled to his knees, jumped up, bulled through the branches and strode toward the "Y" building. He wanted desperately to keep going and it would have taken no more than a touch, but the timing couldn't be wronger. He wanted nothing more to do with that little bitch. He admitted to himself that she was the best, the absolute best he'd ever had. But still he wanted no part of her. It was a feeling. His ambition to be somebody trampled everything else.

Ricki Fernandez was wary. He'd just put the boots to the Dusters. He ostensibly patted the back of his neck, but was actually reassuring himself that the something extra was still there. The long, tempered fighting knife lay in a flat sheath under his jacket between his shoulder blades, from where he could whip it out fast even when crowded. There was an almost hundred percent chance he'd have to use it.

He'd gone to the john, then out on the fire escape for a breath of fresh air, and a little shrimpy guy with glasses came out and started up the usual kind of vague conversation, like guys do when they happen to meet alone for a couple minutes between dances. Ricki was shrewd and he knew practically right away that this was no ordinary shrimpy mutt, but one of the top Rovers. His name, he said, was Joey Groff, and after a few seconds of ransacking his head, he remembered that Joey

Groff was the one the Rovers called the Brain. Ricki was instantly on his guard and his hand automatically started rubbing the back of his neck. But it turned out he didn't need the knife. Groff didn't beat the bushes. He talked plain and fast. He wanted Ricki for the Rovers.

"So, how a-buh-bout it, Fernandez? Get out of this chicken punk outfit. Buh-buh-but you ain't no chicken puh-punk, Fernandez." Groff was a stutterer.

Ricki had lost his edge for the Dusters from the minute Patsy Sean went chicken a short while back. A war leader was supposed to be able to take on anybody in a club, and Patsy could. So what did that make the rest of the Dusters? If you couldn't depend on your club, you were up the alley.

"But since when the Rovers started asking guys?" he put it to Groff. "That don' sound so good."

"Since always. How do you think we guh-guh-got to be Rovers?"

"All the time?"

"This outfit's strictly fricassee, but we heard you had a few good ones. Like you, frinstance."

"And Patsy Sean?"

"He worries too much."

Ricki knew it was the truth, but his shrug was noncommittal. It didn't matter.

"Hokay," Ricki shrugged again. "But I don' tell you nothing about the Dusters. You fine out by yourself."

"Why take the trouble? You live over Brookline, doncha? You better figure on staying down-Butt. You'll get japped outside the territory."

"I don't get japped now."

"You're a Duster, not a Rover," Groff pointed out.

Ricki nodded. Yes, it did make a difference. Who gave a damn about a Duster? "When you want me down there?"

"You better come tonight. You can sleep in the clubhouse."

"No, I got stuff to get home, udder things. Tomorrow's Sunday. I come Monday."

"Then keep your trap shut with Patsy Sean or you'll get a bad time."

"Yeah? Then how come you say he's chicken?"

"There's all kinds-a chicken, Fernandez. Some'll do anything to show they ain't. You dig me?"

"I dig you, man. I don' tell nobody."

"The club's on the north end of Grove Street down the cellar of the old Tri-State Warehouse. The top floors got burned out. You go up the alley around the side. The door's painted red. I'll be there. Just walk in."

"And get my brains beat out?"

"If we were going to do that, chumbo, you'd get it at the line, not the club."

"You mus' have a lot of guys, hey?"

"Any guy you see, he's a Rover. Little kids, too. Just to give you an idea. Take the Number 49 express bus from Midtown terminal, and don't get off for nothing till Grove Street. Here—" he gave Ricki a card from his wallet, "—if the Happy Jacks crowd you going through their territory, show them this and they'll let you alone." Groff laughed softly. "We don't want no guys the Jacks send back with his brains in his lap on account of he broke the rules. You can't go round breaking rules, Fernandez. It makes a bad impression. You better get back outside. I'll drift in another door. But one more thing, chumbo, it's against the rules if you don't show on Monday, but that don't worry me. It's Patsy Sean. Watch him." He nodded once, then went down the fire escape with barely a sound. Groff was the kind who made a point of never making a noise.

Alone, Ricki examined the card Groff had given him. It stated that Ramon Pilar was an Ordinary Seaman and a member in good standing of the Seamans' Union, Local 108. Groff was right. If the Jacks bothered a seaman, the big steamship companies at the end of the Butt would raise holy hell. Not to the city, maybe not even to the state, but down Washington, and that meant FBI.

He lit a cigarette and strolled indolently back to his table near the door outside. He was surprised to find Patsy hunched on the edge of the table, waiting for him.

"What the hell took you so long?" he demanded suspiciously. "You're s'posed to be here till I let you off."

"I got tired of sitting on my ass all night, that's what took so long," Ricki snarled, because he was in the wrong and knew it. "I went to the john, or do I hafta raise my hand like in school again? Crise, who lit your rag, hey?"

Patsy kept looking hard at Ricki, and Ricki scowled back, getting madder and madder, but Patsy made a pacifying gesture before it went too far.

"If you just tole me I'd-a put somebody else on the table," he grumbled. "I tole you this is the important spot, saying hello and watching who goes in. Them mopes taking tickets're too busy making change and taking care of the cloak room."

"So you're sore, hey?"

"Get off your high horse and listen for onct, will you, Spanish? While you were in the rest room, resting, ten Happy Jacks walk in with their

Debs, and over there is Mick Fogarty and some Rovers soused and getting worse, and over there is Vince Kirby and another mess of Rovers and Debs, and right by the bandstand is another pack of them, giving Mooch orders what they want him and the boys to play. I couldn't tell the Jacks to cop a sneak, but I took them aside and pointed out the Rovers. I'm telling you, Spanish, the way they scattered, you'd swear every goddamn Rover and his brother'd had twins. The Jacks took one look and went thataway. It could of been a mess."

Ricki whistled. "*Chinga!* Lucky you stop them in time."

"Damn lucky!" Then uneasily, "I hope they don't come back with the rest of the Jacks. If they do, Spanish, take my advice and go out the window fast."

Ricki had to admit it was good advice, not getting caught between the Jacks and the Rovers, but all the same he couldn't help remembering what Joey Groff had said about there being all kinds of chicken, and he looked it Patsy with veiled contempt.

"I hope nothing else worry you, Patsy," he said.

"The whole damn thing worries me. That dumb Jack Slater, that's s'posed to help take tickets, gets me alone back of the bandstand and says he hears the Rovers is taking new guys and is it okay if he joins up. So I have to bust him in the mouth. I don't like to do it, but crise, a thing like that, and anyways he's a blabbermouth and'll spread the word. I'm not letting no guys walk out on the Dusters if I can help it."

That Joey Groff was one smart feller, Ricki thought; he said Patsy was the bad kind of chicken and he was, and he had to be watched, too.

Patsy slanted him a narrow glance. "Anybody talk to you yet, Spanish?"

"Lotsa them. Mick Fogarty, he called me a lousy spik, but I let it go."

"You're a right guy, Spanish." Then he grimaced and the said a bit plaintively, "All I want to do is hold the Club together, Ricki. I live for the Club. And I ain't letting no mutts from down-Butt ruin it, if I have to mix with Vince Kirby himself. I'll take on Mick Fogarty too, if I have to."

In a burst of insight, Ricki saw why; this was Patsy's last chance to be a big shot. He was probably way over twenty, too old for the club. Outside, he could be one of di Lucca's small-time hoods, but what else? He didn't know nothing but street fighting, and he did as little of that as he could get away with, though he could fight like a son of a bitch.

Ricki felt depressed. Patsy really had him fooled tonight. And even at that, it took Joey Groff to give him the pitch. Yeah, and it had taken Groff less than an hour to size Patsy up. Well, it was time he was getting out of this chicken punk outfit. His brains were shrinking.

His hand slid mechanically to the back of his neck again to make sure the fighting knife was still in its flat sheath under his jacket. He was going to need it once Patsy found out he'd switched to the Rovers.

SIX

Ricki Fernandez thanked God for the early morning fog. He'd gone out to pick up a suitcase stashed with a girlfriend who lived in Lynwood, the first suburb west of the city. He never had to pick up a girl; they flocked around and in a little while got to be a pain in the neck, each wanting him to give up the other for her, writing him letters every day, phoning him day and night at Cuneo's Italian-American Grocery on the corner until—praise God!—good old Cuneo got mad and refused to take any more calls.

He practically had to fight his way out of this one's house after he got the suitcase. She kept weeping and wailing that he was going away and didn't want to see her again, and then, *por Dios!* if she didn't jerk up her dress and try to drag him down on the hall floor—and her mother and father reading the Sunday paper in the parlor with only the dining room in between! Some of his pals had been hooked like that, rolling around on the sofa or the floor or someplace and making so much noise that the whole damn family came trooping in to see what was going on. Then the women grabbed the girl and rushed her off in one direction, screaming and slapping her face, and the men shoved the guy against the wall and told him if it wasn't that the priest wouldn't marry nobody in a wheelchair, they would bust every bone in his body.

Not that the girl did it to get her and the guy caught that way by the family—most girls didn't like to be watched when they were doing it with a guy—but they all had the same idea of getting the guy to marry them, so it came to the same thing.

And here was this dumb chick the same as on the Radio City stage, dress up, pants off, doing her damnedest to get him down on the rug in the middle of a hall her uncles or cousins or brothers were trotting through with two-by-fours or saws or hammers or a mouthful of nails every two minutes.

Ricki wasn't about to get hooked by a chick, and he couldn't give it to her right there in the hall, and there just wasn't any place to give it to her in broad daylight. The scared-sweat poured out, drenching him, and at the very last second he snatched up enough sense to do the only thing that could get him out of this mess. He clipped her expertly on the jaw just hard enough to cool her. He caught her as she fell, hurriedly pushed down her dress, grabbed up her pants from the floor, and backed into the kitchen, pulling her after him by the armpits. He sat her at the porcelain-topped table, curved her left arm and arranged the side of her face in the bend of her elbow. He did not attempt to put the pants back on her, but went out the back door with his heavy suitcase, to avoid her mother and father. He didn't mind the two brothers. They talked the same language, and anyway, they were busy sawing lengths of two-by-fours.

"Leaving already, Rick?" asked one when he came out.

"Yeah. Got some things to do. Anyway, Tina fell asleep at the kitchen table while I was fixing the catch on my suitcase. Must of had a big night, hey?"

"Well, you know, Saturday night . . ."

"Yeah. Big night all over. Tell Tina I'll call her. We can go to a movie tomorrow night."

They laughed and shook their heads. "His girl fall asleep on him and he still comes back for more. That's love for you, worse than having no brains. Don't mind us, Rick. She's a good kid, and we'll tell her tomorrow night at the movies. I think maybe she likes you a little bit, too. See you tomorrow, kid. Take it easy."

Ricki went through the backyard to the street. This way was really closer to the bus stop. Now that it was over, he did not brood about it or heave any sighs of relief or remorse. He dismissed her from his mind and life. A girl like that, you couldn't depend on her. Ricki's relations with girls were simple, direct and casual. He didn't want any complicated chicks like that one. But crise, she was sure one beautiful mouse. You could get worked up just thinking about her. When you cupped your hand, well, her breasts were just about the same shape, though bigger, and they fit so nice....

This being Sunday, he had to hunt for Yutzy Mizzak that had the hockshop. He finally found him playing stuss in the back room of Feinberg's candy store. They went into another back room and Ricki opened the suitcase on the round card table. Nothing ever startled Yutzy in all his years of fencing stolen merchandise, but once in a while he did stare. This time he stared hard and even bent over to stare closer. There were twenty-eight brand new army issue .45 automatics in the suitcase. Ricki took one and slid it into his waistband under his shirt.

"I keep one," he said.

"Maybe you keep them all," said Yutzy. "That's army stuff. Too much of a risk."

"I seen army stuff down your place."

"That's different. Old. This is brand new."

"Never used maybe, but it ain't brand new. Two years I had it stashed away. The heat's off."

"The heat's never off on army stuff, sonny. It turns up, they ask questions."

"In that case, the heat's never off on nothing. It turns up, they ask questions. So don't give me that jazz, man."

"You're a smart boy, Spanish. I give you credit. But you don't know everything. Who does? I'll tell you what I'll do—"

Ricki closed the suitcase, snapped the end catches and fingered his keyring for the right key.

Yutzy was taken by surprise. "Hey, hey, wait a minute," he recovered his commercial poise. "What's the matter, Spanish? Did I insult you? I apologize. On my knees I apologize. We do business together a long time. We're old friends. So let's be old friends."

"You didn't insult me," said Ricki calmly. "But when anybody starts in with, 'I'll tell you what I'll do—' he ain't gonna do it for me. He wants you to think he's doing you a favor. I don't need any half-price favors like that."

"Who said half price? Who said any price?"

"Hokay then. How much? Each."

Yutzy hesitated. This was the trouble with old friends. They get to know too damn much. *Pfui* on them. *Pfui* on this one. He knew to the penny how much he'd make on the guns, and him a little snotnose only sixteen yet. Hmmmm, but brand new .45's. He could get a nice price for them in the right place. Tampa, Ybor City, the Cuban section. Guns sold very good there now. Nice price. A hundred, a hundred and a quarter. Smart boy Spanish, he didn't know that. He didn't know everything yet.

"All right," he threw up his hands, "you know the hockshop business so good, Mr. Spanish, you make the price. Twice as much. I know."

"Ten bucks apiece and another sawbuck for the suitcase. Two hundred and eighty bucks."

As a matter of habit, Yutzy made a despairing noise in his throat, but said, "Suppose I tell you what you fellers tell me when I make a price."

Ricki grinned. "Son of a bitch bastard."

"*Pfui*. With your tongue tied behind your back you do better. Or worse, I'll tell you what I'll do—and shut up this onct. This time you make the price and I pay and say nothing. Next time I make the price and you say nothing. Once, just once, do me the pleasure."

"Hokay. You take the pleasure, I'll take the moo," Ricki held out his hand. "And no more jazz. I got places to go."

Slowly, very slowly, Yutzy Mizzak counted out two hundred and eighty dollars into Ricki's *cafe au lait* palm. His profit would be tremendous on the deal, but he couldn't help it, he found it highly repulsive to part with money. *Pfui* on old friends.

Later, in his pawnshop, he unlocked the suitcase. He hadn't dared to open it in Feinberg's. He thought almost sensuously of the twenty-four-hundred dollar profit he would make when the guns were sold in Tampa. Twenty-four hundred minimum. Brand new army issue .45 automatics in perfect . . .

Wait. Two years, the Spanish had said. Two years. That would be the—oh, no, no!

He snatched up one of the guns and gave a shrill cry of acute financial anguish. A gun is a gun is a gun, but this wasn't a gun. It felt like a gun and looked like a gun but it was a cast iron dummy. He knew all about these guns. Everybody knew all about these guns. But two years is a long time. You forget.

But you have a mind and don't use it, you're a pastrami, a bagel. Or a cop. So he was a bagel. Not even a pastrami.

Two years ago these "guns" were stolen from the storeroom of a marching club that called itself the 76'ers. Very patriotic, very Fascist. They used the dummy guns for drills and in parades. Then they started using them to hit niggers and wops and jews and spiks and hunkies and people they didn't like on the head. They burned crosses in people's front yards. They called somebody a non-American, then tarred and feathered him. They rode a whore out of Lynwood on a rail (Yutzy happened to know she got two hundred bucks from the 76'ers to let them do it.)

But before the 76'ers were put in jail, somebody stole their "guns." The newspapers made a big laugh saying the joke was on the thief. And now who was the joke on? Yutzy Mizzak preferred not to name names.

He'd fix that snotty young Spanish. He'd get somebody to— Slowly a thin smile, as evil as a torturer' knife, slit his ancient face. Why should he throw good money after bad? The snotty young Spanish had taken a gun for himself. So he thought it was a real gun. That was very good, very nice. Just right. A .45 was not a toy. It was a gun you used when you needed it. So there would soon come the day when the Spanish would need the gun.

He, Yutzy Mizzak, did not have to do anything. He did not have to do anything at all, just sit back and watch the newspapers for the death of a hoodlum named Fernandez.

SEVEN

It had begun to drizzle. The fog was thinner near the crest of Lynwood Avenue, but looking back down the hill, Ricki saw it lying thick at the bottom like dirty cotton. He turned up his jacket collar, hunched his shoulders, thrust his hands deep into his pants pockets, and trudged toward the bus stop on the Avenue. He didn't like rain. He could lie on the tenement rooftop in the hottest midsummer sun and purr as it seeped into him, while everybody else was screaming with the heat and the newspapers ran weather stories on the front page.

But rain depressed him and did odd things to his volatile temperament. He hated rain. He heard the car minutes before it turned the corner behind him and there was something familiar about the sound of all that mechanical misery and after one swift encompassing glance, he stepped off the sidewalk and into the leafy concealment of a straggly forsythia bush. At length the car rattled around the corner, appeared to pause, then labored up the hill, steam hissing whitely from under the hood. Yes, it was the car of the *borracho* Chavez. Ricki's eyes were good, but he remembered best with his ears, and he knew the sound of that car. As usual, it was driven by Little Augie Chavez, thirteen, a Junior in the Dusters. His pinched, insufficient face turned jerkily from side to side, like the triangular head of a praying mantis, as he peered through the rain-blurred windshield up and down the sidewalks on both sides of the street. His dark eyes were huge, his jaws hung ajar, and he choked the steering wheel with long, starved hands. He looked both horrified and ravenously hungry. Ricki made sure there was no one else in the car, then put two fingers to his mouth and whistled piercingly. Little Augie looked wildly around, and the car bucked and quivered gradually to a stop, fairly near the curb. It had no brakes. The only way to stop it was to thrust it into low gear and turn off the ignition. It started to roll slowly backward, moving like a man with hiccups. Little Augie jumped out and hastily shoved a length of four-by-four under each rear wheel. That was the brake he used when parking.

Then, at last, he was free to stand up and look around for Ricki. He was, at thirteen, six feet tall and so skinny that he seemed barely six inches wide, yet in a way his diet was perfectly balanced. Seven days a week he devoured bowl after bowl of *chili y frijoles* and never gained an ounce. The other nine Chavezes were fat, sweaty, and surly; Little Angie was usually as happy as a lit box of matches, but not today.

Ricki stepped out from behind the forsythia bush and beckoned. Little Augie came loping across the street like six feet of scaffolding. After all this urgency, all he did was stand and gape at Ricki, horrified.

"I know," said Ricki, "Patsy and the wrecking squad're looking for me. I expected it, but not so soon. How many others are they after? How many'd they get?"

"They caught six, Ricki," Little Augie mumbled. "That's everybody except you and Wally Boyd that went down-Butt with the Rovers last night."

They both spoke Spanish which was easier on the ear than their bastardized English.

"What was done to the six caught ones?" Ricki asked.

"They were thrown on the ground and hit with steel springs, the long ones for screen doors. It is very painful."

"I know. The springs open when swung, and pinch little pieces out of your back when they spring closed. Each time a little more as the skin breaks. They won't do that to me, *amigo*."

"No," Little Augie whispered.

Ricki's head lifted sharply. "No what, *zonzo?*" he demanded arrogantly. "Whipping with screen door springs is too dignified for me, perhaps? Something more degrading is needed. What do they plan? To beat me with yo-yos?"

"I don' know, Ricki," Little Augie's eyes were tragic. "Patsy says you are to be the example. As war leader-to-be of the Dusters, you most treacherously betrayed the Club. You must be made an example. All I know of what they plan is that you are to be taken to the clubhouse and the full membership will be present. The Seniors will sit in the center, the Debs to the right and Juniors to the left. That is all I know, Ricki, but it will be very bad. Whenever your name is mentioned, Patsy is a crazy man. My grandfather says, a once-friend is more to be feared than an always-enemy. I did not know what he meant until I saw how bad Patsy is today. He is demented."

"How did you know where to find me, Little Augie?"

"You were almost taken when you left your house this morning, but there was a police car at the corner with a flat tire being changed. You took a bus and they made me follow with them in the car, of which the engine sickness is unfortunate, but today became much much worse and was to be pitied. It is the coming of rain, I think, so badly it coughed. But even with the sickness of the car, it is very difficult to allow a bus to escape. They cannot have engines, so slow they are. Under the hood must be old grandfathers on bicycles. But my car is not well today. I do what I can but it bounds over the sidewalk and strikes into a tree with an angry noise. It is said that the dear Lord gives his benediction to children and fools, and so it is with my fool of a car, and the tree does not halt its onward progress."

Little Augie's Spanish was more formal and elaborate than Ricki's. The grandfather he quoted had been full professor in an anonymous university before he took to drink and married a prostitute who befriended him. The prostitute became the most relentless example of female deportment and morality in the entire neighborhood, and until her death there was no more upright and virtuous a family than the Chavezes. They were pointed out as good examples to growing children, and were thoroughly loathed.

Somehow, between alcoholic excursions, the grandfather managed to teach Little Augie a sort of Castilian Spanish. The grandfather had but two topics of conversation: one was the ingenious variety of sexual practices in both the ancient and modern worlds. He would explain in minute detail why the palm went to the Ancients, the Isles of Greece in particular, which had a fantastic repertoire, for they worshipped each God individually, and the Gods were nothing if not fancy their pleasures, Aphrodite and Hermes and infinite combinations and explorations being very popular. The grandfather was scornful of modern habits which, he claimed, aspired to nothing more noble than cohabiting in a barrel of hot tar in a windowless basement.

His other topic was more sinister: the artistic appreciation of torture as developed by the most fertile Torquemada during the Golden Age of the Inquisition. Fortunately he was drunk most of the time and no one could understand a word he said. When not with his grandfather, Little Augie used to hide in a broken and unused china cabinet. He was ten when his grandfather and grandmother died within weeks of each other, and he came out of his china cabinet and went out in the street and played with other kids as if he'd been doing it all his life. Or almost. He still did odd things, but not too odd. People blamed it on his grandfather, and as an afterthought, also on his grandmother, the ex-prostitute.

Ricki listened, narrow-eyed, as Little Augie continued. Patsy drove the car after Little Augie ran into to the tree. They almost caught Ricki as he got off the bus to go to Tina's house for his suitcase, but Patsy did not know the car had no brakes. Because of that and the traffic, they had to make a cautious circuit of the block, and by that time Ricki was walking into Tina's house. Neither Patsy nor the two huskies of the wrecking squad wanted any more to do with an ailing car without brakes. They called it Sure Death and snarled at Little Augie to go take a ride on the speedway for himself. They then settled themselves at three different points across the street from Tina's house and waited for Ricki to come out.

If Tina had not been ablaze with desire in her attempt to seduce Ricki in the hall, he would have walked unsuspectingly out the front door of the house and would certainly have been picked up by Patsy and the two wreckers around the corner. But he left by the back door and was almost picked up and warned by Little Augie, except that the car would not operate in any gear but reverse and he went rattling away from Ricki at thirty miles an hour, desperately fighting the wheel for control before he dared turn off the ignition to brake the car. He unscrambled the gears by hitting the stick shift with a wrench. He was on hand when Ricki rang the bell at Yutzy Mizzak's hockshop, but Little Augie was on the wrong side of the street and the traffic was heavy. So he didn't catch up with Ricki until he left Feinberg's candy store after doing business with Yutzy.

"That's all, Ricki," said Little Augie wanly. "But don't go home. That's where Patsy and the others'll be waiting."

"How come you were with Patsy looking for me?"

"I had the car."

"There are other cars, and better ones, in the Club."

"It is just that I was there, I think."

"You were there on purpose, *I* think," said Ricki. "You were there because you told Patsy I joined up with the Rovers. You did, didn't you?"

Little Augie did not attempt to deny it. "Yes, I told him," he said in a dull voice. "I was in the john when you talked to Joey Groff on the fire escape. I just happened to open the window and hear the part about you going down with the Rovers. But I didn't squeal to Patsy, Ricki, honest. I didn't even mention it till this morning down at the club. I thought it was a big thing for the Rovers to ask you to join them. You know, like a promotion. I didn't know Patsy would be mad. He was your friend. I thought he would like it that you were going to a big, important club. And how much it would help the Dusters, I said, to have friends in the Rovers. Never did I think he would go crazy, Ricki, never!"

Ricki believed him, but all the same, the kid should have known. He'd been a Junior in the Dusters for two years. His sense was cockeyed. He read books and things. But then, his whole damn family was nuts, and you couldn't blame the kid for that. The hell with it. The thing for him now was, back to the flat for the rest of his junk instead of fencing it, and get down-Butt tonight. He couldn't fight the whole goddamn Dusters. If it was a chicken punk outfit, it was because Patsy Sean made them that way to keep himself the big shot. That's why he went around with those half dozen muscleheads the guys called the Wreckers. That's the way a guy acted when he was chicken and scared it might show. He'd cripple Ricki for life, that's what he'd do. Like he busted up Teddy Moon's feet with a ball-peen hammer because Teddy fell for a Deb from the Apaches and was shacking up with her. Ricki shook his head. Nuts to being a hero. He'd run for it tonight.

He looked up. Little Augie was standing three feet back, staring, his slack lower jaw agape like an unzipped fly.

"Man," said Little Augie, goggle-eyed, "that's a *gun!*"

"It is much gun," said Ricki, who knew it was a dummy. "It goes in, a little hole only a half inch round, but comes out a foot wide. It takes everything with it. This is a .45, man. It is the *most* piece you can get."

"Comes out this wide for true?" Little Augie held his skinny hands twelve inches apart.

"Sometimes wider, all the way."

"*Ay de mi!* But the fella you shoot, he always die, no?"

"He stops living in one piece, for true."

"*Madre de Dios! Es muy pistola!* But how does one acquire this *grande armamento?* I must have one."

"You're too young, *cabrito*, and don't get any ideas." A lift of his shoulder released a fighting knife from a clip sheath up his right sleeve, and the blade slid ready into his hand.

Little Augie paid no attention to the knife. He had eyes only for the big, ostentatious gun. "I do not want your *pistola*, Ricki. For you, it is a necessity. But to me, most beautiful. I am consumed with desire for such a *pistola*. My uncle will buy it for me. He is a *borracho* but *muy rico*."

"You really get some jazzy ideas, don't you, baby?"

Little Augie looked sad and misunderstood. "All the time I do many things for my uncle. But for me, he has only *maldiciones*. Now I wish a token of regard, a .45 *pistola*—and he will obtain it for me!" He finished intensely.

Ricki was bored with this pointless conversation, furthermore he had things to do at the flat. Thank God the family was away, visiting with the West 116th Street Fernandezes in New York City. There would be no questions about all the wristwatches, gold cigarette lighters and other such trinkets that Ricki was so adept at acquiring.

"I must go now," he said abruptly. "*Hasta la vista.*"

"You do not wish me to drive you in the car," asked Little Augie, but without hope.

"*Gracias*, but there will be Wreckers waiting around my house and I must go quietly."

"*Si*, the car is an abomination of noise, but after I obtain the gun, I will also obtain a silent car. I will obtain many things after the gun."

You're not going to live long, thought Ricki, I can see that. Aloud he said, "I must go. *Hasta luego.*"

"*Hasta luego*," said Little Augie gravely. "Take care, Ricki. Again I apologize for my stupid talk to Patsy. I beg of you, think of me as merely ignorant, not vicious. *Va con Dios.*"

The Fernandez flat was in the middle of the block but Ricki had no trouble. He went through a basement window of the tenement at the end of the block, up the stairs to the roof, across the roofs, and then to be on the safe side, in case Patsy had a stakeout in the hall, he climbed precariously down the air shaft between the neighboring tenements, and slid into the Fernandez flat through the kitchen window, which had a broken lock.

It took him about an hour to gather his loot from the various caches in the walls, floors and ceilings. There were patched and unpatched holes in every room. He wrapped the jewelry carefully in toilet paper so that it would not become scratched and lose value in moving, packed it into an intricately lined and pocketed aluminum suitcase he had made for himself, concealed everything with another quilted lining, and then packed over this his best orlon suit, shirts, ties, socks, underwear, shoes in brown paper bags and the few other odds and ends that belonged to him. These included two additional fighting knives made of metal saw blades, and a genuine pearl-handled .32 revolver, which had once belonged to his grandfather, the one that owned a little cigar factory in Tampa. Ricki had taken it from the office desk as a remembrance in parting. He carefully locked the case and stood it on the floor beside the hall door, ready to go.

Several times during these operations he went to the three windows in the parlor, flattened against the wall and looked down into the street through the narrow gap between the plastic curtains and window frame. It took a little time to spot the watchers, but there they were: a heavy-fisted Wrecker in a truck parked at the corner and the eyes, forehead and hat of another crouched on the sunken steps to a basement flat, peering at him from sidewalk level.

In the opposite direction, down the street, he spied two more Wreckers in the Waldorf Lunchroom, sitting at the end of the counter drinking one cup of coffee after another. That accounted for four of the seven. Two would be up on the Avenue, watching the busses, and that left one, who'd be Patsy Sean himself, for Patsy wouldn't take any of the sludge stakeouts. His best fighting knife lightly balanced in his right hand, his thumb flat to the blade for mobility of wrist, he prowled out into the hallways of the apartment, looking for Patsy. He should have known better. Hanging around halls was another hard-work spot, and maybe a little more dangerous, too, and that wouldn't be for Patsy. He wasn't *that* kind of chicken. The kind of chicken he was, he had to feel important forty-eight hours a day. Patsy would be Directing Operations.

Wait a minute . . . there was a guy, used to be pug, and what you'd call an ex-friend, because Patsy always gave him the brush-off and finally kicked him out of the clubhouse because he came around too much and wasn't a Duster. His name was Mike Maloney and he was around thirty years old. Maloney lived on this street somewhere, and if Patsy was Directing Operations, he'd make someplace Headquarters, and Ricki had a good idea that ex-pal Maloney would be re-palled for the emergency. Among his loot was a pair of Zeiss binoculars he'd lifted during a stroll through Hallowell's Department Store. It didn't take long, window after window, to pinpoint Patsy drinking beer with Maloney and apparently cutting up old scores in Maloney's front room, diagonally across the street. Satisfied, Ricki put the binoculars back into his aluminum suitcase.

He'd gotten into the tenement without being spotted, and could probably get out, but it was better to wait till dark and get away clean and easy. This was no time to fumble. He wasn't excited or scared, just wary. Anyways, it'd be dark in only three hours or so, so what the hell. And he was a little sleepy. He stripped—he had to sleep raw with nothing to catch or bind him—and stretched out on the studio couch in the living room alcove. He went to sleep immediately, untroubled as a child, knowing that the family wouldn't be home till eleven, twelve o'clock and the old man wouldn't come busting in yelling his lousy head off because Ricki was sleeping on the studio couch—Mama's and his bed at night.

There was no transition when he awakened. He was instantly awake and alert and his hand darted down for the haft of his knife between the mattress and spring.

Somebody was in the flat! He glided sinuously out of bed, crossed the room to the wall between the kitchen and the bedroom and tilted his head, listening, his knife instinctively held in the fighting position. Floorboards creaked in the bedroom, but not the heavy creak of a man tiptoeing. You could tell the difference. Too, he heard a kind of soft swish-swish-swish like a girl's clothes being taken off or put on. His ears could remember and identify to an extraordinary degree; he could use them almost like eyes. He listened for a few more seconds and relaxed with a grin. Hell, it was only Sugar putting on her nun's costume. She wasn't with the family because she went to church, on and off, all day Sunday. She was in everything they'd let her in, including the choir.

Dumb little kid. A lot of them went through a religious kick when they were seven or eight or so, especially girls. Little kids could be an awful pain in the ass, and you could special the little girls again on that one, too. So damn prissy. And they were always listening in on you so they could screech, "Oooooh, what you juss said! A curse word. That's against the Church. I'm gonna tell Father Mahon on you!"

He ambled back to the studio couch, yawning. He stretched out, punched up the pillow a couple times, turned on his side, facing the wall, and let himself melt into light sleep. Crise, he sure needed to put in some solid sack time. He felt bushed . . . except, goddamn it, when he remembered Tina pulling up her dress and the sudden pearlescent gleam of her exciting thighs in the dim light of the hallway, and the long surging smoothness of her after she kicked her panties to one side and reached for him.

He heard Sugar come into the parlor and start walking up and down, probably looking at herself in the tall, cracked mirror over the bureau there wasn't room for in the bedroom. He swore to himself. There went his nap, but what the hell, he didn't have the heart to chase the poor little kid. Little kids didn't have much fun, living in flats, all jammed together and everybody yelling at them. No wonder they went on a religion kick for a while. Maybe he oughta be nice to her and say hello or something. There was a chance he might not see her again after today. He rolled over and propped himself up on one elbow, expecting to see a skinny little kid eight, nine years old. All he could do was lay there and gawk like a mope, not even able to think or nothing.

He finally said, "Sugar?"

She whirled around as if she'd been waiting for him to speak. Then she giggled and turned her head and put her hands to her face, but peeked at him from the ends of her eyes. "I can't look, Ricki. You ain't got no clothes on and girls don't look at boys without clothes, an I'm gonna be a nun."

He grinned and said, "Sure, Sugar," and pulled the end of the slip cover across his lap. Couldn't look, but there she was peeking like crazy. She'd come in while he was asleep earlier, and he bet she done her share of peeking then, too. And just like a chick, making believe she wasn't getting an eyeful.

A chick? She wasn't no chick yet. She couldn't be She was his little kid sister Sugar. She was s'posed to be eight, nine years old, and a skinny little pain in the neck, all knees and elbows.

But, *por Dios!* she wasn't no skinny little kid no more. She was a full-growed chick and man, he meant full-growed! Lookit her legs. *Jesu Cristo!* A mouse with legs like that and showed them like that, real beautiful type legs, she was asking for trouble. And goddamn, the boobies! He knew chicks that'd damn near do anything for a pair like that, full and round, but standing right up. *Madre de Dios*, where'd she get them from all of a sudden? Yesterday she was eight years old, today she's got a pair of boobies like this.

He kept staring at her and staring at her, but couldn't convince himself that this was really his little kid sister Sugar. It was a little over four years since he started running with the clubs and not coming home, and even when he was home, just enough to sleep, the only one he really seen was Mama. He wouldn't of come home at all if it wasn't for Mama, and he always slipped her a fin or a sawbuck or more if it'd been a good week, 'cause the old man dinn hardly give her enough to eat on and spent the rest on *bolita* or the lottery. But he didn't know any of them anymore. He wouldn't recognize his brothers if he saw them on the street.

And this wasn't Sugar, not this mouse. His two older sisters were thin and screechy and he'd know them if he heard them a mile away, which you damn well could hear them. This mouse wasn't in the same family.

"Hey, Sugar," he said.

She turned, holding a new, wrapped handkerchief. "Look, in a little cellophane bag all by itself," she marveled. "You buy this, Ricki? Can I have it?"

"Sure, it's all yours Sugar," he said, looking at the heady flare of her mature thighs, which were draped around with some old pinned-up muslin pillow cases, and that black umbrella cloth on her head. Parts of this get-up vaguely reminded him of a nun's habit, but no nun never wore nothing like that, hiked clear up to her hips almost. "What the hell you got on anyways?" he demanded irritably because it was so ridiculous. "Where'd you get it, in the ash can?"

"Just the umbrella cloth. The rest of it Mama gave me from the rag bag. It's my nun's dress. I'm gonna be a nun. I put it on to practice." The smugness leaked out of her voice and, with growing dismay, she looked down at the bunched and lumpy fabric that hung from her. "I know the way it oughta go, Ricki," she said humbly, "but I don't do it so good. It ain't much like a nun, is it? They're so nice and clean and smooth. Now I don' even feel like a nun, I got it so all twisted together. I don't know how to do it, Ricki!" she wailed, tears fattening in her hot chocolate eyes. "It always comes like this when I do it. I look like

Mama's rag bag."

"Look, baby, I dinn mean—"

"I do, I do, I do! And I don' know how to fix it and you don' like me or nothing and you're my favrit brother and I wanted to look nice and everything and—"

"Goddamn it, shut up! And stop crying in your lousy beer, willya, for crisake? Okay okay okay, I dinn mean to yell, but juss stop bawling, it gets me. I'm sorry. C'mere and I'll see if I can straighten it out for you. C'mon, we'll make you a Mother Superior or bust."

As he unpinned the crazy strips of fabric and put them together again, he was conscious of the heat of her body. He knew what she was—and she was his sister! She didn't know it yet, but she would. And she'd be a grab-bag forever. Now she was a virgin, but there were things she was beginning to realize and maybe want. She was not much in the upstairs, but that was not necessary. The hunger, the wanting—that would always be first. Her enveloping breast breathed against his hand as she breathed.

She was not his little kid sister Sugar, she was not Sugar played with a doll made of a white sock, the eyes, nose and mouth put on with a five-and-dime fountain pen. She called the doll Moo-moo. This was a hot little mouse, so filled out, and didn't play with dolls.

Oh crise, if only he didn't have to get down to the Rovers! He would pick out a nice guy, make sure to jap him and Sugar together, and make them get married. But he had to go. It was getting dark. He should be on his way now but he had to wait and make sure Sugar was all right and didn't go out in the streets and get raped, because rape was very bad. It was not that the guy would put it to her. That was not so important. But there were guys that would bust her up with their fists, or cut her, or stomp her belly and other worse things.

He found out quickly that Sugar was all right if she had something to play with and he gave her a cheap rhinestone clip and little earrings to match. The way she acted, you'd of thought he gave her a department store. Just before he left, he promised to write her a picture postcard, and that was even better.

When he left, he kissed her on the cheek and said, "Now you are my favorite sister, and if you need me, you know where I am, the Rovers. *Hasta la vista.*"

EIGHT

He went up to the roof very silently, down to the end tenement and chose a back window of the basement to go out. A hand took his and hauled him up and out and a coldness was like grease in his stomach. But it was only Little Augie, who had been waiting there two hours to tell him that Patsy Sean had called out all the Senior Dusters. Patsy was in a frenzy that Ricki might get away.

"I got a different car," Little Augie whispered. "I made my uncle buy it. Very quiet. We go by the dirt roads at the brook and then out down-Butt. Patsy has Dusters watching all the streets he knows you will have to go for the bus. He will kill me if he knows I take you away in the car. If you don't believe me, look...." He pointed.

The drizzle had died of malnutrition and its shroud, the fog, had gone with it. The first indication of an unborn moon was a feeble luminescence behind shifting clouds to the west. Humidity sloughed away. It was going to be cooler, and everything began to assume form with crystal clarity. Ricki's luck was with him. If he delayed as little as a half hour the moon would be out and he would have been as visible as a dish of black olives on a white tablecloth in the flood of unwarmed light. They'd spot him the instant he stuck his nose out far enough to cast a shadow, and he'd have to run like a son of a bitch and his brother to stay alive. He had a fighting knife in a clip sheath up both sleeves, and if they caught up with him, he'd turn on them with one of his long, honed knives in each hand.

A real knife fighter is different from a stabber or a fencer. He is more like a fast and shifty lightweight boxer, quick to lead, feint, jab, and lead again, always boring in, but he must be still quicker with the counterpunch—or counterslash—beating a thrust already lunging at him. His timing had to be so perfect that it split the lethal split seconds into dangerous fractions. There was nothing so merciful as a knockout in knife fighting. Its only equivalent was in the deadly adroitness of a honed, flicking knife blade across the big neck artery or the final sliding of it up under the rib to pierce the heart. Ricki was exceptionally good and extremely fast with either hand.

He had once tried to teach some of the more agile Dusters the proper manner in which a knife was to be used, but did not have the patience and gave up in disgust, for he could disarm them every time within seconds using nothing more dangerous than a foot-long length of quarter inch dowel.

From the dark at the edge of the tenement, he followed the line of Little Augie's pointing finger and saw two stocky Dusters watching the back of his tenement from the next corner. Farther on were more Dusters, and as his eyes sharpened to the night, he picked out still others scattered east and west on the street and north and south on the Avenue. It was just as he had thought: Patsy had called out all Seniors and Juniors and saturated the neighborhood. His eyes caught the flick of a skirt here, then another there and there and there. Debs. There were Debs, also. Never on foot could he evade them, scattered as they were in depth. The way out now was with Little Augie and the car.

"Patsy put everybody on the streets," Little Augie whispered at his elbow. "They are very mad. He told them you sold them out to the Rovers and soon there would be a bad rumble and many would be hurt, or tortured by the Rovers. The Wreckers worked on Stan Alpine, that also was to join the Rovers, and it must have been bad things they did, because he got up in the clubhouse, very pale and shaking, and said they were all going to be branded C P on the cheeks with acid by the Rovers: C P—that is for Chicken Punk. Now everybody is crazy like Patsy. They blame everything on you, Ricki. I go away from there myself. There will be some Spanish-speaking guys get beaten up bad before tomorrow, I think. Patsy eggs them on. Do you have the Gun, Ricki? I hope you have the Gun. It will take us through anything, the Gun. You have only to point it, that Gun, and everybody will run, much afraid. Just to look at it, you know that it is Gun of great superiority. You did not forget the Gun, did you, Ricki? The Gun, it is like God. It smites with wrath and vengeance and His enemies fall before Him."

"You sound like you been smoking pot," Ricki growled, annoyed as usual by Little Augie's elaborate garrulity. "Yes, I have the gun. Now shut up and let's get the hell out of here. Where's the car?"

"Right here," he pointed at a black Thunderbird at the curb. "It is very speedy and not so noisy like the other. My uncle will buy me anything when I scare him enough. Also, he is very weak from the liquor and needs me. I am glad you did not forget the Gun. It gives you an importance, that gun. More better we go now, Ricki, quick. I wait for you here two hours and all the time I am afraid they will come down and ask why."

"Wait a minute, chumbo," Ricki held back warily. "How come you knew this'd be my way out? Why this special spot?"

Little Augie looked at him in surprise, as if this were something that Ricki should have known, but he explained patiently, "I know you go to your flat when you leave me this afternoon, so I drive over and watch from the alley up there and see you go in here. So, I know here is where you will come out. Also, this is Sordo's way in and out when the guys are after him. We are friends, Sordo and me."

Ricki nodded. Sordo was his youngest brother, the one he remembered best, because once he saw that the little kid was fast and sure with his hands and nice balance on the feet, so he showed him a few tricks, how to use the knife, and Sordo picked it up like *that*. Now he would be about as old as Little Augie. Sordo was the smart one in the family, very shrewd, a planner, and never caught or blamed for nothing, very ambitious for money. Little Augie was smart too, Ricki recognized, but Sordo would go places. Little Augie was crazy smart and some day would get killed doing a craziness. Not real crazy, but a crackpot, queer like all the Chavez family. His heart was good, all the same. You had to understand him a little, was all.

They crouched to keep their silhouettes from showing too much against the corner street light and hastily crossed the sidewalk and ducked into the small black coupe. Ricki took the wheel.

"More better we don't run into trees this time," he said grimly.

"I was going to suggest you drive," Little Augie sounded small and meek and scared. "It is not on purpose that I run into trees. It is that I think of other things. And I don't smoke pot. This afternoon I read the Bible. Old Testament. Then I know He is also the God of the Gun. I am glad the Gun is with us tonight. It is the Lord, thy God. My grandfather, he always read the Old Testament. Very sexy, he said."

"Your grandfather," growled Ricki, irritated, "would find that the washing machine was very sexy too, if he put his thoughts to it."

"No, no," Little Augie protested, "it was only certain things were sexy. Very personal, you understand. Not for everybody. It is an enjoyment that must be cultivated. Not always a *comprensivo* thing, but always *simpático*. He liked to go to the slaughterhouse and watch them kill pigs. But please, *only* pigs. Pigs die without dignity, he said. Some people are pigs. He was proud to be a Chavez, however."

Ricki made no answer.

"What's Patsy doing now—or the last time you saw him?" he asked.

"Patsy?" Little Augie giggled unexpectedly. "He wasn't doing anything, anything at all."

"Just being the big shot, hey? That's Patsy."

"No, no. He wasn't the big shot. He was a very small shot. In fact, he wasn't any shot at all. Nothing, nothing. *Si*, that is now Patsy."

His voice rode on such a strange bubbling note that Ricki darted him a quick sidelong glance. "What do you mean—nothing. Is he drunk or in jail or what?"

"He is in the trunk."

"The *what?*"

"The trunk of the car, right back of us. That is how I know he is nothing."

Ricki said incredulously, "You mean he's dead? You killed him."

"I executed him!" said Little Augie sharply. "Please make note of the difference. He needed to be executed and that is what I performed. It was this way: he was making the Inspection. Like you say, a big shot. He finds me back there and says, 'So here's where that Ricki bastard's coming out. Well, ha, ha, ha. Light a rag, punk. I'm sending some real guys to take care of him when he shows. I said, beat it!' And he kicks my ass very hard. I stick him in the belly with a knife and cut his throat real fast or he yells. Sometimes they yell too loud after a sticking in the belly. You understand it was necessary to do this, Ricki. I have no way to warn you up in the flat. The Dusters, they are all around by now. I cover Patsy with grass and broken branches so he will bleed out into the ground. It is not good to have blood in the car. I know he will empty very fast with a cut throat and I put branches under his legs on a tilt so I know for sure he drains well. He is ready very quickly, but I wait until it is dark, then I roll him in a blanket and put him in the trunk. It might create a disturbance if he is found there before you come out of the flat, maybe the *policia tambien*, and it would be bad if you come out that window with the *policia*. When something must be done, you do it, Ricki, right then. *Verdad?*"

Ricki said heavily, "*Si, es verdad.*" The kid had saved his neck and all that, and maybe did the only thing that could be done, but crise, his explanation and description of it was as crackpot as they came. As crackpot as the grandfather that liked to see pigs slaughtered because he thought people were pigs.

The hell with this noise, he thought. He wanted to be shut of the kid and this car as fast as he could, but he still could see Duster outposts in the streets. Patsy used the biggest Dusters for outposts in case Ricki broke through the first rings of watchers. The outposts had to be big because they were stationed singly. They were the very tough ones, these. He was not afraid of any tough ones, but he didn't want to use a knife on them just because they'd been all steamed up by Patsy. They were really the suckers.

Little Augie was staring through the small rear window. "There is a car behind us, Ricki," he said.

Ricki shot a glance at the rear vision mirror. He was doing about forty through the narrow, winding streets and dared not take a longer look. Briefly, he glimpsed a hodgepodge of headlights. "There are several cars behind us."

"*Si*, but there is a dark green one that is always there. A green one with no left front fender. You know that car."

Ricki nodded, his lips tightening. He knew that car. It belonged to Ernie Straub, eighteen, but bigger than most men, six-foot-four, two-twenty pounds, a weightlifter, very muscular, the biggest and nastiest guy in the Dusters, always squeezing a guy's hand till the guy went down on his knees and yelled. Naturally, Patsy made him the Wreckers' Sergeant. Straub's car was all hyped up and more speedy for sure than Little Augie's secondhand Thunderbird.

Little Augie watched intently. "There is one guy next to Straub up front," he said in a slow voice, counting and moving his head up and down and from side to side to spot the silhouettes against the lights. "Yes, and one—two—God damn—three in the back seat. Push it, Ricki. We better get out of here fast."

"What's the matter with this damn iron?" Ricki snarled. "I'm down to the floor and the best I can get is forty."

Little Augie gasped and smote his forehead in anguish. "The governor," he groaned. "It has a governor on the engine and I forgot to take it off. I am a criminal, a traitor. I have betrayed you, Ricki. I forgot to take off the governor, so many other things I was thinking. *Ay de mi de mi de mi!*"

His mental agony was so poignant that Ricki reached out and patted his knee in reassurance. "We'll lose them, baby," he lied. "A little car like this I can turn on a pinpoint while they have to go round the block."

Little Augie did not brighten. "It is very difficult to turn so fast in the city, Ricki, so many cars and trucks both ways, and Straub has a car of great speed. You have the gun, but if you shoot in the streets we will be shot by the *policia,* or put in the *calabozo*, and I do not wish for them to find Patsy in the trunk."

Ricki said, "Oh crise!" He had almost forgotten Patsy. He should have known better. A long time ago he should have been smarter than to trust a crackpot like Little Augie. This had been wrong from the start and was getting wronger by the minute and soon it would go altogether crazy, and them with it. Crazy and dead.

Little Augie suddenly cried out and pointed ahead, clutching Ricki's arm with his left hand. "The bowling alleys, the bowling alleys. We can run down the alley and Sordo will hide us."

"Sordo? My kid brother? He's in New York with the family."

"No, no. Not Sundays. Bowling is very busy Sundays. Big tips. He works Sundays in the bowling. Pin boy. Quick, Ricki, the turn. Turn *now* and we lose him a little bit, maybe. Sordo will help us at the bowling. We run down the alley between buildings, and there is a side door by the bowling, always open for air. We get in and Sordo will help us. You sure you have the Gun, Ricki?"

"I told you yes, goddamn it. Hold your hat. Here we go."

He twisted the wheel sharply and the small car darted between a bus and a truck, tires squealing, turned right at the next corner, jumping a red light, went a block east on a westbound one-way street, made three more sharply cornered turns, then switched off the lights and drifted up a narrow, unlighted delivery-way behind the bowling lanes. They could hear the constant thunder and crash of heavy rolling balls and falling pins. It drowned out all other noise. Little Augie pointed to the mouth of an alley beside the building and Ricki nodded and went into the darkness, feeling his way along the brick wall. Little Augie was close behind him.

Suddenly he realized that Little Augie was too close, crowding him, pressing him against the building, tying up his right arm, but even as he spun away, he felt himself struck hard, high in the back between the shoulders. He knew he had been stabbed, not clubbed. He skittered on a few feet, then turned, crouching and weaving, snapping his own fighting knife from his sleeve into his hand. His left arm dangled numbly.

"The Gun, the Gun, Ricki," Little Augie panted. "That is all I want, the Gun. I *must* have the Gun."

"Come and get it, punk," said Ricki, then unexpectedly lunged forward, slashed at Little Augie's face and, as the boy defensively lifted the thick butcher knife, Ricki crouched lower and completed the lunge, slipping his long thin knife up and inside Little Augie's rib cage. Little Augie groaned heavily and doubled over, grasping the blade with both skinny hands as Ricki attempted to withdraw the knife and step away. He toppled head foremost, almost pulling the haft from Ricki's pain-weakened hand. Little Augie rolled over on his side, curled in that dying foetal position. His glazing eyes filled his face.

"I only wanted the Gun, Ricki," he whispered, "just the Gun. But run now, please run, just *run....*"

But the time was past for running. A small door opened from the building and a lithe figure flashed into the alley. Ricki had no time for anything. He was slashed, crisscross, twice diagonally on the face—the conventional stroke to blind his eyes, and then the figure dropped low and came up and forward in a killing lunge with a gleam of bright steel at the end of his arm. Ricki felt the knife go in and he tripped backward. His head hit the brick wall of the other building and the world fell away from him.

Out of the darkness above him swarmed the grinning face of Sordo, his kid brother.

"Greetings, brother mine," it mocked him. "I asked my poor dead friend to bring you for a little visit if you were loaded, and I see you are," he rapped the aluminum suitcase with the side of his shoe. "And all for you, eh, Ricki. All for you and none for us. That's the way you always were, you bastard, living it up while we ate *frijoles*. You promised to take me with you once. I waited. Every day I waited. Years. But it slipped your lousy mind, you son of a bitch. Can you hear me, Ricki? Can you hear me? Huh, I thought not. I slid that last one in just where I wanted it. You don't know it, but you've kissed the girls goodbye. Still, you have one more lay coming—when they lay you out in the morgue. Goodbye, brother mine. Don't take any wooden promises." He laughed, snatched up the aluminum suitcase and ran down the alley. The night gulped him.

Ricki was not dead. The curved end rib had turned the knife from quick death to maybe a slow one, but at the moment he was alive. With a dreadful slowness, he began to crawl....

It felt like ten days before he lurched gauntly into the Rovers' Club on Grove Street down-Butt. Joey Groff was alone, writing at a table. He looked up and his jaw sagged.

"Fernandez," he said stupidly. "You're dead. We heard—"

"I spit on the name Fernandez," his voice was so hoarse that the words were scarcely more than a vibration in his throat. "It was my own brother," he made a weak upward stabbing motion. "Don't call me no Fernandez. Call me Joe Blow. That's what I am, and no jazz about it. I'm a lousy dumb Joe Blow, me."

"Sure, Joe, anything you say. What the hell, one name's as good as the next. Come over here. Lay down for a minute."

Groff looked at the ruined face and winced. The crisscrossed knife slashes left thick, ugly welts and looked as though four pie-slice-shaped wedges from different faces had been put together to make this one horror. The left eye was a swollen red pulp, destroyed forever. At least neither the cops nor anybody else would recognize him now, if that was any consolation.

But Jesus, there he was chopped up worse than hamburger and dead by rights, and how the hell did he ever make those four miles from the bowling alleys?

Guts, just guts.

Three months later, Papa and Mama Fernandez went to Tampa.

Nobody wanted Sugar, so she was tossed to the lecherous hospitality of Uncle Pete, who impaled and enslaved her. It was hard to know whether she hated him or was crazy about him in her moronic fashion. He did what he wished with her and she didn't run away.

But every once in a while she stamped in the faces and testicles of big heavy men with her spiked heels. "Why?" she always said when asked. "I dunno. He was a big slob, I guess. What the hell, who cares about a slob. They won't know the difference anyways."

And she always went back to Uncle Pete.

NINE

Sugar leaned against the door of Binnie's flat and slowly rotated her luscious Latin rear end against a raised molding, not because it itched, but because she was unhappy. She always said that when she was down in the dumps, she had to be up and doing, because when you're up and doing, it takes your mind off. Now Veronica was mad with Binnie and Sugar wanted to get her mind off. There was gonna be a scrap and she didn't like scraps. They made trouble. Mugging was different. There was nothing to a mugging but whacking them over the head with a sap. There was never no trouble. She could do it day and night. Her arm never got tired. She was strong in the arms. But a scrap with Veronica was gonna be trouble and she didn't want to take sides.

She liked Veronica and she liked Binnie, too. She liked everybody, she told herself. She never got in no scraps unless they picked on her first or got her mad, and you couldn't call that her fault. Binnie hadn't oughta sit around like that, she thought primly, her kimono open and showing everything she owned. Guys said she had a nice built but Sugar couldn't see it. There wasn't enough, to her way of thinking. But Binnie nearly always acted like a lady and ladies were on the thin side. Magazine pictures of ladies were always thin.

And she hadn't oughta get in no scrap with Veronica neither. Veronica'd mop up the floor with her. Then Sugar brightened. There wouldn't be no scrap. Binnie was too much a lady. Ladies was, like in the movies, different. Greer Garson. People were scared of Veronica but Binnie got respect. From guys even. She guessed if she had to take sides with Veronica and Binnie, it'd be Binnie.

She looked at the closed door through which she could hear Veronica banging around the kitchen, then unconsciously moved along the wall until she was standing to the side of Binnie's chair, like a bodyguard.

The move was as obvious as a public pledge to the Flag. Sugar never was very subtle. Binnie and Midge exchanged glances and Midge made a small well-what-do-you-know-about-that grimace. Till now, Sugar had stuck closer to Veronica than a coat of paint.

"She give you a bad time on the way over, Sugar?" asked Binnie.

"Yeah, bad time. Yellin and screechin'. I almost was gonna sap her one. You know, the cops. Crise. No more-a that jazz."

"She's coming out," Midge warned.

Stolidly, Sugar took the homemade blackjack from inside her jeans and held it behind her back. She was scared only when she didn't know what to do. She was all right now that she'd decided to back Binnie.

Veronica came out of the kitchen, carrying a cold, beaded bottle of beer. She gave Binnie a diluted, yellow-tooth half smile.

"I wasn't really yapping at you, Binnie," she said loudly, "It's jass I'm all on edges. The o'lady thinks my brother Steff busted outta the nut house and's after her on account she signed the papers that put him away, and she won't believe it he got blowed in half with shotguns the lass time. So nobody gets no sleep and the house is a stinking mess. She's got all the furniture stuck against the door and we gotta come and go the fire escape. I'm the oney one. The o'man's shacking up with that lousy mudkicker downstairs. My sister Vera comes around now'n then, much as she can, brings groceries. She's the oney decent one. She'd stay with the o'lady but she's in a house down Five Points. She's okay'n all that, but who'd pick Vera, I dunno. She looks buried by mistake and dug up too late. I like her best when I ain't there. I mean, she's really a good-natured slob. Everybody's gone but me and I go out, I gotta tie up the o'lady with rope or she'll cut her lousy throat. She gets like this since two years, the lass time Steff came howling and kicking in the door to hide in the kitchen closet, the poor bastard. Two months afterwards he took a rake and messed up a guard and they blowed him in pieces with shotguns. I'm talking too stinking much. I can't help it. It's on my chest. But that's why."

"Nobody yells at me," said Binnie. "I don't like it."

"I just tole you it dinn mean nothing, dinn I?"

"Not to you maybe. To me."

Veronica's face became very still. She shook her head. "I won't fight you, Binnie, so don't bother trying. I'm all in. I won't fight nobody tonight."

"Who brought up fighting? Not me. You sound chicken."

"I don't sound nothing. I won't fight. I'm all in. You're wasting your time."

"You'd fight if you got smacked."

"Smack me over the head. Maybe I'll get to sleep for a change."

Midge stood up. "Drop it," she told Binnie. "You won't get a showdown. She knows how it's stacked. I'll see you later."

She went into the kitchen and closed the door. She always left the room when Binnie, Veronica and Sugar got together after the muggings. Any Deb or guy in the Rovers would do the same—get out and go someplace else. If they didn't know the details, they couldn't be blamed if something went sour.

Midge could hear the usual wrangling as they split the night's take, but didn't listen. She looked into the refrigerator but there was nothing she wanted. She finally made a salami sandwich on carraway rye. The way Midge felt, she could of taken on the crazy Polack all by herself. A showdown was bound to come, though. Binnie never started nothing she didn't have figured out. The trouble was, Veronica knew it now, and had more chances to stack it against Binnie for the showdown. Veronica wasn't afraid of Binnie tonight. It was Sugar and herself, specially Sugar. Midge could tell from the way Veronica's washed-out eyes moved and stayed longest on Sugar and how Sugar stood near Binnie with that blackjack sticking out from behind her back. Sugar'd give anything away. She was so dumb, it hurt.

Midge didn't downgrade Sugar. The dumb ones made the best fighters. The brighter you were, the sooner you started worrying about what could sneak up behind your back and clobber you; after that, you were no good in a fight. Sugar didn't think of nothing that wasn't right under her nose. And there was another thing about Sugar; she could *move*. You wouldn't think it to look at her, but she was fastern a starved alley cat and could flick that loaded sap in your face quickern you could blink, even if you was watching for it. And if she gave it to you, one-two-three-four, back and forth, you didn't have no face.

Midge did not go back inside until she heard the hall door open and close and Veronica and Sugar clatter down the uncarpeted stairs. Binnie was sitting with one bare leg thrown over the arm of the chair, smoking a satisfied cigarette. Midge started to say something but Binnie waved it aside.

"Stop worrying about Veronica, will you?" she said. "We patched it up. So forget it."

Midge said, "Sure." But you couldn't patch up a thing like that. All you did was give Veronica time to get organized.

"Is something the matter?" asked Binnie. "You look like a sick cat."

Midge shrugged. "It's my mother," she said. "The old man's been getting in touch with her. He says he's working steady in a lumber yard up New Street. He wants to get together again."

"So what, if he's working steady."

"For him a month is steady. Then he'll pick a fight with her, so's to have an excuse to walk out. Or if she keeps working in the diner, he'll get in a scrap with the foreman at the lumber yard and quit and hang around the house or the nearest gin mill on the money she makes. You know how he is."

"So does your mother. She don't have to put up with it."

"I know, but she always gives him another chance. And now he writes he turned over a new leaf and's got a furnished flat on New Street all fixed up for her to walk in, and he's with the lumber yard over six weeks and maybe soon he'll be put in charge of something. I keep telling her it's the same old jazz, but she believes it."

"Why're you worried about your mother so all of a sudden? You hardly never see her. You're here practically all the time."

"I been seeing her every day before she goes to work."

"Since when?"

"Since two, three weeks," said Midge defensively. "Since the old man started getting in touch with her. So far I got her to put him off, but I don't know how long. And I'll have to go with her. I can't let him take her pay and smack her around too."

Alarm flared in Binnie's eyes. "And walk out on me, Midge? Leave me here alone?"

"But she's my mother."

"All of a sudden."

"It ain't so all of a sudden," Midge mumbled. "I'm the only one she can turn to."

"Who can you turn to? Who can I? Who can anybody? You can't turn to nobody but yourself and in the end it don't make no difference who walks out on you."

"It ain't like walking out, Binnie, honest. Anyways, he'll probably go to work soused some morning and quit or get canned. He ain't never held a job yet, and my mother won't take him back without a job. She's dumb, but not that dumb."

"I knew you wouldn't leave me alone," said Binnie, smiling to break Midge's heart. "I knew you wouldn't walk out."

Midge couldn't stand it when Binnie smiled like that. It made her want to cry, and at the same time beat up anybody who made Binnie unhappy. The smile kind of hesitated around the edges of Binnie's mouth, as though afraid to come all the way out before it was sure you'd like it. It was a beautiful smile and that's what tore you up, the way it hesitated like a little kid that didn't know why its old man beat it up every time he got soused.

"I'll never leave you alone by yourself, Binnie, never, no matter what," said Midge with an intensity that made people wary and even afraid of her. "You can always depend on me. You know that."

"Sure, but you had me scared there for a minute, Midge. You're the only one. I thought I could depend on my sister, but I can't. Loretta's okay, but how'd you like it if your sister was a whore?"

Midge flushed and stammered. Veronica's sister was a whore too, and you could throw it in her face and she'd only laugh, but nobody threw it in Binnie's face.

"She's better than a lot that ain't," she told Binnie.

"Maybe, but I don't want her sleeping around here no more. You never know what you'll catch from a whore. Now you can stay here all the time, Midgie. You won't have to give up your bed for no whore."

Midge didn't say anything, but she couldn't help feeling that Binnie was being pretty rough on Loretta. Loretta was crazy about Binnie. At the same time, you had to admit Binnie was right. Midge didn't know what to think anymore. That was why she got down in the dumps so much. The best thing for her to do was not think—and that started her thinking about old man Salaski, Slaughterhouse Salaski, that got himself mugged tonight, the one that started all the trouble with Binnie and Veronica because Salaski lived right up the street and if he recognized Binnie, there'd be all hell to pay. Midge didn't want to bring it up again but she had to.

"Binnie—" she fumbled. "You didn't *know* it was Old Man Salaski you mugged tonight, did you?"

"Honest, Midge, I didn't."

"That's what I thought. An old guy on your own street. Did—did they beat him up much?"

"*Now* what's eating you, Midge? You know I don't go in for that end of it."

"Yeah, I know. It's—well, you're asking for trouble, going out mugging with them two. Veronica's crazy and Sugar ain't got no sense. They'll kill somebody one of these nights. They give me the creeps."

Binnie regarded her with an expression that was both thoughtful and veiled. "You know something, Midge," she said at length, "you're beginning to worry too much. Be like me and know when to stop. I've had it for one day I'm going to bed."

She went into her small bedroom and closed the door. She swore silently, hands clenched. Was Midge going sour? Much more of this and they'd be washed up. But not yet. It was too soon.

TEN

Midge was still asleep on the sofa-bed the next morning when Binnie was up and dressed in her daytime clothes. She wore a floppy, over-sized man's white dress shirt with the tails brought up and around and tied at the waist, sleeves folded back not quite to the elbows, and in direct contrast, the tight, tight blue dungarees, molded so snugly to the whole area of thighs and hips that instead of making her look less female, it made her more so, provocative and tantalizing.

Her glance at Midge was more appraising than unfriendly. Midge lay curled instead of relaxed and stretched out, and Binnie thought, *all tied up in knots*, which was just the way Midge looked. Binnie went out. She and Midge usually had breakfast together in the Summit Diner up on the Avenue, but Binnie didn't want breakfast with anybody today. She wanted to be by herself. She took a bus to the Rexall Drugs way up at Volk Street and sat at the far end of the counter with a morning paper. Nobody came to Rexall except people that worked around; there was no place to get together. She ordered two hamburgers and a coke and paid no attention to the cold hostility in the waitress's voice. She was used to that.

Binnie went through the paper, column by column, until she found the story about Old Man Salaski on page seven. She leaned forward and read it intently. There wasn't much to read: Artur Salaski, 63, of 109 Midland Street had been found unconscious early this morning by Officers John Gilman and Henry Schneider on the sidewalk of Whelan Street about thirty feet south of Summit Avenue. Salaski was rushed to City General Hospital. Although he had a broken nose and jaw and had been otherwise kicked and beaten, his condition was not listed as critical. Salaski had no wallet and police believe he had been mugged. Under sedation now, the mugging victim would be questioned later when he regained consciousness.

Binnie read the story twice to make sure it said Salaski had been found on Whelan Street, but that's exactly what it said. Whelan Street. But crise, that was practically crosstown from Hacksher Street, where Sugar and Veronica beat him up. Whelan! My God, that was a block the other side the movies on Summit. How'n hell an old guy, sixty-three, ever get from Hacksher to Whelan, and Binnie herself had practically cooled him before Sugar and Veronica went to work? Anybody else, he'd be damn near dead. But this guy, this old Polack, he actually got up and walked crosstown. *Walked.* It gave her a funny feeling. He wasn't human; he couldn't be.

Well, he wasn't dead and that was to the good. At least, nobody'd make a stink about a beat-up old Polack. If they did, they'd spend the rest of their life, because there was beat-up Polacks every night, and who gave a damn?

Nobody.

And who gave a damn about *her?* Okay, Loretta, a whore, and anybody'd tell you a whore was bull-happy. Nix Loretta. Midge? Put a nickel on the drum and save a soul. Nix Midge. Mick Fogarty? Huh. No more'n he could get in. Nix Mick. Vince Kirby? Man, he'd be the one. And almost, too. It was her fault. She tried too hard. She remembered the night. It was when the Dusters gave the jump. That long ago? The Happy Jacks took over the old Dusters' territory, long time ago. He wanted it that night and got it and now he was going nuts still wanting it, but that kind of guy, he'd maybe stick it in cement if it got in his way. She'd get to him, though, she'd get to him, not putting it out for him, but inching him in to want it, and that was the way to do with Vince Kirby. Unless Mick Fogarty took Vince first, and the Mick *could* take Vince if he didn't let down after that first five minutes. That was the Mick's trouble, if you stayed alive after that first five minutes, the Mick caved in, he started to think, he had too much imagination, or something, his timing was off. But crise, during that first five minutes you were *lucky* to stay alive with the Mick, even Vince.

Now what she'd have to do was make the Mick believe that the first five minutes weren't the only five minutes in the world, because nobody, not even Vince Kirby, could stand up against the Mick for *two* five minutes like the first, and the Mick could keep going forever if only he didn't let down.

She knew there was something wrong with the picture, but couldn't put her finger on it. It was the same with her. She could take Veronica, if there were no slip-ups, but then what? She'd be top Deb—but so what? Maybe this one'd want it, or that one, or the other one, and it'd be fight-fight-fight all the time, unless she didn't give a damn and they thought she was crazy, like Veronica. Sugar Fernandez—nobody wanted to fight Sugar the way she could flip that homemade sap in your face from any angle.

Well! all the time she'd been thinking Midge Daly when it was actually Sugar Fernandez, because Sugar never worried about nothing and Midge did, and the one thing you couldn't do was worry.

The Imperials were giving a dance Saturday. Twenty Rovers were going and twenty Happy Jacks. And their Debs. She knew that much from Mick Fogarty. It was arranged so the Rovers and the Jacks wouldn't be no more than twenty, even both ways. This was the first time they'd be together at the same jump, all made up ahead of time, no fights.

There was too much talk about a rumble, and it was like a parade. Nobody won a parade except the cops. So the Imperials' territory was nice neutral ground to set things up for a talk between the Rovers and the Jacks. Nice and neutral was right, because smack in the middle of the Imperials' territory was the 15th Precinct Police Station and Captain Gahagen, and who wanted a territory like that, the bulls ready to kill you?

Binnie didn't care about that part of it. What she wanted was another chance at Vince Kirby. She put it to herself as baldly as that—another chance at Vince Kirby. He was the Rovers and maybe she'd be the Debs and together she'd be both, because she could handle Vince, once she got to him. And she would. If not this time, the next time. A small smile brooded on her mouth.

She ate her tasteless hamburgers and drank her coke, left the surprised waitress a tip, and walked out. She was always hungry after eating, but no matter where you went, the goddamn hamburgers were worse. She took the bus down to Grove Street and stopped in Straub's Delicatessen for a couple candy bars and a pack of Luckies. Rover Seniors hung out a lot here because it was a mail drop and old man Straub took phone calls for free but made it up on sandwiches and coffee. The only one in there today was fat Ed Yates, the sloppy cop, sloppier than usual because he was eating a kosher corned beef on rye and his tan summer uniform shirt was pulled open at his fat neck, as though he'd choke to death swallowing if it were buttoned. And no wonder, the way he gulped chunks out of the sandwich and slurped coffee for a chaser. There were wet coffee spots on his black tie and the front of his pants. Everybody said he was wrong-O and stay away, but Binnie didn't see anything to be scared of. He just looked like a sweaty fat slob in a uniform.

All he saw for a minute was her blue dungarees and white shirt knotted at the waist, and he said noisily, "Another one of the puking cruts. Twenty-four hours a day they're all over. Say, they ever give you any trouble in here, Straub?"

"No, no. No trouble, Mr. Yates," said Straub quickly. "Never no trouble."

"Don't kid me, Kraut. They're always trouble. Look, just say the word and I'll boot this little tramp down the House so hard she'll really be a split-tail."

"No, no, no, please, Mr. Yates. Little Binnie, she's always a lady."

"A lady, huh?" he bit another crescent from his sandwich, grinned and let his eyes slide down to the skintight crotch of her dungarees. "Hey, you got a back room, Straub. I think I'll take her in on suspicion she ain't no lady. A lady, haw! without the 'dy,' you mean. They all are. Look at the pants on her, for crisake. Advertising pays, if you see what I mean. Take a good look. There's a city ordinance on pants like that—indecent exposure, a year and a day in the workhouse. When I say take a look, Kraut, I mean take a look. You're a witness. Here. I don't want you to miss anything." He turned on his flashlight and used the beam as if it were an extension of his finger. "See? She's peddling her muscle or she wouldn't show it off like that. Another city ordinance. Soliciting. Ninety more days in the workhouse."

Binnie didn't move, or hardly breathe. She was scared and ashamed and didn't know what to do—except keep her mouth shut. Above all, keep her mouth shut, no matter what he said. At least the Mick was good for something. He had warned her about Yates. One word, that's all he was waiting for—just one word and he'd be down on her, yelling, "Backtalk, eh, tramp? I'll give you backtalk—the back of my hand—" Slam! across the mouth. But she didn't give him the excuse.

And Straub, he was red as a beet. The Rovers were good customers, but they *did* hang out in his place, so he was afraid not to do what Ed Yates said.

Just by luck, stringy, yakky old Mrs. Straub came in from the back with a big white enameled showcase tray of potato salad. Binnie couldn't stand that high-pitches yak-yak-yak all the time, it never stopped, you couldn't get a word in edgeways, but there was nobody she was gladder to see. Ed Yates shut up like *that*, and immediately started pushing his tie up to his collar, buttoning his shirt, putting his flashlight in his back pocket.

Mrs. Straub shrieked, "Well, ach, look now, if it ain't Mr. Yates from the nice *polizei*. It's been a long time. Only last night I said to the mister, I said, 'It's been a long time for Mr. Yates,' I said, and look, here you are. No, no, you don't go 'til you taste my potato salad, Mr Yates, with eggs it is, special. And a surprise I got! What do you think? You'll never guess. Cheesecake with on the bottom pineapple. Always I tell the mister, I say. 'Mr. Yates, *he* appreciates my cheesecake.' And it means a lot, a little appreciation. Come, we sit down and have a nice kaffee-klatch, and *ja*, with cheesecake. I give you a piece to take home, too. Otto, get Mr. Yates a nice fresh cup of coffee. Something you want, little girl? See what the little girl wants, Otto. Come, Mr. Yates...."

She fastened to his arm with both hands and steered and bunted him across the store to one of the round white marble-topped lunch tables at the side, talking away at the top of her lungs, and he couldn't escape without breaking her wrists. But cheesecake. His mouth watered and betrayed him. He sat down heavily, glowering.

Binnie inched out of the delicatessen, then free, darted across the street through horn-blaring, roaring, cursing Summit Avenue traffic. She was shaking all over as she walked down Grove Street to the Rovers' clubhouse in the basement of the burned-out warehouse. She was still scared—especially after mugging old man Salaski last night. If Ed Yates knew that, crise! he'd bust both her hands with his nightstick. He swore he'd do it to every mugger he caught, and he meant every word. And the way Ed Yates oozed around, talking to this one or that one, usually scaring the hell out of them, he picked up a lot of leads. There was no chance of him getting on to Salaski, it was off his beat, but crise, suppose he did! Crazy Veronica'd resist arrest and get killed or her back busted. Sugar was so dumb, she'd get off easiest, if you could call Ed Yates putting it to you easy. He got randy about twice a month and you could always tell, the way his mouth got all wet and loose when he looked at a woman. That's all he did for two, three days, pick out a woman or a Deb, somebody that couldn't squawk, then go after her and pick her off.

Binnie couldn't stop shaking. That's another thing she'd been scared of, that he wanted a woman, any woman. Binnie didn't want to think about it.

She didn't see a soul in the Rover's Club. It was too early, a little after eight. It was ten, eleven before they began to appear. Unless some Debs or guys were in the sleeping rooms partitioned off in the far back corner. The rooms were used by transients for a number of reasons, but usually they were scared to go home and get beat up by the old man, or they just plain wanted it and had no other place to go.

Binnie drifted across the basement, hoping somebody was ready to get up. She still had the jitters, and wanted somebody to talk to. Her spirits fell. There were ten beaverboard rooms. All ten doors were open. She saw a clothes tree with something that looked like a skirt hanging on it, in the end room. She went down and looked in the door. It wouldn't make any difference if a guy and Deb were in bed. This was morning. At night you left them alone. The bed was mussed, but nobody in it. And it wasn't a skirt on the clothes tree; it was a guy's sport jacket. Furthermore, there were other clothes on a chair, a comb, a safety razor and a carton of Luckies on the bureau. There were five pairs of two-tone shoes on the floor next to the bed. Somebody, a Senior, lived here. They did that once in a while after telling the old man, nuts to you, Jack, and walking out

The carton of Luckies on the bureau reminded her that on account of Ed Yates, she hadn't picked up a pack at Straub's, but hell, the Senior wouldn't mind lending her a pack. She walked curiously across the tiny, cramped room, looking around and wondering who it was this time.

She had a pack of Luckies right in her hand when a guy said at the door, "Put them back, baby. Go ahead. Now." His voice wasn't anything, just cold. He didn't sound mad or nothing. Only cold, and used to telling people. That annoyed her. She didn't like getting told.

She turned, saying, "All I wanted was a lousy pack of cigarettes. Here, look—" she extended her left hand, palm up, "—thirty cents for the pack. I was leaving it by the carton."

In the windowless dusk, he lounged, tall, lean and anonymous at the door. "Put it back. Next time you ask, not take. I don' like it, unnerstan'?"

"One stinking pack a Luckies?"

"I smoke stinking cigarettes? *Put it back now!*"

Seething, she threw the package on the bureau. "You lousy, cheap bastard," she said furiously. "Mick Fogarty'll take care of you."

"You send him around? Hokay. He's that dumb, he needs takin' care of."

"Ha, ha, ha. Parm me if I laugh. You don't know the Mick."

"I know him. Tall fella, cement-color hair. Very good in a rumble. But the Mick, he don't want to fight with me. You see, he fight his way, I fight mine. I take Vince, too. But *por que?* I don' wanna be nobody, and I don' like the fight. I take him already. Jus' fooling around, you unnerstan', I show him things."

"You're a goddamn liar!"

"I don' like it you call me a liar. I think more better you get your ass out of here. Sometimes I get sore. No good."

"I'll go when I'm good and ready," she said arrogantly.

He came toward her and the light of a naked 40-watt bulb, hanging by a single cord from the ceiling, fell full open his face, and she drew in a horrified breath. The light threw harsh, downward shadows from the welted purple double crisscross scars that divided his face into ugly quarters. She had never seen him, but she knew who he was. He was the one they called Spanish, and he came to the Rovers all but dead, bleeding, and with two more stab wounds—one that chipped the bone in his chest, and a deep gash in his shoulder. Miraculously, he had survived, but he never really recovered. He was hardly more than a sparse scaffolding of bones.

They said he was Vince Kirby's and Joey Groff's hatchet man. He had a whole box of knives, they told her, all honed like razors: small, thin ones for the excruciating, intricate work, and heavy, broad-bladed ones for the agony of major mutilations. She screamed and leaped at him, desperately using the judo trick of jabbing stiff fingers at his eyes, and at the same time snatching for his hand with her other for the multiple finger-break.

He said, "Bitch!" weavingly evaded her darting hands, and threw her on the bed. She fought feebly, terror-stricken, for she had seen the gleam of at least one knife, blade in a clip sheath under his left arm and in the struggle, felt the supple narrowness of another held between his shoulder blades. She gave up, she couldn't fight, she was paralyzed by panic. He unzipped her dungarees with a single swing of a hooked finger and slowly drew them down over her hips, then off entirely and on the floor. She couldn't wear panties with those tight dungarees. Her white shirt had become unknotted and rode up just enough to show the exciting, rich undercurve of her rising breasts. His face—that face—contorted into what she thought of as a gloating, evil smile. It must have been a long while since he had a girl. He ran his hands over the clean lines of her hips and thighs. He was gaining self-confidence. He opened her shirt—the bra straps were broken—and gently he cupped her breasts. Numbly, she wondered how he could be so gentle, and yet so fierce, but the fierceness was always there.

Suddenly, the arrogant excitement, the exultation, the ferocity left him.

"Better you get dressed now," he reverted to his empty, cold voice. "Now I think right away you tell Vince. You tell Mick Fogarty. Not good, not good. *Muy malo.*"

And you could see that he was actually sorry for them. *Them!* She stared at him, forgetting that awful face. He was nothing special, just another tall, emaciated Latin boy, a thin white pucker of scar just under his left ribs and a gnarl of it on the back of his shoulder. His black eyes had flashed alight a moment ago; now they were dully bituminous. She dressed hurriedly.

"Sure I'll tell them. Why not? Wottaya think. Two minutes after your big speech, and already you're scared. That's a laugh."

"*Si*, I am scared. Mick Fogarty, he's nothing. *Pfui,* what do you want with a *borracho* like him, *por que?* No, no, no answer. It is not that of which to ask a young girl. But fight? *Si.* Five minutes maybe, then I give him *dos bocas*—two mouths. Maybe before."

"Two what? Mouths? Crise, the one he's got's too big already. But you got a sad waking coming, man. He's bad. What's two mouths?"

"Thus," he drew his thumb across his throat. "He use steel shoes, the brass knuckle, blackjack. *Si,* and the knee, the elbow, the thumb in the eyes, everything else. Me, just one little knife, no more."

"That's dago fighting."

"So. I am Latin fella. We fight, anything goes."

"You're dead, man, long dead."

"No, no. Not tree weeks yet. Then—hokay."

She shivered. "Don't talk like that. It's bad luck. And don't try to fight Vince."

Spanish took a .38 revolver from the bottom drawer of his bureau and handed it to her. He screwed a cylinder of steel wool at the end of the barrel. "The silencer," he explained. "No cops. And see, it's loaded," he flipped open the cylinder to show her. "You can operate it, no."

"I don't like 'em, but I can use 'em. I'm a damn good shot, Spanish, if you insist, okay. I'll shoot the legs out from under you."

"Hokay, shoot straight. Ready?" he stood about eight feet from her, balanced. She threw up the gun and shot without warning, but he was not there. He was to her left, with a long thin knife menacing her from the palm of his hand. He advanced, crouching and weaving in an erratic manner, making a difficult target. She tried to follow him with the muzzle of the gun, but he was always to one side of it or the other, getting closer. She fired two more ineffectual shots, and then he was within three feet of her, bent low in a crouch, menacing her soft underribs with a glittering Toledo steel knife. In another moment, shot or no shot, he was in a position to thrust twelve inches of Toledo steel into her heart.

He slipped to his right on skittering feet, and thrust upward with the long knife. It touched exactly where he had predicted—the soft underside of her left rib case, She screamed and fainted....

A cool wet cloth lay across her forehead when she recovered consciousness and the quartered face of Spanish swam into view, bent anxiously over her.

"I didn't give it to you," he said. "I just touch you to show how it was done. You're not hurt."

"I couldn't hit you," she said. "You're too fast. You can take both of 'em."

"I don't wanna take nobody, I'm waiting for one thing and that's all." He did not elucidate. "You're okay now?"

She did not answer immediately.

"Why don't you take 'em?" she asked.

He brooded at her. "Ain't nobody but one I wanna take," he said. She did not ask whom, but she made up her mind then and there to cultivate Spanish. He'd come in handy.

"What about the rumble Saturday?" she asked.

"No rumble," he said. "Frank Moke is dead and so is Joey Groff." Her eyes widened, but she did not ask why. She said to Spanish, "You goin' to the dance Saturday?"

His eyes flickered. "Me, my face?"

"You're just self-conscious about your face," she said.

"Who wouldn't be self-conscious about a face like this?"

"What—gave you that awful scar on your face?" she asked.

His face resumed its original coldness, and he said in the same kind of voice, "I ran into a barber pole. Now you'd better go."

He left abruptly and disappeared down the dark corridor. She stared after him, unbelieving.

She went into the outer room, but still no one had arrived. She was bored. She left through the side door and walked up to Straub's Delicatessen. The guys would be there by now. Anyway, fat Ed Yates would be gone.

When she walked into the delicatessen, Straub was a profusion of apology. He could not do enough, unless he got down on his knees and groveled.

"That's all right, Mr. Straub," she said. "Anything can happen with Mr. Yates. He's a lousy copper."

Straub did not like to hear that, for he always played both sides of the fence. Yates was okay. And so were the Rovers. He said, "And now what's or your mind, little Binnie?"

She said casually, "Just two candy bars, Mr. Straub."

He went around to the back of the counter, and after a moment's hesitation, he selected two of his most expensive candy bars. He gave them to her over the counter, and she seized them eagerly.

Straub was surprised when she dug into the pocket of her dungarees and paid for the candy without asking for credit, as did most of the Rovers.

Then he had this idea. "What do you say, Little Binnie," he leered, "we go into business, eh?"

She pretended innocence and said ingenuously, "But I don't know anything about business, Mr. Straub."

He said, "You won't have to, Little Binnie. That'll be my end of it. You just handle the trade."

She knew exactly what he meant by trade, and said, "You don't need business, but I'll think it over, Mr. Straub," she said, sidling toward the door.

He tried to go around the counter to intercept her but she knew that gimmick too. This was the oldest dodge in the business, and to hell with it. She got out of the door before Straub reached her.

She felt at odds and ends. What to do with the rest of the day? Not Midge, not Veronica—but there was always Sugar. Yeah. This was the time. Elated, she went over to the Good Luck Cafeteria. Maybe Uncle Pete wouldn't let her upstairs for breakfast, but she'd watch him when he took her tray downstairs to the too damp, cement-smelling rooms.

Unexpectedly Sugar came upstairs for a jelly doughnut and a cup of lousy coffee. Binnie immediately joined her at the table. Sugar looked both surprised and enormously flattered.

"You're the last one I expected to see," she said.

"Why, I like you, Sugar, darling." Sugar reeled in her chair in pure ecstasy. Binnie did not miss this and said, "I liked what you did last night, Sugar."

Sugar looked a little guilty but also resolved to undo the things about which she felt guilty. Binnie knew what it was, of course. Veronica had talked her back into the fold. Now Sugar was switching again.

Her business done, she did not want to hang around Sugar any longer. She patted the other girl's cheek and said sweetly, "You're my gal, Sugar, I know I can always depend on you."

It was only ten o'clock in the morning but she returned to the flat and Midge. Midge was pottering around the flat in her usual seersucker pajamas, ratty as usual. "What do ya think?" Binnie burst forth the minute she walked into the flat. "Groff's dead. The head of the Jacks died too."

Midge did not appear at all surprised. "I knew Groff was going to get it, maybe Moke."

"I should of asked Spanish," said Binnie glumly, "but so many things were going on, I forgot. Who did it?"

"Some greaser called Sordo. Supposed to be a real hotshot with a shiv. It wouldn't surprise me if he was the one that gave it to Moke."

ELEVEN

The dance Saturday night was given by the Imperials, an outfit you couldn't exactly call chicken. Furthermore, the 15th Precinct Police Station and the Youth Center were smack in the middle of their territory. Nobody would start a rumble so close to the House and Captain Gahagen, he'd kill them. Anyway, this was supposed to be a peace talk. Binnie went with Mick Fogarty; Midge had an undersized Senior named Stan Burris, a pugnacious little son-of-a-bitch. The jump was held in the Youth Center. There were no bulls or cops around, although the House was only two blocks away. Instead the two youth workers were there, both six feet two, and weighing about two twenty. They were very popular with the Senior Rovers and the Senior Jacks. They were good Joes.

The Jacks lined up on one side of the room, twenty strong, like dominoes, and the Rovers on the other. They looked at each other dispassionately. Across the floor walked Vince Kirby and the new Jack leader, the one they called Sordo, a tall spic. They talked briefly for a few minutes, then shook hands, nodded, and each walked quickly back to his row of dominoes.

Mick Fogarty was sore. He did not think much of Sordo in the first place, and without a top Jack the others were an easy touch. He tried to make this plain, as plain as Mick could, which is noisy and violent. Vince fixed him with a scowl, said something shortly, and Mick shut up right away. But you could see he didn't like it.

Binnie searched the room for Spanish. He said he'd be there, but there was no sign of him anywhere. And then she remembered the other car that had followed theirs. He'd be there; he never showed his face at a jump. He usually stayed downstairs or outside waiting for trouble. And she knew the kind of trouble he could take care of.

The new visiting nurse was there in a blue evening gown and Binnie was jealous because she looked so good. She was the god-damned wholesome type, and if there was anything Binnie couldn't stand, it was a wholesome-type girl.

A few of the Senior Rovers strutted up to her and asked for a dance. But she was helping the Imperial Debs prepare sandwiches and pour cider. Nominally, this was a teen-age dance, but downstairs in the alley you could get all the liquor you wanted, at a price.

Midge's date was an undersized schmo. He didn't dance with her, but strutted around the Senior Rovers. Finally Midge danced with a tall blond Imperial, who looked like a Swede. The third dance she had with him her date schmo decided it was an offense and tried to start a fight with the Senior Imperial, who merely picked him up by his jacket collar and let him kick there until Vince Kirby came over and took the schmo by the necktie and marched him from the room.

So far as Binnie could see nothing was happening. She expected, with twenty Jacks and twenty Rovers, there'd be some kind of fight, but Sordo had control of the Jacks, and the Rovers were just too damned scared of Vince Kirby. Binnie danced a few times with both youth workers and waited for Mick Fogarty to condescend to give her a jump and leave his crap game and the liquor.

But Mick never showed until the very last dance, and even at that he clodded around the floor reluctantly and certainly not sober. "How's about it after, Chick?" he asked. "I'm hot man, I'm hot."

"Then go upstairs and diddle around with your goddamned cards," she said.

"Aw, don't be like that, baby."

"I am like that and I've been like that for a long time. When you take me to a dance all you do is play cards and get stoned. Nuts to that, man."

"But, baby, we always went back to the club afterwards. What's so all of a sudden?"

"You're weird," she said. "A creep." But he continued to wheedle and she was finally persuaded.

There were a number of Junior Rovers at the club but Mick said, "Get the hell out of here, Juniors, and no back talk."

His reputation as a street fighter awed everybody and they gathered their Debs, and left hurriedly under Mick's glowering stare.

He took Binnie back to one of the sleeping rooms and immediately began to maul her, smearing her with alcoholic kisses. She tried to push him away but he said, "Come on, baby, come on," and threw her on the dirty bed. She knew what was coming. He was going to rip off her dress, literally rip it off, then plunge at her. His idea of love making was a battle, animal noises from one end to the other. When this melee was finally over, he usually went to sleep, but tonight he was wide awake, and still sore that Vince had aborted his fight with any Imperial. They were all chicken punks, and the only thing to do with a chicken punk was beat his stinking brains out.

Now Binnie knew what she had to do. She had to work on Mick. He could take Vince Kirby any time he wanted.

"Honey," she said, making it a semi-question, he'd have to answer.

"What?" he said.

"About Vince."

"What about Vince?"

"You can take him, Mick." she said intensely. "You can take him any time you want. All he does is hold you off, and you kinda peter out. And you don't have to peter out, Mick, you ain't even sweating when you let down."

He looked sheepish and mumbled, "But he don't fight back."

"Sure he does, Mick, he just covers up and waits for you to get bored, then—blam! Just keep on another five minutes, and there ain't no reason you can't keep on forever, with your built. You got it, Mick, you really got it. Use it! You could take over the Rovers."

He said incredulously, "You're nuts, man."

"I'm not, Mick, I'm not. All Vince is, is a cover-up fighter. Just keep on a little longer, Mick. He's only a lousy counter puncher, and you're faster'n he is. You'll smear *him*, and that's the God's honest truth."

Mick was silent for quite a while and then he said, "I think you got something, baby, I think you got it."

"You're damn right I have," she said. "I want my man to be top Rover."

"That's a big order, man." he said slowly.

"If you ain't big enough to fill it, then nuts. Are you big enough?"

"Big enough?" he said more noisily than usual, "You're damn right I'm big enough."

He wanted to make love to her again, but she said, "I had enough 'til you're big enough."

TWELVE

A few days later a new girl moved into the Rovers' territory. She was a huge muscular girl named Edna Vivens. She looked like an adenoidal moron. Veronica, Sugar and Binnie went to Volk Street where her folks had the new flat. Veronica was enthusiastic about enlisting this big nitwit into the Debs. It took some time for Edna Vivens to understand what they were talking about. And then she was eager. Veronica set the initiation for that night in the clubhouse. Several times Big Edna assured them earnestly that she'd be there, not only on time but ahead of time. Binnie thought, the mope didn't know what she was letting herself in for, but that wasn't her business. That evening practically all the Debs, including Binnie and Midge, were in the clubhouse. Veronica had promised them something special. Big Edna was waiting outside the door when the first Deb arrived. She couldn't wait to be initiated.

They took her inside to the partitioned Deb's room beyond the room used by the Seniors. For no reason that Midge could see, Binnie was carrying an inconsequential foot-square piece of dirty half-inch plywood, and when Midge asked her about it, Binnie just laughed.

Veronica had something special for them all right. The initiation, or breaking in, of a new Deb was usually done by a Senior called Joey the Lover. Joey the Lover was a boy who put his heart and soul into his work, and he always made certain that the new Deb would remember her initiation. That was what the Debs expected. However, Veronica had pulled a switch this time. The breaker-inner was not Joey the Lover, but a shrimpy little Junior whose name was Weinie. Veronica thought it the biggest joke ever to have little Weinie break in Big Edna. She explained it in great detail, and said she wondered if they'd ever find little Weinie again.

Then Big Edna was brought into the room, told what the initiation would be and shown her lover. Her face turned the color of mutton fat. She held out her hands as if to ward off the eager Weinie and backed away from him. "No, no, I don't want him, I won't do it, not with him— or even anybody," and she burst into great blubbery tears. Veronica, of course, was furious. She told Edna flatly that if she did not go through with it, they would brand her forehead with the word jerk, using lye. Big Edna backed into a corner and still bawling held a chair in front of her, "I won't, I won't, I won't."

Binnie, standing in an open area by herself, said, "Leave her lay, for crisake. What you tryin' to do, run a slaughterhouse?"

Veronica seized the opportunity to whirl upon her and vilify her in every filthy manner she could possibly lay tongue to, waving her arms crazily as usual.

Binnie said, "I don't have to take that from you, or anybody."

Veronica's pale eyes slid from side to side counting the number of friends who were gathered around her.

Satisfied, she said nastily, "You'll take anything and like it."

Binnie said coldly, "Not from you, baby."

This was Veronica's opportunity. She was surrounded by friends and Binnie had only Midge. With one of her characteristic screeches, she tore at Binnie like a fury, her crazy arms outstretched to scratch the face off Binnie. Binnie caught her left hand in a multiple-finger Judo grip. She threw her own arms down as far as she could, and as Veronica had to go down or have her fingers broken, Binnie brought up her knee and smashed Veronica's face. Somehow or other Veronica wrenched free, leaped backward for balance, then charged again, not making the mistake of letting Binnie get at her fingers. Now Midge saw what the square of plywood was for. As Veronica came in, Binnie took the small board by either edge and jammed it up into Veronica's face, breaking her nose. In a welter of blood and pain, Veronica went backward, tripped, and writhed on the floor. She wanted no more. Binnie stood over her and said;

"If you're done, say so; if not, get up and we'll go round again."

Veronica turned over face downward, covering her mutilated face with her hand, and whimpered. She was done.

She was washed up as top Deb.

Immediately, Veronica's former toadies began to screech for Binnie to be top Deb.

Binnie did not want to be top Deb. She'd wind up on the floor like Veronica. All top Debs had to fight any who challenged, or hold the position by force. She held up her arms and shook her hands for silence.

At this point, she could command silence. When all was still she said she had no ambition to be top Deb, and, turning, threw out her arms, indicating Sugar Fernandez. "There's the one who should be top Deb!" she cried ringingly. The Debs crowded around Sugar, hugging and patting her, uttering various cries of congratulations. Sugar stood there with her mouth open. She didn't know what it was all about. She knew Veronica had been whupped by Binnie, but this part didn't have no connection. What the hell was they congratulating her for? She didn't do nuttin'. It finally took Binnie to convince her that she was now the top Deb and Veronica was out.

"And for crisake, say something to the jerks."

This was right up Sugar's alley. She liked to tell people things, oney nobody never listened. Now they'd hafta. She stood up and glowered at them.

"Okay, you jerks," she said, "anybody that don't do nuttin' that I don't say, or Binnie, gets a bust in the snoot. And that ain't no jazz. Thank you for your kind attention."

Midge walked out of the room without a word and Binnie knew she would not be at the flat that night. In making Sugar top Deb Binnie had violated the things that Midge had always valued. And that was that.

Binnie watched her go without expression. Lately, Midge was definitely a square. Not only had she finally decided to live with her mother up on Elm Street where her father had his alleged flat, but she had started dating a blond boy she'd met at the Imperial's dance. His name, for God's sake, was Bjorn Bjornson, a lousy squarehead. She was well rid of Midge. Now the thing to do was to get Sugar to live with her. That was going to be rough because Sugar liked living with her Uncle Pete Fernandez. Binnie wondered narrowly how much Sugar told Uncle Pete about her activities.

THIRTEEN

Binnie was riding high. She had control of the Debs because she controlled Sugar. Sugar didn't have a mind of her own anyway. Still, things weren't organized yet, and she wasn't getting her cut because the Debs hadn't been taught to contribute to a central fund. She still had to go out mugging with Sugar and the new Deb, Big Edna. They did all right.

She was coming home late one night, about twelve-thirty, and had reached her own street when a man grasped her arm in a grip that was like iron. She twisted to look up at him and her heart fell away. It was Old Man Salaski, the one she and Sugar and Veronica mugged that night and put in the hospital.

He said in his guttural voice, "You're the girl, I know, you take me down that street, for to get mugged, I go the hospital, bad hurt, you're the one, I know, I was tole, now you come with me."

She jabbed up at him with the stiff fingers of her right hand, but he was too tall, too far away and she missed. He slapped her so hard across the face that she was nearly out when he dragged her down into the basement of a flat. He hit her several more times, cursing her for a bitch. All this time he was dragging her across the rough cement floor of the basement. He threw her into the coal bin and from then on it was pure horror. He kept beating her with all his strength. When he was exhausted at last, he dragged her back across the basement floor, up the steps and threw her out into the street.

"I don't think you mug no more," he said heavily. "If you do, you damn fool. More better you be good gorl. You tell police, I tell police. Who makes out better? Move away from this street. I don't like you."

Somehow or other before daylight Binnie managed to crawl to her own flat. The bruises were nothing; it was the pain. He had torn her badly and the beatings could be felt in every muscle. She could not quite crawl up the stairs and that was where she was found when daylight came.

She was taken to the hospital and questioned by the police. All she said was, mocking them, that she had fallen down and stepped on herself. She did not name Salaski. Big Edna was the only one who came to see her, and all she did was sit silently beside the bed and gape out the window. Once however, she asked Binnie who had beaten her. Binnie was in great pain at that moment, and she whispered, "Old Man Salaski." She forgot immediately that she had said it.

Because of lack of room and because she had mended so quickly, she was discharged from the hospital after three days. Again it was only Big Edna who was waiting there at the flat to help her up the stairs. After dark, Spanish came to see her.

He said in that dull voice of his, "Never pick on a Polack. A beating up don't mean nuthin' to a Polack. Don't go out muggin' no more."

He didn't mind Big Edna seeing his slashed face because, if anything, she was even more stupid than Sugar. They left together about ten o'clock.

The next morning Old Man Salaski was found in the basement of his flat, dead from a beating so brutal that he was hardly recognizable. Captain Gahagen immediately threw two teams of detectives into the case. By evening, the police were at Binnie's flat. First, they flatly accused her of the murder. She defied them. They questioned her, then took her down to the Station house, where she continued to maintain her innocence. The police did not believe her. They had all the facts but one. They knew that she had been the decoy to lure Salaski to the mugging. They even knew how much money had been taken from him. They did not know, however, that Sugar and Veronica were implicated. She tried to tell them that she had been going home from the movies that evening, met Salaski coming out and being they lived on the same street he offered to walk home with her. On the way home, she said, they had been jumped by two armed girls. She did not know the names of the girls. The police scoffed that off as pure malarkey. The doctor who had treated her in the hospital admitted that it was possible, although not probable, that she had killed Salaski. The police did not need anything more than a "possible." A grand jury called by the District Attorney indicted her for murder.

Midge came to her cell in less than an hour. The first question she asked was, "You didn't kill Salaski, did you?"

Binnie said, "I didn't Midge, I didn't. Honest I didn't." Even to her own ears the statement sounded false.

Then Midge said, "If you didn't do it, someone else did. And I swear, Binnie, I'll find out."

And that statement sounded no more convincing than Binnie's had. Midge was crying, however. She had promised and Midge always kept her promises.

Midge did not know where to turn. Sugar and Veronica were out. She could not think of any other Deb who'd go that far for Binnie. It was with a shock that she realized that Binnie really did not have any friends, except possibly the Mick.

On a desperate chance she went to the club hoping to find the Mick there. He was. He was playing poker at a round card table in the far corner with Vince and several other Seniors. She interrupted the game and asked the Mick to come outside with her. Standing behind the table was a short squat Italian. She knew who it was. Di Lucca. He was so obviously a man that he made the others, even Vince, look like kids. She took Mick into the small room called an office. It was where dead Groff and Vince had held their conferences. It had been unused ever since. She closed the door and faced Mick intensely. Midge did everything intensely. "Salaski's dead," she told him, watching his open face.

His expression was so flabbergasted that her spirit sank, for she knew that the Mick had no knowledge of Salaski. That evening she went back to the Elm Street flat and her father, who seemed to have turned over a new leaf, advised her to talk to her new friend Bjorn Bjornson. He was in the gangs, her father said and if anybody'd know, it would be a guy in the gangs.

Bjorn was thoughtful when she finally poured out the story to him. He had already heard it through the grapevine. "Who," he asked, "was close enough to Binnie to do a thing like that?" The only one Midge could think of was Big Edna, who had worshipped Binnie. It had been that way ever since the night Binnie had saved her from Weinie, the Junior Lover, and had clobbered Veronica.

At least it was worth the chance. She and Bjorn went down-Butt to Big Edna's flat, but her mother and father said Big Edna was visiting relatives somewhere in New Mexico. They didn't know the address, because Big Edna didn't know how to write. As they left the flat, Bjorn said positively, "They're lying. They know."

Midge thought so too, for the elder Bivens had been shifty about the whole thing. She knew if she went to the police they'd laugh at her, or worse, because she'd been a Rover Deb. Again she did not know what to do. She decided to watch the Bivens flat. After a week of this it became obvious that Big Edna was not there, and would not be back until the murder cooled. Then she had another idea, to watch the Bivens mail box.

After another week a letter came, addressed in a childish scrawl. The only address was the postmark, Weehawken, New Jersey. She took the letter from the mail box with slender fingers. She carried it to Bjorn. It seemed to be of no value. The contents were meaningless chatter, chiefly about school, and it was unsigned.

Weehawken was a large place. The only thing Midge knew about it was that there, on the Palisades, Aaron Burr had shot Alexander Hamilton.

Midge settled down to watch the Bivens mail box again. Finally a letter appeared written in a more adult hand. It was from Weehawken and on the flap of the envelope was the return address of 27½ Boulevard East. She did not take this letter but memorized the address. She went immediately to Bjorn.

She was depending upon him more and more and she had a strong feeling she was in love with the guy. He was cleaner and decenter than any of the Rovers she'd known. Furthermore, the Imperials were not a fighting club like the Rovers or the Jacks. It was a social club and they spent much of their time in the Youth Center one street east of the precinct police station. The Imperials wouldn't fight and no one would fight them, not so close to the House.

Bjorn said that he would go with her to Weehawken. They wasted no time. By six that same day she, Bjorn and three other Imperials were on their way to Weehawken.

It was a tall, narrow apartment house at the lower end of the Boulevard. As they looked up at the windows, they saw a twitch of fabric and the shadow of a figure fleeing into the dark interior. That was the apartment to which they went. The elderly couple who answered the door looked like Santa Claus and his wife. He had a small white beard, well kept, and she was round and red-cheeked. They readily admitted being relatives of the Bivens'. He himself was Mrs. Biven's brother.

But Edna?

Why, they hadn't seen Edna since she was *that* high. They had not the faintest idea where she might have gone, except that there *was* a sort of cousin in New Mexico. They were willing to do everything they could to help, and Mrs. Bivens, regretfully shaking her head, admitted that she could not find it in her heart to like Big Edna, who, she said, should of been a man.

"But," she added, not quite so cordially, "I am sure Edna would not do a thing like that. She comes from a good family. Ain't that right, Mr. Bivens?"

"A very good family," nodded her husband. "My own brother. Edna isn't a bad girl, just homely."

"Of course she's homely," said his wife. "All you Bivens' is homely, and it's a shame. I know the men don't care, but a woman feels it."

She quickly arranged a bogus smile on her face and showed it to Midge, Bjorn and the three other scowling Imperials. "Just a little joke with us, that's all. You wouldn't want to meet a nicer man than Mr. Bivens' brother Dan. We always have him for Thanksgiving."

"Don't you ever hear from Edna?" asked Midge desperately.

"Oh yes. She's very thoughtful. Such a nice card on my birthday. And let me tell you something for your own good, young lady." She could not conceal her hostility any longer, although she managed to put a certain curdled sweetness into her voice, "If I was you, I wouldn't go around saying Edna killed that man. It ain't nice. You'll get in trouble."

"But I didn't say that at all," Midge protested. "I—I just thought she might be able to help Binnie. Just something she heard, maybe."

"The same thing. No difference. You're trying to make Edna as bad as your friend. The police don't arrest people for no reason."

"Not no more," said her husband in the same harsh tones. "They know things we don't. There's a big police college in Jer' City, and that's what they study—arresting the right people. If your friend is arrested, that's where she belongs. And I don't want you coming around no more saying things about my family. Now please go before there's any trouble."

Midge burst into sobs, covering her face with her hands because there were no tears; she was just plain mad but she couldn't afford to get into a scrap with these people.

"I—I'm sorry," she said in a muffled voice. "I didn't mean it that way. I'm all upset. Can—can I use your john for a minute, please?"

She expected a flat refusal, but Edna's aunt was magnanimous. "I know just how you feel, little girl. I get the same way myself. You want to get alone by yourself for a second. Women do." She glared at her husband.

"I'm retired," he smugly told the boys. "It's her idea I'm underfoot all the time. I ain't. I'm just home."

"It's through that door and to the right, little girl." She pointed.

Midge mumbled, "Thanks," and hurried across the living room and through the dining room arch. She'd been listening and was now certain someone was in the bedroom.

She flung it open and a large, yellow-haired woman staggered back with a cry. Midge said, "You're the one I saw peeking out the front window."

"Peek!" the woman tried to sound affronted. "I wash the windows, not peek, girlie. I'm the cleaning lady. And who said you should push in here, huh?"

"I thought it was the bathroom," Midge lied dully.

"Well, you got another think coming. You better go home, like the missus said. There ain't no Edna here."

Midge said, "Thanks for nothing," and went back to the living room.

Edna's aunt was standing beside her chair, clutching the back of it. "You get out of here right now," she said angrily. "I got a good mind to call the cops."

"The cops," echoed her husband. "I'll call them myself."

Bjorn shook his head at Midge, but there was no fire left in her. She walked to the door.

"Well," said Edna's aunt, "I see you found the right door for once."

They left. Downstairs, Bjorn said to one of the Imperials, "Keep an eye on it. All right?"

The other boy looked back at the apartment building. "Okay. But she ain't there, man."

"She ain't," said Midge. "He don't have to stay."

"She might turn up," said Bjorn.

"I'll stick around on the off-chance," said the first boy. "She's just dumb enough."

Midge shook her head, but did not protest. She was at that stage of discouragement when further talk seemed futile. It was a silent drive back to the city.

Then she said woodenly, "Let me off at Midtown Terminal. I'm going down-Butt to see Mick Fogarty. He's got to help her."

"He skipped out, Midgie," said Bjorn. "The cops're looking for him."

"Then I'll talk to Vince Kirby. And don't try and stop me. Let me off here."

There was no way of stopping her. If she didn't go then, she'd go later. Subdued, they watched her get on the bus.

Midge walked into the Rovers' clubhouse on Grove Street within a half hour. "Vince in there?" she asked a Junior, canting her hard little chin at the small room that Vince used for private talks. The young girl nodded dumbly and Midge walked across the basement in a growing silence that followed her like a rolling fog. She walked in without knocking. A tall, emaciated boy in the corner sharply turned his back, but not before Midge recognized him as Spanish, the one with the cut face.

A squat man, sitting behind the table in Vince's usual seat, was saying to Vince, who stood sullenly at the side of the room, "—and I don't want no rumbles, Kirby. The cops know too goddamn much. You got a pigeon in your pack and I want to get my—" He stopped abruptly and looked at Midge.

His face seemed to become darker as all expression seeped from it. Midge's hand was in her purse and very carefully he spread his own hands, open, on the table. He knew what some of these crazy Debs carried in their purses.

Midge knew him by sight. He was di Lucca, said to be boss of the Butt. She was trembling so hard that she had to clench her teeth. All she had in her purse was a rusted and broken .32, but they wouldn't take chances so long as she kept her hand in there.

"I want some help, Mr. di Lucca," she said, ignoring Vince and Spanish. "Binnie Riordan's in jail and this pack hasn't lifted a finger."

Di Lucca shook his head. "Sorry, baby," he said, "but nobody can help that broad. Even if they don't nail her for knocking off Salaski, she'll take a long rap on the mugging."

"But—"

"There ain't no buts, baby. I'm giving it to you straight. You know this Veronica Ferenc? Okay. The cops got her on the mugging too, and she's singing. The Riordan broad's tied up with the killing and the mugging and Christ knows what else by this time. She's bad news, baby. Stay away from her."

"But she don't even have a lawyer!"

"The court'll give her one. Be smart like these guys and stay out of it."

"Because you told them to stay out."

"Yeah, I told them," he kept his eyes on the hand clenched in her purse. "But they couldn't do nothing, just make it worse."

"You could help her."

"Sure, if she had a prayer, but she ain't."

"Look, Mr. di Lucca, all I want is to find Big Edna Bivens."

"She's Catholic," said Spanish unexpectedly.

Di Lucca glowered. "So what? Shut up."

Spanish shrugged, unintimidated. "Catholics stick with Catholics, that's all. You a Catholic?"

"I'll give you this much help, baby." Di Lucca turned from Spanish to Midge, "and I'm telling you, I couldn't do no more if I spent money. She's sunk. Tell her to cop a plea for manslaughter on account of the rape. The D.A.'ll go along with that. And I promise she'll be out in a year. I got the parole board in my back pocket. Fair enough?"

There was a sly, smiling evasiveness on his face and she knew he was lying. He just wanted to get her out of there because of what he thought she had in her purse. She turned to Vince, but he sullenly stared across the room at nothing. She was dismayed at how awfully young he looked all of a sudden, compared to di Lucca. It was hopeless. Di Lucca was telling them what to do and they were afraid not to do it.

But her time was running out. The longer she stayed, the harder it would be to leave the club in one piece.

"You can go, baby," said di Lucca. "Nobody'll stop you. Just don't do nothing dumb, that's all."

Now Midge was really afraid of him. He didn't miss a thing. He nodded at Vince and sulkily, without a word, Vince led her across the big outside room to the exit door. He turned and walked away. She kept her hand in her purse as she went up Grove Street toward the bus stop. To her surprise she heard Bjorn call softly and she stopped, aghast.

"Are you crazy?" she whispered when he joined her. "They'll kill you."

He smiled, shook his head and opened his coat a little, showing her the butt of a gun thrust under the waistband of his pants. "You're the one they might get after, Midge," he said. "We'll have to go by bus. The car got a flat at Bridge Street."

"Oh crise, a piece won't help you none if there's five, six of them.

They'll take it away and bust you up with it."

"Let's go, Midgie. Stick close and walk on the outside. Keep away from the buildings. It's only a half block to the bus."

For the first time in her life, Midge began to cry, but didn't know why. She clung to his arm, half-running to keep pace with his strides. Nobody bothered them and luckily a bus came right along. Midge couldn't have borne a fifteen-minute wait. Three Rover Seniors got on at the next corner, looked around the bus and started up the aisle toward Bjorn.

Midge hissed, "Don't do nothing," and jumped out into the aisle, confronting the foremost Senior, her trembling hand deep in her purse.

"Hello, Tony," she said. "You get off at Ridley, don't you? That's the next stop."

He looked at the way her handbag was tilted up at his stomach and backed away one step. Vince would have slapped it aside, she was that close, but not Tony. He could almost see the gun, hear the report, and feel the slug hit him just over the navel. And he was sure she'd do it. Debs were sometimes worse than guys. They didn't give a damn. And the lousy Imperial had a piece, too, the way he sat with his hand under his coat. He kept backing away.

"Yeah, this is our stop, Midge," he said as the bus slowed; then in furious frustration, "Juss don' come back no more, you lousy bitch. Or you, Imperial. Nobody's lucky twict."

The three of them got off and, looking back, Midge saw them standing on the corner, looking darkly after the bus. They weren't very bright, thank God. They could of phoned ahead and stopped the bus in three blocks, shooting out a tire or something. But they were too dumb, the kind that had to be told what to do and how to do it. Midge laughed and felt better. Bjorn grinned. "This is a helluva time to tell you," he said, "but this is only a cap gun. It's all I could scare up without notice."

"And I got a hunk of rusty iron!"

But there was no real mirth; they had to be too watchful until the bus rolled out of Rover territory. Anyway, Midge was not accustomed to laughter. There'd never been very much to laugh at.

Before they got to New Street, Midge said, "I'm going uptown and try and see Loretta again. She's gotta be in her room sometime."

"She ain't there, Midgie," said Bjorn in an odd voice. "I was up this morning. She, well, she went to Chicago with a guy."

She looked at him and he flushed. "What guy?" she asked. "Luke McGluke?"

"Well—you know what she is," he mumbled.

"Yeah, sure. Binnie's sister, and nuts to the rest of it. Now where is she?"

"I don't know where she is now."

"Now? Whattaya mean, now? You seen her?"

"Yeah, I seen her. She come in about four this morning. Now look, Midge, I didn't do nothing. All I said was, the cops got Binnie—and she acted like crazy. Tried to run outta the flat and everything, but there was two guys at the door."

"Oh no, you didn't scare her or nothing," said Midge sarcastically. "All you did was act like strongarm mutts."

"That's not what she's scared of," said Bjorn evenly. "Her stuff was nearly all packed to go. She don't want to be tied in with Binnie. She's scared of cops, her being a whore and all. She wouldn't even mail Binnie money, for fear of the cops. She said she was getting out of town. But I didn't scare her, Midge. She's been scared a long time. She was ready to run."

A stone lumped inside Midge. Yes, that's the way it would be with Loretta. And why should she take chances after Binnie kicked her out of her own flat—the flat Loretta was paying rent on and sending Binnie money every week? The cops'd give her a bad time. Loretta was only doing what she had to.

Bjorn touched her arm. "What happened at the Rovers?" he asked.

"The Rovers?" Midge came out of her reverie. "Oh. Nothing. Di Lucca was there."

"Di Lucca!"

"Yeah, Mr. Big Shot. Giving orders. Said Binnie should cop a plea. That was after a guy named Spanish said Catholics stick together and was di Lucca Catholic. Di Lucca didn't like it, his buttin' in. Spanish, he don't give a damn about nobody. He's got the cut face. You don't know him. Hardly nobody does. He could of killed Salaski. It wouldn't mean nothing to him, that kind of guy...."

Bjorn touched her arm. "Here's our stop, Midgie."

Midge followed him apathetically out of the bus. She looked around. It was Elm Street and there was the red brick Youth Center and the Visiting Nurse's Office.

"Come in an' lay down for a while," said Bjorn. "You look beat."

She said, "I feel beat," and did not protest when he took her by the elbow and steered her into the Visiting Nurse's office. The nurse, who seemed too meek and mild for this beat but was tough as nails, smiled and took Midge into a small, soothing, green room, firmly made her undress and lie on the most comfortable bed Midge had ever felt. It had a real foam rubber mattress. She said, "Drink this," and obediently Midge drank it, and before she realized it, everything went away, at first mistily, and then altogether.

It was dark when she awakened, and she leaped from the bed like a wild animal in fear of a trap. It took her a few moments to remember that she was not in a trap. However, she did not turn on the light, but fumbled for her clothes by the glow of the street lamp outside. She moved silently into the big room of the Youth Center. It was dark, but at the far side a sliver of yellow light showed from beneath a door. She crossed quickly and listened at the panel. There was a sharp slapping sound, then a voice, possibly Bjorn's: "Come on, come on, what do you want us to do, hurt you?" The voice of Spanish told them exactly what he wanted them to do. Another slap.

Midge kicked open the door, and there was Bjorn towering angrily over Spanish, held in a straight wooden chair by two muscular Imperials. Spanish's face looked worse than usual, blotched red and white. Bjorn held a wet, knotted bath towel in his left hand.

Midge screamed. She couldn't help it. It was pure hysteria. She had seen and heard too much of this with the Rovers; she had done some of it herself when Debs got out of line. She couldn't stand any more of it. Her head was ready to burst from it and she screamed. Forms and colors swam crazily like a mixture of oil paints poured into a pail of water and stirred....

When sanity returned, she was sitting in the wooden chair and Spanish was anxiously patting her face with a wet handkerchief and no one else was in the room. She looked vacantly at him, without recognition. He put his finger to his lips, shook his head and pointed to the door, which was now bolted.

"Shhhh," he whispered. "They think you kill me. They wait outside now to go away with the body. Me. They don' want for you to get in no trouble. More better you trust them. They're hokay." Again he put his finger to the lips of his mutilated face.

"What're you talking about?" she asked blankly, but whispering as he had.

"You scream, hit at them with that." He nodded toward a short length of broken broom handle on the floor. "They go out and maybe think you follow, but you lock the door and faint on the floor. They yell for you not to hit me. Better you tell them it's hokay. They pretty scared, I think."

She nodded. "I'm all right, Bjorn," she said in a louder voice. "I want to talk to Spanish. I'll get more that way than you beating him up. He won't move outta the chair. I got the club. You can stay and listen if you want, but don't try and bust in or he won't talk."

Spanish rubbed the back of his neck. "That's for true," he muttered.

"Don't take chances like this, baby," Bjorn pleaded.

"I stay in the chair, hokay," called Spanish. "I get up, she hit me with the club. You listen out there, I don' go near this one, no."

"Start talking then, man," said Bjorn, "or we will bust in."

Spanish nodded at Midge and she said, "How'd you get here?"

He did not quite laugh. "I am going someplace else through your territory. I don' think Imperials bother me. I'm damn fool. They catch me."

"You're a Rover."

"They think so maybe. Ain' so. I just stay there, like I hide out. I'm suppose to be dead, so I stay that way. Other fella dead they think is me."

"You killed him."

"*Si*. He cut me and I kill him. This is a long time ago. He don' cut my face. That's from my brother. That's why I hide with the Rovers, to wait till I can get him. Forget that part. Has no business with your friend, Binnie Riordan."

"Did you kill Joey Groff?" Midge persisted.

"No. That is my brother, too. I think maybe soon he kills Vince Kirby, too. Then there is a rumble with Rovers and Happy Jacks. It will be a trap, I think. My brother, that's what he likes, the trap. I know how he thinks. I spend a long time figuring how he thinks. He wants for the Rovers to start the rumble, the Happy Jacks hide and the cops bust up the Rovers. Then the Happy Jacks take the whole Butt for their territory. That's how my brother thinks."

"Who is your brother?"

"I don' tell you that. I wait a long time to see him."

He took his hand from the back of his neck and Midge stifled a cry, for he was holding a long, flat, carefully honed knife. "It's hokay," he reassured her. "That's for my brother, not you." He pointed the knife at the door before sliding it back into its narrow sheath. "They don' know I have it," he whispered. "I could of kill them with it, but this fighting knife, I save it special for my brother."

Midge shivered and asked hurriedly, "Who killed Salaski?"

"I don' know. I don' care."

"Don't you want to help Binnie?"

"I don' help nobody."

"But you know more than most people. Did Big Edna do it?"

"I don't know who knocked him off," he said sharply. "I don't give one good God damn. Leave it like that."

"Your lousy Spanish accent slipped, hotshot," said Midge sarcastically.

Momentary alarm flared in his lackluster eyes. "No, no. Is the way I always talk."

"Sure. Because your brother knows you *don't* have a Spik accent. You want to surprise him. But suppose I went around saying there's a guy called Spanish with a phony accent and a cut face, and he's looking for his brother. And suppose your brother heard about it? He might surprise you. And don't lift your hand. You know what I mean. The guys'll bust in that door like tissue paper."

He eyed her speculatively, weighing his chances, but there was no way out of the room except through the door. He shrugged. "Okay, but I don't know nothing about Salaski, except Binnie Riordan turn in my—turned in Sugar Fernandez a half hour ago. But Sugar didn't do it. She's too stinking dumb to do anything by herself. You gotta draw a picture."

"Maybe Veronica drew the picture to frame Binnie."

"I don' think so. She'll get a mugging rap. A year anyways. Turning evidence on Binnie Riordan don't get her off. Too much stuff in the newspapers."

"Did Veronica knock him off?"

"Maybe. I don' know. I don' pay no attention."

"Did Big Edna do it?"

"I told you. I don' care about that stuff."

"No? You cared enough to tell di Lucca that her and him was both Catholic, and Catholics stick together."

"No. A Catholic would of got what I meant, but you ain't a Catholic. I don't know why I said it in the first place, even though your tough friend did me a favor once. I guess maybe sometimes I remember favors. I'll tell you. When a Catholic girl gets in trouble, sometimes the family puts her away in a convent school a little while. Good place to hide, a convent school."

"I never heard of a convent school."

"Catholics know. I'll tell you more. I notice things, unnerstan? Some ways, Big Edna is very tough. You can't beat nothin outta her. Tough talk don't scare her neither. I tell you how to scare her, though. Make her do something against the Church, like when Wienie was gonna break her in. She's most scared of the priest. She beats up somebody, it don't mean nothing to her. But the priest says, putting out for a guy is a sin, she don't let the guys near her. That's how she is. Me I don't say nothing to nobody but you, but what I think is, your friend Binnie kills Salaski. She's very tough. You don't know."

"And you don't know Binnie," Midge backlashed, but she felt very discouraged all the same. Big Edna was becoming less and less of a possibility.

"Why's Mick Fogarty hiding out?" she asked. "Him and Binnie was together nearly every night, specially after Salaski jumped her. He could give her an alibi. Or at least stand by her."

"Him!" Spanish laughed thinly. "He's chicken. He won' help your friend. He hides out in Jersey City, or maybe Philadelphia. I don't know for sure."

Midge made a formless gesture with her hands. "I kind of expected it. They'll let you go now. Wait a minute. I remember hearing you're on 'H,' so what's your goddamn word worth?"

"On 'H?' You mean this," he showed her a hypodermic needle. "*Si*, a little, not much, only when it hurts." He touched the spot under his ribs into which Sordo had thrust the knife. "Once a week about, no more. I don' want to be no crazy mainliner when I meet my brother. I want him to get the most out of every little bit of the present I have for him. I go now. I'll say good luck, but nobody has good luck, what the hell."

He unbolted the door. He paused and half-turned, "If I think of something maybe to help your friend, I'll get in touch. She did me a kind of favor once."

He opened the door and went out, casually rubbing the back of his neck. The Imperials stood silently aside and let him go, although the hands of two of them twitched as he passed. He stopped at the street door, looked back over his shoulder and pointed a finger at those two.

"When you get to want to beat guys up," he said, "you're like the Rovers. No good. Better off dead."

They started angrily, but he was gone, and Bjorn drawled, "He's got a point there." He looked into the little room. Midge was standing dejectedly beside the empty chair, looking at nothing, nothing at all. After a while, she sat down and stared at the floor. It was three quarters of an hour before she came out.

After a glance, she asked, "Where's Angelo?"

"His sister is a nun," said Bjorn. "She's lending a hand. She knows the convent school in Weehawken. Angelo had to stretch things a little, though."

"Big Edna," said Midge without interest.

"They oughta be here any minute, the way Angelo drives. The married sisters're picking her up."

"What're you gonna do?" asked Midge.

"Nothing, Midge, I promise. Scare her maybe, that's all. We dug up some money for Binnie's lawyer, Midge."

"How much?"

"It was a surprise. He only asked a c-note." He lied; it had been five hundred. Bjorn's car didn't have a flat, he had sold it. Bjorn had gone all out for Midge. "And he's one of the best. McKechnie. He's practically got the courthouse in his back pocket. A solid middle-age guy around thirty. All business, no jazz."

Midge revived a little. "That's the first good news today and—"

The street door opened and Big Edna walked in truculently, prodded from behind by Angelo, a swarthy, muscular boy. "My sisters picked her like a daisy," he grinned at Bjorn. "Said they were from her Weehawken aunt."

"—you," said Big Edna in her heavy, clotted voice. And then she saw the bed that Bjorn had placed prominently in the middle of the room. Her eyes widened and began to move erratically, seeking non-existent escape.

"Bring in Wienie the Lover," said Bjorn loudly.

Big Edna wailed, "Mama, mama—Father Daly—" and would have made a dash for the street door if two of the huskiest Imperials didn't give her a rough shove that sprawled her, whimpering, across the bed.

"I ain't gonna stay for this," said Midge, and walked out.

FOURTEEN

Vince Kirby lay on the floor, his broad-boned face against the hard iron leaves of the steam radiator in an obscure room of an obscure fleabag called the World Hotel on Division Street. No one was supposed to know he maintained this shabby hideout. But Vince didn't care about the shabbiness, nor did he care about the sharp edges of the iron radiator that dug into his face. He didn't care about anything, not even the wide-blade knife that stuck up diagonally from under his left rib cage. He never would be aware that the strong, experienced thrust had split his heart apart. Even at the moment of dying, he had been unaware of his death. He had not seen the shadow or the strike come up from the darkness beside his bed. And now he was dead, his face broken from his fall into the rusting radiator.

Now, a long broad knife is not an easy thing to extract from a dead victim. The flesh clings tenaciously, unwilling to part with so intimate an instrument. On the other hand, neither did the killer wish to part with this particular knife. It was his favorite, very handy for chopping, slashing or stabbing. He swore, for now he had to place one foot solidly on Vince's chest, take the knife handle in both hands and pull as hard as he could, which is harder work than it sounds, and he had a congenital disinclination to work in any fashion. He strained and at length felt the heavy knife start to come free.

Then, an unfortunate thing occurred. Someone turned on the ceiling light. It was only a forty-watt bulb, but it seemed like a flaming *nova* to the killer.

"Good evening, Sordo, my brother," said Ricki Fernandez in courteous Spanish. "I perceive that you are in the midst of a difficulty. It is my regret that I cannot offer assistance."

Sordo whirled and crouched, a six-inch switch blade in his hand. Ricki leaned against the far door, indolently scratching the back of his neck.

Sordo gasped, "You!"

"Yes, I," Ricki agreed gravely. "Lazarus risen from the dead, yet still your beloved brother, Ricardo Jaime Maria Cascabel y Fernandez, known simply as Spanish. But please, I beg you, continue with what you were doing and dispose of that ridiculous toy. Is it a knife? How strange. When you are quite ready, we must resolve the problem you proposed." He touched the crisscrossed scar welts on his face.

Sordo was a quick one and did not flounder long in surprise. "You look dead, Ricardo," he said in a chilling voice. "You look more ugly than death. Yet, you still stroll into the wrong places, as you did before. We must correct that habit permanently. Yes, you do look dead. If I sneeze, it may blow you through the window. Take care."

"How true, and I thank you, my brother. How ignominious, to be sneezed through a window. Your reminder is most kind. I shall avoid the window, by all means, and remain here. But pray tell me, what is that strange object you were attempting to remove from the gentleman on the floor? *Ay de mi*, a butcher's cleaver! Have you become a butcher, my brother? How sad. What a degrading fall for a respectable assassin."

"You'll find out what kind of cleaver it is, brother."

"Unfortunately. How ignoble it will be to kill a butcher. Or does one merely butcher a butcher? However, I am a simple man and shall comfort myself in various small ways. Please, I beg you, remove your cleaver from the gentleman. It is almost as repulsive as you, my brother."

Furiously, Sordo wrenched the knife free and turned on Ricki. His grin fairly glittered. Almost languidly, Ricki took the narrow fighting knife from its sheath between his shoulder blades. Compared to the lithe, compact Sordo, so dangerously quick, Ricki looked like a starved, arthritic stork.

"I wish this didn't have to be so short and quick," said Sordo, "but under the circumstances, it must be."

It was. He never had a chance. The needle point of Ricki's knife flickered blindingly in his face like a burst of fireflies, sending him back defensively in surprise, and then, following fluidly, Ricki glided the narrow fighting blade between Sordo's ribs, high up and quite close to the breastbone, through the exact center of the heart.

It was not amazing. For hours and years and every day, Ricki had perfected that flickering feint and the following lethal thrust.

Slowly, sadly, he walked from the hotel. He moved heavily, a man who had lost all purpose and the vital need to live.

FIFTEEN

In her cell on the top floor of the county courthouse, Binnie was so close to hysteria that she could feel the start of a scream gibber inside her head. Her lawyer, a square-faced man with harsh gray hair, kept droning the same thing over and over until frantically she wanted to shove the leaden pillow into his mouth.

"It's the only thing, Miss Riordan, your only chance. The district attorney will accept a plea of manslaughter and—"

But Binnie was not listening, for she saw Midge hurrying toward her cell with one of the matrons. She clung to the bars and cried out, "Oh, Midge, Midge, please, please, get rid of this lousy mouthpiece. Please, Midge, please, get me a decent lawyer. I don't want to take the rap. I didn't kill Old Man Salaski. I didn't. Honest to crise, I didn't! Get me out of here, Midge. I'll leave the Rovers. I'll do anything you want. I'll get a job—anything, anything!" She reached abjectly through the bars, grasping as if Midge were her last hope. Tears dribbled down her face. "I'll get down on my knees, Midge. They want to put me away, maybe even the Chair. Please, please, please, please . . . She dropped to her knees and groveled, babbling incoherently.

It was humiliating to see, but the matron was unmoved. "You can get up off your lousy knees. One of your sorority sisters came through with a confession—signed, sealed and delivered. You won't burn, damn it."

"Big Edna," said Midge in a small voice. "She said she'd never let nobody do anything to you, remember? You know, on account of you not letting Veronica get her initiated by Wienie."

Binnie started slowly, unbelievingly, to her feet, and then came up with a furious surge. "She did it and let me rot in here all this time?" she screamed. "Look at me! Look at me. I'm a mess. Where is she? Where is she, Midge?" She stopped and looked arrogantly at the matron. "Okay, sourpuss, let me out. Don't just stand there. Come on. Snap it up."

The matron smiled grimly. "Not so fast, sweetheart. It seems like there's a little charge of some muggings. The judge won't send you up for a minute more than ten years. He's a soft-hearted old bat." She walked away, laughing.

Binnie's jaw wobbled. "Ten—years? That's just jazz, ain't it, Midge? She's just being a bastard, ain't she?"

Wordlessly, Midge shook her head. "And there's nothing I can do about that, Binnie," she said in a still smaller voice.

"You—can't?"

"Well now, at least it's not manslaughter, Miss Riordan. Don't let the matron upset you. She's antagonistic. I'll look into—"

Binnie snapped, "Shut up. I'm thinking." She raised her face to Midge. "Get me Vince Kirby," she ordered.

"They—they found him dead this morning, and Mick Fogarty's hiding out. Di Lucca's kind of running things, using a guy named Reilly for a stooge. Di Lucca won't do nothing. I talked to him."

Binnie bit her lip, her face white and strained. She snapped her fingers. "Spanish!" she said. "Get me Spanish. He's on the inside."

"Sure. Okay, Binnie. Right away."

"Move, move!" Binnie yelled. "And tell the matron to get this crud out, too."

It was an hour before Spanish came walking draggingly up the corridor with the matron.

"You took your goddamn time," Binnie snapped at him. "What's the matter? You look like the wrath of God."

"*Si*, that's what I am, the wrath of God. Midge found me just in time, I think."

"Just in time hell. It's an hour. Look, you owe me a favor."

"Ah, so that's why you are nice to me that time—so I owe you the favor."

"You owe me a favor. It's money in the bank."

"Hokay," he said drearily, "I owe you a favor. But you're not much good, I don't think."

"Who cares what you think. I want the favor. Now listen . . ." she moved closer to the bars and lowered her voice. "Somebody turned me in to the cops. Then somebody turned Veronica in. But I had to turn Sugar in or she never would be here. See what I mean?"

"I see."

"Okay. Now I want you to find out who turned me and Veronica in and didn't turn Sugar in."

Spanish shrugged his skeletal shoulders. "I know that. Sugar talks too much to a man. Pete Fernandez. He's a pigeon. I know it for years."

"And you didn't do nothing about it?" said Binnie incredulously.

"Why should I? I don' care. Now you got your favor. I go now. I don't think I live so long. I don' feel like it."

"Okay, but get me di Lucca before you drop dead. And don't say nothing to him about Pete Fernandez, understand. If I tell him who the pigeon is down-Butt, he'll get me out of here. Only he'll get me out of here first, *then* I'll tell him."

"I don' tell nobody nothing no more," said Spanish in the same dead voice. "Just that you want to see him, is all."

"And tell him it's important, make sure."

"When I tell him, he knows it's important. He'll come."

"Okay, okay. Now beat it. I want to think some more."

Spanish said, "Better you think less. Too bad I owe you this favor." He walked away.

Midge was sitting in Angelo's car with Bjorn when di Lucca drove up in his black Caddy and hurried into the courthouse.

"Well, that's it," said Bjorn. "If she gets tied up with di Lucca, it's the end."

"And there used to be nobody like Binnie," said Midge, feeling crushed. "Nobody at all."

"You got it turned around," said Bjorn. "She used to be just like the rest of them. Maybe a little smarter, maybe a little worse . . ."

THE END

LORENZ HELLER BIBLIOGRAPHY
(1910-1965)

As Frederick Lorenz

Novels:
A Rage at Sea (Lion, 1953)
Night Never Ends (Lion, 1954)
The Savage Chase (Lion, 1954)
A Party Every Night (Lion, 1956)
Ruby (Lion, 1956)
Hot (Lion, 1956)
Dungaree Sin (Chariot, 1960)

Stories:
Backbite (*Justice*, Jan 1956)
Big Catch (*Justice*, July 1955)
Living Bait (*Justice*, May 1955)

As Dan Gregory

Three Must Die! (Graphic, 1956)

As Laura Hale

Novels:
Wild is the Woman (Rainbow, 1951)
Lovers Don't Sleep (Falcon, 1951)
Kiss of Fire (Rainbow, 1952;
    reprinted in Australia as *Kiss Of
    Death,* Phantom, 1953)
Woman Hunter (Falcon, 1952;
    reprinted in Australia, Phantom,
    1953)
Desperate Blonde (Beacon Australia,
    1960)
Lessons in Lust (Beacon, 1961; re-
    write of *Woman Hunter*)
Sensual Woman (Beacon, 1961; re-
    write of *Lovers Don't Sleep*)
The Zipper Girls (Beacon, 1962; re-
    write of *Wild is the Woman*)

The Marriage Bed (Beacon, 1962; re-
    write of *Desperate Blonde*)

As Larry Heller

Novels:
I Get What I Want (Popular, 1956)
Body of the Crime (Pyramid, 1962)

Story:
Blood Is Thicker (*Guilty Detective
    Story Magazine*, Mar 1957)

As Larry Holden

Novels:
Hide-Out (Eton, 1953)
Dead Wrong (Pyramid, 1957)
Crime Cop (Pyramid, 1959)

Stories (alphabetical listing):
...And Death Makes Ten (*Detective
    Tales*, June 1947)
Another Man's Poison (*Shadow
    Mystery*, Apr/May 1948)
Any Corpse in a Storm (*Dime
    Mystery Magazine*, Aug 1949)
Anybody Lose a Corpse? (*Mammoth
    Detective*, Aug 1946)
The Big Haunt (*10-Story Detective
    Magazine*, Oct 1948)
Blackmail Means Homicide (*15
    Story Detective*, Feb 1950)
Bloody Night! (*Dime Mystery
    Magazine*, Oct 1949)
Bodyguard (*Thrilling Detective*, June
    1951)
Bullets for Beethoven [Dinny Keogh]
    (*Mammoth Mystery*, June 1946)

Coffin Key (*Detective Tales*, Oct 1951)

A Corpse at Large (*Ten Detective Aces*, July 1949)

Corpse in Waiting (*New Detective Magazine*, Nov 1950)

A Corpse to His Credit (*Dime Detective Magazine*, May 1947)

Criminal at Large (*Suspense Magazine*, Summer 1951)

The Crimson Path (*Detective Tales*, Sept 1947)

Cry Murder (*New Detective Magazine*, Oct 1952)

The Crying Corpse (*Ten Detective Aces*, Sept 1948)

Death Brings Down the House (*10-Story Detective Magazine*, Apr 1948)

Death Carries the Mail (*F.B.I. Detective Stories*, Aug 1950)

Death for Two! (*Detective Tales*, Dec 1952)

Death in Dirty Linen (*Shadow Mystery*, June/July 1947)

Death in Six Reels (*Doc Savage*, July/Aug 1948)

Death in Thin Ice (*Shadow Mystery*, Feb/Mar 1948)

Death Is Where You Find It (*Suspect Detective Stories*, Nov 1955)

Die, Baby, Die! (*Detective Tales*, June 1948)

Don't Crowd My Shroud (*10-Story Detective Magazine*, Dec 1948)

Don't Ever Forget (*Detective Story Magazine*, Mar 1953)

Don't Wait Up for Me (*Triple Detective*, Fall 1955)

The Eighteen Screaming Corpses (*Detective Tales*, Jan 1948)

The Expendable Ex (*Dime Detective Magazine*, June 1952)

Face in the Window (*Detective Tales*, June 1951)

Fall Guy (*Detective Tales*, Aug 1953)

Forger's Fate (*Dime Detective Magazine*, Apr 1951)

The High Cost of Chivalry (*Dime Detective Magazine*, Dec 1951)

Home for Christmas (*Thrilling Detective*, Dec 1947)

House of Hate (*10-Story Detective Magazine*, Apr 1949)

Humpty-Dumpty Homicide (*Detective Tales*, June 1949)

If the Body Fits— (*Dime Mystery Magazine*, Dec 1947)

If the Frame Fits— (*Detective Tales*, Dec 1951)

I'll Be Home for Murder! (*Detective Tales*, Apr 1948)

I'll See You Dead! (*Detective Tales*, May 1947)

In Her Mother's Best Bier! (*Detective Tales*, Dec 1948)

Keeping Honest (*Doc Savage*, Winter 1949)

Kickback for a Corpse (*All-Story Detective*, Apr 1949)

Killer's Kiss (*Detective Tales*, Aug 1949)

Lady in Red (*Detective Tales*, Oct 1948)

Lady-Killer (*Dime Detective Magazine*, Dec 1952)

Lethal Boy Blue (*Detective Tales*, May 1949)

Love Me, Love My Corpse! (*Detective Tales*, Aug 1948)

Make Mine Mayhem (*New Detective Magazine*, Jan 1949)

Man with a Rep (*Detective Tales*, Dec 1949)

Mayhem at Eight (*New Detective Magazine*, May 1950)

Mayhem's Mechanic (*Detective Tales*, Sept 1946)

Morgue Bait (*New Detective Magazine*, Dec 1951)

Murder and the Mermaid (*Dime Detective Magazine*, Oct 1952)

Murder Never Gets Too Old (*Private Detective*, Jan 1950)

Never Dead Enough (*New Detective Magazine*, Sept 1947)

Never Turn Your Back (*Mike Shayne Mystery Magazine*, July 1959)

Nightmare (*Detective Tales*, Oct 1952)

No Dead End (*Triple Detective*, Spring 1955)

On a Dead Man's Chest (*Thrilling Detective*, Apr 1953)

One Dark Night [Dinny Keogh] (*Mammoth Mystery*, Dec 1946)

One for the Hangman (*Suspect Detective Stories*, Feb 1956)

Operation—Murder (*F.B.I. Detective Stories*, Aug 1949)

Orphans Are Made (*Mobsters*, Feb 1953)

Out of the Frying Pan… (*15 Mystery Stories*, Oct 1950)

Port of the Dead (*New Detective Magazine*, July 1947)

Prelude to a Wake (*Dime Detective Magazine*, Feb 1952)

Red Nightmare (*Dime Mystery Magazine*, July 1947)

Sailor, Beware! (*Detective Story Magazine*, May 1953)

Save Me a Kill (*New Detective Magazine*, June 1953)

Self-Made Corpse (*Detective Tales*, Apr 1949)

She Cries Murder! (*New Detective Magazine*, June 1952)

Sing a Song of Murder (*Dime Detective Magazine*, Aug 1952)

Snow in August [Dinny Keogh] (*Mammoth Mystery*, Aug 1946)

The Spice of Death (*Private Detective*, Dec 1950)

Start with a Corpse [Dinny Keogh] (*Mammoth Mystery*, Jan 1946)

There's Death in the Heir [Dinny Keogh] (*Mammoth Mystery*, Aug 1947)

They Played Too Rough [Dinny Keogh] (*Mammoth Mystery*, Mar 1946)

This Shroud Reserved (*New Detective Magazine*, Oct 1951)

Those Slaughter-House Blues (*Mammoth Detective*, Feb 1947)

A Time for Dying (*Dime Detective Magazine*, Aug 1951)

Too Many Crosses [Dinny Keogh] (*Mammoth Mystery*, Feb 1947)

Tragedy in Waiting (*Invincible Detective Magazine*, Mar 1951)

The Trouble with Redheads (*Mike Shayne Mystery Magazine*, Apr 1959)

Two-Headed Killer (*15 Mystery Stories*, Feb 1950)

Undressed to Kill (*New Detective Magazine*, Sept 1949)

Vicious Circle (*Detective Tales*, Nov 1949)

The Voice That Kills (*15 Mystery Stories*, Aug 1950)

Wake of the Ermine Chick (*15 Story Detective*, Dec 1950)

When Cops Fall Out (*Detective Tales*, June 1953)

With Hostile Intent (*Fifteen Detective Stories*, Dec 1954)

With Love and Bullets! (*Detective Tales*, Feb 1953)

Written in Blood (*Ten Detective Aces*, May 1948)

You Can't Live Forever (*New Detective Magazine*, Aug 1952)

You Die Alone (*Fifteen Detective Stories*, Oct 1953)

You'll Die Laughing (*Detective Tales*, Oct 1950)

You're Killing Me (*Detective Story Magazine*, Sept 1953)

Dinny Keogh series:
Start with a Corpse (1946)
They Played Too Rough (1946)
Bullets for Beethoven (1946)
Snow in August (1946)
One Dark Night (1946)
Too Many Crosses (1947)
There's Death in the Heir (1947)

As Lorenz Heller

Novel:
Murder in Make-Up (Messner, 1937)

Stories:
Blood Money (*Suspect Detective Stories*, Nov 1955)
A Tasty Dish (*Suspect Detective Stories*, Feb 1956)
Twilight (*Short Stories*, Nov 1956)
The Hero (*Mystery Tales*, Dec 1958)
The Last Hunt (*Adventure*, June 1959)

As Burt Sims

Television Scripts:
1953: "Death Does a Rumba" (Season 2, Episode 12, *Boston Blakie*)
1953: "Island of Stone" (Season 2, Episode 1, *Chevron Theater*)
1954: "Tailor-Made Trouble" (Season 1, Episode 11, *Waterfront*)
1956 - 1959: Seven episodes of *Sky King*
1958: "Beautiful, Blue and Deadly" (Season 1, Episode 14, *Mike Hammer*)
1958: "Texas Fliers" (Season 1, Episode 18, *Flight*)